THIRTEEN STRIPES

Edward Robert Belding

THIRTEEN STRIPES

~ A Wetherill Mystery ~

Thirteen Stripes
A Wetherill Mystery
© 2023 Edward Robert Belding

Dedication

for Will and Chance—

the future of the family name is in your hands

When all our weak resources fail,
When friends forsake, and foes assail,
Thy sure assistance let us share,
And chase the monster, fell Despair.
Compell'd to seek his native hell,
In torments let him rage and yell!

from

HOPE, AN ODE

by Peter Markoe

PROLOGUE

· · · · · · · · · ·

John Hancock fancied himself a general. Such a bold idea came to him two months prior when a messenger on horseback saved him from being captured by the British on the eve of clashes at Lexington and Concord. Back then, he regretted not being able to lead thousands of armed militiamen on April 19, 1775. He regretted not being able to garner some fame and credit for causing King George's Regulars to retreat to the safety of Boston. But now, perhaps, fortune would bless Hancock with a chance to command the armed forces laying siege to Boston . . . a chance to drive the usurpers into the sea.

At the age of thirty-nine, John Hancock was already a primary leader of the colonial rebellion against Parliament and the King of England. He was serving as the President of the Second Continental Congress, which was still meeting in the bustling city of Philadelphia, Pennsylvania. Hancock had been here since May 10, 1775. Now it was the fifteenth of June. A pleasant day—warm and clear with a gentle southerly breeze shouldering great promise and optimism. However, proud John was soon to find out that his chance to be general would slip swiftly away. He was not going to be chosen Commander-in-Chief by the majority of delegates from the provinces that made up this assemblage careening toward independency. It was not in the cards for proud John. It would never be.

Delegates were looking for an experienced military man—one who could hold up against daunting odds and lead a rag-tag, yet-to-be-formed army successfully throughout a long and difficult war. Such a man had to be seasoned in combat. But above all, he had to be able to pull the southern colonies into the pending fray, which had already begun north around Boston, Massachusetts.

Hancock did not measure up in John Adams's estimation. But the sharp-tongued, fellow New Englander knew who could. Adams fancied a gentleman farmer from Virginia—a tall, stout fellow with a fair measure of military leadership experience from the last war. A modest, virtuous forty-three-year-old with a brave heart. Mister Adams spoke ever so eloquently of Colonel Washington during the debate over who was most suitable to lead the future Continental forces against a vastly superior British war machine. Adams sounded convincing. The debate was short-lived. Colonel George Washington was unanimously selected by the delegates.

Hancock never stood a chance. He was tepidly disappointed, but did not show it then. He was gracious in congratulating the first Commander-in-Chief and looked forward to the man's acceptance speech scheduled for the next day. Beyond that, the fate of what the Continental Congress was creating remained in God's hands.

News of this bold decision by Congress spread like wild-fire throughout the city of brotherly love. Local reaction to the news was mixed. Quakers paid it no mind. Loyalists felt that whoever had been chosen to lead a rebel army was bound to embarrass himself in short order and fail. Many of those favoring independency applauded the choice and were glad a true military leader, not a rabble rouser, had been chosen quickly. Among the most radical Whigs, there were few whispered doubts. Now it was time to wait and see.

Official word of Washington's selection had to wait for Congress to draft his commission as General on the seventeenth of June. Couriers were then sent forth with signed and sealed missives containing the momentous decision by the congressional delegates. Important patriotic folks had to be put on notice. Plans had to be made to escort the Commander-in-Chief north to reach his army gathering outside of Boston in the fields of Cambridge.

Word also had to get to Captain Abram Markoe, a founder of the Philadelphia Light Horse Militia. This wealthy merchant had arrived in the city only five years ago from the island of St. Croix. He was the grandson of Pierre Marcous, a Huguenot who fled France in the late-seventeenth century and settled in the West Indies. Abram came from a large, affluent family of ten children raised by Peter Markoe and Elisabeth Farrell Cunningham. They considered themselves Danish subjects, since St. Croix was in possession of Denmark at the time, thus, all members of the family were loyal to the Danish crown. Abram Markoe became the owner of four sugar cane plantations and over a hundred slaves. After his first wife, Elizabeth Kenny Rogers, died, Abram left his young, free-spirited son, Abraham, in charge of the plantations and came to

Philadelphia to expand his mercantile interests. At this time, his other son, by his first wife, was studying in England. Peter became disenchanted with his study of law and decided to become a diletante, poet, and playwright. He would soon join his father in Philadelphia.

Abram Markoe, now in his late forties, had quickly ingratiated himself to the wealthy, influential citizens of the city of brotherly love. He became a darling of those expressing Whig sentiments. In 1773, he wed twenty-year-old Elizabeth Baynton, daughter of fellow merchant, John Baynton. This marriage cemented Markoe's popularity among the elite of the city. Two weeks after the first Continental Congress met in Carpenter's Hall, September 4, 1774, twenty-eight men of wealth—mostly members of the Schuylkill Fishing Company, the Gloucester Fox Hunting Club, and other fraternal orders—met and organized the Light Horse of the City of Philadelphia, also known as the First City Troop. Although he was still a Danish subject and a resident of Philadelphia for only a few years, Markoe was elected Captain of the troop of horse. His outfit, consisting mostly of the sons of wealthy local merchants, had already served as escorts for the likes of Adams and Hancock, as well as other delegates, on their sojourns to New York City and back in May. Both Adams and Hancock knew their new General would be safely delivered north by Markoe and his men.

The time had come for a troop of gentlemen of fortune to escort General George Washington to his so-called army. The man's safety had to be ensured in crossing the Delaware River, in forging through New Jersey, and making it safely into New York. There was no better band of skilled horsemen to turn to than the Philadelphia Troop of Horse. And no better officer than Captain Abram Markoe to lead them.

1

A CLUTCH OF RED ROSES

· ·

(Saturday, June 17, 1775)

The new seamstress for the Markoes had no business strolling for so long in the garden on the sun side of the manse. Mistress Elizabeth, the second wife of Abram Markoe, had given the woman explicit instructions that the gold silk banner had to be completed before the twenty-first of the month. Why, the sewer did not know. For what purpose, she could only guess at. For whom the gaudy banner was intended was another mystery. Ruth Mount, a mature, plain-faced woman amply scarred by the pox and other unfortunate circumstances, assumed the thing she was ordered to work on was intended to merely test her ability. If it passed young and pregnant Mistress Elizabeth's discerning eye, then Miss Mount might keep her job. If not, then she would move on to wherever her real boss chose to send her and select another name to go by. For now, she liked being Ruth Mount.

So far, the work assignments had been easy but tedious. Boring actually. However, the former Elizabeth Baynton was kind to a fault and allowed her free servants frequent breaks from the monotony of their assigned tasks. Not so much the kitchen help, who were mostly slaves brought along from Abram Markoe's plantation in St. Croix a few years ago. The house servants, free or slave, were numerous and falling over each other eager to please. Ruth Mount, or whoever she really was, knew how to take advantage of the situation even though she had been hired a mere month ago when Mistress Elizabeth learned she was expecting her second child. Her first pregnancy had been a difficult one. Thus, three maids were hired at the beginning of May—a needle-woman, who introduced herself as Ruth Mount; a nurse/mid-wife, Cornelia Emmons, who was skilled at making potions and remedies for all sorts of aches and ills; and a chamber maid, Anna McClew, who was also hired to look after the first-born child and, in a few more months, the little one on the way. McClew was a striking, flame-haired Irish beauty and the youngest of the three new hires. She was even younger than Mistress Elizabeth. Ruth Mount wasted no time taking a fancy to this ripe plumb.

The new seamstress liked her fresh-hired peers equally well, but for different reasons. Cornelia Emmons had previously worked for a wealthy family Mount had also worked for—until the master of the house passed away. The seamstress hoped that Emmons might be trusted to spy on the Markoes and relay any pertinent information she discovered. The new chamber maid, however, was so innocent and naive—a slender sprite unsullied by the ways of the world. Anna McClew was just the sort Ruth Mount was looking for, but not for spying. Such a ripening young thing held much potential as a fair lover.

Ruth wore the accepted servant's uniform insisted upon by the Markoes. A light blue gown. White apron. White mobcap. One could tell the servants apart only by the color of the ribband each wore attached to the cap. Mount's was usually royal blue. It dangled down below her gathered chestnut hair and rested on her broad shoulders. Small breasts hid behind the bodice of her simple gown. Her wide hips and broad thighs kept their secrets behind the ample folds of her garment which reached to her tight-laced shoes. She was a large-boned woman who failed to radiate beauty. She admired beauty in others and the things around her. She was fully aware of her shortcomings and limitations. She had full confidence in her skills.

The seamstress paused. She had reached her favorite flowers in the east garden. She ran calloused fingers over the heads of a clutch of red roses. They felt like soft, warm velvet. So opposite from the thorns which she avoided, even though they fascinated her as well. She loved such silent, ominous beauty. Ruth reached for her cutting tool in the pocket of her apron and used it to separate a thorny stem from the nearest bush. She would bring this prize rose to Anna McClew—thorns and all.

Mount's place of solace was originally intended to serve as a spice garden. But flowers came to bloom like a conquering horde of bright and beautiful lords. Their warriors were a legion of industrious bees. These insects shared the space with Miss Mount and she was most careful not to disturb them as they made their rounds. She knew her place in the order of things. A reasoned, pragmatic doer—one who trusted only those worthy of her trust. She was content to spend precious moments of her free time enjoying nature's wealth. She was not envious of those who had benefitted from material gain—either by honest means or not. Ruth was willing to take chances, but to do so on her own terms. She was determined to succeed by employing her own cunning and wile. That is why Ruth seized the opportunity to make good money by spying on the Markoes . . . much more solid coin than she could make from honest work. A stroll in her master's garden always allowed her to forget about the right and wrong of what she was up to. Admiring beauty in nature was a right proper antidote for acknowledging sin.

The seamstress had to admit that she had yet to explore the extent of Mister Markoe's holdings. This out-of-the-way estate was burgeoning with potential—a slew of strategic hiding places suitable for nefarious and pleasurable activities. In time, Ruth planned to find them all. Markoe's new mansion stood between Chestnut and Market streets on the outskirts of town. The wealthy plantation owner, turned merchant, had purchased a city block's worth of land between 9th and 10th streets back in 1772. His large house sat fifty feet back from Market Street. A post and rail fence surrounded the entire estate, save for an elaborate marble entranceway in front. Stables, carriage house, and detached kitchens lay in close proximity to the manse. So did wonderful orchards and brilliant flower gardens like Ruth Mount's favorite on the east side. An abundance of stately walnut trees remained where they had stood for decades. Beyond them lay the hay fields stretching to the Schuylkill River.

Yes, Abram Markoe was no stranger to flaunting wealth. He had the wherewithal and the potential to become an important figure in America's struggle for independence. He was fast becoming a darling among the leaders of the rebel movement. This was why certain parties most loyal to the British Crown felt the need to spy on Captain Abram Markoe. Ruth Mount was the first chosen to do so. She had learned much already and had dutifully reported such to her real boss. She liked her situation. The sewing work was humdrum at times, but the snooping about and reporting in to the agent in charge was exciting. For this reason, Ruth wanted to stay on this assignment as long as she could. Find out as much as she could. For the pay, yes. For the King, of course. But mostly for the thrill of it all. The decision for how long she was to keep up her clandestine assignment was not hers to make. Nor was it up to the Markoes. Her true boss would make that decision. He was the one who paid her well and coached her on what to do. He was the one who told her of late to keep an eye on those who came to visit Abram Markoe . . . find out who they were and what their purposes might be.

Here was yet another reason for Miss Mount to linger in the east garden. She had a clear view of visitors approaching on the paving stones of the horse shoe entranceway to the welcoming door of the manse. There seemed to be an increase in the number of visitors coming to see Markoe ever since the delegates of the Continental Congress came to town. Today was no exception.

As Ruth was taking inventory of her favorite growing things— the roses, of course; the holly hocks and foxgloves; such spices as horehound, madder, wild clary; and even the ornamental higuerilla imported from St. Croix—a man approaching on horseback caught her eye. His fine stallion was clattering hooves on the stones that made Markoe's entranceway before Ruth could lift her skirts and emerge from the garden to greet him.

The handsome rider spotted the servant woman, shouted his 'halloo!', and reined in his mount with a skillful flourish. The jet black steed was gleaming sweat from obviously being coaxed to a demanding pace. It was a hot, clear day, and a meager breeze struggled to bring relief. The rider was sweating too. He removed his black forage cap, shook his golden head, and mopped his brow with a scarlet sash. Ruth assumed the man to be no more than twenty. His eyes were blue as the sky and his lionel hair was tied back with a black ribband. He wore a tight-fitting stable jacket that matched his eyes. A scarlet standing collar framed his clean-shaven face. The seamstress found herself counting the plated ball buttons on his broad chest. If she had been attracted to men, this one would have been worth sharing a few stolen moments in her master's garden.

"My good maid," hollered the rider, "I have good news for your master! Where might I find him?"

Ruth courtsied like a young innocent. "Master Markoe was up and out early this morn. He supervises his slaves in the hay field beyond the carriage house. He has yet to return."

The rider gave a nod, put his cap back on, and checked the leather pouch at his belt. "I shall ride out back then." He patted his belt buckle. "I have here an envelope from Major Thomas Mifflin, himself . . . for Captain Markoe's hand only."

Ruth smiled in a flirtatious way. "What news of import might you carry, good sir?"

"Not for the likes of you," scoffed the rider, looking down a prominent nose. "You might be a Tory!"

The young courier followed his insulting words with a laugh and dug a spurred heel into the flank of his stallion. He and his lathered horse sped off in the direction of the carriage house. They were quickly lost from view.

Ruth Mount flashed a crude gesture with her left hand in the direction of the nearest hayfield. She hated the haughty behavior of men of wealth—especially a young macaroni who held no title but acted entitled anyway. She feared the American colonies were close to replacing the British ruling elite with their own superior class—one that would be worse to bear. Not to be as much envied as despised.

The seamstress shook her head and drove dark thoughts away. She whirled about in her garden like a little girl at play. The cut rose, intended for sweet Anna McClew, was held securely in her hand. Ruth headed for the servant entrance facing the nearest kitchen house. She was already late getting back to her sewing chores. But she now had a plausible excuse, thanks to the rude but handsome rider. Mistress Elizabeth would swallow her account. Best of all, she had some ripe news to share with her real boss.

2

KILLING KINGS

· · · · · · · · · · · · · ·

(Sunday, June 18, 1775)

"I have a problem here, gentlemen," admitted Captain Abram Markoe with his hard island accent clinging to each syllable. "Major Mifflin requests thirty of our mounted men outfitted and prepared to escort General Washington safely into New York . . . twenty in the fore . . . ten in the rear behind the wagons . . ."

"When would that be?" interrupted one of the youngest fellows at the round game table in the center of a well-lit room in Philadelphia's two-story Tun Tavern. The twenty-three-year-old was the son of a popular local brewer and already a budding merchant in his own right. Another coltish chap, exuding entitlement but lacking a title, went by the name of Robert Hare. He was crowned with his own curly amber mane untied for this occasion, deep brown eyes, round face, full lips, and an unsewn scar on his chin from a fall off a horse.

The other card players, besides Markoe, looked up from their hands and waited for their Captain's response.

The founder and leader of the city's first troop of horse put his three Commerce cards down and spoke in sober tones: "Well, Mister Hare, to date the plan is to leave from here at dawn on Friday the twenty-third. That means we have this day to add names to my list in order to reach thirty. The rest of the wait time is for taking care of personal affairs, checking equipment, and saying our farewells. Already, I have visited the lads at Christian Sam's Gloucester Hunt Club and the lads at the Schuylkill Fish Company Lodge. More than a score have volunteered so far for the upcoming escort of General Washington and his train . . ."

"How many of us?" Hare interrupted again.

"I need six more volunteers," Markoe declared. "That is where you lads of Saints George, Andrew, and Patrick come in. Several of your fraternal mates are already in my count . . . but I need six more, and for good measure a few alternates."

The tallest man at the table, thin favored and upright, piped up: "All of us in this room are willing and able to join up." This Benjamin Randolph cocked a confident blue eye and showed the side of his face that sported a dueling scar. He flashed a cocksure smile and a set of perfect teeth. "Give us a pint of ale, a pinch of snuff, a pipe of tobacco, and a mere rumor of rebellion . . . we'll be ready."

"You have made my task of selecting easy, Ben," Markoe said as he scooped up his three cards and eyed the 'widow' cards face up on the table. The Captain was an optimistic, confident man— always ready to impress and cajole. His premature gray hair made him look respectably older than he was. His sad brown eyes under thick black brows exuded care and concern for those in need of attention. His large, flat nose, full lips, and unremarkable chin marked him as an honest, non-threatening soul—one who led out of compassion rather than instilling fear. His men saw him as an equal.

"Not so fast, my jaspers," came the gravelly voice of the horseman who sat opposite Markoe. Blair McClenachan, already a well-respected financier and second-oldest at the table, was an uppity, red-faced Irishman with ample freckles to prove it. He had dressed in finery for an evening of leisure. Fancy lace hung loose around his thick neck. His green silk vest lay open to reveal his ample girth. A striped silver and black waistcoat hung on the back of his chair. McClenachan, the wealthiest man at the table, completed his thought: "Rain showers may have prevented some of us from arriving on time. To be fair, we should wait a bit. See who comes through the door. Then we can figure out how to pick the six of us."

"Well said, Blair," the Captain exclaimed. "How do you propose the six be chosen?"

"Another round of Commerce ought to do it," said the same gravelly Irish voice.

Markoe disagreed. "I say we finish this round. Let it be the last of this chancy game, Blair. After the late ones have arrived, may I suggest we try our hand at my version of this card game . . . one I call Three Pips."

"Is that the one where the court cards are thrown out?" asked Billy West, Jr., a nervous sort who rarely spoke but fidgeted a great deal. He was short in stature and temper, but long on loyalty to the cause.

"Exactly," Markoe said.

"You should call your game Killing Kings, Captain." The voice was owned by Will Pollard, the rider who had delivered Mifflin's request on Saturday and had confronted Ruth Mount. This son of St. George, so popular with the upper class single ladies of Philadelphia, was not sweating now. He was out of uniform and casually dressed for a gentleman's evening out. Will wore a plain white tow shirt under a linsey vest of sailor blue. He set straight in his chair—composed and relaxed. Not one scar spoiled his boyish face. He flashed straight teeth behind full lips. Pollard was grinning, but he meant his words to be taken seriously.

His suggestion roused a few laughs from well-watered throats and a snatch of a rebel song: "We are sons of liberty . . . no longer sons of loyalty . . ."

Captain Markoe smiled back. "I shall keep that name in mind, Will."

The modest gathering of patriot gentlemen at the Tun Tavern completed their last round of Commerce. John Mease, a staunch Presbyterian from Strabane, Ireland, showed the best hand—a flush of three hearts led by a queen. The twenty-nine-year-old paid for the next round of house ale brought by two comely tavern maids— the Mullen sisters, who were daughters of Sam Mullen, minehost at the Tun. The glad recipients of the warm, foamy brew drank and chatted about the latest news from the Second Congress and the latest news from beleaguered Boston.

Other patrons were in the main room. Half of them stood at the bar listening to jokes told by Minehost Sam. The other half occupied small tables close to the walls. Their main topic of conversation was the possibility of all-out war visiting their dear city. No one here had to speak in hushed tones. The Tun Tavern, at the intersection of King Street and Tun Alley a short distance up from Carpenter's Wharf, had become a meeting place for patriots. The Society of St. George met here regularly; so did the Society of St. Andrew upon occasion, as did the Society of St. Patrick. The first meeting of St. John's Masonic Lodge was held in this very same building—one of many structures Joshua Carpenter had built in the previous century. The Tun was a warm, old place. It housed a modest number of ghosts. The exterior sported a long front porch, four large front windows, five dormers, and stout chimneys on each side. Such a popular place it used to be when the King's name was praised in toasts. Such a popular place it remained when the names of the leaders of the rebellion were raised in toasts. The likes of Ben Franklin, the Adams brothers, John Hancock, and most recently, George Washington, were now hailed by the whiggish crowd. There were loud, boastful words of praise for other rebel leaders as well—voices loud enough to scare even the ghosts.

Three late-comers to Captain Markoe's meeting finally traipsed in. They were dripping wet from having crossed town on horseback in the rain shower. They removed their soaked outer garments and hung them on pegs to dry. The trio grabbed pints of Hare's Ale at the bar and sauntered over to the oval table where empty chairs waited for them. Apologies and excuses for lateness were given by the three. They were accepted by those already at the game table.

Abram Markoe welcomed the three by name: "Tench Francis, Sharp Delaney, Alexander Nesbitt . . . glad you could make it afore we put the cards away for the night."

Their Captain proceeded to get them up to date on his recruitment of volunteers to escort General Washington on the twenty-third. He mentioned that Major Mifflin had informed in writing of this honor and that Major Generals, Charles Lee and Philip Schuyler, would be accompanying the Commander-in-Chief. Then he addressed all present about how the choosing of the final six men needed would be done.

Markoe explained: "We have nine of you vying for the last six horses in the escort party. One round of a game of my choosing will decide who goes and who stays behind. Don't feel slighted if you lose because any brother left behind will serve as escorts for other dignitaries in our city—certain ones who will not be accompanying General Washington. Most of them will have cause to go somewhere in these trying times. And those who stay put may call upon you to protect them . . ."

Sharp Delaney, a copper-haired son of St. Patrick, interrupted,

"Who will lead the unlucky ones?"

Markoe responded assuredly, "I am putting Sam Morris in charge of the rest of you. Christian Sam is more than worthy of the task. Those left behind will take orders from him."

"Are you saying, Captain Markoe, you intend to lead the new General's escort?" oily-tongued Ben Randolph asked.

"'Tis obvious as my nose. Ben," Markoe said. "Indeed I do . . . an honor not to pass up. But more than this, I feel flattered that our troop of horse has been invited to serve. So, we can all share in the glory whether we go or stay."

Huzzahs went up in the game room and near empty pints were raised in unison. The Mullen sisters rushed out from the bar to replenish the horsemen's vessels. The names of Markoe and Morris were oft-repeated in a spate of toasts. The men were fully aware that Sam Morris had always been Markoe's choice for second in command. It had already been decided that if Markoe was not able to continue as leader then Christian Sam would assume the captaincy of the troop. Another election would not be needed.

Things quieted down quickly after the cheers and toasts. The men wanted to hear what Markoe had to say about his game. Their Captain shuffled the cards deftly and let Sharp Delaney, sitting to his right, cut the deck. Markoe then dealt three cards to himself face down. Did the same to John Mease on his left. Then Tench Francis, Robert Hare, Blair McClenachan, Ben Randolph, Alexander Nesbitt, Will Pollard, Billy West, Jr., and finally Sharp Delaney. Markoe then placed three cards face up in the center of the table to create the widow. He placed the rest of the cards face down next to the last widow card.

The men picked up their cards and studied them. Four horsemen rearranged their cards to suit their liking. The rest simply waited for instructions from their leader.

Markoe did not disappoint: "Dealer goes first, then clockwise for the round." He glanced once again at his nine of clubs, nine of hearts, and jack of diamonds. Then he pondered the widow for a breath's span. It featured a six of clubs, seven of clubs, and an ace of hearts. He announced, "Kill the jack!" Then he placed the face card down to start the castoff pile on the other side of the widow line.

"One lobsterback down," Will Pollard acknowledged.

The comment garnered a rumble of confirmation from the others.

Markoe smiled and picked up the six of clubs and seven of clubs from the widow. He placed his nine of hearts face up in the widow line, then drew a card from the leftover stack and placed it face up next to the nine.

"What you must do," instructed Markoe, "is get rid of your face cards, for they do you no good in this game . . ."

"Same for the King of these provinces," inserted Will Pollard before his Captain had finished his instructions.

The Private received a modicum of support from his peers.

Markoe ignored the fuss and plowed on: 'You may hold to your hand or replace one or two cards selected from the widow to forge a better hand. Whoever holds the best hand at the end of this round not only gets to join the escort team but also gets to ride at the front of the line and hold our standard."

Such news was greeted by hearty cheers. The Mullen girls came running again with pitchers to refill ale cups.

On the tide of merriment at the Tun floated one minor complaint. Alexander Nesbitt barked, "The first banner you designed, Captain, suffered a tear when we escorted John Adams to New York. Any chance of a whole new flag?"

Markoe nodded in the affirmative. "I happen to have my recently-hired seamstress working on a second standard . . . one which I have redesigned. I've added something to the canton, which I will keep a surprise till the twenty-third. I am confident my sewing maid will be finished by then."

"What'll be the fate of the first flag?" asked a concerned Tench Francis.

"The same maid will mend it," Markoe said. "You who stay behind will use it as Christian Sam wishes."

The Captain's words were received warmly. Well-lubricated throats voiced approval.

Markoe decided the time had come to review the possible winning hands in his game: "A 'tricorn' of highest sum wins a round. If none, then a 'flush of same suit/highest sum wins with diamonds first, hearts second, clubs third, spades as last resort. A 'sequence' has a middling chance of winning with a 10-9-8/

unsuited being the highest possibility. A 'pair' shows two cards of the same suit or same number. Last is a 'point' which shows the least value sum/unsuited."

The participants had no questions at this juncture for their Captain, because his rank order of winning hands was quite similar to a round of Commerce.

John Mease, seated to Markoe's left was ready and eager to kill. He called out "Kill the queen" and promptly laid down his face card on top of Markoe's discarded jack.

His move was saluted by others raising their cups and taking a good swallow.

Mease, with sleeves rolled up and brows furrowed with determination, picked up the nine of hearts and ace of hearts from the widow. He laid down an eight of clubs face up. The slender, dark-haired fellow, whose son was also in Markoe's horse troop, then plucked a four of clubs from the face-down stack and put it face up in the widow. He smiled at his new hand and winked confidently at his chances of joining the escort team.

Tench Francis did not appear as optimistic. Deep furrow lines striped his pale forehead. His thin lips creased his frown. He was a born worrier, and his hand gave him something to worry about. A seven of hearts, five of spades, and four of hearts held the cause. The widow, now all clubs, promised little and offered no solace. Tench picked up the five of clubs and replaced it in the widow with his four of hearts. He was the first to put his hand face up on the table for all to see. Then he got up and strolled over to the bar. Tench knew his lowly pair of fives had not put him in good stead.

Robert Hare, the brewer's son, killed his queen of clubs and laid down a ten of diamonds. He picked up the four of hearts and four of clubs from the widow to go with his four of spades. He fetched the king of hearts from the face-down stack and promptly killed it, much to the glee of his peers who raised their cups a second time to praise his luck. Hare picked again from the stack and placed a four of diamonds face up in the widow line. The curly-haired optimist knew he had a winning hand, but he offered no tell on his round face. He decided not to show his cards.

Blair McClenachan was next to make a move. He cleared his throat, took one last look at his nine of diamonds, three of spades, and jack of clubs. Sighed. Killed his jack. Laid down his spade card.

The others took little notice of the dead jack. There was hardly a mumble or a hand gesture.

Blair picked up the ten of diamonds and four of diamonds from the widow. He plucked a three of diamonds from the stack and placed it face up in the widow line. Onlookers shot him queer looks for making such a move, but he countered with a slight grin. He also decided to keep his new hand to himself for the time being.

Ben Randolph studied the widow with skeptical blue eyes. He was next. Before he made a move, he gave McClenachan a sideways glance. The man had left Ben meager opportunities. Randolph plunked down his two of spades and picked up the eight of clubs. He was left with a pair of eights and an ace of clubs. Ben threw his cards down in disgust. He remained at the table however, to nurse his pint of ale and wait to see who did worse than him.

Alexander Nesbitt was not a patient man. He did not like waiting while others before him set the bar for success or failure. He picked at his face pitted by small pox. Nesbitt was a slender fellow—quick on his feet and always willing to take chances. Black straight hair crowned his small head. It was cropped short and free of the constraints of a ribband. His temper was short as well. Those who knew him well tried hard to avoid riling him. Alexander put down his two of hearts and picked up the three of diamonds from the widow. He was left with two threes and the two of diamonds. Nesbitt did not show his cards. He was embarrassed by them and did not feel they were strong enough to qualify.

Will Pollard wasted little time making his move. He felt lucky. He held an ace of diamonds, a two of clubs, and a six of diamonds. Will put down his ace and six. He picked up the pair of twos from the widow. Pollard beamed with pride at his good fortune. He placed his three humble pips face up on the table for all to see.

The others congratulated Will on his tricorn hand by toasting his good luck. Robert Hare, who had not shown his cards yet, was especially effusive with his praise. He predicted that Pollard would get to carry the flag.

Billy West, Jr., shook his long, golden-brown hair in an attempt to chase away any doubts about being able to best Pollard's hand. He held a five of diamonds, a jack of hearts, and a king of diamonds.

He promptly killed his jack and king.

His peers cheered doubly loud and shouted, "Kill the King! Kill the King!"

Billy ignored them and the Greek chorus at the bar He picked up the ace of diamonds and six of diamonds from the widow. He put his flush face down next to Pollard's tricorn and boasted that his hand was good enough for second place.

Sharp Delaney was last to go. He took his time making a move. The widow left him a two of diamonds, three of spades, and an ace of spades. He held a ten of clubs, ten of hearts, and a queen of diamonds. Delaney killed his queen without fanfare. He picked up the three of spades. There was little else he figured he could do. Sharp placed his precarious hand face up on the table.

This move ended Markoe's round of Kill the King.

Players who had not revealed their hands turned their cards face up on the table. Captain Markoe perused each hand. He called out the names of the men who had garnered superior hands. Tench Francis, Alexander Nesbitt, and Ben Randolph were not mentioned. Their pairs did not measure up. Sharp Delaney's pair was good enough to qualify as the sixth man chosen for the escort team. Robert Hare's tricorn of fours bested Will Pollard's tricorn of twos for winner of the round and the opportunity to carry the new standard of the Philadelphia Troop of Horse.

Robert Hare received the majority of toasts from the rest. Captain Markoe received a goodly share, including one for Elizabeth, his pregnant wife. Toasts were also given to Markoe's homeland of St. Croix, and one to his son, Peter, who was sailing from England and expected any day soon. The final toast was to all the absent, hard-riding. hard-drinking lads of the horse troop.

Before the lively, well-lubricated gathering adjourned, Captain Markoe reminded those on the escort team to be on his fallow field at dawn the next day for drills and inspection of equipment in preparation for the Washington assignment.

"I expect each man selected to be on his best horse," Markoe insisted, "sober, wide awake, and on time."

All cheers were in the affirmative.

3

13 STRIPES

· · · · · · · · · ·

(Monday, June 19, 1715)

Since arriving from New York a month ago, Enoch Mortaine, special adjutant to the Philadelphia Wharf Inspector for the West India Trading Company, had no desire to visit a public tea room. He preferred the sign of the Blue Anchor down on Water Street, where he could enjoy a stiff pint of ale in the presence of strong, seaworthy man. Mortaine always played work sober. He consumed his off hours as close to drunk as a gentleman dared. He managed his vice as well as he managed his service to the King. His true boss thought highly of him and had given him important clandestine responsibilities of late. Spying on wealthy merchants was one. The trading company and certain government officials were interested in keeping an eye on merchants suspected of involvement in smuggling operations between the islands of the West Indies and the thirteen colonies. One of their best agents, Enoch Mortaine, had been sent to Philadelphia for such a purpose.

The most recent assignment brought the stocky, well-attired Mortaine to Widow Chandler's Tea House on the east side of Front Street above Walnut Street. At the hour of five on Monday, June 19th, Mortaine started his stroll up the cartway from Carpenter's Wharf. A slight northerly breeze failed to tame the late day's heat. Mortaine did not care. His choice of a burgundy-hued waistcoat over a ruffled chambray blouse was too heavy for such a summery day, but he wanted to look the part of a prosperous gentleman. A modicum of discomfort did not matter to Enoch Mortaine. That his planned meeting with a woman of humble means went off without a hitch was what counted most. Mortaine usually met the women in his life, wedded or not, in ordinaries—places and women with sullied reputations. This was another vice he played discreet. Such trysts could go unnoticed in the less desirable places. The Sign of the Blue Anchor was one of those places.

Mortaine adjusted the uncomfortable powdered wig crowning his large, square head. He tugged at a lacy sleeve. He was satisfied with his disguise. He also liked the name he called himself since arriving in Philadelphia. He whispered it to himself as he stood in front of a quaint white-brick narrow building, crowned with a pair of gables and a slate roof. The facade sported two tiny-paned windows and a blood-red door. The large black and white sign above the door indicated that Enoch Mortaine, or whoever he really was, had found the correct, pre-arranged rendezvous place—Widow Chandler's Tea House.

Thinking he was early, Mortaine lingered in front of the establishment. He saw no one he recognized sitting by a window. Two women, strolling arm and arm, passed the refined looking gentleman but ignored his bow and bending of his leg. They entered the tea house. He suddenly realized his hireling might be inside already. The woman he had hired to spy on Abram Markoe and his family was sharp enough to shy away from the windows and sit in a shadowed corner. Besides, Miss Mount was always early. Strictly business. She was eager to gain hard coin for easy work. She was probably already inside sipping some of King George's finest tea.

Mortaine opened the thick red door and set off a tinkling of bells. Three patrons acknowledged him with a skeptical eye. They mistook him for a fop playing the role of an up-town dandy. His soft brown eyes and clean-shaven face held no hint of menace. He posed no threat to these patrons. Mortaine hid his dark side well. After all, he had years of experience handling all sorts of situations and people—from ruthless, obnoxious folks to sweet, malleable souls. The ones who had crossed him in England, male and female, were either severely maimed or dead and gone. He had exuded charm and innocence, so far, in the colonies. His reputation here was unblemished. He was still an unknown to most citizens of the city of Philadelphia. His gentleman's disguise seemed to be working.

One woman in a powder blue gown, snow pale apron, and equally white mobcap sat alone in a far corner. She was staring at the man who had just entered the tea room. She remained tight-lipped, neither smiling nor frowning. Mortaine acknowledged the woman by touching a black brow with his pointing finger. He walked stiffly across the sanded floor and bowed adequately.

"Miss Mount, such a pleasure to see you here." Mortaine glanced around the room to check and see if any patrons were paying attention. None bothered. They were busy with their teas, cakes, and gossip of the day.

Mortaine took a seat opposite Ruth Mount.

The woman flashed hazel eyes and a barely perceptible smile. Above it, a heart-shaped patch on her cheek covered a pox scar. "I ordered your favorite souchong bohea. Figured you did not want to waste any time. What took you so long?"

Mount did not wait for an answer because she expected none from her never wrong boss. He remained silent, admiring the craftsmanship of the cherry wood table at which they sat. The sewing maid raised an ungloved hand. The tea server on duty rushed over with a steaming pot of tea and poured a cup for the only other male patron in Chandler's. The nervous server said not a word and skittered to another table.

A fair day for a stroll in this city," Mortaine offered as he started to play with his teaspoon. "'Tis a bit hot and things have slowed down on the wharf."

Mount glared at her boss while taking a sip of her camomile tea. She held her cup with the refinement of a noblewoman. Finally she said, "I was early, thanks to luck . . . so, in that sense, you were not late. It turns out, Master Markoe's son arrived by ship from London this morning and I was able to gain a ride in from the master's coach driver, who has gone on to fetch Peter Markoe. My excuse for coming into the city is my need to purchase certain bolts of cloth, threads and other sewing things to finish a cursed flag. The thing must be completed before the twenty-third of this month, or I'm out of a job."

Mortaine's hireling set down her tea cup gently while keeping her eyes on her boss.

"So Markoe threatened you?" Mortaine asked before he took a sip of his tea and made a face.

"In so many words he did so . . . that wealthy, spoiled cock in the yard. All because he's promised the men in his precious horse troop . . . each one a rich, spoiled cock as well. They've demanded a new flag for their latest foolish adventure."

Mortaine lowered his cup and pushed it away. "You must be talking about Captain Markoe's escorts for the rebel army's new general?"

"My work on the flag must be completed on the twenty-second," groused Mount. "What's worse are the Captain's revisions for the design, which was originally given him by a Mister Folwell of this town. I was doing quite well on the midpoint seam, the center shield and knot, the golden scrolls, and the bay horse head. Even the Indian on the left and the angel on the right of the center shield pose no problem. The motto lettering is easy, for it is a specialty of mine. I must say, the flag to this point is a handsome one . . . even the Virginian commander shall be pleased with it . . ."

"So what's left to be done?" Mortaine asked with tepid interest, as he reached for a lemon-glazed sweet cake waiting for him on a silver tray in the center of the table.

"The prig wants laurel vines embroidered on three sides of the yellow silk field . . . a silver fringe at three edges. Worst of all, blue and silver stripes alternated at the canton where our union crosses customarily sit."

"Let me guess," said Mortaine, after a polite mouthful of his sweet cake. "He wants thirteen stripes obliterating the crosses."

"Thirteen stripes in the corner," affirmed Miss Mount, "one for each of the rebel colonies,"

Mortaine placed his elbows on the table and cupped his hands under his double chin. He focused on his hireling's eyes. "This work you are doing for Captain Markoe is all so fascinating, but not the work I mean for you to concentrate on. Get the damn flag done on time and keep your job so you can find out what I need to know."

Miss Mount reached into her bag of newly purchased sewing materials and extracted a folded piece of vellum. She pushed it over to Mortaine. "You will find the names of some of the members of the troop of horse on there."

Mortaine unfolded the half-sheet of soft parchment and read the names aloud. They were all unfamiliar to him and piqued his interest. "I count nine names with three lined out. Any meaning to this?"

"I fetched it from what the Captain tossed away recently." Mount took another sip of her tea and purposely ignored what remained on the sweet cake tray. She wanted to avoid getting as stout as the man sitting opposite her, but she was not that far removed from his shape. Her ample servant's gown hid broad thighs and thick ankles. However, her chest was no match for her buttocks and hips. She would have made a fair anchor for a small ship.

The seamstress decided to continue: "I have no idea what import this list might serve . . . perhaps something to do with those selected to escort the rebel general. There must be a master list hidden somewhere . . ."

"No doubt," mused Mortaine, as he stuffed the assumed partial list in his pocket and another morsel of cake in his mouth. "I need more names. Find as many as you can. Find them all, my good woman. I am sure one or two members of the troop can be coaxed back to our side. We need at least one soul in the troop to spy for us . . . help us out in some way."

"I will try my best," Mount asserted.

"And find out who will be visiting Captain Markoe in the next few months. This task is of equal importance, Miss Mount."

"I told you of Peter Markoe."

"Yes, but he is not worth our worry," Mortaine said while shaking his head and ignoring his tea. "That carpet knave is chafe in the wind . . . a spineless dandy . . . a student of law who now fancies himself a bard. Smuggling is as coarse to the likes of him as is hard work."

Ruth Mount sought to change the subject: "Lady friends of Mistress Markoe visit often and arrive by coach in chatty groups."

Mortaine frowned. "You will learn nothing from the likes of those twits. Concentrate on the guests come to see the Captain . . . particularly anyone visiting from the islands. My sources inform me something big is afoot in the smuggling business. It has something to do with outfitting the rebel army this General Washington plans to organize."

Mount protested: "Master Markoe is a Danish subject. I doubt he'd get in deep with smuggling for the patriot cause."

"Far as we know, ever since the man brought his wealth to Philadelphia and flaunted it for all to see, he has loudly proclaimed which side he is on.

"He might simply be taking sides to turn a profit," Mount suggested.

"Any merchant would sell his soul to increase profits . . . especially rapacious Danish merchants with ties to the islands. Most of them are soft on the rebel cause much to the chagrin of their king's advisors. This Markoe chap may be one of the worst . . . a skulking danger to our King's interests . . ."

Mount was not convinced. She cast a frown of doubt.

Mortaine had more to say: "Abram Markoe is a complicated and conflicted fellow. He identifies with this independency cause against England, yet he remains staunchly loyal to the Danish king, though he denies barbaric viking roots when in the company of his pecunious horsemen. This I have been told."

"I have observed the man with his family and servants in his new castle," Mount said. "I have overheard his ranting about the maltreatment of King Christian's British-born wife. He seems loyal to his Denmark, but not so keen on its addled king. In fact, I have heard him curse the king and his advisors."

"Keep an ear on such matters, Miss Mount. It may develop into something useful."

The seamstress nodded that she would.

"Oh, and it reminds me," Mortaine continued. "Any truth to the rumors about our good rebel captain from St. Croix taking liberties with the help, black or white, when his blossoming wife is distracted?"

Miss Mount scoffed but refused to blush. "No less so than his moneyed peers, judging by the boasting and bragging I've heard in other places I've worked."

"Has he favored you with his lusty eye?"

Mount snapped, "I'm too old for his bother and new to his house." She paused to finish her tea with one last sip. "Besides, you well know, Mister Mortaine, I am not inclined to reciprocate any man's advances. I mock them if they dare."

"Your business, Miss Mount, not mine nor the King's. How about the other two maids who were hired same time as you?"

"Cornelia Emmons is a widow and older than I am," observed the seamstress. "Captain Markoe pays her no mind. The woman is friendly enough, especially around Mistress Elizabeth and her daughter, but not so with the master of the house. If you ask me,

I think widow Emmons is afraid of him. Her first love is her herbs and spices and the potions she brews. She visits the garden more than me."

"I shall keep her in mind," noted Mortaine. "Her skills may come in handy in the future. Which way does she lean?"

"In politics or affairs of the heart?"

"Politics . . . Tory or Whig?"

"Never asked her," answered Mount. "She's been mute on the subject. I would have to say she's a fence-sitter . . . more like a Quaker, though she is not of that persuasion."

"Find out for certain," Mortaine instructed. "Guide her to the side of the loyal sheep."

"I will try my best, sir."

"What of the other new hire . . . the Irish girl. What's her name again?"

"Anna McClew is a shy, sweet thing," sighed Mount warmly. "She will come around to obeying me more than her master. Come winter, little Anna shall be sharing a bed with me and warming my toes. For the time being, Anna is merely an innocent—neither harmful or helpful to either cause."

"How about the others . . . ones in service to Markoe longer than you?"

Mount was careful with her response. "I've heard stories of Master Markoe diddling some of the kitchen slaves he brought with him from St. Croix. But I have no proof. Such gossip is more about his randy son, the junior everyone refers to as Abraham in order to differentiate him from his father."

"What have you heard about this stoat?"

"Abraham is in charge of the family plantations on the island—a huge sugar cane operation requiring a great number of slaves. According to the oldest kitchen slave at the manse, this son has sired four by black wenches. I've been told all of these half-breeds have been sent off to Denmark to be educated."

"I have heard similar stories about rutting Danes on the islands," Mortaine mused more to himself than to the seamstress. "Such news about the dalliances of a son, and possibly the father, might serve useful to us down the road."

"Perhaps in Virginia," Mount countered. "Not of much use in

Pennsylvania. Such behavior, wherever one goes, in high-born circles renders praise more than rebuke. In the dark, the hue of the mistress matters none but the number of mistresses counts for much."

"Ah, such wisdom from the likes of you, Ruth," Mortaine said as he looked around the tea room to make sure no one else was listening to their delicate conversation. Only Mount was listening. Mortaine continued in a whisper anyway. "Another reason why I hired you."

"Why, because you know I would never become entangled with the passions of a man? Especially one in favor of the rebel cause?"

"That and more, my good spy," Mortaine beamed. "Just keep gleaning more dirt on our Captain Markoe. So far so good."

"Anything else, before you pay for the lovely teas and cakes?" Mount queried firmly. "Before you pay me and fetch a coach for my return to the manse?"

"Yes, yes, of course." Mortaine reached for his coin pouch tucked in the folds of his voluminous shirt. He plunked down several whole silver coins and divided them into two small piles—one smaller than the other. He placed a hand over each pile. "Before I decide which trove is bound for your sewing bag, woman, there is one last item of business before we set a time and place for our next meeting."

Ruth Mount's eyes were fixed on the hand which shadowed the larger pile. "What matter have we not discussed?"

"We are in need of a password, should one be required by you or me, or anyone we bring into our confidence. Something of import is starting to boil. It may be in a larger pot than the two of us can handle. Others may have to join our circle to assist us. You and I will have to know and trust these folks. They must identify themselves by words we can remember—words we will use to identify ourselves." Mortaine stared at the seamstress long and hard, then he completed his thought. "The choice of words is yours to make, Miss Mount."

Ruth did not hesitate. "Two words have been stitched into my thoughts of late. I will never forget them."

"Those words are?"

"Thirteen stripes," Mount whispered.

The first time thirteen stripes appeared on an American banner was probably when Captain Abraham (aka: Abram) Markoe presented his design to the Philadelphia Troop of Light Horse in 1774/5. This standard is described adequately by Charles J. Lukens of Philadelphia: "The . . . flag is formed of two sides very strongly hemmed together along the edges, each side being of two equal pieces attached together by means of a horizontal seam, the material of the flag being a light bright yellow silk . . . The canton . . . is 'Barry of thirteen azure and argent'. The azure being deep ultra-marine, the argent silver leaf. The achievement in the center of the flag is: Azure, a round knot of three interlacings, with thirteen divergent, wavy, bellied double foliated ends or, whereof two ends are in chief; and one in base as per margin. The scrolled edging of the shield is gold, with outer and inner rims of silver.

"Crest, (without a wreath) a horse's head bay, with a white star on the forehead, erased at the shoulders, maned sable, bitted and rosetted or, and bridled azure. Over the head of the charger is the monogram L. H.

"Beneath the shield, the motto 'for these we strive', in black Roman capitals of the Elizabethan style, on a floating silver scroll, upon the upcurled ends of which stand the supporters, DEXTER, a Continental masquerading as an American Indian (probably of the Boston tea party, Dec. 16, 1773), with a bow or, the loosened string blue floating on the wind, in his left hand, and in his right, a gold rod upholding a liberty cap, with tassel azure, the lining silver, head dress and kilt (or ga-ka-ah) of feathers, the former of five alternately of gold and of dark red . . . The quiver is of gold supported over the right shoulder by a blue strap; its arrows are proper. A continental officer's crescent, gold, suspended around the neck by a blue string, rests just where the clavicles meet the sternum. The mocassins are buff with feather tops, . . . alternated dark red, and gold. The Indian has deep black hair, but his skin is intermediate between the Caucasian and the aboriginal hues, rather inclining to the former, and his cheek is decidedly ruddy, almost rosy. He approaches the shield in profile as does also the SINISTER SUPPORTER which represents an angel of florid tint, roseate cheek, with auburn curly hair, and blue eyes, blowing a golden trumpet, with his right hand, and holding in his left a gold rod. His wings are a light blueish gray with changeable flashes of silver. His flowing robe from the right shoulder to the left flank is purple. These supporters not being heraldic in position and motion for human or angelic figures, their left and right action have the natural and not heraldic significations."

4

MISTER POLLARD'S PISTOL

$\cdot\,\cdot$

(Wednesday, June 21, 1775)

No self-respecting man with moral fortitude would dare walk alone at night down the cartway. But the so-called Enoch Mortaine was not burdened by respect or morals. He had survived many a sojourn down the rough, unlit stretch which connected Front Street to Water Street in Philadelphia. A waning half-moon provided enough light for this one man rushing to meet up with another before midnight. Mortaine had one more secret business matter to attend to before George Washington's entourage headed north on the morning of the twenty-third.

Mortaine had dressed plain and humble for the occasion. It was a cool night, but he wore no fancy outer garment as he had done when meeting Miss Mount at Chandler's Tea House. Now his outfit consisted of a thick nankeen shirt, long leather vest to keep the chill from his bones, and crocus trousers, over coarse-thread hose, tucked into black walking boots above the ankles. He wore no wig nor ribband to tie back his tangle of chestnut hair. His locks flared out from under a black fisherman's wool cap. The King's agent wanted to look like any other waterfront bloak on his way to refreshment and merrymaking at the Sign of the Blue Anchor. So far, he was succeeding.

The Assistant to the Chief Wharf Inspector was tending to his special assignment. He hurried down the cartway because he did not want to be late this time. The latest change in plans was much more important than keeping an eye on the Markoe family. Word had been passed down from a superior in the morning. Immediate action had to be taken. Priorities had changed overnight.

Mortaine reached the broken wooden fence where he had met his man a few times before. He slipped into the shadows behind a gap in the fence. There he waited. He did not have to wait long.

An arm suddenly coiled around his shoulders and a knife blade was pressed against his throat. The air in Mortaine's lungs was thrust out in one gasp. The cold steel of the flat of the knife kept him from crying out. Mortaine failed to catch his breath. He felt his knees give way. He would have collapsed then and there, but whoever was choking him from behind would not let him fall. His nostrils did catch the tangy, sweet scent of one who was a loyal friend of hard liquor.

Mortaine managed to catch enough wind to manage a whisper: "Thirteen stripes . . ."

Immediately, the large, strong man let go of Mortaine. His victim fell like a sack of clams and held a trembling hand up to his throat. He felt dizzy and disoriented. The half-moon seemed to be winking at him—mocking his plight. Mortaine closed his eyes tight and imagined sitting comfortably at a table at the Sign of the Blue Anchor. In an instant, he forgot how close he had come to death.

Rough hands grabbed Mortaine under his armpits. He was yanked up to a standing position. His errant fisherman's cap was placed back on his tangled hair

"Sorry, mate, for the rude welcome," the deep-voiced greeter burred with a whiskeyed breath. "Had to be sure . . . lucky I remembered the password."

Mortaine, still fighting to catch his breath, managed nothing better than a whisper: "How'd you come by it?"

"Don't know the chap, but he know'd me . . . whispered it to me . . . never met him afore . . . prob'ly won't never see him again. He'd be one of your kind most likes. Caught me at the Blue Anchor this once. You prob'ly know'd of him."

Mortaine recaptured his voice but kept it low, just above a whisper. "I did pass the words to my superior. No one else. Must have been the one I gave your name to. That chap is already on his way back to New York. You can forget about him and put your mind on the new business at hand."

"No problem," said the man in the dark. "Long as the coins is good."

"What are you calling yourself now?" Mortaine asked.

"Call me Pip for now . . . maybe somethin' else after you pay me."

"Fair enough, Pip. Fine with me. And you can call me Enoch from now on."

"Maybe we'll get to share a pint at the Blue Anchor, Mister Enoch, afore this new matter's been settled."

"Maybe so," Mortaine said. "Sooner than later, I hope. Were you civil to my superior?"

"Wouldn't be showin' here if'n I weren't," Pip offered after he spat loudly. He changed the subject: "Some Quaker I know'd vouched for me . . . praised my work as a drover for him, though I can't recall doin' so. All I know'd is the widebrim got paid well by your boss to introduce me to a certain Levi Hollingsworth who's servin' as a quartermaster for a certain Captain Abram Markoe."

"So you already know of the new plan?" Mortaine said.

"Somethin' 'bout this here Markoe escortin' the new commander of the rebels part of the way to Cambridge, so I've been told."

"Why is this Hollingsworth fellow interested in you, Pip?"

"Lookin' for a drover . . . a rebel drover."

"Whose side are you on?" Mortaine asked.

"Whichever pays the most," Pip admitted without hesitation. "Been down on my luck of late . . . a few debts here and there, don't you know. I'm in need of some real hard coin . . . no script . . . nothin' clipped for the likes of me."

"I see," said Mortaine. "So this Hollingsworth fellow hired you to be part of the escort train?"

"From what he tells me, a score or so of the horse troop will be escortin' the new commander to a point above the city of New York. Hollingsworth needs a practiced drover for the troop's supply waggon. This drover turns out to be me . . . for a short wain and a two-horse team. I must report to Captain Markoe's manse afore dawn."

Mortaine was careful and cautious with his last question: "Did the one who gave you the password inform you of your more important responsibility during this journey?"

"Not a word," Pip announced boldly. "But I'm sure as the sun 'tis somethin' I can handle if'n the money's good."

"You get paid half this night," Mortaine instructed, "and half when you return to Philadelphia. You'll meet me here at this very same spot . . . same time . . . on Saturday, the first of July. If you are successful in doing what you must accomplish, you might return earlier, but you must wait till the first to get paid."

"I can live with that," Pip muttered. "I'll have enough pay from Captain Markoe plus your first half to live on till then."

"Good then," Mortaine sighed as he reached for a dueling pistol hidden behind his belt. He handed the expensive weapon to Pip. "This piece was stolen from the saddle pouch of a horseman named Will Pollard. He happens to be one of the men picked by Captain Markoe for the escort team. He's a carefree, careless chap who rides around town with one pistol at his belt and one in his pouch in case he loses one."

"Appears the lad's done so," mused Pip as he fingered the uncocked firearm in the moon's feeble light.

"You can feel his initials carved on the hilt," Mortaine instructed. "So we know who owns it—a gift from the man's father worth a pretty coin or two."

"How'd you come by it?" Pip asked.

"That's for me to know and never tell," snapped Mortaine. "Keep it on your person . . . at your belt till you are half-the-way through the Jerseys."

"Then what?"

Mortaine responded crisply: "You pick the exact place and time."

Pip took a guess: "For to dispatch Captain Markoe?"

Mortaine managed a chuckle: "No, Pip. The Crocian is small fish in this game."

"Then who?"

"A certain General, newly appointed," offered Mortaine. "And please leave the murder weapon where it can be easily found."

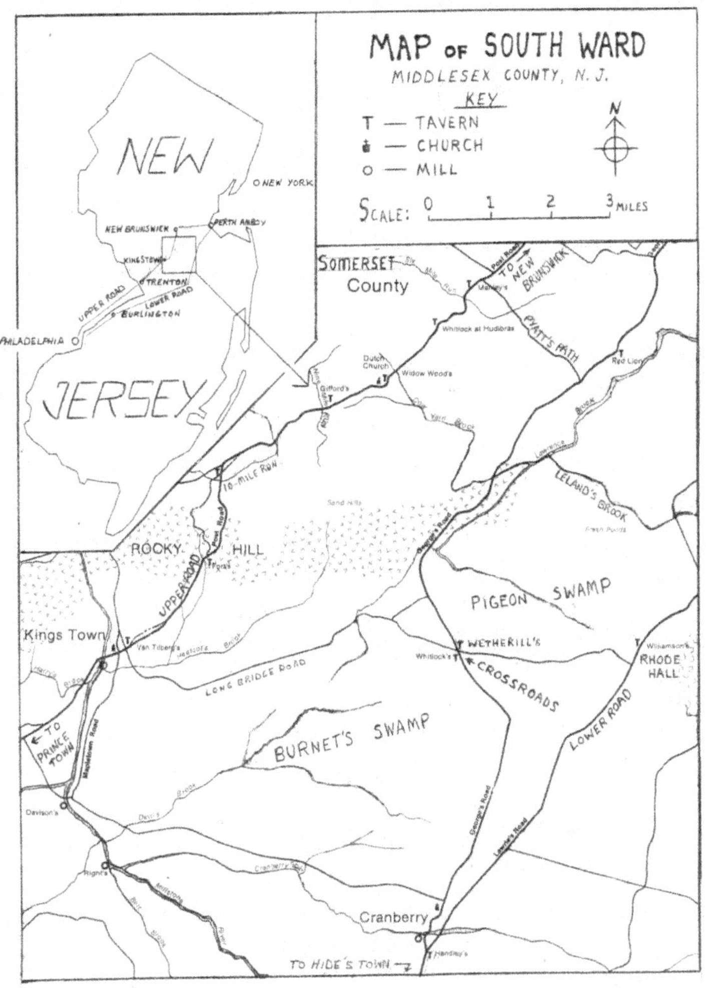
MAP OF SOUTH WARD
MIDDLESEX COUNTY, N.J.
KEY
T — TAVERN
— CHURCH
O — MILL
N
SCALE: 0 1 2 3 MILES
NEW
JERSEY
NEW YORK
NEW BRUNSWICK
PERTH AMBOY
KINGSTOWN
TRENTON
UPPER ROAD
LOWER ROAD
BURLINGTON
PHILADELPHIA
SOMERSET
County
Post Road
TO NEW BRUNSWICK
Lindsey's
Whitlock at Hudibras
PYATT'S PATH
Red Lion
Dutch Church
Widow Wood's
Gifford's
Mill Brook
Lawrence Brook
LELAND'S BROOK
Fresh Ponds
10-MILE RUN
Sand Hills
ROCKY HILL
Gross
PIGEON SWAMP
UPPER ROAD
Kings Town
Van Tilberg's
Westcotts Brook
WETHERILL'S
Whitlock's
CROSSROADS
Williamson's
RHODE HALL
George's Road
LONG BRIDGE ROAD
TO PRINCE TOWN
Middletown Road
LOWER ROAD
BURNET'S SWAMP
Brook
Davison's
Devil's Brook
Right's
Cranberry Brook
Millstone River
Cranberry
Lindsey's Road
TO HIDE'S TOWN
Handley's

5

AN UNFORESEEN INCIDENT

(Friday, June 23, 1775)

Twenty-one-year-old, Puddin' John Barricklow, stoop-shouldered and sporting a down look under a royal blue tricorn with gold trim, stood on the stone steps of the entrance to Manley's Tavern. He was cursing again. This time his target was old Jacobus Lake and his cabbage waggon pulled by a sway-back mare. The farmer was trying his best to navigate the ruts in the King's Highway, which Whigs preferred to call the Upper Road. This former Native American path connected Trent Town to New Brunswick. It was the preferred way for husbandmen to get their produce to market. But to Puddin' John the road did not belong to anyone—not even King George III. The addled young man deemed it neutral land sitting between Somerset and Middlesex counties. Over the years this wide road had been violated by greedy farmers and reconfigured by authorities. In Barricklow's troubled mind, someone had to guard the road, keep it pristine, and not allow just anyone to ply it. That someone was a self-appointed ward of the old road whose birth name was John Barricklow. He earned his nickname before his teen years.

Puddin' John felt the need to curse at the oldster who was clucking to his horse. Jacobus Lake was moving too slow. More important traffic was rumored to be approaching soon. Local folks on either side of the boundary usually paid the Dutch fool no mind. Everybody knew Puddin' John was a bit touched in the head. That's how he earned his nickname. Ever since he was a wee lad, he had behaved strangely. He loved to play in the road. He was often pulled, kicking and screaming, out of the rut puddles by a parent, older sibling, or concerned neighbor. Even back then the strange boy insisted the road was his to guard.

Over the past decade, traffic on the King's Highway increased greatly. Stage waggons, horsemen, and produce vehicles of all sorts used the road from dawn to dusk. Puddin' John ignored some but heaped his wrath on others. He loved to chase after waggons whose drivers would not obey his commands to stop. He threw stones at horses and vehicles upon occasion. But most of the time he hurled curses into the wind. Puddin' John had never done a day's work. He claimed to be too busy patrolling his road—a task too important to be left to someone else.

The gathering of men inside Manley's, as usual, paid no mind to Puddin' John's antics. This was always as it had been for many years, except when some accosted wayfarer halted in the road and threatened Barricklow with bodily harm. Such instances were rare. But when a stranger to these remote hills took umbrage at Puddin' John's words or stones, and strove to assault him, patrons at Manley's came to the rescue, sent the stranger on his way, and pulled Barricklow to safety. Little did the current patrons know, on this rainy late Friday afternoon, June 23, 1775, two of their number would have to come to the road guardian's aid.

The usual foul-weather crowd of locals was gathered inside Manley's establishment. Not much could have been accomplished in the surrounding fields in the middle of a lengthy rainstorm. After tending to doable chores, thirsty men came acalling to their favorite watering place. Also in attendance were members of the Ratters, a local hunting club from Cross Roads, who got caught in the downpour while scaring up worthy game in the Sand Hills. They had abandoned their hunt on orders from their leaders—Vincent Wetherill and his older brother, John, Jr. They were the sons of John Wetherill, noted long-time Assemblyman representing Middlesex County, and, recently, a delegate to the New Jersey Provincial Congress in Trent Town. Two months ago, both sons had returned to the area to manage their father's thousand-acre plantation in his absence. This gave opportunity to revive the Ratters Hunt Club which had been dormant for several months.

The Ratters had all decided to trace Six-Mile-Run out of the woods and along the Upper Road to Manley's. They left their horses and hounds tethered in minehost's stable barn, much to the dismay of the overworked slaves seeking shelter there. Generous

John the Younger gave each slave a modest coin. warned them to stay a safe distance from the tethered hounds, and concentrate on the needs of the horses.

Vincent Wetherill, a tall, strapping twenty-six-year-old, led the hunters across the muddy yard to the rear entrance of the humble tavern. They carried their weapons with them, for they did not trust to leave them with minehost's slaves. The bedraggled line of soaking wet Ratters, following the Wetherill brothers, included young locals Benjamin Hull, John Caywood, Cutlope Hancock, Johnny Davison, Rob Marshon, and Ike Higgins. They tramped in noisily, left soaked outer garments on pegs along the walls of a narrow hallway, and proceeded to the already crowded bar where they were greeted warmly by Minehost Manley and the patrons who had chosen not to crowd the porch where Puddin' John held sway. Before the first pints were poured, Manley instructed the hunters to prop their muskets and rifles against the wall by the main entrance. They complied then slaked their thirst.

Loud conversation went hand in hand with the drinking. John, Jr., asked why so many farmers were out on the porch. Manley explained proudly that General Washington's train of waggons was expected to pass by on its way to New Brunswick. Minehost explained that one of the Emmons boys—Benjamin, or 'Little Ben' as most folks called him—had galloped up from his homestead north of Kings Town with the grand news. Emmons had stopped at Manley's to quench his thirst and spread the news. He told those gathered around him of the train slowing to a crawl in managing Rock Hill in the rain. Washington's entourage was late by hours, but still hoping to make Brunswick by nightfall.

"The new General's in need of a heap of luck," Manley quoted Little Ben as saying before he gulped down the last of his drink and headed to the door . . . his castor hat beaded with moisture, his buckskin shirt and breeches soaking wet. But he stomped out spritely, according to Manley, and said before opening the door: "Got to tell the folks at Waldron's next." Then the Emmons lad was gone. Manley remarked that Puddin' John paid no mind to the messenger. Nary a curse or a stone was thrown.

Minehost's news convinced John, Jr., and his Ratters to hang around. They retreated to tables with their cups and requested the big-boned serving maid come pour another round. At one table, the elder Wetherill brother, dressed like his peers in hunting leathers, spoke excitedly about what was coming: "When our new Commander-in-Chief makes it here, we will have to go out on the porch and help Puddin' John cheer on the waggon line!"

Cups and bowls were raised. Cheers reached the rafters. Only Ike Higgins, seated alone at a corner table, kept his bowl of Jersey lightning to his lips and offered no huzzah. He drained his vessel quickly and rushed to the bar to fetch another. The Irishman was known for not taking sides. He trusted the leaders and the laws of neither side. All the rest of the Ratters were ardently Whiggish in their convictions and looking forward to signing up for service in the local militia. They were glad to hear that General Washington was on his way to New England. Finally, the Congress had made the right move in putting a true military man in charge of a soon-to-be-organized Continental Army. Today, in a short time, these South Ward locals would be able to cheer on their new leader—their new hero. Ike was not amused. He had survived this far without heroes. He needed none now.

"Maybe the Virginian will set foot in here?" Vincent Wetherill was speculating from the table nearest the bar. He was taller than his brother and stronger. When he spoke, the Ratters tended to listen more attentively than when his older brother spoke to them. Vincent possessed an aura that commanded respect. And he could back up his word. His sibling was a better business man—a negotiator who knew when to back down. Vincent never backed down and he instilled that spunk and spirit in his admirers—especially the German, Cutlope Hancock, and the Irishman, Ike Higgins—whether drunk or sober.

Those who had cheered John the Younger's words now raised their voices louder after Vincent's words. They looked forward to sharing a pint with the welcome stranger from Virginia.

When the clamor died down, Minehost Manley expressed some doubt: "Washington's train is way behind schedule . . . Don't think the man has time to dawdle in this outland."

"Nobody of high station has ever stopped at this hole," Abe Gulick, a Somerset local from Six-Mile-Run, chided. He was ensconced with the hunters at Vincent's table.

The pair of statements garnered a heap of guffaws and chuckles. Drinking vessels were drained. Refills were in order. Ike was at the bar again replenishing his bowl of Jersey lightning.

Will Donaldson, a farmer up from Ten-Mile-Run on the Middlesex side, managed to get a few words in edgewise: "John the Elder's been here often. He's sure important to the likes of us on our county side." He was sitting with three fellow husbandmen at the third center table.

"That old penny pincher's got my vote next time around!" exclaimed Dollis Hageman, a well-respected Dutch farmer whose land also lay on the east side of the Upper Road. He was seated next to Will Donaldson.

There was loud agreement from those who lived on the far side of the King's Highway and a muted, but respectable, amount of noise from the throats on the Somerset side.

"Where is John Wetherill?" asked a yeoman in the rear of the crowded main room. "He's missing a great event!"

John the Younger spoke in defense of the notable absentee: "My father would love to be here with you all . . .. be here to greet our Commander-in-Chief. But he cannot be in two places at once. He's no shape-shifter. He is now serving us well at the Provincial Congress in Trent Town. I am sure he was among the deputies who took the time to greet General Washington down there."

Suddenly there was a call to toast the Provincial Congress and one for John Wetherill. Cups and bowls were drained once more. Wetherill's elder son, far from penurious as his father, offered to pay Minehost Manley for another round. The husky serving maid was kept busy.

Now the cheers were for the Wetherills in the room. Drinking continued inside, but for some it continued outside as some men drifted to the porch where the long, broad roof protected them from the rain. Most of the Ratters gravitated to the porch. By then, Puddin' John Barricklow was standing in his road with one side of his tricorn uncocked. He was waiting silently for his next victim to come along. The spectators noticed that the queer fellow cradled a few stout stones in his left hand. They also noticed that the wind had died down and the resultant straight rain was letting up. Those not lost in idle conversation either stared hopefully at the gray sky or watched the stoic fool in the mud.

Cutlope Hancock, who was done with drinking, asked Vincent Wetherill if he should fetch Puddin' John out of the rain.

"No, Cut. Let him be."

The German stepped back from the lip of the porch. Other Ratters made room for the stout, barrel-chested man. He flashed his deep blue eyes and gave his close-cropped head a shake. Being a man of few words, Cut assumed his usual silence. His feats of strength spoke volumes for him. He was also known to be the best shot among the Ratters. His peers had ample reason to give the German his space.

Ike Higgins, allegedly born Ichabod Higgins of murky parentage, stood the farthest away from Mister Hancock. He had his reasons. The German, over the few years he knew the Irishman, had developed a strong dislike for him—Ike was a heavy drinker, careless to a fault even when sober. Trouble always had an easy time finding him. Proof was apparent on the scars and nicks which abounded on his face. He looked less like a hunter and more like the hunted. His homespun shirt was mud-streaked as were his bearskin trousers. He clutched his vessel of Jersey lightning and nothing else. Ike was the only Ratter on the porch who carried no firearm. His job on a hunt was to scout the area and rouse the game for others to shoot at. Ike was content to do so. He knew his place among gentlemen farmers and he knew which ones to keep a safe distance from.

All the Ratters had hoped to head back home to get to Cross Roads before dark, but the news of Washington's approach convinced them to stay. This was done in the name of curiosity and respect. They grew silent in the waiting. Watching Pudding John parade in the puddles failed to hold their interest. The minutes slipped by ever so slowly. The rain turned to a fine mist. The sun decided not to bother announcing Washington's tardy appearance.

Puddin' John, now brandishing a debarked tree branch, started up again. He was cussing loudly and pointing his weapon down the road in the direction of Nine-Mile-Run. The Ratters on the porch lifted their firearms and pointed them in that direction as well. Vincent Wetherill poked his head in the door and shouted for others to come see the approach of Washington's train. As many as could fit on the porch followed his command. The rest, including Manley, crowded at the open door. A few flies took advantage and buzzed in to search for treasures.

A trio of Somerset farmers, who had been early in sharing the porch made a dash for the shelter of a nearby leafy tree. They wanted to be first to greet the General. A half dozen children of slaves came running from the stable trough with full buckets of water. They had been instructed to service horses in the approaching train—the ones that could not get to the front trough near the hitching posts. These boys found another tree near the road. They chirped and cheered as lustily as the farmers.

First to trot into view was a uniformed horseman seemingly unbothered by the mud and the rain. This lead scout sat erect in the saddle and surveyed the spectators with eagle eyes. He liked what he saw and flashed a bright smile. Well behind the scout was another uniformed horseman holding a limp gold banner affixed to a long staff. The amber-haired young man spotted the crowd of cheering onlookers on Manley's porch and pointed the standard at them. Then he waved it for all to see. When the thirteen distinct stripes of blue and silver were revealed, the welcomers cheered their loudest, for they recognized the import of the unique design.

Twenty mounted men, dressed exactly like the first two, followed close behind the escort with the standard. Each sported a dark blue flat-topped forage cap, a stable jacket of the same hue with a standing collar of scarlet. Their pantaloons were gray and their short boots black. Even in the rain, these handsome fellows were a grand sight for the humble farmers from two counties.

Cheers erupted again when the advance guard from Philadelphia sloshed by. They did not halt their prize mounts until General Washington, himself, had pulled up parallel to Manley's tavern door and shouted a command to stop. The tall well-put-together gentleman farmer from Virginia was dressed in a full tarred cloak over his new blue and buff uniform. A gold-trimmed blue/black tricorn kept the rain off his brow. He seemed to pay no mind to the foul weather or the poor condition of the best road the Jerseys had to offer. General Washington, indeed, looked the part he was supposed to play.

The Commander-in-Chief acknowledged the loud reception

with the wave of a gloved hand. But he flashed no smile and remained tight-lipped. Washington barked out a few commands to his aides and the captain of his escorts as he remained in his saddle and tugged at the ornate clasp of his voluminous cloak. Spectators caught but a glimpse of the General's new uniform when he raised his sword hand to salute those locals standing on the porch of the tavern. Those who raised their guns in reply could see the fine job Washington's indentured servant, Andrew Judge, had done on sewing the uniform. It fit the Commander-in-Chief perfectly. History would soon forget who made the forty-three-year-old Virginian look so dignified. History would as speedily forget who sewed the banner with the thirteen stripes and the names of those who stood on Manley s porch. But, at least, all had a hand in lifting the spirits of the soon-to-be famous handler of crisis after crisis.

Those clustered around the Commander-in-Chief, remaining on their mounts, also caught the attention of the men on the porch. At that moment, Major Thomas Mifflin had the Virginian's ear. A nervously twitching Major General Charles Lee was close by, as was a dour Philip Schuyler and Lt. Colonel Joseph Reed. A cheer for Reed, a Jerseyan, emanated from the porch. One local called out the Colonel's full name.

There were a number of delegates returning to their home provinces in the line, but they sat snug in carriages. A few bothered to pull leather window flaps aside and stare out to see what the delay was all about. Two delegates took advantage of the stop by emerging from their respective vehicles to find the tavern ordinary which sat between two oaks behind the Manley house. Charles Lee dismounted and did the same. A stable slave intercepted the disoriented trio and escorted them to the door of the outhouse.

The rest of the train's personnel, consisting of the supply waggoneers and the rear escorts, waited patiently for movement to resume. A few waggoneers called out to slaves to bring their water buckets to thirsty horses. The young bucks under the tree sped down the line, sloshing the contents of their buckets as they ran.

A number of the lead escorts gathered at the front trough to allow their mounts to drink. One of these men sported a scarlet ribband on his forage cap. This marked him as Captain. When Abram Markoe's roan stallion reached the trough, Puddin John was there to lodge a complaint. He started in with a rude harangue about the failure of the train to keep moving along. Then he threatened to charge the Captain for watering his horse.

"I'm the ward of this road," declared Barricklow, while raising his stick and showing the stones in the palm of his other hand. "Pay up for the Adam's ale and move along . . . or suffer the consequences!"

Markoe let his horse drink. He smiled civilly at the obvious tom fool and decided to chat with one of his men.

Puddin' John realized he was being ignored. He was getting nowhere at the trough. He shrugged his shoulders and took off on the run, sloshing down the line past the coaches and following the slaves to the supply waggons. The uncocked flap of his tricorn danced up and down as he ran. His progress was cheered by a few patrons watching from Manley's porch. To encourage the daft fellow turned out to be a mistake.

Barricklow found the last waggon in the line to his liking. With a suspicious eye, he took full measure of the sullen, silent driver and marked him as a violator of a host of rules. Puddin' John started berating the man. He pointed his staff menacingly and showed the stones again. Pip James ignored the ninny just as Markoe had done. He slouched his shoulders and pulled the hood of his tarred cloak lower on his broad forehead. The driver of Captain Markoe's supply waggon simply stared straight ahead. Behind the vehicle, a rear guard horseman was laughing at the blue language employed by Puddin' John. This time the ward of the road did not get discouraged.

The self-appointed ward dropped his branch, selected a stone, and flung it with all his might at the side of the supply waggon. The missile snicked against the ribs of the vehicle and fell harmlessly to the ground. At the sound, a few heads turned to see what was going on. Many of the guards in the rear were laughing now. The slaves with water pails stopped running. They stood in place anticipating trouble. A few locals on Manley's porch strained their necks to see what the commotion was all about at the far end of the line. Even General Washington, who was growing impatient and about to give the command to proceed, turned his head and gave a look.

Vincent Wetherill was the first to act decisively: "Ike, go fetch Puddin' John before he gets us all in trouble . . . he will listen to you."

Ike spat off the porch, put down his empty drinking bowl, pulled his wide-brimmed hat down lower on his shaved head, and bolted along the shoulder of the road. He garnered cheers of encouragement from the Ratters he left behind, except for Cutlope Hancock who remained his taciturn self. Cut felt no need to encourage one who always created more trouble than he was worth. He felt Vincent had made a mistake in sending Ike to fetch the fool.

Before the Irishman could reach the last waggon, Pip James climbed down from his seat board and grabbed Puddin' John by the collar. He lifted the foul-mouthed fellow off his feet then threw him down in the mud. Barricklow was reduced to flailing his arms and sputtering in an attempt to catch his breath. Pip stood over the irritating rube, waiting for him to get up. But Puddin' John stayed put. He was moaning now, slapping the mud with empty hands.

Ike finally reached Puddin' John. He ignored the much larger man standing there and attempted to pull Barricklow out of the muck. He did not succeed. The waggoneer shoved Ike down on top of Puddin' John, Higgins gave out a feral grunt, popped back up on his feet, and faced the snarling bully. Ike grinned, called the man a bastard, then presented him with a brace of Gaelic curses—the meaning of which was known only to himself.

By then, someone else on Manley's porch sensed the inevitable and sprang into action. This Ratter had rescued old Ike from harm many times before. Now it was time to do the same once more. No one else watching the little drama unfold at the end of the train seemed to care or dare to try help Ike Higgins.

Cut handed his heirloom rifle to Vincent Wetherill and abandoned the porch in one bound. He sped down the line of vehicles faster than bow-legged Ike could ever manage. The German did so with the grim determination of a hungry wolf. Those who knew Cut Hancock knew better than to make him one's foe. Those who got in his way suffered dire consequences.

Before the German completed his run, Ike had taken time to flick mud off his homespun shirt. Then he bull-rushed the teamster, took a swipe with his fist, and hit the larger man square in the ribs. Pip James staggered back. Struggled to catch his breath. He came out of a crouch with a look of shocked surprise on his stubbly face. He quickly removed his cumbersome cloak and flung it up on the seat board. Pip pulled a knife from under his striped Holland jacket and pointed the blade at Ike's heart.

Ike readied his fists to deliver another blow, but Cut appeared and shoved the Irishman aside. Cut delivered a mighty kick to the waggoneer's right calf. The leg buckled, but the knife-wielder reached for the side of his waggon and caught his fall. Pip kept the knife in his left hand—the same hand he was using to keep himself upright. Cut seized the opportunity by slamming his fist down on the man's support arm. The crack of bone was heard by horsemen behind the last waggon, dignitaries in the nearest carriage, and a few waggoneers.

Although Pip now owned a broken arm, he was not done. Having lost his knife, Pip lunged forward and attempted to strike the German with his good right fist. He missed when Hancock dipped under the blow. Cut slammed his own right fist against the waggoneer's jaw. Pip went down like a sack of clams. He lay face up and motionless, blood trickling from his mouth.

Ike scrambled over to the downed man and checked to make sure he was still breathing. The Irishman put his ear close to Pip's mouth. The man was very much alive and reeking of rum. During the process, Ike allowed his fingers to trace along the man's belt. He found a pistol, but no money pouch. He seized the weapon and slipped it behind his own belt. He took a quick look around for the large knife the man had wielded but failed to find it. Then Ike helped Cut get Puddin' John to his feet. The entire unforeseen incident took but a few minutes, yet the delay, felt by others in Washington's train, seemed like an eternity. There was no cheering when the two rescuers shouldered the odd fellow back toward Manley's porch. Barricklow was swearing again but just above a whisper.

A waggoneer and two horsemen, who had dismounted, came to the rescue of the fallen man. Pip was out cold. The three men rolled Pip on to his cloak. Another waggoneer came to catch a corner of the cloak. The foursome carried Pip all the way to Manley's porch and deposited him there as gently as they could. Pip James became the focus of everyone's attention.

Captain Markoe, face crimson with anger, dismounted and

strode over to the porch. He let fly harsh words for those in his way, but fortunately most of the words were in a tongue rarely heard in the South Ward. Only Cutlope Hancock understood what the Captain was saying.

Cut stepped forward to intercept the Captain. He apologized in his mother tongue: "Deeply sorry for what's been done."

The two men stared unflinchingly at each other. All eyes were on the yeoman and the wealthy merchant. Many were expecting the worst. The rest saw nothing good in the outcome. Fists against an officer's sword was never a fair fight.

The German finished his apology of sorts: "The drover pulled a knife. The outcome might've been worse."

Markoe nodded. He understood the farmer's German and replied in like manner: "My man is out cold, thanks to you. It is apparent you broke his arm. I should have you arrested and thrown in the nearest jail. How will you compensate me for your actions?"

Cut simply stared at the gentleman. He had nothing left to say.

The Captain continued his rant: "My man cannot handle a horse team with only one good arm, even if he came to. So I am out a teamster. And we must be on our way . . . no more delays. The General is already two hours behind schedule."

Major Mifflin, who had dismounted and approached the porch, had something to say. He had been sent by Washington, himself, to speed things up.

"Let me handle this," said Mifflin as he stepped in front of Markoe.

The Crocian took a grudging step back, but voiced no objection.

"Who claims highest status on this porch?" demanded the Major.

Puddin' John piped up in a raspy voice: "I am the ward of the Upper Road . . . you must address me first!"

There were a few nervous chuckles on the porch.

Ike still held the brash fool's arm. He tightened his grip on the man's limb to silence him. The move worked. Barricklow flinched, but made no sound.

Minehost Manley, still at his door, spoke for all on the porch: "John Wetherill's son, by far . . . he can speak for the likes of us."

Vincent Wetherill was about to step forward, but his older

brother was quicker. John, Jr., reached for Major Mifflin's gloved hand and gripped it firmly. Their handshake lasted too long as far as the Philadelphian orator was concerned. He pulled his hand free quick as he could.

John the Younger had his words ready: "One of my hunters rides on horseback to fetch the nearest doctor at Three-Mile-Run. I will be paying Doctor Lerner for his efforts. Minehost has agreed to place your driver in his finest bedroom at no charge. My men will carry this poor fellow up the stairs and place him in a soft bed."

Mifflin nodded his approval, but his darting eyes indicated he expected more.

John, Jr., did not disappoint the Major: "I do apologize for the behavior of my peers. I am truly sorry for any delay they may have caused. Please tell General Washington that I . . . that we . . . are deeply sorry. We wish him only the best. Each one here supports the cause. We plan to do our part to defend it."

Ike Higgins frowned, but voiced no correction to what his superior had said.

The Major gave a modest bow and thanked the porch spokesman for his kind words. "When your father returns from his duties in Trent Town, tell him we appreciate all he has done for the cause. Be sure you encourage him to lead in this struggle . . . in any way his age and health allow him to handle."

Wetherill's older son bowed and indicated he would relay such kind words to his father.

Vincent Wetherill seized an opportunity to add his two-pence worth. He had enough of the exchange of niceties. He wished to end the delay and get Washington's train moving again. His brother and Major Mifflin were wasting precious time on more verbiage than necessary. Vincent had a solution to Captain Markoe's dilemma and he meant to propose it.

The younger Wetherill introduced himself to the Major and the Captain. Then he said: "Mister Hancock is a stellar waggoneer in his own right. He has often been called upon to manage my father's transport of wares over long distances. As you have learned, Cut fears nothing. Allow him to make amends for his untoward actions against the limbs of your unlucky teamster. Have Cut take the man's place . . . up to Brunswick Town . . . no farther."

Many on the porch liked the idea. Their grunts of approval indicated such.

Major Mifflin smiled. Captain Markoe cast a frown of doubt, but did not object. Both flashed a signal to their commander, who remained stoic as ever in the saddle. Washington looked none too happy over the latest delay, but he had no choice other than getting used to them. He could not even imagine what fate had in store for him. And this was only the beginning.

Major Mifflin turned to Abram Markoe just to make sure he was amenable to Wetherill's suggestion. "What say you, Captain?"

Markoe repeated his nod of approval. He was not too keen on his injured waggoneer's attitude or behavior anyway. Perhaps the German would be an improvement. Pip James left a great deal to be desired. When Markoe returned to Philadelphia, he planned to lodge a complaint with the gentleman who had recommended Mister James. So the Captain's less-than-stellar hire might not be missed, if the man Wetherill recommended proved serviceable up to New Brunswick. Markoe felt confident he could find another man in that river town where Washington's entourage planned to stay the night. Markoe would be able to retrieve his broken-armed teamster on the way back through this God awful countryside. This was a trivial concern compared to what was most important— to make a good impression on the Commander-in-Chief. So far, Washington had praised the flag design, but little else. This latest incident with Pip James did not help. Neither did the soreness in his legs and back caused by having to walk his horse up the notorious Rock Hill. Markoe had stumbled twice and fallen once in the process. Nothing was going well for the Crocian.

Markoe responded to Mifflin's question: "Fine with me, Colonel."

He turned to the two horsemen who had helped carry Pip to the porch and ordered them to escort Mister Hancock to the supply waggon.

Cut stepped forward, rifle in hand.

Captain Markoe asked in English: "Do you agree to Mister Wetherill's proposition?"

"Yup," said Cut in kind. "Long as I can hitch my horse to the back of your wain. Keep my rifle with me. And I need to get back to my wife quick as I can."

Ike let go of Puddin' John's arm and stepped forward also. "I should be ridin' with the likes of you, Cut."

The German waved at Ike as if swatting a pesky fly. "Nein, Irish . . . no more woe. Fetch my horse. Lead it to the supply waggon."

Ike scuttled off the porch to do as told.

Cut followed the horsemen to the last waggon in the line. He was accompanied by the two waggoneers who had helped lug Pip James to Manley's porch. Ike was not far behind astride Cut's horse.

After dismissing Ike curtly, Cut tethered his horse to the back of the supply waggon. He climbed up to the seat board, cradled his rifle in his lap, took hold of the reins, and uttered a few words in English to his charges. The pair responded with a snort and snicker, then clomped forward when the waggon in front lurched into motion.

General Washington's train headed toward Three-Mile-Run. New Brunswick was a good two hours away if the rain kept to mist. Disaster had been avoided . . . and the only one who knew was just coming to in a fine, soft bed in Minehost Manley's best upper room.

<h1 style="text-align:center">6</h1>

WHEN RATTERS MEET

• •

(Thursday, June 29, 1775)

It was supposed to be a day of fasting, humiliation, and prayer called by patriot clergy throughout the thirteen provinces. Supporters of the independency cause were supposed to refrain from gorging themselves and drinking to excess. But all that supposing was being ignored at the Wetherill Tavern fronting Rescarrick's Road in Cross Roads on the night of June 29, 1775. Good Mary Woods was in her second year under the employ of Thomas Wetherill, son of Freeholder, George Wetherill, and nephew of Assemblyman, John Wetherill. She reigned supreme in the tavern kitchen and had prepared a fine meal for the members of the Ratters Hunt Club. Its members had come together for their end-of-the-month meeting in the cramped game room of the tavern. All the meats Good Mary prepared this night came from the game the Ratter lads had killed on their second venture into the Sand Hills. There was venison, of course. Wild turkey roasted to perfection. Diced raccoon, possum, and squirrel all contributed to Good Mary's critter stew. Early squash and beans were served from a steaming pot lugged in by Good Mary's half-breed son, Little Ned. Sweet breads and samp pudding finished off a meal that no red-blooded hunter in the South Ward could refuse—even on a fast day. Besides, the sun had gone down and the fasting had been set for dawn to dusk.

No soul at the game room tables felt guilty, even when helping himself to second and third portions. The hunt club members had earned what they ate—not from when General Washington had passed through and a downpour that day had forced the Ratters to seek shelter at Manley's Tavern, but on the twenty-sixth when Ike

Higgins, the so-called 'Ward of Pigeon Swamp', guided them to the best hunting spots in the untamed area.

Ike was the newest member of the Ratters. Only Cutlope Hancock had voted against admitting him as a member. After all, the prodigal indenture of old John Wetherill was bad luck in Cut's book. He still had a knack for befriending trouble. As far as Cut knew, the Irishman possessed no firearm. But Ike could manage Thomas Wetherill's hunting hounds very well and he was good at beating the bushes to scare up game. So, except for Cut's reservations, Ike Higgins was welcomed into the club as a conditional member. Since he was Good Mary's mate, the club members could not bring themselves to vote with Cut. The Wetherill Tavern's cook was too damn good. Besides, Ike had stayed away from serious trouble ever since Old John had conjured up a position of employment for the Irishman. And Good Mary was keeping her man in line. She was watching what and how often he drank. Mary made sure her mate downed no more than she did, or anything stronger than she chose. But that was only when Ike was in her presence. Women were never allowed into a Ratter meeting.

The only recent trouble Ike had been involved in, if it could be trouble started by him, was the incident on the twenty-third when he came to the aid of Puddin' John. The fate of the waggoneer was the first topic of discussion at the hunt club's feast.

"I hear tell the teamster with the broken arm took off in the middle of the night," said handsome Johnny Davison, as he passed a platter of venison to Rob Marshon on his right.

"I heard the same," added Benjamin Hill, who dared elaborate on any subject whether versed in it or not. "Past midnight without a trace . . . never revealed his name . . . hardly said a word to anyone . . . even to Doc Lerner."

"Maybe the waggoneer headed for Brunswick Town to catch up with Washington's train," John Wetherill, Jr., offered. The elder son of the Assemblyman, sitting at the head of the longest table, was dressed in a lacy white cotton shirt and claret-hued silk vest. He looked more like a gentleman merchant tending to a business matter than a hunter of wild game or a manager of his father's plantation.

"Doubt that," John Caywood countered. He was sipping from

his bowl of Wetherill hard cider and contemplating another slice of venison.

"Prob'ly headed south . . . to Philadelphia," surmised Vincent Wetherill, who sat at the opposite end of the longest table. He, too, was dressed in finery. His wife had selected his outfit to wear for the occasion—a striped camblet shirt and swanskin jacket. "That driver'd never be able to catch up to the General's train on foot. Washington must be north of New York by now. The escort horse troop are heading back. That Captain Markoe prob'ly found a better driver in Brunswick and coaxed the fellow to stay on all the way to Philadelphia."

"Ike and Cut may have done this Captain, you speak of, a favor," chimed in Thomas Wetherill, who was taking a break from tending the bar in the main room of his tavern. He sat at a small table by the game room door. He was wiping his hands on his voluminous stained apron which protected his fall front breeches and expensive linen stockings. He flashed a broad grin at the local hunters who were enjoying the meal his cook had prepared for them. These were his best paying customers.

"What say you, Cut?" asked John the Younger.

"Don't know," Hancock responded. He was concentrating on a large bowl of Good Mary's stew. Cut was in the process of ripping chunks of oat bread from a fresh-baked loaf and dipping them in the bowl. Some he allowed to float on top before scooping them up with a large wooden spoon. Eating was always more important than talking as far as the German was concerned.

"How did it go once you got to Brunswick Town?" coaxed John, Jr., in an attempt to elicit more information out of the taciturn man.

"Easy ride to the Indian Queen," offered Cut. "Cap'n Markoe offered to pay for a room . . . let me stay the night . . . turned him down . . . took my pay for services rendered . . . got on my horse . . . found George's Road . . . headed home."

"So you never learned of your replacement?" asked John, Jr., who was glad to hear Cut finally open up.

"Nein," said Cut curtly.

"Anything worth remembering during the ride to Brunswick?" Vincent asked. He had drained a pewter cup of his father's cider and was signaling Little Ned to fetch another pitcher.

"Nein," Cut repeated. "'Cept one horseman claimed to be missin' a thing of great value . . . lost between Philadelphia 'n Brunswick Town . . . never learned what he'd lost."

"Lost or filched?" Ike asked. He was fussing over his bowl of samp pudding at the small table next to Thomas Wetherill. Most of the hunters in the room were surprised that Ike was paying attention to the conversation. Usually, at such gatherings, the Irishman kept to himself and concentrated on the food and drink—particularly on the drink.

Cut was reluctant to acknowledge that Ike was in the room. However, without looking in the direction from whence the question came, he responded with brevity: "Might'd been either."

Ike was not done. He posed another question: "How 'bout the knife the prat pulled on us?"

"Lost," Cut snapped. "Might be in the wain . . . but I paid no mind to fish for it . . . someone'll find it."

John the Younger inserted himself back into the conversation. He felt it was going nowhere. "None of this talk of missing waggoneers and weapons matters to us this night. We have more pressing matters worth discussing. Plans for next month need to be addressed—plans for what us Ratters intend to do in July."

"And what we may be called upon to do," added Vincent loud and clear from the other end of the main table.

"What is your guess, little brother?" asked John, Jr.

Vincent ignored the slight by his sibling. He knew his brother meant no harm and that he could thrash him in a fair fight. The others in the room felt the same. They paid no mind to the brotherly prattle.

The Assemblyman's younger son was glad to gain everybody's attention. "We have taken the oath. We are the eyes, ears, and strong limbs of the South Ward's Committee of Safety. No getting around it, we'll be beating the bushes, chasing dawn suspected sympathizers of the King. Things are heating up . . . won't be long afore our rousting of such inimicals turns into all out war."

John, Jr., was ready with a reply. Use of words was his strong suit—a valid reason for him to head up the local Committee of Safety. "I hope you are wrong on your prediction, little brother. The

Campbell lads over at Fresh Ponds have toned down their praise for the King of late. So have Willy Smith, Ben Drake, and John Cook. The tar 'n feathering of Mister Kearney last month put the fear of God in the worst of the King's sheep."

A spate of silence followed Wetherill's words, but Jonathan Combs, one Ratter who skipped the last hunt, was first to challenge the leader. Combs was a staunch supporter of independency and a hater of Parliament. He was quick to express his feelings about the future. "General Washington is not going all the way to Boston to lead a parade. Things are turning black up there. Won't be long till we see redcoats marching down the Upper Road. They and their supporters like the Campbells, Smith, Drake, and Cook will soon be stealing from us . . . all because we've not prepared."

Hendrick Van Dyke, a neighbor of Combs at Fresh Ponds, was less pessimistic. "If redcoats dare visit us, Ratters will be waitin' for 'em with muskets at the ready!"

A chorus of coarse throats was raised in affirmation. But a few voices were far from strident.

John, Jr., stood, raised his right arm, and quieted those in attendance at the meeting he had called for back when certain members of the Ratters were standing on Manley's porch. "We may be willing, Henry, but I am leary of how prepared we are. More good men are needed in order to give us a fighting chance . . . more men who can shoot. The call to form a militia company came down at the start of the month. We are late getting organized."

John Caywood voiced his concern: "Your father is among those delegates to the Provincial Congress who voted for raising militia companies in every city and township. I hear Old John is adamant about this issue. We should have been one of the first to organize. What is the problem?"

Thomas Wetherill offered his take on the delay: "My uncle and most of his peers have done what they could, but the stall and the wait involves Congress in Philadelphia passing down guidelines to each province regarding minute men and regular militia. If you are fit, willing, and able, all in this room will get your wish soon."

"No need to wait around on our arses," exclaimed young Andrew

McDowell, Jr., from Rhode Hall. For this exciteable man, the future was now. "What can we do to prepare?"

Johnny Davison offered his farthing's worth of advice: "Keep your powder dry and aim low, lads . . . and elect a damn good captain!"

Davison's words were greeted with a keen measure of nervous laughter.

Vincent Wetherill attempted to speak over the noise: "We can do more 'n that."

"What do you suggest?" his brother asked.

"I say we hold a shoot in the nearest fallow field. Invite all good men, between the ages of fifteen and forty, who dwell in the South Ward for a competition with muskets and rifles at a hundred and two-hundred yards. We'll find out who is fit for the challenge and who is ready to join the militia."

Thomas Wetherill liked the idea. "Your idea would make your father proud, Vincent. I suggest you hold the shoot same day as the pedlar's fair. By doing so, you'll draw a goodly number of participants. You'll need a few barrels of free cider for the contestants, spectators, and those wagering on the outcomes. Mister Whitlock, 'cross the way, and I can take care of the thirsty souls."

"Good idea, uncle," said John, Jr. When does Mister Whitlock plan to hold his next fair?"

"Middle of the month, as I recall him telling me just the other day," Thomas said. "Yes, Saturday, fifteenth of July."

"Suits us fine," John, Jr., said. "We can plan two hunts—one afore the ides and one after."

"Can't interfere with the first reaping," objected Jonathan Combs. "Got to make up for last year's failures, God willing."

"Understood," said the older Wetherill sibling.

"So the second week is out," Combs added.

"So schedule a hunt on a day in the first week," John Caywood suggested. "And one for the last week of the month . . . say the seventh and the twenty-eighth. Make 'em close by."

After a measure of unfettered discussion and another round of drinks, the men in attendance voiced unanimous approval of the dates and having the two hunts close by.

John, Jr., eventually turned to Ike Higgins, who was staring at his near empty drinking vessel and keeping his thoughts to himself.

Wetherill roused the Irishman from his reverie: "Ike, what say you 'bout the Ratters visiting Pigeon Swamp twice next month?"

Higgins gave a bleary-eyed glance in the leader's direction. He asked Wetherill to repeat the question then called for little Ned to fetch him more rum.

John, Jr., rephrased his question before Little Ned snatched up the empty bowl in order to refill it.

Ike nodded to show that he understood the question. "Fine fer me 'n the haints in the swamp. The drier it be in there, the better fer to hunt. Hope the gods gets stingy wit' rain."

"Then it's settled," declared John, Jr. "We spread the word of our shoot. Vincent and I will organize the event . . . and select the judges . . ."

"Ones who ain't blind!" interrupted Hendrick Van Dyke, possesser of a quick tongue and simple wit.

John, Jr., plowed through the laughter. "We'll make keen eyesight a determining factor on who will judge. Anything else in need of discussion?"

Silence reigned until the Ward of Pigeon Swamp, of all people, destroyed it. "What 'bout them wit' pistols?"

The older Wetherill sibling in the room employed a squinting eye of suspicion in the direction of the newest member of the Ratters. He doubted Ike meant no more than posing a bit of verbal mischief in the midst of a serious discussion.

"Few of us in these parts own a pistol or have use for one," contributed Vincent Wetherill. A pistol won't do much 'gainst a lobsterback unless he's close upon you with his bayonet."

"Just askin'," said Ike.

Johnny Davison came to the Irishman's defense. "Would not hurt to open the shoot to those few who harbor a pistol. My father owns a dandy piece. I know Old John owns a pair. I've heard Mister Lawrence boasts of owning a dueling pair . . . and . . ."

"All right, then," interjected John, Jr., as fast as he could. "Those in favor of including pistols in the shoot say 'aye.'"

There was only one man in the room who failed to respond.

"All those against, say 'nay.'"

Cut's voice was loud and clear with the sole negative vote. He had reasons known only to himself.

John, Jr., saw no need for further discussion on the latest issue. "The ayes have it. Our shoot will include pistols at twenty-five yards . . . a fair dueling distance."

For some reason, known only to himself, Ike Higgins was grinning.

7

THE FAILED ASSASSIN

(Saturday, July 1, 1775)

The Philadelphia Troop of Horse, led by Captain Abram Markoe, returned to the city before dusk on the first of the month. A crowd of patriots was there in front of the Tun Tavern to cheer them on and welcome them back home. The men were weary but glad to be back in the city of brotherly love. Captain Markoe remained on his horse and addressed the throng of welcomers before dismounting and leading his men into the Tun to slake their thirst and celebrate their success. The proud merchant told the welcomers, inside and out, that General Washington had been safely handed over to the Connecticut guard which was to escort the Commander-in-Chief the rest of the way to Cambridge, Massachusetts, where his forces waited for him to take charge. Cheers rang out for the Commander-in-Chief. There were also cheers for the lesser generals who accompanied Washington. While outside, Markoe concluded his impromptu speech by informing onlookers that nothing untoward occurred during the journey to New York. He purposely failed to mention the fate of the teamster who broke his arm. Nor did he bother to mention that the poor fellow had been left behind to mend at a tavern in Middlesex County in East Jersey. Markoe saw no need to account for a lowly waggoneer who had vanished before the troop of horse had returned to Manley's Tavern to fetch him. The missing man was just not worth mentioning.

Little did the Captain know that Pip James had already returned to the city and was hanging out on the waterfront. No one welcomed the failed assassin back. Only a few unsavory patrons at the Blue Anchor bothered to acknowledge his presence, or question his appearance. He sported a black and purple brawler's mark on his jaw. His left arm was wrapped firm and fine—cradled in a linen sling. None of Pip's few associates dared ask him what had happened. He was a mean bastard through and through, and they knew better than to rile him up. The constant blue scowl on his unshaven face was enough to warn anybody who approached not to ask questions. Often he drank alone.

While Captain Markoe and his men were enjoying themselves at the Tun Tavern before returning to their estates, nettle-browed Pip sat in the deep shadows of the Blue Anchor. He was nursing a pint of the cheapest rum the tavern offered. He was staring at nothing worth staring at. He was thinking of his recent setbacks. Pip had already spent most of the half-bounty money Enoch Mortaine had given him. In his present condition, finding work was nigh onto impossible. He was of no use to the owner of the stable where he had previously been employed. Pip did not even bother to return there. Perhaps he could find a job on the docks soon as he parted with the sling.

His precious knife was gone—vanished in Jersey when a rustic bumpkin broke his arm and tattooed his jaw. That same bastard, or someone of his ilk, had stolen the expensive dueling pistol Enoch Mortaine had found for him—the weapon he was supposed to have used to slay that new General. Now, the same scamp who filched his knife was probably walking around with a fancy dueling pistol. Maybe the culprit was one of the chaps who carried him up to the room in Manley's Tavern. Pip was not ready to forget his losses. He had a plan.

Yes, the failed assassin had lots to be pissed about. He had made new enemies he did not even know. He had received blame for the incident which delayed the new General's train at Manley's. That is why Pip slipped out of the South Ward tavern before the Philadelphia horsemen returned to fetch him and bring him back to the city. He feared Captain Markoe might have asked him too many questions—ones causing the ex-teamster to lose his temper and blow his cover . . . or worse. By leaving hastily in the night, Pip avoided such an embarrassing confrontation. However, he lost an opportunity to find out who stole his weapons. Pip promised himself that he would return one day to that cursing fool's road and make sure those who snaffled his weapons paid dearly for their deeds.

At least Pip was successful in making it back to Philadelphia on his own. He had purchased a horse in Maidenhead. Rode most of the way back to the city. The crossing of the Delaware at Trent Town was accomplished without incident. When he reached Bristol, Pip sold his horse for less than he paid for it. He had no need for a mount in Philadelphia. He walked the rest of the way and made it back with time to spare before having to meet Mister Mortaine, as promised, on the first day of July. His goal was to get the rest of the money owed him. If Mortaine balked because Pip had failed to dispatch General Washington, then force would have to be used to gain what was owed him. The agent for the King was no match against the one good arm of Pip James.

Another pleasant moonless night cast its black cloak over the cart-way. Enoch Mortaine navigated half its length by memory. He had second thoughts about going alone because his brutish hireling would probably be in a foul mood after the bloody jack fool failed to complete a murderous task. Mortaine assumed that Pip still possessed a keen knife. If their discussion did not go Pip's way, the grim fellow might just employ said weapon. But Mortaine was no fool. He carried a truncheon this time . . . just in case. He was used to handling surly types. It came with the responsibilities associated with his secret position. A good thrashing always turned a recalcitrant underling into an obedient servant. It worked on slaves and trained dogs like Pip. So Mortaine strode forth unaccompanied and somewhat confident he could handle whatever the dark held for him.

Mortaine wore the same homespun shirt and leather vest he wore to their last meeting. Dressing down for such occasions gave him a false sense of security. It made him feel stronger and tougher than he actually was. Comfort was also a consideration. This time, he wore decent broghams on his feet—a soft pair sporting big brass buckles.

Enoch Mortaine found the broken fence without much stumbling in the dark by feeling for it with his truncheon. He struck a fence post with his weapon. It made an ugly noise which echoed down the length of the cartway. The sound was greater than what Mortaine had wished for, but, at least, it would serve to signal his arrival at the rendezvous spot. Now all he had to do was slip behind the fence and wait.

Long did the King's agent have to wait. Midnight came and went. Still no Pip. Not a soul passed by. Mortaine whittled away the time by reflecting on what had gone wrong. Last he heard, from more than one reliable non-associator source, General Washington was alive and well . . . on his way to join his rabble of an army. No source offered a clue as to what went wrong regarding the assassination attempt. Very few knew about the plan anyway. Only Pip could provide the information needed so that Mortaine could complete his report to his superiors. This was the main reason he decided to wait for the bumbler well beyond midnight if he had to. Next time, he hoped to have a better plan with more than one bloak in on the action. Relying on one assassin had not worked.

Mortaine had also learned of Captain Markoe's triumphant return. The merchant from St. Croix and his troop of horse had distinguished themselves. Thus, the attempt to implicate a Philadelphia horseman in the assassination attempt had failed. Abram Markoe had not been embarrassed. In fact, the city was still celebrating his return. The Danish citizen was fast becoming an American hero.

Markoe had to be brought down a peg. Mortaine was now assigned to do just that. So far he was failing. Markoe was succeeding— ingratiating himself to wealthy and powerful Philadelphians . . . and more and more leaders of the patriot cause. The man had to be profiting from his endeavors. Getting wealthier from smuggling, so Mortaine's superiors kept telling him. Mortaine had found no evidence of it yet. He would eventually. Markoe would suffer the consequences, see the light, and back out of supporting the wrong side in the pending battle. Mortaine knew what to do—be more cunning than Markoe. Plan better. Employ clever underlings. Pip James seemed to be too stupid for such work. Clumsy. Hot-tempered. Mortaine considered letting go of the fellow, or, perhaps, giving him an assignment even a field slave could carry out. He wished Pip had Ruth Mount's brain, but God did not work that way. He also wished Miss Mount did not hate men so much. She was handsome enough for Enoch's taste, but her heart was hard as his truncheon and wicked to boot. There were rumors that she had sent her father and an unwitting suitor to early graves. Mortaine could believe it.

Enoch spent the rest of his wait time on the ill-starred events of the past few weeks. Things were going from bad to worse—seemingly getting out of hand. Regulars were being pulled out of Jersey and New York. They were shipping out to Boston because things were getting ugly there. Thus, the potential for trouble across the Delaware and across the Hudson had gone from possible to probable. Committees for Safety were identifying loyalists who refused to take patriot oaths. Rabble elements were tar and feathering neighbors marked as supporters of the King and his ministers. The same rabble were hanging royal leaders and sympathizers in effigy. Many English ships were not permitted to unload in colonial ports. The main culprit cargo was of course the tea shipments of the East India Trading Company. Much of it had been destroyed by raiding parties attacking the ships and/ or warehouses being set ablaze. Coffee was spared such a fate and becoming a popular drink among the rebellious subjects. Enoch Mortaine felt the authorities were doing too little too late. The King and his advisors were concentrating too much on Boston and nowhere else. The Continental Congress was proving that the colonies could form a united front and that the colonists could work together to oppose the King's wishes. Enoch figured the rebel movement only needed roughly a third of the population to put up a formidable fight. Loyalists would need half the population, but it did not appear that many neutrals were about to change their minds. Most Quakers would never take sides and neither would the many souls taking a wait-and-see approach. It was too early for many to take sides. The loyalists were slow to react and organize themselves. They put great stock in the might of the forces protecting them. But Enoch knew these forces were insufficient and stretched too thin. He also knew there were elements in England that had no stomach for war and wasting revenue on such an inevitability. In the darkness blanketing the cartway, Mortaine could peer into the future, and it was just as black as it was bleak.

Still, Pip had yet to appear. Where was the failed assassin?

Probably drinking away the last of his first installment, thought Mortaine. It seemed way past midnight, but he could not tell for sure. All he knew was that Pip was late . . . very late. Maybe the bumbler would not show at all. Maybe Pip wanted nothing more to do with dispatching rebel leaders. That Pip was out there unaccounted for might prove to be a problem in itself. A tongue loosened by too much rum, or something better, might wag the truth in the wrong places. Maybe this chap might have to be eliminated.

Mortaine caught the sound of shuffling feet approaching on the cartway. He gripped his truncheon tightly in his right hand and peered into the darkness. Starshine on a clear, moonless night failed to reveal a thing. Luckily Mortaine detected the odor of cheap spirits way before the hireling reached the gap in the broken fence.

Pip spoke first: "To hell with the thirteen stripes nonsense. Give me the rest of the bounty money!"

Mortaine took a step in the direction of the rude voice, raised his truncheon, and brought it down smartly. It thwacked loudly against a fence rail but did not crack the wood.

Pip had avoided stepping into harm's way. He stood in silence. Those who knew him well, and those folks were less than three, claimed he had 'Indian eyes' and could see in the dark. Pip had sensed the blow coming and successfully avoided it. If he spoke now, the man floundering in the dark would stand a better chance of finding him with the truncheon. Pip wanted the money owed him, not another injury.

Mortaine stood silent for a moment also. His inability to see in starshine put him at an embarrassing disadvantage. Finally, he cleared his throat and decided to speak. "You are late, Pip."

"That I am," said the would-be assassin, "but I'm here now. I want what's owed me. No need strikin' a faithful servant."

Mortaine spat in the direction of the broken fence. "You don't deserve a penny more," countered the Tory operative. "I've been told General Washington is scheduled to arrive at Cambridge on Monday or Tuesday. I hear his journey through the Jerseys was accomplished without incident, my good Pip. So what went wrong?"

"Not my fault," growled the hireling.

"You are the only one who knows and the only one who can tell me."

Pip was quick with his explanation. "I was set upon by three bumpkins half-the-way to New York. Not one of Markoe's men came to my aid. I had to fend for myself."

"Is that so?" queried Mortaine ruefully. "A strapping, mean bastard like yourself. with fighting skills feared by so many down at the wharfs . . . and armed to boot. I find it hard to believe that a few farmers got the best of you."

"Broke my arm, bruised my jaw, and loosened two of my teeth. For such, I deserve the rest of my pay."

"Washington is very much alive," observed Mortaine. "You were supposed to make sure of the opposite. Since he lives, you don't get one penny more of the bounty."

"Ain't fair, Mister Mortaine. Not only was I attacked, but I was robbed of my weapons . . . lost my knife and the pistol you found for me."

"Jesus be damned!" cursed Mortaine as he slammed his truncheon against the fence again. "Now you tell me the pistol with the owner's initials carved on the hilt has been stolen. If that firearm ever gets back to its owner, and he is told who it was taken from, then anybody with a spider's fart of intelligence might figure out who you are really working for. Even Abram Markoe will be able to figure it out."

"They'd never trace the plan back to you," said Pip. "I got my story ready and it don't include you. Besides, when my arm heals, I'm goin' back into Jersey to fetch that pistol and bring it back to you. Give me a month's time. But till then, I'll need the rest of my pay."

Enoch Mortaine hesitated. He was debating what to say next. Should he murder Pip now by bludgeoning him to death, or should he let him live to serve another day?

Mortaine chose his words carefully. "I cannot pay you the rest, Pip. 'Tis a matter of principle. "

"Yes, you will, or . . ."

"Hear me out," demanded Mortaine firmly while raising his truncheon to deliver a blow. "Don't dare threaten me or threaten to wag your tongue to whomever might pay to listen to what you have to say."

"Better be what my ears want to hear," countered Pip, "or it's my maulies you'll be listenin' to."

"How about this." offered Mortaine while ignoring the threat. "You keep your mouth shut and you continue to work for me through July at a higher sum than the amount you would have gotten for using the pistol."

"Doing what, pray tell?"

"I need a keen-eyed man to snoop 'round the docks and learn what's being smuggled into Philadelphia from the islands—particularly St. Eustatius, Nevis, St. Croix, and Montserrat. I'll drop in at the Sign of the Blue Anchor each Wednesday at the end of the day. You report what you have learned."

"You'll pay me each time?"

"Handsomely, Pip."

"Agreed. I'll keep my jaw tight shut 'cept for a morsel of food 'n a sip of rum. I'll retrieve that pistol in August, promise."

"Fair enough," said Mortaine. "By then, I may have another job for you to do."

"Another slaying?"

"Perhaps," mused Mortaine. "It depends on the nature of the business of Captain Markoe's guests in the next couple of months."

"Hope it's Markoe hisself," added Pip. "I took no likin' to the man . . . too uppitty and sure of hisself. He sure did not take a likin' to me right from the start."

"We will see," said Mortaine. "We will see."

8

A STROLL IN SOUTHWEST SQUARE

· ·

(Wednesday, July 5, 1775)

It was a far pleasant day for a stroll in Southwest Square. The spacious park, one of five designed by William Penn and Thomas Holme a century ago, was as good a place as any for Enoch Mortaine to meet up with his hireling, Ruth Mount. The block of green lawns and leafy trees and garden beds surrounded a tiny duck pond. Many of the well-to-do elite of Philadelphia frequented the place to bask in the sunlight, take in the pristine air as advocated by old Ben Franklin, and show off their finery. Children and servants also frequented the place, especially those who lived and worked for the owners of estates nearby. Southwest Square was indeed a safe place for the innocent by day . . . not so much after nightfall.

Mortaine, dressed in his finest wig, light summer surcoat of brown sateen, and a wisp of white lace cascading from his cravat. had completed his walk once around the pond. He had traded Saturday's truncheon for a sporty lacquered cane with an intricate chased silver top. He used it now to support his weight as he looked around for Miss Mount. Their after-dinner meeting had been planned for this location because it was not far from the Markoe manse. It was within easy walking distance along Walnut Street. The hour for the meeting was convenient for both parties, especially Mount who had been given more free time after completing the troop flag with the thirteen stripes on time—the one used for escorting General Washington up to New York. Many in Philadelphia had learned that even the General had praised the flag and was intrigued by the stripes in the corner. Captain Markoe, upon his return, was nothing but effusive in his gratitude for Ruth Mount's efforts on sewing the flag. Thus, she was rewarded more free time. This gave her a better chance to snoop around and gather information for her other master—the so-called Enoch Mortaine.

The King's agent decided to rest his feet. They were giving him some discomfort while circling the pond. His new walking shoes had raised blisters on both feet. He wanted to remove his footwear and silk stockings, sit at the edge of the pond, and soak his feet in the cool water. But that would not be a proper exercise for a gentleman of his stature—one providing such a vital service to his King in these troubled times. Instead, he found a stone bench in the shade, sat down, and waited for his accomplice to appear.

No sooner had Mortaine sat dawn, than two women dressed the same in powder blue linen frocks, white aprons, and white mobcaps approached. They were arm and arm, sharing whispered words, and smiling. They moved at a leisurely pace and did not appear to notice the finely dressed man on the bench. This pair of paid servants seemed comfortable in a world of their own creation.

Mortaine recognized the maid with the royal blue ribband dangling from her cap. He wondered when the woman was going to stop and acknowledge him, or pretend not to know who he was and continue strolling on by. Mortaine could only guess about the boyish, young woman accompanying Ruth Mount . . . the one sporting a red ribband.

The sewing maid stopped suddenly; smiled, and made eye contact with the man on the bench. "Dear brother, sorry I am late, but duties at the manse have to come first as you know."

Mortaine arose from his bench, stood erect on his sore feet, and bowed to the one he did not know.

"Oh, my goodness," said Ruth Mount, "my apologies for not introducing my sweet companion, Miss Anna McClew."

The speaker, beaming with pride, withdrew her arm from the Irish girl's grasp.

Miss McClew bobbed a dainty curtsy in a rehearsed sort of way. Her cheeks blushed crimson. Dark eyes attempted to broadcast innocence.

Ruth Mount gave her companion a fond glance and said: "May I introduce the family member I told you about. This is my younger brother by half, Azariah Willett.

McClew, red-haired and possessing more freckles than stars in the sky, courtsied again and added, "A pleasure to meet you, Mister Willett . . . for sure I am."

Enoch Mortaine, suddenly announced as Azariah Willett, lost himself for a second in the young woman's soft, green eyes. Then he recovered. "Likewise, Miss McClew." He wanted to say more but the words failed to come.

Ruth Mount rescued her boss. "I told my companion you wished to discuss certain family matters with me in private, Azariah. Here is as good a place as any."

"I shall continue the walk alone round the pond," sighed McClew, again using her rehearsed voice. "And leave you two to be discussin' what has to be discussed." She turned to her special companion. "But promise me, dearest Ruth, to walk round the pond when you're done with your brother."

Mount smiled affectionately. "I promise, Annie. Anything for you. And I mean it."

McClew courtsied again then started walking away. She looked back only once to trade smiles with Ruth Mount.

When McClew was out of hearing distance, Mortaine made a tart observation: "I see progress is being made, little sister."

"On many fronts, Mister Mortaine. Some of it for you to know . . . some of it for you never to know. Suffice it to say the bed sharing has already begun. But what I do after my first sleep and before my second sleep shall remain a secret."

"I expect no less," said Mortaine. "Come sit on the bench with me, Ruth. My feet are killing me. I shall be in a better mood if we sit down."

The man did and the woman did not.

"Been sitting most of the morn," groused Mount. "I prefer to stand in the shade of this tree you've selected to sit yourself under . . . such a fine choice on a warm day. You are showing good judgement, little brother."

"Suit yourself," said Mortaine. With that he leaned back on the bench and let out a labored sigh. His next breath included a question: "Azariah Willett—is that really your brother's name?"

"I have no brother, whole or half," said Ruth. "Least, that I know of. My mother never spoke of one. She was in her cups most of the time . . . never did she know how many little ones she had."

Mortaine gave an understanding nod. "I think I shall employ the Willett name when the need arises."

"You might have need to use the name if and when you come in contact with any of the Markoes. Anna McClew knows it now and her gossip about me will soon include the mention of my brother, Azariah Willett."

"I thought you have complete control over this young lass?"

"No person can control a woman's tongue," opined Mount officiously. "One can only hope and pray my Anna uses hers discreetly . . . and to bring me pleasure, of course."

Mortaine felt suddenly hot and uncomfortable. He shifted his weight on the stone bench. It did not help. The man made an awkward gesture with both hands and attempted to change the subject. "Enough of this talk of names and partners and whatnot. Let us get on with why you are here, Miss Mount. Let us be done by the time your little Anna completes her circle of the pond."

"Grand idea," declared the rompish woman, who loved to see a man squirming nervous in her presence.

"Good then," said Mortaine, as he swallowed with difficulty. "What about Captain Markoe's guests?"

"There has been only one—his grown son, Peter."

"I am not talking about that twit," growled Mortaine. "He poses no threat to our purpose . . . no more than a hair on my arse. I hear the buffer's lines of verse reek of self-indulgence . . . the pitiful work of a narcissist."

Ruth Mount smiled at her boss's critique of a middling poet. "Peter has been reciting some of his sing-song patriotic verse of late. Nothing worth remembering. Doggeral if you ask me. But it does show he favors the other side."

"The rebels can have him," sneered Mortaine. "When they run out of musket balls, they can hurl his precious words at the Regulars. For now, let us forget that effete bard. I want to know who is coming next to visit Captain Markoe."

"I have learned much about a certain wealthy plantation owner from St. Croix," admitted Mount. "The man's visit is eagerly anticipated by the Captain. He has spoken highly of the man these past few days. Arrival date? From what I have gleaned so far, this guest shall arrive early in August."

"Does this fellow have a name?"

"Colonel Johan Gottfried Krause, an officer in the West Indian Guard and proprietor of the sprawling Annaberg Estate in the King's Quarter of St. Croix. The King of Denmark has named a lagoon nearby after this man."

"Can't say I've heard of the chap," confessed Mortaine with another sigh.

"A loyal Dane," Mount added, "and a warm friend of the Markoe family, so I've been told more times than I care to count. Appears this character is coming to Philadelphia to inspect a school run by the Moravians—the same order that has done missionary and educational work among the slaves of St. Croix, according to master Markoe. Seems this Colonel Krause admires their efforts and desires to send his two youngest sons to the school."

"That would be Nazareth Hall," observed Mortaine. "An innocent enough excuse for visiting Philadelphia."

Ruth Mount offered more: "The man does have a few business matters to attend to, but I have yet to learn the nature of them."

"I'm sure a man of his stature has more on his mind than enrolling his offspring in a boarding school."

"Agreed," said Mount.

"As I understand it, that institution of learning happens to be in dire need of financial support. See if you can find out about any other reasons why this Colonel Krause is visiting our Captain Markoe. It may prove significant to us to learn what 'business matters' this fellow has in mind."

"I will do just that," Ruth said confidently.

"Any others?"

"Visitors, you mean?"

"Yes," demanded Mortaine. "Who else shall be gracing Markoe's steading?"

"The usual gaggle of Miss Elizabeth's clucking hens for tea and gossip," sneered Mount. "Oh, and John Folwell, that reknowned designer I may have mentioned to you earlier. He is soon due for another visit. Captain Markoe wants the man to inspect the work I have done on the flag. He wants Mister Folwell to add a few finishing touches to the design. Then he plans to commission James Claypoole to gild and silver a separate version of the flag.

This is going to cost my master a handsome sum."

"The flag business is of no interest to me," huffed Mortaine. "Concentrate on the Colonel from St. Croix. I suspect his business matters may have something to do with smuggling contraband."

"Doubt it," Ruth offered. "But you are better at sniffing out such sport than I am."

Mortaine managed a smile and forgot about his foot pain for a moment. "Well, I am glad to hear you admit I am better at something."

Ruth Mount was about to offer a smart retort, but she caught a glimpse of her paramor approaching.

Enoch Mortaine spotted the young maid also. "Time to end our chat, little sister. May I suggest another place for Wednesday, the nineteenth. Lets make it the gate at the Christ Church burial grounds . . . weather permitting . . . same hour."

With that said, Mortaine handed Ruth two gold coins which she promptly slipped into the folds of her frock before Anna McClew drew close. The sewing maid had just enough time to hand Mortaine an updated list of the members of Markoe's troop of horse.

"You've done well, my dear sister," remarked Mortaine with a wink. He stood with difficulty to acknowledge Miss McClew's return. He managed a slight knee after he had finished praising Mount.

Ruth also acknowledged the return of her dear Anna with a nod and a smile. She offered her arm to the blushing Irish maid. Anna entwined hers comfortably and off they went for another circling of the pond.

Mortaine watched the pair disappear among the trees. Then he took off in the opposite direction. He needed to contact certain higher ups about this Colonel Johan Gottfried Krause. Mortaine felt in his bones that he was on to something big. He ignored the fact that his feet were killing him.

9

A TEST OF SKILL

(Saturday, July 15, 1775)

The day of the most recent pedlar's fair at Cross Roads in the middle of July was as good a time as any for the local folks to gather, spread gossip, and share the latest news. A bright sun officiated the proceedings. The sky went about remaining clear. It had not rained since an evening shower on the fourth of July. The ground was dry and thirsty. Pessimists considered it a drought. Optimists held out for rain coming soon. An intermittant breeze kicked up dust from the roads where most folks had gathered. Judging by the noise and merriment, the optimists outnumbered the pessimists.

Women outnumbered the men at this event. Thomas Wetherill's daughters—Abigail, Rebecca, Ann, and Sarah were in attendance. Vincent Wetherill's wife, Abigail, whom everyone called 'Abia', was able to attend because Old John's house slave, Sarah, was watching Vincent and Abie's two-year-old back at the manse. All such women were honing their gossiping skills while the men were attempting to outdo one another in swapping accounts of the news. Besides talk, folks of all stripes gathered to see the latest items being promoted by the handful of pedlars who had ventured out from New Brunswick by plying George Rescarrick's Road. By this time, most locals referred to the byway as Georges Road.

The carts and waggons of the pedlars were filled with dry goods, consisting of finery and fluff for the women and hardware and leather goods for the men. Pedlars also contributed the latest news and the ripest gossip from the bustling town on the Raritan. Topics ranged from predictions on when the war would begin in earnest to the true tale of the woman in Morris County who had been wed seventeen years and just gave birth to her twentieth child.

Old John Wetherill's name was always bantered about at these occasions, especially when he was absent from them. Folks knew he was still in Trenton at the Jersey Provincial Congress. The latest report circulating was that the well-respected representative of the people allegedly took umbrage at fellow delegate Hendrick Fisher's assertion that harmony between the colonies and England would soon be restored. The feisty local politician maintained that it was too late for such an idea to work. Most folks at the fair sided with their Assemblyman. All the fasting and all the praying in the world were not going to turn things around. Fisher was dead wrong. Wetherill was surely right. War was inevitable.

But war was not going to spoil this pedlar's fair. Merriment and joy reigned where Ridge Road crossed Georges Road. There was reason to celebrate and remain optimistic even with the prospect of war looming and drought continuing. Folks who had been inoculated for the pox in New Brunswick, which included all the pedlars and a goodly number of locals, shared their experience and urged others to make the trip into the city. Additional positive news came from a few folks who had ventured up from Prince Town to experience the fair. They brought word of Reverend John Witherspoon's beautiful daughter, Anne, being married to the Reverend Samuel Smith.

Such positive news was balanced by rumors of the troubles facing Richard Cayford, a known loyalist who had been accused by a Committee of Observation of attempting to enlist men to fight under British General Thomas Gage, stirring up slaves to kill their masters, and interfering with the justified efforts of the Committee. All of this was still in the rumor stage, but at this gathering, the tyrant King's friend had to be punished. What was open for discussion was an appropriate punishment for the scoundrel—tar and feathers was considered, but hanging won out.

Also of interest, especially for those fearing the worst in the months to come, was the story of a local miller who stirred up the debris at the bottom of his pond, observed gas bubbles floating to the surface, and decided to ignite them with a lit candle. The result, so claimed one of his neighbors who was in attendance at the fair, was like an explosion of gunpowder. This account spawned a lively discussion among the farmers present about whether or not the miller's debris contained saltpetre. This led to the patriots in the crowd promoting the idea of farmers helping the cause by culling saltpetre from their barns and yards where their animals were kept. Everyone knew that large quantities of gunpowder would be needed for the pending conflict. It was in short supply, as were firearms. Those who were too old or too young to fight could still do their part. Making gunpowder from saltpetre, sulpher, and charcoal would be a crucial contribution to the cause.

Off in the distance the sound of musket fire could be heard above the noise at Whitlock's fair. There were no hunters in the fallow fields behind the inn, but there were several men eligible for the militia muster rolls who had gathered to take part in the Ratters' target shoot. They had come from miles around, not only to demonstrate their prowess with favorite muskets, rifles, and pistols, but also to discuss plans for raising a company of militia and electing officers. Companies had already been formed in Somerset County. Exercises had already been held at Bridgewater. Abraham Ten Eyck had been elected captain. So far, over four score of fit men between the ages of sixteen and sixty had volunteered in the neighboring county. But Middlesex lagged behind in forming companies. The South Ward was way late in this game. However, the Wetherill brothers—John the Younger and Vincent—meant to do something about it.

The Wetherill slaves, under the leadership of Old John's trusted Pharoah and Boss, had erected target posts in Burnet's fallow acreage at distances of twenty-five, one-hundred, and two-hundred yards. The shortest distance was meant for pistols only. The middle distance for muskets. The longest distance for rifles. Each pair of grooved posts, with a cross bar set at four feet above the ground, was placed a safe distance from the next.

The targets had been cut from broad pine wood planks at Dean's Mill. Three waggon loads had been brought to fallow ground the day before the event. Each thick target square sported a broad whitewash 'X'. A target was set in the grooves of the two posts and rested on a crossbar. Any contestant with a musket had to fire off three shots in less than a minute in order to qualify for the next round. When a contestant finished a round, the target was pulled from its posts and handed to a runner—a young slave of one of the contestants. The runner brought the target to the judges who then counted any holes in the white. They carefully measured the distance of each hole from the center of the target. When all seventeen musket men completed the first round, the judges selected the best three targets for the champion's round. The same process was used for the rifle competition at two-hundred yards. There were fewer entrants using rifles than those sporting muskets. The pistol competition was saved for last. As it turned out, only three men brought pistols.

John Wetherill, Jr., took charge at the judging table, which had been set up under the lone tree in the fallow field. He was sharply attired in a royal blue waistcoat, blue knee breeches, silver gray hose, and shiny buckled shoes. An officious white wig crowned his head. He was responsible for registering the contestants and, at the same time, encouraging them to sign up for the militia. Few contestants were eager to sign their name, or, if they could not read nor write, afix a distinctive mark after Wetherill had carefully printed their full name.

Thomas Wetherill was absent from the judging table, because he had to tend to business at the tavern across from the Whitlock Inn, while the pedlar's fair was in full swing. However, his father, George the Freeholder, had taken his older son's place at the table. He was his usual exuberant self for the occasion—loud, overbearing, and overly dressed. His white wig sat high above his broad forehead. Lace surrounded his fleshy neck in cloud-like fashion. His full-skirted knee-length red coat and matching breeches, both trimmed with gold piping, had no equal at the shoot. Old John's brother meant to be the center of attention. And he was.

George Wetherill was not happy with the paltry number of men who were signing up for militia duty. Before the first round of firearms competition began, he demanded to address the competitors and the onlookers. John, Jr., voiced no objection. Neither did Vincent, who was in the midst of inspecting the weapons and ammunition to be used. The other two judges remained silent. They knew better than object to the will and whims of the Wetherill who was called 'Windy' behind his back.

George got up from his bench then proceeded to stand on it. As he scanned the crowd that stood before him, he rolled his brown eyes and cleared his throat. He placed one well-shod foot on the judge's table. That was enough to capture everybody's attention.

"I must assume to be addressing liberty boys at this friendly shoot," roared the Freeholder proudly. "Am I correct?"

Many in the throng crowded closer to the judge's table and shouted that the loud man was correct.

"Good then," George continued. "You all know the real reason you are standing with me in this dry and dusty field. In the past couple of months the King's Regulars have murdered or wounded hundreds of our fellow sons of liberty in small towns and villages outside of Boston."

Grunts and jeers emanated from George's audience. A few raised their guns and stabbed the air.

"The same might soon happen here in our South Ward . . . Regulars marching down the Old Road from Brunswick town . . . Regulars searching for powder magazines . . . Regulars confiscating the firearms you are holding now . . ."

"Never!" interrupted a man with a musket in the rear of the gathering. His shout was followed by cheers of support.

George responded quickly: "Never means you all are willing to give up your lives for the cause of liberty, whether here on your own soil or far from here . . . even in another province if necessary."

Cheers of affirmation followed the Freeholder's words, but they lacked the intensity that he had generated before. Second thoughts were gaining ground.

George sought to recover his momentum. "We are late in preparing for the worst, my good men. The farmer King and his Parliament are pleased to see that New York and the Jerseys are ill-prepared and uncommitted. Up to now, we have been good at hurling words and writing things down. 'Tis time for action. Our Provincial Congress shall direct all townships to raise militia companies . . . craft a plan for local defense . . . secure a stock of essentials—powder, lead, and suitable firearms. Our Committee of Safety has already begun to address these concerns. Now, the time is ripe to commit yourselves to defending the Cause. What say you?"

The cheers in favor of George Wetherill's inspiring words

were loud. Louder than before. Voices were accompanied by the stomping of feet and the thumping of musket butts. The air glazed over with rising dust.

George raised a gloved fist and the men quieted. "Each of you can start, if you have not already done so, by gleaning saltpetre for the making of gunpowder. Second, you must locate as many working muskets and rifles as you can. At present, we have few too many firearms and not nearly enough black powder. Some of our brothers in New England are brandishing pitchforks and scythes. They are a pitiful match against the Brown Bess and bayonet. Third, there is a crying need for decent horses. Soon we'll need to be raising a troop of horse . . . hopefully, as sharp and smart as the escorts for General Washington when he passed through here last month. What I'm telling you is that there are several ways you can contribute to the cause of liberty. The best army and the best navy in the world will be coming at you. You must get ready. Whether you serve as a minute man, a courier, a scout, a waggoneer, or a drummer boy, you will need to prepare. If you are fit and able, the time is now to sign up."

In the midst of rumblings, pro and con, one voice shouted: "What about officers to lead us?"

"Who dares lead the likes of us?" came another shout from another voice.

George Wetherill responded with booming authority: "Those of you committing to serve this day will gain the opportunity to elect your company officers. Folks greater than me shall decide who leads the regiments. My brother informs me of his being encouraged by lofty peers to accept an officer's position in the soon-to-be Middlesex County regiment. Who among you would not like to be led by John Wetherill himself?"

The crowd reaction was a mixture of cheers and silence. Many doubted the old man was up to the task healthwise. But none voiced opposition to the idea.

"Enough of this talk," shouted a fellow brandishing a musket in the row closest to the table. Others voiced the same sentiment. They wanted to get on with the shoot.

Windy George had much more to say, but his brother's elder son gave him a signal. The Freeholder bowed to his audience and stepped down. He took a seat at the judge's table. John, Jr., thanked him and assured him that his words had to count for something.

Several of the first men lining up told John Wetherill's sons that they would join up only if their Assemblyman was willing to lead them. Vincent and John, Jr., promised they would relay such sentiments to their father soon as he returned from the Provincial Congress in Trenton. The number of men who now stepped forward to sign up for militia duty pleased all the Wetherills in attendance . . . especially George Wetherill.

Soon the preliminary rounds of the target shoot commenced without incident. There was a bit of arguing but no fighting. Mister Whitlock had provided a stout waggon burdened with two large barrels of cider. The vehicle and its horse team were positioned on the far side of the lone tree. Stones had been placed at two wheels to keep the waggon in place. One of Whitlock's slaves had been quick to hammer in a spigot tap on the first barrel. Another Afric stood at the ready with a dozen long-handled ladels in hand. All the partakers who stepped forward to down a ladel's worth complained that it was not hard cider. But on such a dry and dusty day, the first barrel was drained during the first hour of the shoot. The second was down to half empty within the next hour. John, Jr., was glad he had requested plain cider for the event. Whitlock was also glad. His cider was not up to John Wetherill's standards, but on this day it was appreciated just the same. Plus, it was cheaper than the hard stuff and a safe bet to keep tempers from igniting. For the sake of a civil shoot, any drunken shootist was not allowed to participate in the competition. Furthermore, Vincent and John, Jr., wanted sober men to sign up for the militia—not one who would forget the next day what he had signed up for.

All the finalists turned out to be sober as the judges. There were three in the musket competition. David Chambers was using a ten-pound English militia musket. All three of his shots at one-hundred yards were located in the crux of the white bars. Twenty-three-year-old Abraham Dean sported an old English dog-lock musket weighing close to nine pounds. He managed to get all three shots in the crux of his target, but his third shot sat at the very edge of the crux. Rhode Hall's Johnnie Van Arsdalen employed a fairly new Dutch musket weighing close to eleven pounds. He had almost the same results as Dean, but one of his shots lay just outside the crux. The second volley at one-hundred yards would decide the musket champion.

Rifle finalists were also three in number. Sam Wetherill, George's thirty-year-old son, wearing no hat over his loose and free sandy brown hair and flashing his haughty brown eyes, shouldered a smoothbore fowler six feet in length. He put three pieces of lead in the crux of his target at two-hundred yards. Cutlope Hancock, challenging with his heirloom jaeger hunting rifle which weighed close to eight pounds, also placed his shots in the crux. Sand Hills own Willie Bastedo, just turned twenty-one, used a Pennsylvania rifle which was close to seventy inches long and weighed nine pounds. He was good for two shots in the crux and one just outside but still on a white stripe. They were scheduled to go at two-hundred yards again after the musket finalists were done.

The three men who showed up with pistols were slated to go one round at twenty-five yards after the riflemen had completed their final round. To everyone's surprise, Ike Higgins showed up with a pistol. His mate's son, Little Ned, who was now ten years old and sprouting fast, announced the fact to all who would listen. He boasted that Mister Higgins was going to do well with his new pistol. Ike let Good Mary's boy carry the pouch, which contained an unloaded dueling pistol and its paraphernalia, This was after they left the boy's mother behind at the fair. Thomas Wetherill had allowed Mary a short break from her kitchen duties when the first pedlar's waggon rolled in. She needed to restock her sewing materials and find a bolt of ozenbrig cloth to make Ike some work shirts. The one Ike was wearing to the fair was patched at the elbows and frayed at the collar. Little Ned's blouse was in the same condition. Mary hoped the dry goods pedlar would remedy the situation and provide her with the materials that would help her avoid embarrassment.

The second contestant in the pistol competition was tall, lanky Abraham Terhune. He was a fresh-faced lad, barely sixteen, but casting a sharp eye and a look of confidence. Terhune showed up at the judge's table with his father's old constable's .55 calibre pistol. Vincent Wetherill examined the piece and deemed it fit and proper for the competition.

Simon Van Dyke wanted to enter his slave, Alpha, in the pistol competition. He claimed that his scorched boy could hit a dollar tossed at fifty yards with Van Dyke's silver-mounted French officer's pistol. Many in the crowd jeered Simon's intention and voiced objections to having dark wood participate in the target shoot. The Dean brothers were quite vocal about this matter and did not let up.

The youngest Aaron Dean in attendance spoke for the majority: "Your boy holds even chance of hittin' the tosser afore he hits the coin, Simon. How 'bout you try such a trick right here now? You toss the coin 'n see who gets the lead first!"

Dean's chiding comment garnered a fair measure of guffaws and laughter from his kin, the Applegate lads, the Davison contingent, and others. A red-faced Simon Van Dyke quickly handed his .48 calibre pistol to Hendrick, his son. The twenty-two-year-old, blessed with straw blond hair—clubbed up behind—and keen blue eyes, was a fair shot in his own right. The crowd erupted in applause for Simon's second choice. His son immediately became the betting favorite to take the pistol competition. Ike's name was mentioned the least.

David Chambers, looking handsome and confident in his hunting skins, toed the mark set one-hundred yards from a fresh target. He prepared his heirloom musket and fired off a round. He reloaded in quick fashion. Fired again. Did the same routine a third time and finished well under a minute. A slave ran to the target, removed it from its moorings, and came running fast as he could with the heavy wooden square. He placed it on the judge's table and scampered back to safety. The Wetherills—George, John, Jr., and Vincent—plus Jonathan Combs, sporting a turkey feather in his tricorn, were serving as the judges for the finalists. While they examined the target, many of the eliminated contestants and betting onlookers pressed close.

Combs called out the placement of the three holes in the wood: "Two in the crux apart by an inch and one on the northeast arm half-the-way from the corner . . . so two holes in the center and one on a white arm!"

Cheers rang out. David Chambers's name was chanted by his supporters.

Abraham Dean stepped to the line. He sported the oldest of the three muskets still in the competition. The weapon had been used in the Indian Wars, and used often for hunting in more recent years. It was a bulky .79 calibre piece, but Dean was strong enough to handle it well. However, he was not as quick as Chambers between shots. Dean made up for this shortcoming by exuding cocky confidence and showing a steady hand. Abraham managed to finish his last round in just under a minute, as he had done in his first round. A diminuitive target runner came staggering in under the weight of Dean's accomplishment. The young slave plopped it down on top of Chambers's target, bent over to catch his breath, then ran back from whence he came. The judges promptly examined the three holes in Dean's wood.

After conferring with his peers, Combs announced the findings: "Three shots in the white, but all beyond the crux."

Groans outnumbered cheers in the crowd. No one bothered to call out Abraham Dean's name. The judges placed his target under David Chambers's target.

That left Johnnie Van Arsdalen to conclude the musket competition. The twenty-four-year-old maintained a cool and calm demeanor as he stepped to the line. He was also dressed in a deerskin outfit. He wore a wide-brimmed hat at a jaunty angle. He was stronger than Aaron Dean and even handsomer than David Chambers. Van Arsdalen was the crowd favorite and he knew it. He fired off his three shots with alacrity and flare. He finished well before Vincent Wetherill shouted that time was up.

The third runner, a slight boy dressed in raggedy hand-me-downs, tripped and fell while attempting to lug Van Arsdalen's target to the judge's table. He picked himself up, wasted no time dusting himself off, retrieved the target, and completed his chore. Those gathered around the table made way for the slave and greeted him with cheers.

The judges took charge, inspected the third musket target, and measured the distance from the center to the hole farthest out. One hole was close to dead center on the crux, but the other two were far out on the white northeast stripe and southeast stripe. Jonathan Combs called out these results. John, Jr., placed Van Arsdalen's target over Dean's target but under Chambers's winning target.

The crowd applauded the results. Losers of bets forked over script and coin to winners without incident. No arguments erupted. No fisticuffs ensued.

John, Jr., praised the crowd for its civil behavior. He congratulated the three musket finalists for their efforts. He added: "And you, David Chambers, will have your winning square hung on the wall in the game room of the Wetherill Tavern after your name has been painted in blue on a white stripe. The same fate awaits the winner of the rifle competition."

With that said, Sam Wetherill stepped to the mark with his smoothbore fowler in hand. He prepared the sleek weapon for firing and wasted little time getting off three shots.

But timing was not accounted for in this competition, because it took much longer for a rifle to be readied for each shot as opposed to a musket. The weapon's advantage over a musket was better accuracy and longer range.

Wetherill's runner was quick as a rabbit. After he plopped the target down on the judge's table, there were instant oohs and aahs emanating from the crowd. The judges pointed to the three holes in the crux—two very close together near the center and one an inch to the left. Sam was beaming. He was sure he had won.

Cutlope Hancock gimped to the mark. He lifted his father's jaeger hunting rifle from his shoulder and prepared it for his initial shot. He calmly took aim and squeezed the trigger. The thundering of his weapon caused some in the crowd to cheer for no reason. Cut appeared unmoved by the commotion he had caused. He took his sweet time preparing for his second shot and even longer for his third. His runner was quicker getting to the table than Sam Wetherill's had been. Even the runner garnered some cheers. The judges were also quick with their observations.

Jonathan Combs announced their findings: "One hole dead center . . . and a close pair at the right border of the crux."

The crowd erupted with applause. John, Jr., placed Cut's target square next to Sam's square. This move indicated that the judges had not made up their minds on who the clear leader in the rifle competition was. They had decided to wait until the third contestant had completed his round. Chiding words were exchanged between the supporters of Wetherill and the supporters of the German. However, the taunting did not fall to fisticuffs. After all, the Hancocks and Wetherills were neighbors.

Willie Bastedo readied his Pennsylvania rifle for his first shot. He was nervous. Sweating. He cast the down look of a contestant already defeated. Three shots later he still held to his frown. Even his runner, rushing up to the judge's table, did not give any sign that he held a winner.

The three judges examined the target wood and saw that poor Willie had not come close to besting either Sam or Cut.

Jonathan Combs, poker, faced and deep-voiced, called out the results determined from the last rifle target: "None in the crux . . . all three holes rest outside on the southwest stripe."

Cheers and chants erupted, but not for Willie Bastedo and his Pennsylvania rifle. The clamor was all about Cut and Sam, with the majority favoring a Wetherill. The German did not mind. He had ambled over to the cider waggon. He paid no concern over the judges now trying to decide the winner of the rifle competition. The distances between holes on the two targets had to be remeasured and compared. For those milling around the judge's table, debate and discussion became heated. Good money was riding on the final decision.

Finally, Jonathan Combs raised both arms and quieted the crowd. "Close it is," shouted Combs, "But it all comes down to best shot or best cluster of shots. Cutlope Hancock was dead on once, but Samuel Wetherill put his three shots closer together . . .

Combs was interrupted by raucous shouts. Most voices favored Sam. The judge decided to announce the winner after the noise died down.

George Wetherill decided to take advantage of the situation. He climbed up on the bench again and waved at the crowd. "Before we announce the winner of the rifles and move on to the pistol competition, let me announce that each winner shall be rewarded a cask of my brother's eight-year apple brandy!"

His words gave rise to more cheering and roars of approval. George beamed at the response. John, Jr., did not. The latter knew his father would never give away a single cask of his reknowned brandy. But his uncle's impulsive word was not to be challenged.

Thus, the younger John voiced no objection. Neither did Vincent who was busy inspecting pistols.

Once the noise of the crowd subsided, George Wetherill concluded his remarks: "Of course, such a prize for each winner comes with a caveat of sorts. I am sure the winners will sign up for militia duty in order to receive the brandy. As for the rest of you, a free pint of ale at the Wetherill Tavern after the pistol competition for all those who have affixed their mark for militia duty."

The loudest cheers of the day erupted from throats thirsting for something stronger than Whitlock's cider. George gave a final wave to his appreciative audience then stepped down. Many in the crowd pressed forward, eager to join the militia. George's magic words had done the trick.

Minutes went by before Jonathan Combs dared to announce the winner of the rifle competition. He pronounced Sam Wetherill the champion. Cheering flared again. A scuffle broke out between Sam's supporters and a pair of Cut's supporters. The two favoring the German got the worst of it. The 'friendly' debate died quickly when the crowd turned its attention to the three contestants who had signed up for the pistol competition. Interest was surprisingly high, especially among the gamblers who had yet to win a bet. They hastened to put hard coin or script on best shot and overall winner. Most gave the Irishman, Ike Higgins, no chance in either category. Opinions were evenly divided over the chances of the two Dutchmen.

The judges decided to split the Hollanders and sandwich the so-called mackerel snapper in between. Vincent Wetherill flipped a coin to see which Dutchman would go first. Abraham Terhune called heads and won the toss. That meant Hendrick Van Dyke would go last. No objections were raised. The single round for pistols was ready to begin.

Terhune toed the mark, assumed a rigid dueling stance. took aim, and fired his constable's pistol. He prepared his weapon for a second shot, employing the steady hand of an experienced shootist. But it had been a few long years since he had fired the thing. He was admittedly rusty, but his pistol was not. Its blue finish gleamed in the sunlight and caused several in the crowd to wager on his firearm to win the competition.

Ike Higgins possessed a more stunningly beautiful piece but he had yet to pull it out of the bag Little Ned was carrying. However, no matter the excellent condition of his pistol, most bettors would not change their minds about Ike. They doubted the Irishman had showed up sober. They were amazed he was competing at all. For as long as folks could remember, Ike Higgins possessed no firearm. That was one of the rules Old John Wetherill had set when the Irishman was appointed Ward of Pigeon Swamp. There was one exception. Since joining the Ratters hunt club Ike was allowed to borrow a musket for hunts in the swamp but nowhere else. All this did not matter now. Men at the competition were curious about what Ike was hiding in the bag.

Abraham Terhune completed his three shots. The target was brought to the judge's table by a bow-legged slave who took his time walking the twenty-five yards. This gave ample time for folks to gather round once more. Gamblers pressed the closest. Terhune's three holes were in the crux but wide apart. Not one was close to the center. Jonathan Combs announced it a fair-to-middling showing. There were no cheers of support for Abe Terhune.

While everyone was distracted by the target on the judge's table, Ike extracted his pistol and the elements needed to secure his first shot from the bag Little Ned was holding. When he had readied the English dueling pistol for his first shot, Ike raised it above his head and captured a gleam of sun on its polished surface. That caught the attention of most of the men in the crowd. They closed in to see what the Irishman would do with such a handsome piece.

"How'd you come by a gentleman's pistol, Irish?" asked Robert Nixon, who had ridden his horse up from Hide's Town to enjoy the pedlar's fair. The stout visitor stood closest to where Ike had positioned himself.

"Won by chance off a not-so-lucky plum," Ike responded without taking his eye off the target awaiting his first shot.

"Must have been a rather desperate wealthy man," observed George Wetherill, who had left his bench to witness the final competition close up. He owned a pair of English single-shot dueling pistols, though he had yet to use them. If he had been younger, he might have dared compete.

"The gloak was down . . . almost out when I'd fleeced 'im," Ike boasted. "But me cards was better . . . me hands was clever boots. Now stand away. Let me fire me piece."

Nixon, Wetherill, and the rest standing too close took a few steps back to allow Ike to get off his first shot. The .55 calibre lead ball slammed into the right post which held the target. Splinters of wood exploded into the air and fell to the ground. There were several gasps and a few twitters of laughter. George Wetherill scolded those who might have been distracting the shooter. The crowd grew silent.

Ike fumbled with reloading his pistol for his second shot. Only he broke the silence: "A wee bit o' rust you'll find on the likes o' me . . . but I'm tryin' me best fer little Ned's sake. So thanks fer the quiet."

Little Ned was standing close by, clutching the empty bag with both hands. A look of hope and trust was in his large, brown eyes. He focused on the pistol.

"The boy talked me into this hamble," Ike explained, as he took aim in a far too casual way and fired off his second round. This lead found a corner of the target board but missed the white.

Certain upstarts in the crowd were about to respond derisively but George Wetherill raised a gloved fist and Robert Nixon scowled. That was enough to let silence reign.

Ike said nothing more. He prepared for his third and final shot. He knew he had no chance to win, but he still had something to prove to Little Ned. The Irishman had never given up in any situation—be it a game of chance, a brawl, or any other dangerous predicament. He had taken many severe blows in his life, but on each occasion he had picked himself up and persevered. More times than not he found himself on the losing end, but ever so often he tasted victory. So rare a triumph, but so sweet when it happened.

Ike stepped to the mark. He fixed a sober eye on the heart of the target. He steadied his extended arm and squeezed the trigger. A spark from the flint ignited the black powder and the third lead ball whistled straight and true towards the crux of the target. The resultant hole was but a smidge off center. It was grand enough for Little Ned to rush up to Ike and give him a hug.

As the target runner brought the evidence in, cheers rang out in favor of Ike's moral victory. He had saved his best shot for last and had impressed his diminutive admirer.

The target was dropped on the judge's table and immediately placed under Terhune's better showing. Ike and little Ned stepped away from the mark to allow Hendrick Van Dyke to prepare for his first shot. They headed to the cider waggon much to little Ned's delight.

Cutlope Hancock was there to greet them, but not to offer praise. The Irishman was in the process of placing his prize pistol back in the bag Ned was holding open. The German reached for the weapon and snatched it out of Ike's hand. Cut held it high and examined the firearm, especially the haft.

Ike attempted to grab the weapon back, but Hancock kept him at arm's length with his free hand. Little Ned stared in awe at the German's show of strength. He stood frozen in place with his mouth agape. He had been taught that Cutlope Hancock was a man to fear.

"See these initials here carved on the handle," observed Hancock as he waved the pistol. "They don't match up with the name of the man you filched this from."

Ike stopped struggling and stood seething but calm. "Yer guessin', Cut . . . only guessin'."

"I learnt the name of the drover I replaced when I got to Brunswick Town," the German claimed. "They called that fool Pip James . . . or at least that's what he was callin' hisself back in June."

"Give it back, Cut. I won it fair."

"This here is a dueling pistol. The twin of it is still owned by the one who truly owns this one. His initials lay carved in the grip."

"So I got the one 'n the owner's got t'other," said Ike. "Who's goin' to a bother comin' this far fer to find it?"

"Well," said Cut, "whoever might be 'WP' for one and Pip James for the other."

"Let 'em visit . . . one or both. We'll take care o' 'em as we done when first we met Mister James."

"Nein," spit Cut. "You'll be on your lonesome the next time around, bog hopper. Don't mention my name when either man comes callin'."

With that said, Cutlope Hancock handed the pistol back to Ike. He turned and headed towards the judge's table. Cut made it in time to see John, Jr., place Henry Van Dyke's target on top of the other two in the pistol competition.

10

DANISH GAMES

· · · · · · · · · · · · · · · ·

(Wednesday, July 19, 1775)

A handsome open coach stood at rest not far from the corner of Arch and 5th Streets. The driver, dressed in a hunter green outfit and high hat, calmed his horse with soothing words as he waited for his well-paying passenger to return from a visit to the Christ Church burial grounds. The squat fellow did not mind the wait. He had pulled under a tall walnut tree and was enjoying the cool shade. He also enjoyed a nip of rum from his flask ever so often. Life was good. It was a pleasant, blue sky day offering a warming temperature and a cool breeze from the west. The roads from the wharfs to the cemetery had dried out since the heavy shower of two days ago—a badly needed rain for farmers in the countryside, but not so much for coachmen in Philadelphia. The patient fellow reached for his flask again.

The gentleman passenger did mention that he had to meet someone at the cemetery gate. Words to that effect had been said to the driver almost an hour ago when he helped the large man into his coach. Nothing else had been said until they reached their destination.

Upon exiting the vehicle, the passenger exclaimed: "My sister has already arrived!"

The coachman turned and saw a large-boned woman standing in front of the open gate to the cemetery. She was clutching a bouquet of flowers—the only thing outstanding about the woman. She was wearing traditional, unspectacular servant's attire.

The passenger handed over a few coins to make half the fare. He declared: "The rest upon my return. I shall not be long. My sister and I are paying a visit to the grave of a dear family member. Your patience is appreciated, my good man."

The coachman tipped his high hat and urged his passenger to take all the time necessary. He pocketed the unbitten coins without counting them and climbed back up on his perch. He watched the gentleman hitch toward the drab, unsmiling woman. They certainly seemed an unlikely pair of siblings. But the coachman paid them no mind. Instead, he gazed at his snickering companion and considered how lucky he was to have been paired with a better looking mare. When he lifted his head and glanced back at the open gate, no one was standing there.

Ruth Mount bustled along the path leading to the oldest stones in the graveyard. She clutched a modest bouquet of hollyhocks and foxgloves surrounding a single red rose. Enoch Mortaine, looking quite dashing in a shiny blue-black waistcoat, buff knee-length breeches, and brightly polished black shoes, struggled to keep up. His feet were still bothering him.

"Why the rush, sister?" Mortaine said with a forced smile.

"Because, dear brother, I've heaps of chores to tend to . . . besides, I miss my little Anna already."

Mortaine fell farther behind the woman. He was struggling to catch up when he asked: "Why did you not bring your new friend along this time?"

"Miss McClew is sore afraid of ghosts," answered Mount crisply, "especially the haints hovering about where the dead lay. So she decided to spend her free time in the garden where I stole these flowers. I left dear Anna there and trudged eight long blocks to get to the cemetery gate. I should be the weary one . . . not you."

Mortaine ignored the change of subject and the slight about his inability to keep up. He decided to stay the course: "Miss McClew is superstitious then?"

"To a fault, my brother," snapped Mount as she purposely picked up the pace.

Mortaine sighed and made a more concerted effort to close the gap, but his elegant shoes were pinching his toes and his feet continued to complain. He considered gout as the culprit rather than blisters being the root cause of his misery. Due to his excessive drinking, he felt he was a prime candidate for such a malady, but he also knew the woman he was following did not care. Mortaine wondered who the real boss was in this endeavor. When he felt miserable, he was most vulnerable—off his game and finding it difficult to lead.

"Who are those flowers for again?" Mortaine asked in a rush as he tried to get his mind off the pain.

"Sarah Knowles, our dear, sweet grandmother," said Mount, as she pointed the bouquet up the path. "Just a wee bit farther, little brother, and we'll find her stone."

"I wish you would stop calling me brother," insisted Mortaine, as he peered into the well-landscaped distance. "There is not a soul around. Why are we pretending to pay respects to a poor soul who is blood-related to neither one of us? This place is our own for the moment. Lets make the most of our time and then get out of here."

"Soon as I drop these flowers and we find the bower bench I spied the last time I was here . . . then you can rest your poor, fagged feet."

"Thank you for your concern, Miss Mount," replied Mortaine acidly. "For a moment I thought you were purposely torturing me."

Mount smiled, "Long as your coins are good and you keep your pistol hidden, there'll be no abuse of your limbs . . . though I am tempted by such a pleasuresome thought, now and again, to cause you pain."

Mortaine frowned. "I'll wager you dream of such often."

"You are wrong, little brother. Miss Anna McClew fills my dreams . . . and, occasionally, one for my dear old grandmother. None of my dreams involve you or pain."

"This Sarah Knowles might just be your kin, but she's no kin of mine," Mortaine said while struggling again to change the subject and remain in charge.

Ruth Mount pointed to a faded stone listing to the left. She tossed the flowers near its base. "Mine neither, but it is the oldest stone I could find in the yard and it provides an excuse for us meeting here. Besides, it allows another name for me if I should chance to need one. This Sarah passed in 1721. By now, few will remember her or her name."

The seamstress turned her back on the stone and found the path which led to the bower bench. She sat down quickly and started smoothing out the wrinkles in her mundane gown.

"Come sit here, old man," Mount commanded. "Tell me what

you have learned of Captain Markoe's mystery guest."

Mortaine gladly took a seat on the hard wooden bench. He stretched his legs and folded his hands in his lap. "Tell me first, then I will tell you what my superiors have allowed me to say about this Colonel Johan Gottfried Krause."

"Very well then. Refined ladies, first. Questionable gentlemen, second."

Mortaine let Mount's latest slight pass. He was more interested in what the woman had discovered of late about the Danish Colonel from St. Croix.

"Nothing of substance, really," started Mount. "The date of Colonel Krause's arrival remains the same—early in August, but how early you may know better than me."

"I can say without a doubt, the man should arrive during the first week in August," stated Mortaine. "If the weather holds to fair and the seas stay calm, Colonel Krause might step on the docks by the first or second of next month."

"Leaves us little time to prepare for him," Mount observed.

"Let me handle the preparations," Mortaine said. "What have you learned that will be new to my ears?"

"This Krause fellow appears to be a favorite of the King of Denmark."

"How do you know?"

"Captain Markoe was telling his wife about the lagoon I mentioned when last we met. He waxed on about shallow pools and mud banks located on the south coast of St. Croix. For as long as Markoe could remember, the place used to be called the King's Lagoon. But the name was changed recently to the Krause Lagoon, in honor of the Dane who used his slaves to dredge and widen the waterway."

Mortaine was ruminating again with a frown. "Should have named the lagoon after any one of the slaves who lost his life during the endeavor."

"I am certain several Africs perished in the process," asserted Mount, "but Markoe was all praise and admiration for the Colonel's efforts. I assume the Danish royal court feels the same about this Krause fellow."

"What else?"

"I have learned that the man left Denmark in 1754 and sailed to the islands. Seems he stayed on St. Eustatius for a brief spell—long enough to wed a Heyliger girl in 1759. By the next year, Krause was definitely settled on St. Croix. He established a profitable sugar cane plantation, which he named 'Annaberg' after his wife, Anna Caroline. All the while, Krause worked his way up the ranks of officers on the island. He was commissioned a Colonel in the West Indian Guard in 1770. Krause is forty-seven years old and in the best of health—a large man with a huge appetite and a roving eye. He can handle his liquor as good as any sailor. The Colonel has five admitted sons and a few in hiding on his plantation . . ."

"What do you mean by 'hiding'?" Mortaine queried.

Mount shook her head with confidence, but her words were not precise: "Captain Markoe has merely implied on more than one occasion that most Danish plantation owners eventually succumb to lust. They have their favorite wenches. Such black motts are treated better than the rest. Dane wives appear to tolerate such behavior and pretend to be ignorant of such Danish games."

"I guess our Captain has not admitted doing so to his dear wife?" Mortaine asked with a wink.

"Mistress Elizabeth knows only of her stepson, Abraham, and his escapades with a certain ebony wench of some repute. I surmise that this Abraham gladly remains behind on St. Croix because of his liaison with said wench."

Mortaine stroked his shaven chin and pondered out loud: "I wonder how we can use such information against the Captain and the Colonel."

"Not such a startling thing on any of the islands, or, for that matter, here in the colonies," Mount observed. "Men are beasts, easily aroused. They think most times with their loins."

Mortaine chuckled. "I suppose you have need to worry about me then?"

"Only if my Anna arouses some needful devil in you. Then 'tis the man who should fall to worry, not me."

Mortaine waved his hand as if shooing a fly. "But what about the Captain and your Anna?"

"Captain Markoe minces around the topic of affairs in the presence of his green wife," said Mount. "He is such a fawning soul around women . . . a definite weakness. Anna has no need to fear him."

"I shall remember this," Mortaine sighed with a yawn. "Any woman might make the Captain pliable. Markoe might loosen his tongue in the presence of a woman . . . might let something important slip out."

"Yes," affirmed the seamstress. "But that is as far as he will fall. The Colonel, however, may be another story. He has frolicked with many a woman—slave and free. He has sired some half-breed kin. He has a number of 'hiding' sons."

"So when the honored guest arrives, you must watch him carefully," advised Mortaine.

Mount offered a knowing smile but said nothing.

Mortaine continued: "No need for more talk on the matter of Danish games. What else have you learned?"

"Not much left to tell," Mount confessed. "I did hear of the many travels under sail taken by Colonel Krause during these past few years. He thinks of himself as a roving ambassador of sorts for his king's interests. At least, that is how Captain Markoe put it to his wife when I listened at the door to their sitting room."

"I have learned much the same," Mortaine sighed. "This fellow has some connection with the Dutch East India Company as well as the Danish West India Company. I believe the man is cooking up some sort of money-making scheme."

"What makes you think so?"

"I've been told Colonel Krause's plantations—he is heavily invested in more than one, don't you know—are not doing well. Market prices for sugar are on the verge of dropping. And the weather has not been kind of late south of these colonies. The price of imports, such as lumber and flour, are going up. Good for farmers and merchants here, but not so for plantation owners on the islands. Krause and his peers are already feeling the pinch. Some have resorted to smuggling contraband and privateering to get around customs and make profits. My higher-ups are certain Krause is into selling contraband of the worst kind."

"And what would that be?" Mount asked.

"Not at liberty to say at this juncture," Mortaine replied. "Suffice it to say we want to catch Captain Markoe in whatever scheme his friend, Krause, is hatching. After the Colonel arrives, you will serve as the eyes and ears at their get-togethers. My higher-ups and I are counting on you, Ruth."

Mount nodded. "Long as your Spanish bits and the King's silver are good, I shall do my best."

Mortaine nodded as well. "I suggest we meet at the beginning of August to share anything new. What say you?"

"Noon on Wednesday, the second of August, will be fine," said Mount. "Graveyard again?"

Mortaine paused to inspect his surroundings. He had to admit: "Such a peaceful setting. I shall look forward to meeting here again."

The agent to the King took a moment to reconsider what information he could share with his underling. Finally, he found suitable and safe words: "What I can tell you is that our government has learned of King Christian's advisors putting pressure on him to sign a neutrality edict preventing all Danish subjects from participating in an American rebellion. I am guessing Krause wants to gain same sort of contraband deal before the edict is signed by his king. This may be why Krause is coming to Philadelphia. It may very well be why he intends to visit Captain Markoe. Now we may have an opportunity to catch two crows in the same nest."

Mount rushed her observation: "Whether Markoe gets involved in Krause's scheme or not, it appears the Danish monarch's edict will put my master in a difficult bind."

Mortaine agreed with a smile and a nod. "Likewise a few other Danish subjects who are soft on the bastard sons of liberty. If such frog-eating colonists honor their ruler's wishes and we subvert Krause's scheme, then you and I shall celebrate a double victory."

Mount posed a wide grin and showed decent teeth. "I might have to demand a few more Spanish bits."

Mortaine rubbed his hands together as he responded. "If you come through for us, Miss Mount, then you will prove worthy of a handsome reward."

"But in order to do so, Mister Mortaine, you need to tell me all you know. That way I will learn what to look for and what to plan."

Mortaine hesitated. He was not sure what to say. His superiors might not want certain facts and speculations about Colonel Krause being bantered about. But he had come to trust Miss Mount more and more. She possessed no heart of spades—the cruel kind Pip James owned. At least she gave no sign of such yet. True, she had been insulting at times, and demanding as well. But she always came through for him.

"Do not share this information with anyone . . . not even your dear Anna. Is that understood?"

Mount nodded and cast honest eyes in Mortaine's direction.

"Good then," whispered the King's agent, as he glanced about but did not see anyone else other than his hireling in the graveyard. The only noise in the place came from the throats of songbirds high in the trees. This was a perfect time and place to impart sensitive information. Mortaine continued: "Colonel Krause has cooked up a deal involving a great quantity of munitions—something General Washington's rebel army desperately needs. The Colonel is coming to Philadelphia to arrange a sale of arms to procurers for the rebel cause."

"Does my master know of his friend's purpose?" asked Mount.

"Not that we know of . . . not at this juncture, anyway. This is the first you heard of such a scheme . . . am I correct?"

"Captain Markoe has said not a word about such . . . at least not within my hearing. I've also checked his letters after they were opened and left unattended. Nothing mentioned on this matter."

"Krause will most likely ask Markoe to find him a procurer for the munitions transaction . . ."

"My master has many connections," interrupted Mount. "But I have not heard the names of any involved in firearms, lead, or black powder."

"That is good," said Mortaine. "What I want you to do is this. When you get confirmation that Colonel Krause is actually peddling munitions, I want you to somehow get word to Captain Markoe that your half-brother is a munitions procurer for the rebels."

Mount waved a hand in front of her face. "Impossible. Can't be done."

"You are a most clever woman, Ruth. I know you can pull it off if you put your mind to it. Your reward will be great."

"You better have a second plan ready," said Mount.

"My higher-ups have two plans in the works," said Mortaine

with his usual confidence. "The one I've shared with you is mine alone. And I'm counting on you to carry it out."

"If your plan works, I look forward to counting lots of your money, little brother. That is why I shall give it a try, but I can't promise anything."

"All I ask is to make the attempt to invite me into the Colonel's game. I'll take it from there."

Mount stood, straightened her apron, and started down the path toward the open gate. Mortaine rose to follow. He hobbled after her.

Mount glanced over her shoulder and used her firmest voice: "Tell me all I need to know about you as a munitions procurer, Mister Azariah Willett. I do not want to slip up when in the presence of my master and the Colonel."

Mortaine gladly provided enough factual and fictive details to satisfy the seamstress before they got to the gate. Then he asked her if there was anything else she required.

"Nothing," was her response. Then Mount added: "Don't ask your coachman to wheel me to Markoe's manse. I did not like the way your beefy driver was staring at me as I stood waiting for you at the graveyard gate. He may have a good memory and bad intentions."

Mortaine grunted but said nothing intelligible.

"Besides," Mount concluded, "I shall look forward to a long walk back so I can come up with a strategy for getting you involved in the next Danish game."

11

BAGGIN' A COON

· · · · · · · · · · · · · · · ·

(Saturday, July 22, 1775)

"Hush," whispered Ike, as he grabbed little Ned's arm and pulled him down in the moist soil that carpeted most of Pigeon Swamp. He adjusted his red Monmouth cap with one hand and held firm to the boy with the other. "Hush yer mouth 'n use yer keen eye to spot this critter."

Ike was also on his knees, hiding behind the upturned root base of a large, fallen tree. He had streaked his face with black char for hunting—his nicks and scars were nicely hidden. Ike started loading his pistol, eager to take aim at a raccoon busy foraging for his morning meal at the edge of a spring pool in the heart of the swamp. The Irishman had chosen a perfect time to take Good Mary's son on a hunt. It was another fair day warming to the eighties with a whisper of wind coming from the southwest. Ike had picked his hiding spot well. The wind was in his face, hence the racoon failed to pick up the scent of the man and boy come to do him harm. The swamp was dead silent save for the occasional twitter of birds and the buzzing of mosquitos which were letting nothing stand in their way of finding innocent blood.

Ike handed the empty gun sack to Little Ned, who had been watching every move the Irishman had made in loading the pistol. Killing the raccoon did not interest the boy as much as getting a chance to fire the pistol—a chance at anything, moving or not.

"Let me take a shot," whispered Little Ned, who was wearing a patched pair of raven's duck trousers cut down to his size and a dirty homespun shirt with the sleeves rolled up. The trousers and the shirt were too large for the boy's thin frame. They allowed him plenty of room to grow.

Ike ignored the boy's request. He noticed that the raccoon had lifted its head . . . alerted by something. The critter seemed poised to dart off into the safety of the underbrush.

"Just one shot," repeated Little Ned.

Ike continued to ignore the boy. The request had been made often since their rising at dawn, all through Good Mary's magnificent breakfast, and all along the path in back of the Wetherill Tavern which led into the swamp. The Irishman always said no as the boy's mother had instructed him to do. Mary did not want her only child shooting himself in the foot with a firearm. After all, Little Ned was only ten. And, besides, his fingers were too small. These were adequate excuses in a caring mother's book. When Mary said no, Ike obeyed—of course, only when it came to denying the boy his wants and wishes. Other than that, the Irishman was want to do whatever he wished as long as his mate was out of sight. Ike did not dare cross Good Mary. She had tamed his drinking and his propensity for making it easy for trouble to find him . . . but again, that was only when the woman was around.

Ike half-cocked the hammer of the single-shot pistol. With his free hand he ran a finger over the flint. It felt sharp and firm. He reached for a small bag of black powder and carefully poured a measure of it down the muzzle and tamped it down with a ramrod. He then wrapped a lead ball in a linen patch, put it in the muzzle, and tamped it in place. Ike finally dropped a small amount of fine primer in the flash pan. He cocked the trigger full back and signalled Little Ned to keep still.

The boy had taken note of every step in the loading process. He knew his time to shoot the pistol was coming soon.

Ike peered out from behind the roots of the fallen tree. Using his better eye, he took aim. The raccoon flicked its striped tail and commenced a defiant hissing sound. But this defense was all for naught. Ike squeezed the trigger. The flint struck the frizzen causing sparks to find the primer. The powder flashed and ignited the powder in the barrel. The lead ball blew the head off the raccoon. The rest of the critter fell into the lapping water at the edge of the spring pool.

Little Ned was up and racing towards the kill before Ike managed to pick himself up from the mud. The empty sack which had held the pistol and its accoutrements fluttered like a flag as the boy ran.

He tripped and fell, but picked himself up without hesitation and reached the fallen prey before Ike took one step. Little Ned pulled the lifeless form to dry ground and prodded it with a stick to see if there was any life left in it. Not a twitch.

Ike came scrabbling with pistol in hand.

Ned greeted him with: "Your best shot, Mister Ike . . . better than the one at the target shoot!"

Ike patted the fuzzy rust on the boy's head and said: "At a greater distance too, I reckon."

"My turn, next," insisted the boy as he stopped poking the dead carcass and tossed the stick into the water.

"No turn at baggin' a coon till ye takes a turn at reachin' twelve. laddie," pronounced Ike. "'Tis the promise I gave yer mum."

"Then let me take hold of your pistol till you're ready for next time."

"Well, 'tain't loaded now," considered Ike, as he inspected his purloined firearm. He used his free hand to scratch his nicked ear while he debated what to do in his mind. "I guess it wouldn't hurt none. Besides, this here is a big old coon. Gonna take up the full insides o' me huntin' sack. Don't want me gun gettin' soiled in there. So I'll put the pistol gear in me money pouch 'n pockets . . . you lug the piece."

Ike handed the dueling pistol to Little Ned. The boy beamed with appreciation. He grabbed the thing and started aiming it at the roots of the fallen tree, the nearest large rock, and a blue jay on a sweetgum branch objecting to poachers in his kingdom.

Ike pulled out a hunting knife that John Wetherill had given him when he was appointed Ward of Pigeon Swamp. He proceeded to cut the ringed tail from the coon's corpse. He handed the trophy to Little Ned who accepted it with pride. Ike picked up the rest of the critter and stuffed it in the bag. He decided to carry the bag since the boy was gleefully burdened with the pistol and the tail. Ike went back to the fallen tree to collect his paraphernalia.

The unlikely pair of hunters found the path they had used to get far into the swamp. About halfway back to the Wetherill Tavern they found a flat rock on which to rest a moment. Little Ned climbed up on the rock and stood there. He took aim with the pistol at anything that was worth aiming at. Ike paid no mind to the boy's game. He leaned against the rock, hunched his shoulders, and flicked bits of dried mud off his hunting trousers. He started at the knees and worked his way down to his heavy boots. Even with such grooming, Ike knew Good Mary would scold the boy and him fierce for returning filthy.

Little Ned broke the silence first: "How come the letters on this pistol grip don't square with the letters in the name Mister Cut gave you at the fair?"

"Can't read 'em meself, so I don't know," said Ike. "You tell me."

"Mister Cut says you took this piece off of Pip James . . . but the letters here say 'W' and 'P'."

"First o' all," confessed Ike, "I'm borrowin' that there pistol . . . intend to return it to a rightful owner when next we meet."

"You told me you won this pistol fair and square."

"True on that," said Ike. "I won the chance to borrow the thing till I needs it no more."

"So who is the owner of these two letters I'm looking at?"

"I won a chance to hold the pistol 'n this so-called Pip James won his chance afore me."

"What about the owner before that?"

"Not me worry," said Ike, "so sure not yer worry."

"So you'll be keepin' hold of this thing till after I'm twelve?"

"Least by then, me lad," Ike stated confidently. "But by then you'll find a pistol o' yer very own . . . 'n mayhaps, a musket."

"So I can join the militia." said Little Ned with equal confidence.

"Not our fight, little one. You 'n me are sittin' out this here battle."

"But you've been made a member of the Ratters, Mister Ike. All them hunters seem eager to sign up."

The Irishman cracked a wise smile. "All them lads has no scars from bein' at the wrong end o' a whip 'n a brandin' iron. Patriot's laws are goin' to be harsh as King's law fer the likes o' me. The luck I own will drop the same on either side o' the fence. Me best chance is to mind me own business in this here swamp. I knows where to hide if either side comes lookin' fer me 'n I knows how to survive on coon meat 'n such."

"I want to join up," said Little Ned proudly. "Gain me a chance to fire a musket and march about."

"Suit yer own self, boy," said Ike. "But remember who ye are.

When the likes o' you reach the takin' age, the rebel war may be done, 'n if not, many a soldier don't want to be fightin' 'longside a half-breed."

"When I show 'em what a good shot I am—even better than you, Mister Ike—they will have to welcome me in."

"They might be desperate 'nough to take ye earlier than yer hopin', Neddy. I'd be a mite careful what yer wishin'."

"I ain't 'fraid of no redcoat," declared Little Ned, as he took aim at the sun pending above the trees.

"Neither is the likes o' meself," said Ike, "long as we're hidin' in this here swamp."

"I don't want to hide," challenged Little Ned. "I'm ready to fight."

"If'n we hadn't a hid back there," said Ike, as he pointed down the path he had marked out a year ago, "our game bag would set empty."

Little Ned chose to ignore Ike's logic. "Hiding's for cowards."

Ike spat against the rock. "Whether fate wants ye a coward or a hero, now ain't the time fer makin' choices. Yer mother's makin the call on this . . . fer both you 'n me. End o' story."

Little Ned did not argue. He leaped off the rock and trotted down the path. "Follow me, Mister Ike!"

The Irishman pulled away from his perch and hobbled after his little charge.

"Hurry," cried the boy. "Redcoats are comin' this way. We must give 'em a warm welcome."

Ike was grinning ear to ear. "Lucky fer the lobsterbacks there ain't no ball in that there pistol!"

12

AT THE BLUE ANCHOR

. . . .

(Wednesday, July 26, 1775)

The closest road to the Philadelphia wharfs dotting the west bank of the Delaware River was not favored for taking an evening stroll. Ruffians, thieves, and scoundrels involved in nefarious activities ruled the night on Water Street. The deeply shadowed way was their turf. Strangers were nothing more than victims or suspects in crime. And the victims were fools to dare walk the length of the rutted, foul-smelling road. Even strangers up to no good were taking a chance.

Along this scandalous road sat the Blue Anchor Tavern—a modest, listing toward decrepit, ordinary. It was a meeting place for rummies and rogues. A place to plot and plan the next big move. A place to hatch some preposterous scheme, surely against the law, but immensely profitable if it could be pulled off. Usually such schemes involved the stealing of all sorts of cargo being brought in on the ships at dock. Rumors of riches and goods flew in the Blue Anchor like wave foam in a gale. Precious items just had to be aboard certain vessels, and the best thieves were destined to get their hands on such. A bribe might have to be given, a throat might have to be slashed, a risk might have to be taken—no matter what, the place to conjure up a successful plan was the Blue Anchor . . . late at night when the innocent were sleeping.

Enoch Mortaine, dressed down in an undyed shirt and flapfront trousers, walked briskly down the cartway and turned right on to Water Street to get to the Blue Anchor. He was wide awake and feeling confident. A stout knife was at his belt.

Upon reaching his destination, he paused under a pair of sputtering lanterns hanging from the talons of a real anchor the original minehost had long ago painted ghostly blue.

The lanterns gave off enough light to reveal the large oaken entrance door. Mortaine reached for the iron handle, but he did not go in. Something caught his eye high on the door. He stared at two fresh letters carved in the wood. A smear of blood stained the base of the letters. The King's agent wondered what the 'H' and the 'L' stood for. He made a mental note to ask Pip James about the fresh carving. Mortaine had many important things to discuss with his hireling, so he decided to save such a minor detail for last. After all, the letters were probably nothing worth remembering. The man shrugged and entered the disreputable establishment.

On this warm and overcast Wednesday, the Blue Anchor was very much alive with hearty drinking—mostly cheap ale and rum favored by seamen. Lusty songs were being sung—most about women charmed and women lost. Games of chance involving pitiful amounts of money gleaned from low wages were being played under poor lighting. Supper was being served—caveached fish on coarse, stale bread. Few patrons were interested in food. Most preferred their cups. Many kept hungry eyes on the bar maids who were gliding from table to table bearing vessels of cheap spirits. This was no gentleman's crowd, such as the one at the Tun Tavern. Spittoons were near to full. The sawdust on the floor was slick with mysterious liquids. One tattooed patron, with vest ripped and seaman's trousers torn, was passed out and curled up under a table. Nobody paid him a bother.

The close air in the place was a warlock's brew of brine, sweat, and smoke from cob pipes. This was a laborer's sanctuary—a place for a schemer to find a willing soul who would do anything for money. The Blue Anchor was where Enoch Mortaine had found Pip James when he first came down from the city of New York several weeks ago . . . a place both men loved to visit.

Mortaine crossed the floor of ill-defined stains. He found his hireling sitting by his lonesome in the darkest corner of the room. Pip was hunched over a pint of kill-devil rum staring at nothing in particular. Enoch noticed that the man's arm sling was missing. The grim fellow wore no shirt, just an aurin leather vest which revealed his muscular arms. As Mortaine got close, he noticed that his man sported no fresh scars on his pocked face.

Mortaine slid into a grimy seat opposite Pip and signaled the nearest serving maid. Eventually, she glided his way. Her shadow loomed large. It plunged the already Stygian corner into starless night.

"What'd be yer fancy, sailor?" the plump maid asked in a rushed, roupy voice.

"Two pints," chimed Mortaine, ignoring the seaman's reference but hoping to pass as an alongshoreman. He had purposely failed to wash his trousers . . . same for his yellowed, sweat-stained shirt. In his mind, his disguise was working. "Ale for me, fair maid, and your best rum for my fellow alongshoreman here."

The round-shouldered woman flashed no smile. She cast a skeptical eye on the gentleman pretending to be a common laborer. Her face remained ghostly pale and unreadable in the dim light. She swiveled her broad hips and hurried off. Mortaine watched her struggle through the crowd in order to make it to the caged bar where a sweating keep under barely adequate candlelight was bellowing out orders and making demands.

Mortaine turned his attention to the one who was the main reason for venturing into such a dreadful place. He used an upbeat voice: "So, my good Pip, what news have you brought me?"

Pip failed to make eye contact. He brought his near empty rum pot to his lips, took a long pull on his drink, then plunked down the vessel hard on the table.

"Nothin' much," he muttered.

"Skip the nothing and bring on the much," insisted Mortaine. "We've less than a week to prepare."

Pip's thick brow hovered low over unfocused eyes. At that moment, the bar maid deposited two pints and scooped up the coins Mortaine had left for her on the table. Pip finished off the pint he had been nursing and reached for the new one.

"What are we preparin'?" Pip asked in a low voice of disinterest.

"A warm welcome for a weary seafarer," Mortaine said with the keen optimism of a successful merchant. He took his first sip of the cheap, bitter ale, winced, and completed his thought. "I'll get to all that later. What's come in from the islands?"

"Nothin' out of the ordinary," said Pip. "Cacao, indigo, coffee bean, molass, 'n sugar—the usual stuff gettin' off-loaded. Some fine rum, I'm told, came off the latest sloop from Nevis." Pip looked down at his vessel of rum and frowned. "Has to be better'n this foul stuff they're servin' here at the Anchor."

"What's being loaded on the island ships?" Mortaine asked.

"Salt beef, corn flour—worms 'n all, butter, plus a goodly 'mount of lumber. You know . . . the usual goods to suit the needs of the islanders. But I did notice a grand amount of hardware which was loaded on a large ship bound to return to Montserrat."

"What exactly, pray tell?"

"Axes, hoes, sugar-hatchets, 'n witch kettles," Pip answered.

"That means a step up in production," mused Mortaine, "even though there's a glut on the market in sugar production." He shook his head, took another sip of his warm ale, and winced again. "When will they learn how to pull in the reins down there?"

"All the jabber 'mongst the seamen come to port was about the promise of good times comin'" said Pip. "'Specially with war brewin'. Many a bloak was braggin' 'bout makin' good coin either by legal ways or not."

"I'm afraid those men are correct," sighed Mortaine. "There is always money to be made during a conflict, especially when it comes to smugglers, pirates, and privateers. Are the salts gabbling about anything else?"

"The usual malarky 'bout mermaids and monsters up from the depths," said Pip. "One salt off the last sloop from St. Eustatius got his ear cut off in a fight over who makes a better soldier—Irishman or Welshman."

Mortaine offered a slight grin. "Who won?"

"Well, the winner with both his ears fixed to where God put 'em lies fast asleep under that there table." Pip pointed to where the tattooed man was still in repose under the table Mortaine had passed. "He's Irish through and through."

"I assume you have been able to avoid such trouble."

"Yup," said Pip after taking a modest pull of his rum. "Ain't found a new knife to my liking and my left mawley arm's still on the mend . . . still wrapped tight in linen." Pip lifted his bandaged limb to show it off. "So I've been behavin' myself."

"Good," said Mortaine. "Keep it that way . . . at least for another week."

"Why? What's brewin'?"

Mortaine leaned close over the table. He whispered just loud enough to be heard by his hireling. "I'm working on a plan which involves a certain guest of Captain Markoe . . . a prominent man from St. Croix due to arrive by ship either on the first of the month or a day or two after."

"So you want me spyin' on that one ship?"

"Yes, of course."

"The name of this here vessel?"

"You will be expecting a sloop called the 'Caramaw', flying the Danish king's flag," Mortaine explained. "A vessel owned by a friend of Colonel Johan Gottfried Krause—the guest our Captain Markoe will be hosting while the man is in Philadelphia."

"What particulars am I lookin' for?"

"Find out all you can about the Colonel and the crew," Mortaine answered confidently. "Find out who is accompanying this Dane and what he carries off the hold."

"Wouldn't you be better at findin' what'd be in the hold of the sloop?"

"Since being summoned here from New York, I've sat in the weights and measures room of the Counting House and checked the ledgers of what has been shipped out and what has come in," Mortaine stated in an officious tone. "But all such information is secondhand. Often times what's on the books is not all that comes in and out of the hold. I want a first-hand report of what is hidden below decks of that sloop. That's where you come in, Pip. Check what is on board and what comes off."

Pip frowned in the gloom. He did not look forward to doing clandestine inventory work. He liked causing bodily harm better. Slaying someone for money was the best chore of all.

"How 'bout givin' me a weapon so's I can take out this Krause fellow soon as he sets foot on the dock," requested Pip without any show of emotion. "Then I won't be wastin' my time or yours snoopin' among the rats 'n such on a ship."

"My superiors want none of that rough stuff this time around," scoffed Mortaine, as if offended. "We need to find out what this Colonel is up to and what part Captain Markoe will play in it. For that to play out, these two men must be kept alive. Do what I say and complete what must be done. Report to me soon after Krause is whisked away to Markoe's estate. After the sloop comes in, I shall visit here each night. Make sure you do the same."

Pip managed a sour laugh. "If'n you visit here too many times, Mister Mortaine, you're bound to get an ear cut off . . . your arse buggered . . . or worse."

Mortaine countered with his own laugh. "My good man, I like this damn place. Besides, I am always armed and can take care of myself. I would not be serving my King in this capacity if I were not. You worry about yourself, Pip. I will take care of me."

Mortaine dropped a fist of coins on the table and Pip scooped them up like a gambler who had won big. The agent kept an eye on the quick, gnarled hands of his hireling. He was impressed with how fast Pip moved when he wanted to.

He remembered something he wanted to ask his man about. "By the by, I noticed certain initials freshly carved upon the Blue Anchor's door. Any story behind the pair?"

"You mean the crook 'H' 'n lazy 'L'?"

"Correct."

"You'll have to ask the stagger 'n jag bloak kissing the floor under that table over there." Pip pointed his good arm in the direction where the tattooed man lay in repose. "I hear tell that bog trotter's mean as they come . . . 'n a superstitious bastard when sober. Got into a brawly in the road . . . cut up the Welshman real bad in a close-to-fair fight. Then he cuts off the ear of the taffy 'n stuffs it in the owner's mouth. But the bloak ain't done with his game. He marches to the door of this place 'n wipes his bloody fingers on the wood. Then he takes his knife 'n carves them letters you're askin' 'bout."

"Who's initials are they?"

"Neither Welsh nor Irish, so I have been told."

"Then who?"

Pip took a long pull on his latest rum and sighed. Then he whispered, "Somebody higher up than the Pope hisself."

13

A TIMELY ARRIVAL

(Tuesday, August 1, 1775)

John Runger's newest sloop, fresh out of St. Croix, was anchored in the channel of the Delaware River waiting for the incoming tide. The Danish captain of the privately owned 'Caramaw' stood at the portside rail scanning the wharfs which dotted the river bank on the Philadelphia side. He was a short plug of a man, dressed in an ill-fitting dark blue uniform featuring large brass buttons and much gold thread. A black clipped-brim hat hid his bald pate. A partial halo of mostly gray hairs peeked out from under the brim. His eyes were an unreadable blue-gray. This captain held to silence. He gripped a spyglass tightly in one hand and held firm to a rail with the other. Everything about him spoke of patience and firm resolve.

"Hvor laenge?" said the stout passenger standing next to the captain on the command deck. He had started in a crisp, clear Danish tongue, but always retreated into English when moved to do so. "How long, Captain Cruger?"

"I am telling you not much for long," the Captain replied in imprecise English. "Must wait we will till the waters reach to deadman's beams."

The one in charge lifted his spyglass to his better eye and scanned the bustling docking stations. "A reception crew I do see at the timbers of Penny Pot Landing."

Colonel Johan Gottfried Krause, an imposing Dane from any angle, squinted into the distance. He held a gloved, saluting hand over his sea-green eyes. A copper-skinned mulatto boy, in the midst of his fourteenth year, stood to the Colonel's left doing the same thing. They were dressed alike in dark gray waistcoats and bone-white knee breeches. Neither wore a wig. The former tamed his tawny mane with an iron-gray ribband knotted at his neck. The boy let his copper red curls fly free in the breeze.

"Fortaelle?" Krause suddenly shouted. "How can you tell?"

Captain Cruger handed his spyglass to the good friend of the owner of the vessel. "One of your greeters has hold of a handsome standard. In the westerly wind he waves such a thing. See it?"

"Oet gar jeg bestemt," smiled the Colonel from St. Croix after employing the Captain's spyglass. "I most certainly do. Must be Abram Markoe's own banner. I count tretten—thirteen stripes at the canton . . . just as he described in his last post to me."

"Guess there's to be no doubt whose side takes your friend," the Captain opined.

"Ingen," Krause mused. "No doubt . . . I hope good Abram remains my friend after I complete the reasons for my visit."

"Luck for good during your stay in the colonies," Cruger said.

Krause handed the spyglass to the mulatto boy still standing quietly by his side. After doing so, he spoke in somber tones to the Captain. "Jah, I will require all luck not assigned by chance to others. One thing in my favor is the paltry few Danish subjects who have chosen the rebellious side in the conflict. At least my time here shall be brief."

"Amen to such," offered Cruger. "May God the almighty fend for you where fate steers your ship, Colonel."

A handsome carriage and a fine team of horses, sent by Captain Markoe, waited on the shade side of the stone Port House south of Vine Street. A well-dressed coachman was snoozing on his seat board. Several paces to the fore, and sweating in the sunlight, were two members of the Philadelphia Troop of Horse. They remained silent in their saddles. Robert Hare and Will Pollard were in full uniform for the occasion. Each wore a round black hat bound by a silver cord and accentuated by a buck's tail. Each wore a dark brown short coat faced and lined with white. Gray French pantaloons over short riding boots completed their distinct outfits. They were uncomfortable in the heat but stoic just the same. It was an honor to have been chosen by their Captain to receive and escort such a distinguished guest . . . and a double honor for Robert Hare to carry the troop's standard.

Private Hare decided to break the silence: "You ever find that missing pistol of yours?"

Will Pollard jerked his head as if yanked from a deep thought. "Nope. The partner of the one at my belt must have been stolen. Haven't a clue when or where, much less who's the filcher."

Hare wanted to pursue the subject. "As I recollect, the dueling pair is a gift from your father."

"True," Pollard said, "and such a fine, precious gift to me . . . my reward for joining Captain Markoe's troop. But on my third assignment, I lose half the gift."

"Must've disappeared on the escort journey up to New York in June," Hare surmised.

"Shortly 'fore we left from here, but not after I checked my saddle pouch in Brunswick Town," Pollard guessed. "I remember placing one piece in the pouch two nights prior to leaving Philadelphia. I did not have cause to check my saddlebag till we reached Brunswick. 'Tis then and there I discovered it missing."

"Long gone by now," Hare speculated soberly. "But I'd not fret over the one lost. You still have a good one at your belt, Will."

"'Tis the one I'll use on the bastard who filched the other."

"Doubt such a fate hides in your cards, Will."

"If I get the chance to escort Captain Markoe's guest on the rest of his journey, then I might be able to retrace my steps across the Jerseys."

Hare flashed a skeptic's frown. "Slim chance to none of ever finding the pistol. You've a better hand finding a fair maid suitable for bedding down in the Jerseys."

"Maybe I'll win in both departments and you'll be sorry you ever doubted my luck," Pollard laughed as he waved his troop sword in the direction of the incoming sloop.

Hare was not finished. He wiped some sweat from his brow and offered: "You could post a notice of your loss in Dunlap's Packet . . . the one which sells well in the Jerseys."

Pvt. Pollard rolled his piercing blue eyes and flashed a doubting Thomas smile. "You're forgetting one thing, my friend. The filcher, or filchers, most likely can't read a lick, nor can the ones who know 'em. I'd be wasting good script on such a posting."

Robert Hare chuckled at his friend's words, but he did not disagree. Instead, he focused his attention on the trio of alongshoremen huddled together half the way down the Penny Pot wharf timbers. One was taller than the other two, larger all around. and the owner of the meanest scowl Hare had ever seen. This stout fellow was unshaven and amply scarred. His left arm was thickly wrapped in filthy linen. He could have easily passed for a land-bound pirate down on his luck.

"See the tall bloak on the dock," said Pvt. Hare, pointing the standard pole in the direction of the three men assigned to haul Colonel Krause's luggage and paraphernalia from the sloop, once they had caught the mooring lines and secured the vessel. "Does he look familiar to you?"

Pollard looked to where his fellow trooper was pointing. He studied the unkempt man for a long moment, then said: "Can't place him . . . can't say I know him."

"I'd swear he's the drover we left behind, Will . . . on the Upper Road before we reached Brunswick Town."

"You mean the chap who had his arm broke in a fray against a few yeomen?"

"Yes, that's the one," Hare said with conviction. "He may know something about the fate of your missing pistol."

Pollard scoffed at the idea. "By the looks of him, I wouldn't trust that rogue even if he had just confessed to a preacher. Doubt he ever met a word of truth. Besides, he's probably not the one you're so convinced he is."

"Well, I do remember the bastard with the broken arm was up and gone by the time we returned to the tavern where he was supposed to have waited for us," Hare persisted. "He could have made it back to Philadelphia and found work down here on the docks."

Pollard entertained such a possibility for a second, then he quickly said: "If it's as you say, then this fellow will not want to talk to any member of our troop. And, if we corner him and make him talk, he will deny ever serving in Washington's train. Forget him, Rob. He's worth nothing to me."

By this time, the trio of alongshoremen was springing into

action. The 'Caramaw' was soon secured and a gangway plank was dropped into place. Private Ballard signaled to the coachman to roll the carriage closer to the ship. Both horsemen sprinted ahead and saluted the large man being escorted down the broad plank by the sloop's commanding officer. A few curious onlookers followed the coach. They wanted to catch a glimpse of the latest notable to visit their city. They were pointing at the red-faced Dane and the tawny boy following in his wake. Gossip was already starting to fly in the northwest breeze. Behind the captain and the passengers came the three porters who had rushed aboard the sloop to fetch whatever had to be carried to the waiting coach. All three struggled with bags, satchels, and cases of unknown things.

Colonel Krause saluted the flag that Robert Hare was holding high. He shouted something in Danish, but Hare failed to catch it. Neither did Pollard.

Captain Cruger flashed a wide grin, then translated the Colonel's words into English: "A handsome banner . . . better even it looks up close."

Hare and Pollard each gave a nod. The coachman chuckled. A few of the spectators donated a polite cheer.

Krause ignored the responses. He turned to the grimy porters and barked at them in coarse English. They were to lay their burdens on the wharf timbers and return to the sloop to fetch four large wooden cases in the hold. He insisted these cases be loaded into the coach first.

Two of the three alongshoremen serving as porters bowed respectfully. They wore matching soiled shirts and patched fall front trousers of Russia drill. The tallest one stood straight as a gravestone. He refused to bow. Never did. Never would. This one wore nothing under his bister-hued vest—no doubt, in order to show off his muscles. His trousers were black and worn shiny at the knees. The other two waited for the tall one to give a signal.

The man in the vest turned suddenly and the other two followed close behind up the gangway. Robert Hare watched them disappear into the bowels of the ship. He was sure he was right about the identity of the bull-large fellow. Will Pollard ignored the three alongshoremen. He was more interested in the nattily dressed Dane and his scorched-wood boy.

Colonel Krause was in the midst of giving orders to his mulatto. He instructed the boy to climb up and sit with the coachman. Markoe's driver dipped a shoulder, extended a gloved hand, and pulled the boy up to his seat board. Both swapped words of introduction in thick accents culled from islands—Ireland for the coachman and St. Croix for Krause's boy. Each complimented the other on fine outfits provided by equally wealthy masters. In quick time, the odd pair was chattering away in fairly decent English.

The three porters, with the help of a few crew members of the sloop, emerged from below decks with four long wooden cases. After struggling with the heavy containers down the gangway, they rested them on the wharf for a breather and commenced arguing over how best to lug them to the coach.

"Ingen, ingen!" Colonel Krause shouted in his motherland tongue.

The captain wasted no time translating for the procrastinating alongshoremen. Cruger hastened back to where the cases sat. He ordered two of his crew members to come off the plank and pick up one of the cases. He instructed the two shorter alongshoremen to place one case atop another and carry both to the coach. The last case he left to the tallest fellow to manage on his own. Not one hauler—crew man or alongshoreman—was happy with the arrangement, but Captain Cruger alerted them that his noteworthy passenger would reward them well for their efforts once they succeeded in completing the task.

The race was on. The tallest man reached the coach first and wedged the rope-bound case into the passenger compartment as per the broken English directions of the gesticulating Colonel. Next came the two bowlegged seamen straining all the way. The first man relieved them of their burden and placed their case next to his.

The last two porters had not made it too far before having to lay their burden down. They had only staggered a few paces from their starting point. Captain Cruger sensed the pair's incompetence before the Colonel started bellowing again. He shouted to the tallest man to come to their aid. The grim fellow strolled back towards the gangway and plucked the top case off the other. He flaunted his strength by lugging the case with one arm. Spectators cheered his efforts. His second case was quickly set on top of one of the other two in the coach. Right behind the crowd-pleaser were his less-impressive partners, struggling with the fourth mysterious container.

When all four cases were secured in the coach, and it was declared that the stout Colonel would be able to fit inside the heavily burdened vehicle, Captain Cruger bowed to his passenger and wished him well—in Danish, of course. Krause, employing the same language, thanked the captain for transporting him safely to Philadelphia. He then took several silver rix dollars from his bulging money pouch and meted them out—one to each alongshoreman. He gave the rest to Captain Cruger to give to his crew.

Colonel Krause held on to the last dollar. He asked the tallest man a simple question in Danish and in English: "Hvad hedder du?" followed by "Your name?"

The one so addressed glanced at the horsemen studying him much too intensely. He lowered his brimless cap to no avail, so he shielded his eyes with a large hand. Pip James had to think quick. What came to him first were the initials carved in the door of the Blue Anchor by an equally dangerous man.

"Hendrick Lau," muttered Pip. "Hendrick Lau's the name my dear mother gave me."

"A good German name," declared Krause in his best English, as he tossed the last silver coin to Mister James, who now wished to be called Hendrick Lau.

Markoe's pair of horsemen remained silent on their mounts. Neither knew a cabbage head by that name.

Captain Abram Markoe and his honored guest, Colonel Johan Gottfried Krause, retired to the host's spacious library to enjoy an after-dinner apple brandy and a clay pipe of Virginia tobacco. The welcoming mid-afternoon repast had been deemed a success. It was measured by the second and third helpings of roasted shad, boiled potatoes, and succotash devoured by the large man from St. Croix. Krause even had seconds on the mince pie, and, in the process, consumed every bit of the crust, as a commoner would dare to do. Between mouthfuls, the Dane had only words of praise for the food. He thanked both host and hostess, in two languages, for such a warm welcome and tasty meal.

In the midst of dessert and drink, the Colonel sent his mulatto charge, whom he had introduced as Asher his faithful chamber servant, to fetch a large, square box which sat atop the wooden cases and luggage stacked in the entrance hall. Asher was quick to do as told. He had been instructed to present the item to the mistress of the house. The boy returned to the dining area, bowed before Elizabeth Markoe, and placed the gift for her on the table. He made another bow and backed away. Asher assumed his standing position behind the Colonel's chair.

Captain Markoe's wife, dressed in yellow-flower linen and pink silk lace across the bodice, reddened with delight. Her blue eyes sparkled with anticipation. Elizabeth wrestled with the scarlet ribband holding the box lid tight. Her husband came to her aid with a carving knife, which he brandished like a gallant knight of old, and freed the lid from its binding. He lifted the lid ever so gently and placed it next to the opened box. Markoe reached into the container, removed a handful of packing straw, and pulled an ornate wire cage with a porcelain base from the box. Trapped inside the golden wires of the cage sat a blue and red songbird affixed to a swinging perch. All members of the host's family—which included the Captain's son, Peter, as well as baby Lizbeth, fast approaching the terrible twos—and the few servants in attendance applauded the Colonel's beautiful gift. Krause nodded in the direction of the hostess and instructed her in his best English to wind the key at the base of the cage. Elizabeth Markoe did as instructed, then let go of the key. Immediately, the sweet chirping of a painted bunting filled the dining room. What followed were sighs of joy and a twitter of laughter which lasted nearly as long as the song.

Markoe's daughter, dressed in a pristine white smock and restrained in Anna McClew's lap, slapped the table with her tiny hand. Lizbeth wanted the bird to sing again. Her mother obliged the tike two more times. When Lizbeth demanded an encore and was ignored, she started to cry. Mrs. Markoe instructed her nanny to take Lizbeth to the upstairs nursery. When Anna McClew and her charge were gone, Elizabeth apologized for her daughter's outburst and thanked Colonel Krause for the lovely gift.

The guest flashed a red-lipped smile and muddled through his response in English: "For you each, a gift for sure . . . but you men must wait . . . maend sidst."

By the time the men had retreated to Captain Markoe's favorite room, only the host had not received his gift. He was familiar with the games his guest liked to play and so he forgot about the gift in the offing. Markoe had more important things to worry about. He was simply glad to be sitting comfortably in his favorite room with an old friend. His library provided gentlemen a degree of privacy not found in other parts of the bustling mansion. The library was situated where many other rooms could be easily accessed by common doors, corridors, and even a secret passageway, up and down, hidden behind an oak panel. Markoe often slipped down the staircase which connected his private bedchamber to his library. He always had difficulty sleeping—a restless sort ever since childhood. For the sake of his wife's delicate condition, Markoe slept alone. And, when he could not sleep, at least he could unwind and relax with a good book under candlelight or tend to some business matter or letter writing at his cherry wood desk. The chair and desk design, as well as the shelving configuration for his vast collection of books and the hidden stairway, had been designed by him. Even the latest version of his horse troop flag, which stood in the corner near the summer-dormant fireplace, had been designed mostly by him. The boy named Asher stood next to the flag stand admiring the details on the standard. He had grown weary of perusing the spines of books and was trying to keep his mind occupied while the grown men in the room chatted on about doings in St. Croix and the world at large.

Colonel Krause failed to stifle a belch, then failed to apologize. Abram and Peter Markoe continued sucking on their pipes, pretending not to notice their guest's rudeness. Only one person made note of the Colonel's eructation. Actually, she was making note of every sound and word emanating from the library. Ruth Mount sat on the bottom step of her master's secret stairway, out of sight behind the moveable oak panel. A thin shard of candlelight at the edge of the partition was not adequate for allowing findings to be written. Miss Mount had to put everything salient to memory.

She had seen the portly guest just once so far. This was when he and his alleged servant boy were ushered up the steep front steps of Markoe's manse and into the entrance hall at noon. Mistress Elizabeth had ordered her entire staff—free, indentured, and slave—to line up in two rows against the blue walls trimmed in white. The wainscotting had recently been painted a rich ivory. The help shied from brushing against it. After the initial greeting by host and hostess at the door, Peter Markoe was introduced, then all the staff members one by one.

When it came to Ruth Mount's turn to be introduced, Mistress Elizabeth touted her position as personal seamstress. Ruth curtsied as she had been instructed to do, but grudgingly so. She made eye contact with the honored Dane and saw only lust in his gaze. Ruth felt he was undressing her one petticoat at a time. She did not like this man.

Captain Markoe accompanied his wife down the line of servants. When he stood before Miss Mount, he informed the Colonel that she was the person responsible for sewing the horse troop standard. Krause winked at the woman and offered another red-lipped smile above his double chin. Ruth curtsied again but reciprocated no smile.

As she pressed her ear to the crack where the panel almost kissed the frame, Ruth reflected on that first encounter. The Colonel's every word must not be forgotten. She was glad his voice reached her loud and clear. Ruth was also glad she had found the hidden staircase early on during her free time when the Markoes were preoccupied elsewhere. She now enjoyed a perfect lair for stealing the secrets of suspect gentlemen. Her real boss will be pleased indeed, she thought.

Colonel Krause, playing distractedly with his pipe, spotted the aforementioned flag in the corner of the room. He kept to English this time. "Is that the one the escort today carried?"

Abram Markoe glanced to his left to see what his guest was staring at. "Oh, the troop standard you mean?"

"Jah, that's the one . . . over where my Asher is standing."

"No, Rob Hare was holding the flag we used to escort General Washington to New York . . . the one getting weathered a bit."

The Colonel took a sip of his apple brandy cordial, admired the glass, then belched again. "For what is this other one?"

"My wife's seamstress has made a new one for me," Markoe stated proudly. "I have improved the center design and added vines at the border. An artist in town has been commissioned to work the final design."

"Interessant," mused Krause. "Very interesting. You I commend on your inventive skills, Abram . . . and my compliments to your sewing maid for such fine work."

Ruth Mount blushed behind the oaken panel. She frowned at the same time. She was not eager to hear what would be said next.

The Colonel made a selfish request: "Perhaps, dear Abram, you might convince her to make a flag for me . . . something simple, of course. I like the stripes and the golden field. I like not your filigree at the edges . . . just a handsome flag for my new ship, if I ever get around to privateering."

Such a statement was pursued by a twitter of laughter from the two Markoe men.

The Captain offered a timely reply: "Of course, Johan . . . anything for a brigand from the islands. I shall summon Miss Mount on the morrow and you may tell her exactly what you desire. I understand she has ample cloth remaining from her work so far."

"Du er far venlig," Krause said. "You are too kind, Abram. So selfish of me for such a favor to ask."

"Not at all, Johan. My Miss Mount shall be more than glad to please you. She will start working on your flag in the morning."

Ruth winced in the darkness. She wanted to curse her bad luck out loud, but she held her tongue. She caught the implication, accidental or on purpose, threading through her master's words. Oh, how she hated wealthy men. Oh, how she hated all men.

The manly conversation turned to more important matters. The formerly silent and polite Peter Markoe finally spoke up. He was gaily dressed in a burgundy robe cinched at the waist by a broad yellow sash. Low-heeled leather shoes, sporting paste-stones of various hues, shod his feet. His voice soft and gilded with affectation: "Tell us, Colonel Krause, what brings you to Philadelphia?"

The Colonel shifted his rump a bit in the soft leather of the chair, cleared his throat, and answered evenly: "In this beautiful place, I am starting a visit to Nazareth Hall. I intend to visit there on the morrow. As you may, or may not know, the Moravian School has fallen into financial straits. Their missionaries on St. Croix continue to do wonders educating our slaves . . . keeping them passive and meek. I intend to offer the school what I can afford in the way of assistance. I also want to inspect their program for future reference. One of my younger sons is in need of a proper education and some strict disciplining, which are both wanting on our island."

Markoe complimented the Colonel on his suddenly improved command of English. Krause's verbosity genuinely surprised the host.

The Colonel smiled proudly. Both guest and host were aware that the islander only pretended to be challenged by English.

Markoe added: "My best coach is at your disposal, Johan. I would join you on your jaunt to the Hall but I do have pressing business matters to attend to. However, I shall consider helping the Moravians as well. I am fully aware of their exemplary work among my own plantation slaves."

"Most kind and generous of you," Krause gushed. "I will need no escort this time. I am going to take my chances in the wilderness beyond the city limits."

The Markoes both laughed. Krause gave them a puzzled look, but said nothing. He returned to his glass of liquor.

Captain Markoe finally spoke: "The wilderness you speak of hides far to the west and north of here. If you dare venture that far out, you will need my entire company of horse to protect you."

"Jah, then I shall venture no farther than Nazareth Hall," Krause promised. "I should return before dusk."

"Before you set out, Johan, and after a breakfast to your liking, I will bring you to our sewing maid. That way she can start immediately on your request . . . hopefully complete the thing before you have to return to St. Croix."

"Det lyder godt og godt," Krause responded. "All well and good, but one thing I must correct."

"What might that be, Johan?"

"Runger's sloop is taking on a supply of corn flour and salt beef . . . leaving port, bound for St. Croix, on the morrow. I will not be aboard . . . neither will Asher. I have business to attend here,

New York, and Boston before I am done. I told of this in my last letter."

Peter Markoe chimed in: "Even my father's full troop of horse can't get you into Boston these days."

"Jeg undskylder," Krause said. "I apologize. What I mean is a need to find Hans Febiger, if I can. Hans, as you may know, is a fellow Crocian and a loyal Dane . . . and damn good, I hear, with stones in a game of kag. Rumor has it, he has joined the rebel cause, as you have, Abram. I received word, before I left St. Croix, that Hans joined the Massachusetts militia in April. He was made a captain in May. Now he's throwing stones at Regulars."

"Does this Dane have what it takes to be a leader of men?" Peter Markoe asked in a voice feigning experience in martial pursuits. He owned none.

"I understand his uncle raised him on our island after his father died," Krause continued. "The uncle made sure Hans received a proper military education. He has only been in the Boston area a few years, but has established himself in horse trading and such. The man is not even close to having your level of success, Abram, but successful and popular just the same . . . not bad for an orphan from Faaborg."

"Impressive," mused Peter Markoe. He raised an eyebrow to show his displeasure over Krause addressing his father and ignoring him.

His father was not so moved. Abram Markoe changed the subject: "You may visit here as long as you like, Johan."

"My plans are to settle certain accounts here, arrange for some sorely needed supplies to be shipped to St. Croix, and make arrangements for my journey to New York and beyond. For such matters, I've allotted the time of a week."

"Well, you don't have to worry about transportation, Johan. My best coach, larger than the one employed today and fit with new springs, will be at your disposal by next week. The same trustworthy coachman shall be at the reins . . . and a team of four strong horses instead of two."

"Mere end venlig, Abram. More than kind . . . God bless you."

"Just don't leave before you allow me to open the gift you have brought me," Markoe said with a chuckle.

Krause frowned. "Your son and your wife opened their gifts when I deemed it proper to do so. But yours must not be opened till I am far from here."

"Why all the mystery, Johan?"

"Kun et spil," Krause confessed, "but a game played by my rules. Please bear with me as I obey my king and follow my heart at the same time. After some prayer and counsel at Nazareth Hall, I shall be able to tell you what you need to know."

A long silence ensued. By then, Asher had found a volume of maps to his liking and was leafing through the pages. The three gentlemen sucked on their pipes and sipped their drinks. Ruth Mount counted the leaden seconds.

Finally the conversation resumed. The three men covered various mundane topics. Abram Markoe went over his schedule of activities planned for his guest. The demonstration of skills by the troop of horse and the tour of the estate had been moved up to Thursday, August 3rd, in order not to conflict with Krause's visit to Nazareth Hall. The horsemen's drills would start at 6 a.m. and last until 8 a.m. The tour would follow and be accomplished before noon. Markoe had nothing planned for Friday so that the Colonel might attend to business matters in the city. Saturday was reserved for a fancy reception banquet in Colonel Krause's honor at the Markoe estate. Many of the city's dignitaries and several of the Congressional delegates had been invited to attend. Sunday would be a proper day of rest and the time to start preparing for the Colonel's journey to New York.

The Colonel scolded Markoe for fussing over him. He insisted there was no need for a banquet. But the Captain argued that he wanted to do more. He had hoped his guest would consider staying longer in Philadelphia. The two bantered back and forth on each other's plans.

Meanwhile, Peter Markoe lifted a teakwood box he had been cradling in his lap. Krause had given it to him as a gift. It contained expensive inks and quills—the kind a writer of delicate verse would employ. He placed the box gently on the side table nearest him. He brushed at nothing in his lap but stroked his breeks just the same with slender fingers and well-manicured nails. The younger Markoe decided to put an end to the civil back and forth between the Captain and the Colonel. He was getting bored, and, at such times, he was prone to stir the pot.

"How goes things with our poor, dear Queen Matilda?" Peter asked with an asp's tongue when the other two men had paused to sip their spirits.

This was, indeed, a touchy subject for any Dane to discuss. Caroline Matilda was the sister of King George III of England. At the age of sixteen, she was married off to the unstable lout, King Christian VII of Denmark. At first, the new queen was quite popular with Danish subjects. Her supporters called her 'the English Rose'. Her union with Christian was supposed to have put the so called 'frog-eaters' in Britain's back pocket as far as alliances and diplomatic matters were concerned. At worst, the 'flame-haired Vikings'—as English nobles referred to the Danes—could be counted upon to remain neutral if the rebellion in the American colonies flamed into an all-out war. But this union of royals grew tenuous at best. Things went awry when King Christian's personal doctor, Johann Strunsee—a second-rank professional from common German stock—wormed his way into the position of chief advisor to a king who was deemed incapable of making decisions on his own. Christian was most interested in drinking till drunk and carousing with common tarts. He loved to order such women to dress in men's clothing, and, as they paraded about, satisfy his compulsion to masturbate.

Doctor Strunsee took charge in 1770 and initiated many reforms which angered most Danish nobles and the Queen Dowager, Juliana. The last straw involved rumors about a burgeoning affair between the good Doctor, nicknamed 'Cicisbo', and Queen Caroline Matilda, who had been virtually ignored by the 'strutting cock' king. The alleged affair between the king's private doctor/chief advisor and the queen resulted in rumors and suspicions as to the paternity of the queen's second child. Thus, conservative nobles and the Queen Dowager, in concert with the military guard, planned a coup against Strunsee and his cabal of bureaucrats. After dispatching the good doctor and declaring Christian insane the plotters intended to put Frederick, the king's half-brother, on the throne.

Strunsee and Matilda were arrested at a masked ball in 1772.

The doctor's right hand and head were cut off. The head was placed on a stake for the public to view. His body was drawn and quartered. Riots and burnings by commoners ensued. Queen Matilda was exiled to Elsinore Castle. She was forced to leave her children behind. The English were incensed over the treatment of their 'Sweet Rose' by the Danes. King George demanded that his sister be moved to the castle at Zell in Hanover, which was referred to as 'England's Germany'. This situation brought England and Denmark to the brink of war.

Peter Markoe asked again: "Tell us, Colonel Krause. What is your take on the queen's status?"

Krause grudgingly brought the listeners up to speed, using the best English he could muster. "On my visit last to London, I ran into Nathaniel Wraxall, a special agent to King George. He spoke of his concern over the health of Queen Matilda. She did survive the pox outbreak a few years ago, but, since then, was putting on weight. She was looking very sickly. Matilda was depressed over the loss of her children and equally depressed over her looks. Her personal doctor prescribed stewed rhubarb to conquer her ills, but this foolish remedy did nothing for her malaise. I was surprised to hear from Wraxall that he was involved in a plot to free Matilda and restore her as Queen of Denmark with the help of certain Danish nobles and military support from King George."

"What nobles would dare such a foolish enterprise," Peter Markoe speculated more to himself than to Krause.

"Not at liberty to divulge their names," confessed the Colonel. He plowed on: "King George merely gave a tepid promise of support and only if, and when, the restoration succeeded. Needless to say, the attempt fell apart. Poor Caroline Matilda succumbed to a 'purple fever' outbreak in Zell two months ago. With her passing came the abandonment of any hope to get rid of Christian and his new advisors."

Peter Markoe spoke with heightened enthusiasm: "I must write a poem—an elegy to the Rose Queen."

"Do that, little Peter," urged the Colonel. "Use the ink and quill I have given you to honor her."

Abram Markoe finally contributed: "I tolerated King George's sister before she conspired with the German doctor, but after, I despised her as much as I've despised that scamp Christian all along. Who is left to admire?"

"The head of foreign affairs, Andreas Peter Burnstorff," Krause said. "The man's a strong proponent of Danish neutrality. He is not keen on Britain keeping Denmark on puppet strings, but he also fears a homeland rebellion if Denmark sides with the American colonies."

"I trust him not," Markoe opined.

"Why?" insisted Krause. "Because you are such a rebel against the farmer king?"

"But of course," said Markos with unblinking eyes. "I want Denmark ready to declare war on England when the time comes. I want St. Croix on our side. I want all Danish subjects here and there and everywhere in favor of the cause."

The Colonel raised his pipe to interrupt Markoe's rant. "Not so hasty, Abram. Neutrality always works in favor of a merchant. Neutrality means Denmark will not bow to Britain's demands. Be happy with such a fate, my good man."

"Being happy with such is not in the cards for me, Johan."

The Colonel bit his lip and sighed. He knew he was getting nowhere trying to change his host's mind. "For now, let us say no more about our dear motherland's predicament. We should move on to lighter subjects."

Behind the oaken panel, Ruth Mount smiled to herself and sighed inaudibly. She had heard more than enough and had put it all to memory. She had discovered Krause's purposes in coming to Philadelphia. Her boss would be pleased. Ruth was sure she would be paid well. The silent sewing maid rose to her feet and climbed the narrow stairs to her master's bed chamber. She wondered why the Captain preferred to sleep alone. Ruth never could.

14

MEETING MISTER LAU

· ·

(Tuesday, August 1, 1775)

Enoch Mortaine found his hireling at the same table in the same dreary corner of the Blue Anchor. The man was hunched over his rum pot, whiskered chin almost touching the near-empty vessel. He projected a hangdog look—no gleam of promising prospects in his dull brown eyes and no smile of recognition on his sun-blistered lips.

"Thirteen stripes," blurted Mortaine as he approached the table. The password was little more than a joke now . . . something said to lighten the mood. "What's ailing you, Pip?"

The large man waved a calloused paw at his generous boss and pointed a grimy finger at the chair opposite his.

Mortaine pulled it back and sat down quickly. He was better dressed than the last time he visited the disreputable tavern, but not by much. This time his ozenbrig shirt and checkered vest were clean. So were his flap-front leggings. Only his hob boots showed signs of where he had walked to get to the tavern. He stomped both feet and clots of muck escaped to the floor.

"What, pray tell, struck you, Pip—lightning or a coach and four?"

"Back is hurtin' fierce, Mister Mortaine," answered the hireling with a wince. "Also the arm what was broke is actin' up . . . all due to a day of heavy luggin' down on the dock."

"You're a mean, strong fellow, Pip. All you need is a bit more rum, a frolic with a bow-legged woman, and a good night's sleep."

The base man spit on the floor. His eyes smoldered with anger. There was a bitter taste in his mouth. His words held the same flavor. "First off, call me Hendrick Lau from now on. 'Tis what all new friends have started callin' meself startin' with today. As for the rest, I'll take another rum if you're payin' . . . forget about the whore 'n the bed. Doubt if I'll find either after I'm done here."

Mortaine ignored most of what the fellow said. He signaled the same well-fardled bar maid. She scurried over, took his order for a pint of ale and a pot of rum, and fled as quick as she came.

"Okay, Hendrick Lau," Mortaine said slowly, as if practicing the pronunciation of the man's new name. "What have you learned about dear Colonel Johan Gottfried Krause?"

"A generous bloak who's carryin' some mighty heavy wooden caskets bound secure with nautical ropes thick as a gaunt woman's wrist."

"Interesting," mulled Mortaine as he stroked the stubble on his chin then counted out suitable coins for the serving maid. She returned as soon as the first coin hit the table. Pip, alias Hendrick Lau, grabbed for the brimming rum pot as spiritedly as the bar maid scooped up Mortaine's coins.

The agent for the King continued: "Ever find out what is in those containers?"

"Me 'n some other bloaks pulled four caskets from the sloop's hold, plus many boxes and satchels from the deck. Never got a chance to poke in any of the Colonel's belongin's. But the caskets had initials burned into their lids—two said 'AM' 'n two said 'CF'. There were other such caskets in the hold, but we was told by the first mate to pull out only a certain four."

"How many cases altogether?"

"I counted eight more in the hold. The rest of the containers was fiskens and tuns of perishables, far as I could tell."

"Well, we can assume that two of the cases are meant for Captain Markoe, judging by his initials burned in the wood. But we do not know who in this city will receive the two containers marked with 'C' and 'F'."

"Have not been here long enough to know many," confessed the now Mister Lau.

"Same for me," added Mortaine, "but I will find out. How about the man himself?"

"You mean Krause or Markoe?"

"The Colonel, of course," said Mortaine. "I understand Captain

Markoe was detained on a business matter and he sent two of his dragoons to receive Krause."

"Correct," replied the hireling. "A mounted pair posin' in full dress. One held the troop's banner, which the Colonel made a fuss over. He spoke some in Danish, which I did not understand, 'n some in English . . ."

"Krause wants us to think his command of English is poor," Mortaine interrupted.

Pip ignored the agent's comment and said, "He paid us well in Danish silver."

"Anything else?"

"A half-breed boy servant shadowed the Colonel to the coach," said Pip. "I did not catch his name. But Krause caught mine. 'Fore he rewarded me with another coin, he asked for my name. So I gave him 'Hendrick Lau', 'n I've worn it ever since."

"What name do you intend to use when you head north to find the dueling pistol?"

"Does my name matter?"

" Yes, if I need to send someone to find you. The name you're going to use will help to track you down."

"My work is over at the wharf," Pip declared. "Soon as my back is right, I'm fixin' to head out . . . usin' this here new name . . . maybe not." Pip paused to take a pull of rum. Then he remembered something: "Krause's sloop is takin' on flour 'n beef . . . headin' back to St. Croix at high tide tomorrow. At least that is what I've been told by Captain Cruger of the Caramaw."

"Good to know," mused Mortaine. "So the Colonel shall remain here but his ship will not. I wonder how long he will stay in Philadelphia. And what are his plans for returning to St. Croix?"

Pip opined: "Judgin' by the weight of his luggage, the Colonel plans on stayin' for a long spell."

"So, then, I may need you for some dirty work if the need arises," said Mortaine. "That is reason enough to know what you'll be calling yourself in the Jerseys."

"I'll be usin' the new name, Mister Mortaine. I'll be found at Manley's Tavern along the King's Highway . . . a place north of Kings Town by some few miles."

"Fine then," Mortaine asserted. "Good luck finding the pistol.

After you have succeeded, bring the weapon back to me."

"If the money's right," grinned Pip.

"You lost the damn thing," countered Mortaine, "and you failed to use it. I should not have to pay you anything for finding it."

"But you will," said Pip, still burdened with a broad grin.

"I might consider such," Mortaine sighed. "Luckily, the money I work with does not come out of my own pouch."

"Then you won't mind rewardin' me a modest amount of coin for retrievin' the missin' firearm?"

"You'll get your large reward after you've dispatched a rebel leader, Pip. 'Tis what you were originally hired for. Don't fuss over piddling amounts."

"'Tis Hendrick Lau now," Pip insisted. "Don't forget the name when I come to collect the reward you speak of. Hope it'd be comin' more to soon than late."

"I am hoping the same, Mister Lau," Mortaine said. "The sooner the better."

15

A SIMPLE REQUEST

(Wednesday, August 2, 1775)

Mistress Elizabeth's sewing parlor was in the next room over from the nursery on the second floor of the spacious Markoe manse. Ruth Mount sat alone close to the tall window facing east overlooking her favorite garden. Her chestnut hair was tucked neatly under a white mobcap. Her blue cotton gown and white apron were void of stains. Both were free of wrinkles. Ruth wore no shoes while sitting at her work station. It was a luxury she allowed herself whenever possible.

The proficient seamstress had started work on an infant's smock—one of many to be completed for Mistress Elizabeth's yet-to-be-born second child. Ruth had taken much time selecting materials, thread, and tools from tables and drawers which lined the windowless wall. Once she sat at her work station, she wanted everything she required to be at arm's length so that she could finish the gay smock in one setting.

But Ruth Mount was soon distracted by droplets of water still clinging to the panes of glass that made the window. The sky was clear—almost cloudless, with a bright, early morning sun doing its best to dry up the moisture left by a heavy, pre-dawn shower. However, it was not yet warm enough to open the window. Mistress Elizabeth preferred all windows shut tight anyway. Captain Markoe felt the same. Ever since coming from St. Croix, the master of the house fell victim to such superstitions about evil vapors in the air, and keeping doors and windows shut whenever possible to avoid said vapors from seeping in. Ruth was not from the same school of thought on the matter, but she obeyed the Markoes to avoid falling out of favor. She was satisfied with the amount of fresh air she gained during her free time in the garden below the window.

There was no compulsion on her part to crack the window open on the sly.

The seamstress was also distracted from her work by worrying over what to say to her master and his guest when they came to her. She doubted that Enoch Mortaine's scheme would work. But worse, she doubted herself. She would have to sound convincing and speak of things culled from pure fiction. Somehow Ruth would have to summon the courage to sound convincing. She had had a pleasant and productive sleep with Anna McClew up to and including the rain storm. The morning repast in the servant's kitchen had proved substantial and delicious. Two bowls of camomile tea had helped calm her nerves. Yet she was still on edge. Tense. Afraid she would stumble over her words when confronted by the two wealthy gentlemen. Ruth gave the pale yellow ribband on her cap a tug, then got back to work. Daydreaming and dread both had to be put to rest. Work was the cure.

The parlor door was ajar. The sewing maid heard two loud voices conversing in a foreign language out in the hallway. She quickly picked up needle and thread, and pretended to worry a hem.

Captain Markoe ushered Colonel Krause into the sewing parlor. He neglected to close the door behind him. Asher, the servant boy, remained in the hallway, but Ruth could see him peeking in.

Markoe addressed his guest: "Here is my little seamstress, Johan . . . busy at her tasks so early in the morning."

"Ja, godt," grunted the Colonel.

"How are you managing, Miss Mount?" Markoe asked in a rutilant voice. He was dressed in a rich man's riding gear, highlighted by a short burgundy hunting jacket.

"I am progressing well, sir," Ruth said, as she put down her equipment and attempted to stand in order to curtsy.

"No need to abandon your work, Miss Mount. Please remain seated," insisted Markoe. "My guest has admired the effort you put into the pair of troop standards. He likes your work and has a simple request to make of you."

The Colonel, also dressed for riding—but in a coach rather than atop a horse, cast lickerish eyes at the seamstress. Ruth felt him undressing her again with his eyes. Krause was also moistening his lips with his tongue after noticing that she was shoeless. His mouth and teeth glistened menacingly in the sunlight streaming in through the window.

The Colonel produced his best English: "I have in mind a flag design of my own—one to fly on a ship I plan to build. Something stark, but pleasing to the eye . . . not as pleasing as you, Miss Mount, but pleasing just the same."

"You have material left from the work on my standards, do you not?" Markoe asked sharply.

"The golden silk I have aplenty," admitted Ruth. "And a modest amount of blue—light or dark. As for greens and reds, I have little. Black I have, but not in broad cloth."

"That will suffice," concluded Markoe with a wave of his hand. He turned to his guest. "Any of those hues suit your fancy, Johan?"

"Ja," Krause responded. He clasped his hands behind his back and leaned into the sunlight. "Gold for the field . . . azure for the striping. I require nothing more, Abram. No snaking vines. No fancy fringe. No figures nor words dancing in the center. My wants and desires are plain and simple."

Markoe turned to his seamstress. "What say you, Miss Mount? Can you shape a flag of, lets say, three foot hoist and four foot fly to be finished by Sunday evening? Colonel Krause is leaving on the seventh."

"A large order," Ruth said firmly.

"Do you mean size of the flag, or the time restraint, or both?"

"Size is the challenge," admitted Ruth. "The larger the flag, the more stitching involved. Thus, the more time it will take."

The Colonel gave a chuckle. "Size should not worry a woman of your age and experience. I am sure you can handle any of my requests."

Ruth flashed a sour face and squinted a knowing eye. She had cut through the wealthy Dane's implication like a knife through butter. She wished, in her heart, she could have used the knife to cut him to the bone right then and there.

Captain Markoe, seemingly oblivious to the game being played by his guest, said: "Miss Mount shall craft the largest flag she can in the time allotted. Are you happy with that, Johan?"

"Ja . . . of course, of course," the Colonel replied. "Long as my flag can be seen a fair distance away, no complaint will I show."

"Miss Mount will do her best," said Markoe with finality.

Ruth's countenance still held to sour. She, in fact, looked suddenly weary and sad. It was time to take advantage of a challenging situation.

"Is anything ailing you, Miss Mount?" asked Markoe in a concerned voice.

"Yes, there is, kind sir."

"Tell me. You may trust the Colonel to keep in confidence whatever you say."

Ruth looked down at the polished floor. She spotted a hole in her hose and wished she had kept her shoes on. She also saw her reflection in the sun-struck floor boards. The seamstress smiled inwardly at the clever frowning mask she was wearing. She raised her head slowly and cast sad, honest eyes in her master's direction.

"My dear mother is ailing," Ruth sighed softly. "She lies in a poor state suffering from the throes of the pox. Hovering close to death . . . so says my brother who has journeyed all the way from New York to inform me of her condition."

Captain Markoe's eyes spoke of sincere concern. His guest managed a polite sigh.

Ruth continued: "My brother remains in this city seeking passage by ship to New York. Hopefully he can make arrangements for the two of us by the middle of the month . . . the sooner the better for my mother's sake."

Ruth allowed a faux tear to find her cheek. She wiped it away and took a deep breath. She decided to stare out the window again. By now, the storm's tears on the glass had vanished.

"I assume you are requesting a leave, Miss Mount?" asked Markoe in a business-like manner.

"I was getting around to asking soon as my brother sends word of the date of our leaving. I shall return as soon as I am able."

"This is an untimely request," said Markoe, as he started pacing in a tight circle, his riding boots clicking against the floor boards. "You have not been in my hire for very long. I will have to counsel with my wife. Perhaps I should talk to that brother of yours."

The Colonel leaped into the conversation between master and servant. "May I make a humble suggestion, Abram."

"What do you have in mind, Johan?"

"Since I will be journeying up to New York in your most spacious coach on the seventh of this month, I am sure there will be enough room for my Asher, Miss Mount here, and even her brother. This will give your seamstress incentive to complete my simple request on time . . . and provide a chance to return by way of your coach at an earlier date than she predicts."

Markos stroked his clean-shaven chin. "What say you, Miss Mount, to Colonel Krause's kind offer?"

Ruth arose from her low chair near the window, but kept her shoeless feet firmly planted under the table. She managed an awkward curtsy, then sat back down immediately.

"I shall be most indebted to you, kind sir," Mount said with as much sincerity as she felt necessary. "But I must inform my brother of your offer soon as I can."

"This is a large city," the Captain interjected. "Where exactly is this brother of yours?"

"You might find him at the Port House on Water Street attending to business matters," said Ruth, "or in a room he is renting above the Tun Tavern on King Street. He is a procurer of munitions. Certain dealings have given him an excuse to bring me the bad news in person."

The Colonel suddenly turned away and coughed. Phlegm caught in his throat and caused him to struggle for air. The Dane turned red-faced. Markoe slapped his guest hard on the back. With a difficult swallow, Krause regained his composure.

Krause bent a knee to the seamstress. "You will please forgive my rudeness . . . must be from the snuff employed after breakfast."

"Shouldn't use the devil's weed so early in the day, Johan," warned Markoe. "Such a remedy for your breathing difficulties will be the death of you."

The Colonel frowned. He did not want his train of thought interrupted by his host. There was an important matter to discuss—a crucial matter related to his main purpose in visiting the colonies.

But Captain Markoe was not through dispensing unsolicited advice. "I suggest the counsel of our midwife, Cornelia Emmons. I hear she works wonders with roots and spices. My wife swears by her magic." He turned to his seamstress. "Miss Mount, please visit

Miss Emmons to see if she can lift your spirits with an elixir. While you're at it, ask Miss Emmons for something to clear the Colonel's stubborn head."

Krause chuckled and held up a hand. "Not to worry yourself on my account, Abram. One of these days I will stumble upon something better than snuff to clear my head. I will take care of myself my own way . . . not by some witch's brew. No need to fret over this Dane."

The Captain smiled at his mulish friend and decided to waste no more words of advice on him. He turned to his seamstress instead. "Colonel Krause and I will be attending a meeting of the Order of St. George at the Tun Tavern tomorrow night. I hope to find your brother there. By the by, does he carry your surname?"

"In truth, he is my half-brother," Mount said. "He goes by Azariah Willett, in memory of my dear mother's first departed husband."

Markoe nodded. "I shall look forward to meeting Mister Willett. By tomorrow, I shall have counseled with my wife on the feasibility of allowing you a leave on such short notice. After doing so, I will sit down with your brother and discuss this matter."

Colonel Krause added: "I am most interested in meeting your brother, Miss Mount." He gave a quick glance toward Markoe. "May I sit in on your meeting?"

"By all means, Johan," said Markoe. "That is why I am putting off finding this man till the morrow. You will be at Nazareth Hall most of this day and you will need your rest when you return. Best to find Mister Willett on Thursday. He might wish to join us for the tour of my estate and the drills by my troop of horse, which I have planned for you."

"Jah, fine by me," the Colonel said.

Captain Markoe was about to wish his seamstress a productive day and turn to leave the parlor, when Ruth Mount spoke up: "I nearly forgot to ask . . ."

"What pray tell?" said Markoe, who was now most concerned with getting the guest on his way to Nazareth Hall.

"How many stripes?"

Markoe turned to his guest and repeated the question: "How many stripes on your flag, Johan?"

The Colonel offered a toothsome grin. "I dare not ask for less or more than thirteen when in Abram Markoe's house."

The Captain matched the Colonel's grin. "A good choice, Johan . . . a very good choice."

16

TRICKING THE PIG

· · · · · · · · · · · · · · · · · · · ·

(Thursday, August 3, 1775)

A fine roan mare was hitched to the nearest post by the open gate to the Christ Church burial grounds. The mount was enjoying a patch of grass and clover under the shade of an elm. This was a rented horse, trained to accommodate the queasiest of riders. Her latest was, indeed, not accustomed to employing her kind to get around and his riding skills were poor at best. But the mare was a patient dame who knew the streets of Philadelphia well. She had been plodding them for seven years. Her master down at the stable down on Water Street was kind and gentle. His fee to gentlemen in a hurry was steep, but they always returned with a laudable word or two about her abilities. She did not care about all that. Being fed her oats, watered well, and brushed thoroughly by the stable slaves were her only concerns. Now she could rest a bit in cool shade on such a fair and clear day, while her well-dressed rider was paying his respects to a deceased loved one inside the gated cemetery. At least, that was the excuse the fellow had given to the mare's master at the stable. The horse did not care about the reasons or excuses either. Life was good only if it was uncomplicated. For now, it was good as the grazing.

Behind the open gate two figures strolled down the path just as they had done on their previous visit. One kept to an even pace. The other was hindered by a limp. This time, however, they paid no attention to the grave of Sarah Knowles. They headed straight to the bower bench. A pair of wren tits nesting there took flight noisily and lodged their complaints about being rudely disturbed from a safe distance in the nearest birch tree.

Both parties sat close and kept their voices low. Things had gotten serious in one day—very serious.

The man, dressed in a coffee-brown waistcoat and cream-colored breeches. spoke first: "You need to find out what is in these wooden cases Colonel Krause brought to Markoe's manse."

"How am I to accomplish such a thing, Mister Mortaine?" asked Ruth Mount, who was dressed in her usual servant's garb plus a gray shawl of her own making. "I'm told each case is heavy as a yearling ox and bound with sturdy seaman's knots."

"Where are they stored?" Mortaine asked.

"All four are now in the anteroom off the welcoming hall behind the nearest door."

"Is the door locked?"

"No," Ruth said with conviction. "I have seen the Colonel's servant boy go in there to fetch various items. Most of his master's luggage is in there as well."

"Hmm," mused Mortaine. "All such dunnage must be for his future plans." The King's agent paused to collect his thoughts. "But you have access to this room, if Krause's boy does. Am I correct?"

"Yes, of course," scoffed Ruth.

"So give it a try when the boy is not about and Markoe's other servants are occupied elsewhere. I shall double your stipend if you bring me back useful information."

"Since you make it worth a try, Mister Mortaine, it will be done . . . but I cannot promise anything. This is a man's work you're having me do."

Mortaine smiled. "You are man enough for this task, Miss Mount. Use the wiles and strengths the good Lord has given you, then get word to me of your findings as soon as you can."

The seamstress nodded. "I shall do my best."

"Good, now tell me what you have learned about our new guest."

"I was privy to a conversation in my master's library—the Captain himself, Peter Markoe, and their guest, Colonel Krause. The Colonel's boy servant may have been in the room, but I could not see any of them because I was hiding behind a false wall."

"Yet, you could hear their voices well enough?"

"Clear as a preacher at his sermon," Ruth said. "As if I was sitting with those three men in a front pew."

"Good," Mortaine declared, while matching Ruth's smile. "So you can account for every word uttered that evening."

"Most certainly . . . 'tis what you pay me for."

"So get to it, Miss Mount. My time is valuable."

"The first topic was that damn flag," started Ruth. "The one I am so weary of sewing. Colonel Krause was fawning again over the horse troop's standard and then asking my master if I could make a flag for him . . ."

"That should be no problem for a person of your talents," interjected Mortaine.

Mount scowled: "I have no choice in the matter. The next day, the two gentlemen visited me in the sewing parlor and posed their request for a striped flag—blue and gold . . . to be completed before the Colonel departs."

Mortaine leaned closer. "And when would that be?"

"Monday the seventh at dawn."

"By what means?"

"Captain Markoe's best coach and four."

"What destination and by what route?"

"The Colonel is visiting Nazareth Hall this day . . . something about schooling for his youngest boy and helping out the Moravians financially."

"Not important to us," quipped Mortaine. "I want more about his plans for next week."

"The Colonel is off to New York and then to Boston," answered Mount. "My master insists that the Lower Road be taken through the Jerseys. He gave no reason."

"Less traveled and faster than the Upper Road," Mortaine ruminated to himself. "And that poses a problem for my plans."

Ruth Mount ignored Mortaine's vexation over the chosen route. Instead, she offered: "The Colonel claims he has business to attend in New York and a certain Hans Febiger to contact in Boston."

"I know not the nature of Krause's business matters in New York, but I have heard of this fellow named Febiger. He is a Dane, don't you know, and probably another pawn in Krause's game. This Febiger will not be found in Boston. He is an ardent rebel like Markoe and is probably shining Washington's boots in Cambridge. I will solicit my superiors about this particular Dane. Go on, Miss Mount."

"The Colonel did promise to inform his host about more of his plans at a later time. I should learn more by then."

"Good," said Mortaine. "Anything else?"

"Their conversation drifted to my master's schedule of activities for the Colonel after his return from Nazareth Hall. Captain Markoe will be giving his guest a tour of the estate, and the Philadelphia Troop of Horse will be demonstrating their equine skills. There will also be a formal reception for Colonel Krause on Saturday."

"Does not give us much time to enact my plan," fretted Mortaine. "But we will have to adjust and press on. What else did you learn?"

"Too much on the doings in Denmark . . . mostly about the demise of our King's sister and the failed plot to remove the Danish king from the throne."

Mortaine held up a hand, palm out. "I know all about poor Princess Caroline Matilda and that lunatic ruler of Denmark. No need to make me ill, Miss Mount. Move on to more palatable stuff."

"Nothing more to say," stated Ruth bluntly. "The conversation fell to Denmark's status if war breaks out here. The Colonel spoke of neutrality and the Captain spoke of Denmark siding with the rebel cause."

"Nothing unremarkable there," concluded Mortaine. "We know where Captain Markoe stands, no doubt. But the problem lies with the Colonel. He is no Quaker. Did he offer any clues this morning in the sewing parlor?"

"No hint of his favoring the rebel side . . . except for settling on thirteen stripes for his flag. He maintains the flag is for a ship he plans to build."

"No doubt a privateer," mumbled Mortaine.

"He also warmed to me in a most ungentlemanly manner," confessed Ruth.

"By his actions?" asked Mortaine.

"By his words . . . methinks he longs to ravish me."

Mortaine clucked like a skeptic. "You should be flattered, Miss Mount. A simple servant maid sought after by a man of his station."

"I don't give a fig about the man's rank or his wealth," insisted Ruth. "If he dangles his pestal near me, I shall have need to employ my cutting blade on his person."

Mortaine was still clucking. "Such a move might put a damper on my plans. You must comport yourself in a cooperative manner when in the presence of Captain Markoe's guest. If he happens to harm you in any way, one of my cohorts will deal with him quickly and harshly . . . that is, after we learn what he is really up to."

"I may be quicker and harsher, Mister Mortaine. I am alerting you now. The Colonel will not get close to me. Till then I am playing your game as best I can. I told my master, in the presence of the Colonel, that our dear mother is gravely ill and on her death bed in New York. I told them you had come to Philadelphia to fetch me. The Captain was not pleased with my request for a leave in order to see our dieing mother."

Ruth Mount paused to catch Mortaine's reaction to her scheme. The man remained, stone-faced and said nothing.

The sewing maid continued: "The Captain insisted he must counsel with his wife. The Colonel, on the other hand, appeared moved by my situation and has offered to allow you and me to accompany him and his boy servant by coach all the way to New York."

Mortaine came alive with a broad grin and a slap on his knee. "Brilliant. Miss Mount . . . simply brilliant. You have played this well . . . better than expected."

"I think Captain Markoe is skeptical of this ploy," said Mount. "He plans to meet you at the Tun Tavern to confirm what I have told him. I understand that he and the Colonel will attend a meeting of the Order of St. George at the Tun tomorrow evening. You better be at the bar." She paused and gave her boss a hard stare just to make sure her directions were registering. Then she continued. "By the by, I told the Captain your name is Azariah Willett and that you are a procurer of munitions . . . but I did not say for whom. I told him you were renting a room at the Tun."

"Beyond brilliant," exclaimed Mortaine. "I could kiss you, Miss Mount."

Ruth stiffened her back and cast cold eyes. "I suggest you don't try, dear brother. Remember always that I carry sharp instruments in the folds of my gown. I create tears as easily as I mend them."

Mortaine sought to ignore the threat. "You are correct about everything . . . except that I am renting a room down the street from the Tun. But I will work around that item. Tell me what I need to say in the presence of the Captain and the Colonel."

Ruth relaxed her spine a bit. She cupped her hands in her lap and gave her boss all the details he needed to know.

Mortaine put the information to memory. He concluded the meeting by instructing Miss Mount on what she needed to do beyond finding out what was in the mysterious cases.

"We need to tame the Colonel . . . loosen his tongue to get him to talk," said Mortaine, more to himself than to his cohort.

"Spirits will not work on that one," advised Mount. "Imbibing to excess and gluttony at meal time appear to be virtues in his book."

"Then we must allow such to work in our favor," posed Mortaine. "How about that fellow maid who came on board the same time you did— the one you said knows her roots and potions?"

"Cornelia Emmons, midwife to Mistress Elizabeth?"

"Yes, that's the one," Mortaine said with sudden enthusiasm. "Why not ask her to recommend some magic brew which will make one drowsy and passive—something to ensure our good Colonel turns most cooperative."

"Miss Emmons hardly speaks to me or Anna," Mount admitted. "She prefers the company of the kitchen slaves from St. Croix."

"Still and all, I would ask her about such a potion," maintained the agent. "Say it is for you or for Miss McClew."

"Obtaining such from Cornelia is one thing," said Mount. "Administering it to a rude shoat like the Colonel is another."

Mortaine laughed. "Remember, Miss Mount, swine eat anything and everything."

17

A COOL RECEPTION

(Thursday, August 3, 1775)

The meeting of the members of the Order of St. George at the Tun Tavern started late and ended early. Nothing much was accomplished save for excessive drinking and toasts to the leaders of the rebellion, Captain Markoe's guest from St. Croix, and Markoe himself. Events of the day were reviewed. There was much boasting and bragging over the fine demonstration of skills by the troop of horse on the Markoe estate early in the morning. Colonel Krause, dressed in a wealthy gentleman's finery from snow-white wig to shiny silver-buckle shoes, gave his effusive impression of the horsemen's drills and tour of the Markoe estate which had followed the demonstration. Captain Markoe followed with an invitation to all members of the Order of St. George to the formal reception planned for his guest on Saturday. Those members in attendance voiced their gratitude and accepted the invitation.

When the meeting adjourned, the Captain and the Colonel excused themselves from the card game in the rear room and headed for the crowded bar. A few members of the Order of St. George were already there mingling with non-members and discussing salient topics of the day. One man stood alone in a far corner. He was nursing his third pint of house ale and watching the others gabbling away. This fellow was dressed in no outstanding manner—his outfit consisting of a silver-gray waist coat, black vest, black breeches, white hose, and buckle broghams. Anyone there would have pegged him as a man of business—an honest one, more than likely. His hair was tamed back with a neat black ribband. His brown eyes were clear and bright. He could have passed for anybody's unremarkable brother. He was no match for the Colonel's lacy attire nor the Captain's blue and black military look.

Captain Markoe reached the bar before his lumbering guest did. He hailed minehost, but shouted out to everyone: "Is Azariah Willett here?"

That call turned many heads but only one man responded to it. The chap at the end of the bar raised his pint. Markoe pointed to an empty table close to the bar, and the man got to it before the Captain and the Colonel completed their requests for liquid refreshment—madeira for Markoe, peach brandy for Krause.

When all three had reached the table, introductions were made, chairs were pulled out, and seats were taken.

"Your sister informs me that you have brought her sad news, Mister Willett," said Captain Markoe rather coldly.

"My half-sister, actually," said the supposed Mister Willett. "We share the same mother, but have different fathers unknown to both of us."

"I see," pondered Markoe, sniffing the air surrounding the base man. "And your mother's condition?"

"Poor, at best," offered the man playing Willett. "That is why I rushed down to your fair city to tell dear Ruth of our mother's losing battle against the pox. I fear her days on earth are numbered. So I came as fast as I could."

"I understand you would like to escort your sister back to New York," inquired Markoe.

"I know this matter is on short notice," said the King's agent and employer of many names. "But, yes, that is the hope. Ruth is my mother's favorite and it is her wish to see her daughter one last time."

Markoe took a sip of his wine and made his decision. "I have discussed this matter with my wife. We both agree that Miss Mount has become invaluable to us. She is a diligent worker who knows her craft. She has taken the young, less experienced nursery maid, Miss McClew, under her wing and is teaching her things that are beyond my understanding. Miss Mount sits well with all my other servants and she attends to my wife's every demand. In other words, we would hate to miss her even for a day."

"I understand," the imposter said, feigning sincerity and sadness.

The Captain nodded, then plowed on. "However, my wife and I are no martinets. We shall grant your sister a leave of five days and expect her back by Friday the eleventh before dusk."

"I have been unable to book passage until Wednesday the ninth," the alleged Willett said, still offering a downcast look. "She will not be able to return at the time you have allotted her."

Markoe waved a dismissive hand. "Colonel Krause has an alternative plan that may work for all involved. What say you, Johan?"

Krause plunked down his glass of brandy and wagged his tongue in loud, imperfect English. "I will tell you this. A few days from now, for New York I leave by coach. Join me. Two days up, two days back . . . and a day for your poor mother."

Mortaine took a polite pull on his ale and paused long enough to bluff that he was seriously considering the Colonel's generous offer. "You are too kind, sir. Does my sister know of this opportunity?"

Markoe jumped in. "She most certainly does. I'm surprised she did not get word to you right away, Mister Willett."

"I've had business matters to attend to which have taken me away from this city. Most recently, I was out at the Frankford Mill to see Oswald Eve. I returned from another pressing matter just a few hours ago. So this is the first I have heard of the Colonel's more than generous offer."

Captain Markoe accepted the excuse with a nod. "For the record, let me say that I support Johan's offer. After all, you will be riding in my coach pulled by my four horses guided by my best driver. He will make sure your sister returns safely at the appointed time."

"I see no reason to refuse your offer, then," said Mortaine. "I will simply hasten through my business matters here and be ready to depart at the appointed leaving time."

"Good then, Mister Willett." Captain Markoe did not offer a hand to shake. He did give the man the particulars as to when the coach was departing and where to meet up with the vehicle. Then he added: "What may I ask is this business that brings you all the way down to our city?"

Mortaine glanced right and left, then leaned over the table and spoke in a low voice. "Munitions . . . black powder mostly."

"For the cause?" asked Markoe in an equally low voice.

The King's agent said nothing, but he did nod in the affirmative.

"There is need for such up your way?" asked Markoe in a whisper.

Mortaine nodded again.

Colonel Krause felt the urge to join in. "Any need for firearms?"

Markoe gave his guest an awkward glance. Mortaine did the same. A seemingly long silence ensued.

Mortaine finally picked an avenue to pursue. "Pressure is being put on gunsmiths up my way to return to England soon as possible. Those 'round Philadelphia have not yet been pressured to leave. My responsibility down here is to convince gunsmiths to stay and to inventory what firearms they have on hand."

"A noble pursuit," commented Markoe.

"Something I shall look forward to discussing with you about on our journey, Mister Willett," beamed the Colonel.

"I shall look forward to such," said the man successfully posing as Ruth Mount's brother.

Captain Markoe stood, signaling the end of their confrontation. The other two followed his example. Mortaine extended his hand and the Captain reluctantly shook it.

The imposter had tried his best. He felt he had succeeded. It was a long time since his last victory.

18

A GIFT FROM ST. CROIX

· ·

(Friday, August 4, 1775)

Ruth Mount found the round-favored Cornelia Emmons puttering about in the garden on the sunny side of the Markoe manse. It was late in the morning and warming nicely. The women's free time rarely coincided, so Ruth decided to make the most of their meeting. It was already in the high seventies with a wind shallow as an elder's breath, but Cornelia was playing the part of an old spinster. She had a heavy shawl, one that Ruth had knitted for her, draped over her shoulders. Miss Emmons was a coarse-looking woman with narrow copper-brown eyes nestled under thick black brows; an owlish nose and several scraggly hairs under it; thin, pensive lips; and a large mole rising above a patch of whiskers on a long chin. The only attractive thing about her was a bright green ribband affixed to her mobcap.

"Cornelia, my dear, good morning to you," Ruth shouted loudly. She knew Miss Emmons loved to play a game of hard of hearing.

The older woman failed to look up from her gathering chore. She did not bother to wave for Miss Mount to come closer.

Ruth did so anyway, invading the fellow servant's personal space and leaning close to show interest in what Miss Emmons was harvesting.

"What have you there?" Ruth asked, louder than necessary.

"Winter savory for one," Cornelia responded without making eye contact. "And oregano for my usual aches and pains."

"I'm not feeling well myself, dear sister."

Cornelia Emmons straightened up. She looked into Mount's tired hazel eyes. The older woman thought she saw a mite of truth in those younger eyes. Cornelia smiled. She never missed an opportunity to give advice and render a cure for whatever ailed any person who came to her. Cornelia relished helping others and making them dependent on her. She liked being called 'sister' after having experienced a life of abuse and abandonment by relatives and former associates. Besides, she owed Miss Mount a favor for the beautiful shawl.

"What'd be the matter with you, my dear?" Cornelia asked in a motherly tone.

"I find myself in a blue mood, sister . . . so vexed am I about my mother's condition, which I told you about at breakfast. But I failed to tell you what effect the sad news has brought upon me. My stomach is in knots and I have been unable to purge myself of my last few meals. This feeling has made me uppity and tense. I am unable to concentrate on a special task I must complete by Sunday."

Cornelia took inventory of the herbs in Captain Markoe's prize garden. She stroked her whiskered chin and fell into deep concentration.

"Not much to offer from here," said Cornelia finally. "The beans of the purple higuerilla over there might prove effective if administered carefully in small measure. However, the beans are not yet ripe. I do not know how potent they might be at this stage."

"Is there a danger in trying them?" asked Ruth.

"Only if you swallow too much of its bean paste, or powder form, at one time."

"If you happen to, what might occur?"

"Lethargy, to the extreme," said Cornelia calmly, "convulsions, vomiting, violent purging, then death—a very painful way to end your life."

Ruth pretended to wave the thought of death away with a swipe of her hand. "I think I will pass up the castor bean . . . might you recommend anything else?"

Cornelia checked her tiny basket of herbs and adjusted her shawl, then said: "I'll see what I have in my room. I am sure I can find something gentle enough for your delicate constitution."

"I would appreciate that very much, sister."

Ruth hugged the woman then watched her waddle towards the door to the warming kitchen behind the manse. When Cornelia Emmons, burdened by her full basket of herbs, had disappeared from sight, Ruth walked over to the ornamental higuerilla. Using her cutting tool, she split open several spiny pods, each containing three seeds. She removed several castor beans and placed a large quantity of them in her apron pocket. For good measure, she lopped off a few whole pods and secreted them away in the folds of her servant gown.

When the seamstress had finished her secret chore, she whispered a few words of gratitude: "A gift from St. Croix . . . so generous . . . so generous is fate to me."

19

SEAMAN'S KNOT

· · · · · · · · · · · · · · · · ·

(Saturday, August 5, 1775)

Ruth Mount did not fret over missing out on the banquet room festivities. She was by herself in the anteroom off the reception hall with the door wide open. She could hear the merry voices of those invited to attend the feast in honor of Abram Markoe's guest from St. Croix, Colonel Johan Gottfried Krause. She could also hear the hired strings busy at playing lively tunes emanating from a corner of the spacious banquet room. So far, everything was favoring her plan.

Miss Mount was cleaning up after completing her first assignment. All the imitation flowers her mistress had purchased for the occasion had been put to use. She had been assigned to arrange the flowers into tiny bouquets and help attach them to the bodices of the women guests who wished to wear them. The 'stomacher', a Danish custom, became an instant fashion statement among the elite wives of Philadelphia who had been invited to the Markoe fete. Not one faux flower head remained. Rich, delicate gowns burdened by hoops and panniers had been enhanced by the sewing maid's creations. A few of the women even complimented Ruth on her efforts.

When the talented servant finished tidying up, she went to the door, took a peek up and down the hallway, and saw that the man-servant stationed by the entrance door was seated and comfortably snoozing. No one else was in the main hallway. All the guests were about to take their seats for a sumptuous dinner and all other servants, slave or free, were tending to their chores in the banquet room or other rooms. Miss Mount did not exit the anteroom and go to her second assignment in the warming kitchen. Instead, she took one more look, ducked back into the room, and closed the door without making a sound. The solitary window, with curtain pulled aside, allowed enough light into the sparsely furnished room. It was a gray, breezy day with thunder rumbling in the distance. Ruth could make out the pile of luggage set aside for the Colonel's overland journey. She could also see that two wooden cases marked with the initials 'AM' had been separated from the two marked 'CF'. Each pair of long, stout containers was stacked, one on top of the other, in a separate corner of the room. Ruth decided to work on opening the top case scarred with the supposed Abram Markoe initials. She gave the case a shove. It refused to budge. She sighed resignedly. There was no way she was going to be able to coax the top one off by summoning all the strength she possessed, but, if she had, she would have been unable to lift it back on top of the other by herself.

Ruth cursed the Colonel's name and she cursed Enoch Mortaine's also—in a whispery voice that would not have disturbed a mouse. Then she got down to the task at hand.

The intricate knots binding each box reminded Ruth of the Irish configurations she employed in her knitting work. She puzzled their snaking pattern, rummaged for proper tools in her sewing bag, and attacked the first knot. The seamstress poked and prodded, tugged and pulled, reddening her calloused hands. She gritted her teeth and strained her limbs for what seemed an eternity. Her fingers ached. Finally, the knot came undone and the thick rope ends fell from the sides of the top case. Ruth wasted no time. She attacked the knot at the other end of the top case. Not long after, she heard footsteps in the hallway. Ruth stopped what she was doing and retreated to the darkest corner of the anteroom. She pressed her back against a small door that hid a secret passage she had never used.

The footsteps faded. Ruth went back on the attack. The second knot came apart more easily than the first. She lifted the lid off the top case and put it to the side without making a sound. A broad fold of sealskin protected whatever lay underneath. Ruth lifted the covering and studied the contents of the case—long, black muskets were arranged uniformly in what appeared to be two layers of six muskets each—heavy, menacing firearms separated from one another by strips of woolen cloth. At the butt end of the top row, Ruth found a folded piece of vellum. She pried it up with a weary finger and unfolded it. She brought it to the window to make out the letters penned on it. At first glance, the letters appeared to be initials of individuals similar to the 'AM' on the lid of the box.

In her softest voice, Ruth read the first line aloud: "1M T5N TH152L" Then the second: "L5SS F9V5." She read the rest. They were set in similar configurations of letters and numbers. Ruth finally reached the last figures. She paused to consider whether they kept to the same pattern or not. She read them to herself: "Cl5NT1CT W 89NGH1M."

Ruth refolded the vellum sheet and carefully slipped it back where it came from. She dared not take the thing. She had no means by which to make a copy. At least she had memorized the first and last lines. That would have to be enough to satisfy Enoch Mortaine. She had no idea what the letters and numbers meant. This would be a chore for her boss.

The seamstress quickly lifted the lid and set it in place. So far, things had gone surprisingly well. Ruth felt proud of the progress made. She promised herself to demand more remuneration from Mister Mortaine.

The hardest part proved to be reknotting the nautical ropes. The knot patterns were hard to duplicate, and, no matter how hard she tried, the tightening of each knot proved difficult. Ruth was already arm weary when she started on the first knot. She was doubly so and in much pain by the time she finished the second knot. These bindings were not as tight as when she began, but they would have to do. Only the practiced eye of an old salt would notice the difference.

Ruth gathered her tools into her kit bag and headed for the door that hid the secret passageway. She did not dare use the door to the welcoming hallway. She heard footsteps again. Ruth quickly entered the darkness and closed the door behind her. She felt her way along a narrow passage until she came to another small door. She pressed her ear to it but heard nothing. She opened the door and found herself in her master's unoccupied library. Relieved to find familiar surroundings, Ruth rushed across the room. She slid the panel back and ducked into darkness again after sliding the panel back in place. With heart still beating fast and sweat upon her brow, the seamstress found the stairway to her master's private bedroom and cautiously climbed it.

The worst of her tasks had been accomplished . . . so she thought.

20

PIP'S LUCK

(Sunday, August 6, 1775)

Pip James, who now preferred to be called Hendrick Lau, considered himself a resourceful soul—a cross-eyed-wench-and-cheap-rum man. He was proud of being niggardly with his money and dishonest in his business dealings. Why not. He had been beaten down by fate since he was born—a London street urchin and a failed indenture in the American colonies. Pip was a born loser who still liked to win even if it meant flaunting the King's laws and bending the rules. It was never beneath him to steal in order to obtain things for free. His latest acquisitions fell into this category. For starters, Pip 'borrowed' a knife from a sleeping man in the Blue Anchor, the night before he got word from Mister Mortaine about Markoe's coach destined to ply the Lower Road come Sunday. The weapon would be needed for what Pip had planned. But he needed more.

An early stage waggon out of Philadelphia on a fair and pleasant Friday included a passenger by the name of Hendrick Lau. He was dressed like an alongshoreman in a stained blue Russia shirt and flap-front trousers. Wiry stubble crowded his scarred face, but his head was shaved bald. A rust-red woolen seaman's cap sat high on his large head. He sat alone opposite a young couple who dared not look him in the eye. Lucky for them, the fierce-looking Mister Lau got off at Trent Town right after being ferried across the Delaware River.

The menacing stranger could have remained on the stage waggon with the frightened pair all the way north to his destination, but that did not suit his plans. Without acquiring his own means of transportation, he would be at a distinct disadvantage. Trent Town was a good place to find what he needed. The couple who remained on the stage waggon were relieved to see Mister Lau get out and walk away.

Mortaine's man spent all of a rainy Saturday on foot searching for a serviceable horse and a fair-sized cart. He felt he needed such in case dead bodies had to be disposed of discreetly. But first, grim Pip James had to tend to more basic needs. He found cheap, watered-down rum in four different ordinaries before dusk. He found a whore down on Queen Street before midnight, close to the stone bridge which arched over the Assunpink Creek. After his inexpensive encounter, the sky opened enough for a half moon to cast its glow. Pip was feeling lucky—the rum had proved passable and the whore was not cross-eyed.

After finding Quaker Lane and trudging its muddy length in feeble moonlight, Pip stumbled upon more good fortune. Instead of entering the Fox Chase Tavern looming on the far side of Brunswick Road, Pip decided to inspect the horses tethered in front of the publick house. The front of the place sported adequate lantern light hung high over a freshly painted red and green sign. The owners of the steeds were all inside the Fox Chase enjoying something better than cheap rum. As luck would have it, one of the patrons had come by horse and cart. Pip checked the gelding and found the beast fit enough for his needs—on the old side, judging by its wayward teeth and sparse mane, but muscular in the withers and newly shod. The cart and harness gear appeared to have aged well. One wheel sported a few new spokes. The wheel hubs stuck out a bit too far for Pip's liking, but he felt he could manage somehow if they became an impediment on a narrow trail. The sides of the cart could have used a fresh coat of paint. But, all in all, this rig seemed a sound free bargain.

Pip trusted that the owner would emerge much later from the tavern. Hopefully, flat out drunk. Realize his loss and stagger home on foot, giving such an unlucky chap a chance to sober up along the way . . . and form a logical explanation for his loss.

Pip untethered the horse, climbed up on the seat board of the cart, and headed north on a rutted and muddy Brunswick Road, which locals also referred to as the Upper Road or the King's Highway. The half moon lit the way and the trail left by muddied wheels. Pip clucked to the horse and kept it at a slow, steady pace.

He was in no hurry. He gave the wheel trail no nevermind. There was no urge to rush in order to gain his revenge. He trusted that luck would prevent any patron of the Fox Chase from tracking him down. Logic told him that any thief would have headed back into Trent Town and points south. He was confident the road north would be hassle free. All he had to do was reach Manley's Tavern, inquire as to the whereabouts of a certain pair of thieves, and do them in. Then he planned to meet up with Enoch Mortaine on the Lower Road. If he could pull all this off by Sunday evening, then he might consider himself a very lucky man, indeed.

Pip was certain the cart was large enough to hold two bodies. He smiled and praised himself out loud for being so damn fortunate in such a brief period of time. He looked forward to returning to Philadelphia with a pistol and two knives under his belt . . . to leaving behind a pair of rotting corpses hidden well . . . never to be found.

21

TRUE COLORS

· · · · · · · · · · · · · ·

(Sunday, August 6, 1775)

Even with the window of the sewing parlor closed shut, Ruth Mount could hear morning bells in the city of Philadelphia peeling loud and clear. A steady, wind-whipped rain was falling yet stalwart souls were venturing outside to attend worship services in nearby churches. Ruth wanted to go and so did Anna McClew but their domestic duties and the foul weather denied them the opportunity most other servants took advantage of. It was supposed to be a day of rest, but Ruth had a flag to finish and Anna had a mischievous child to attend to. Thus, the seamstress for the Markoes worked feverishly on her stitching of blue bars on a yellow field in the sewing parlor, and Miss McClew entertained the Markoe baby next door in the nursery, hoping the energetic child would soon be ready for a nap. If things went according to plan, Anna would be able to come chat with Ruth as soon as Lizbeth fell asleep.

As Miss Mount was want to do, the door to the sewing parlor was always left open. Ever so often, Ruth looked up from her tedious work in anticipation of her favorite one dropping in to rescue her from boredom. Minutes dragged by slowly until footsteps sounded, coming down the hallway. Ruth looked up but no smile formed on her lips. Colonel Krause rushed in, pushing his boy, Asher, in front of him. The man made sure the door was closed before he grabbed Asher's arm and approached to where the seamstress was sitting. A table to her right held most of the unfinished flag. The rest was draped over her lap.

"Making progress, Miss Mount?" asked the Colonel, who was dressed in damp Sunday finery, which gave evidence of having attended an early morning service. Asher was bedecked the same and damp as well. Both males gave off the odor of wet dogs.

"I shall make the deadline," said Ruth firmly, "as long as I'm not interrupted."

"We will not take up much of your precious time, my dear," said Krause in his best condescending voice and surprisingly passable English.

"What is it then?" said Ruth, not taking her eyes off her stitching.

"Show Miss Mount what you found, Asher."

The boy looked up at the Colonel, then reached in a deep packet and pulled out a sewer's cutting tool. He placed the object on the unfinished flag adorning the table then took a step back.

"Where did you find this dainty blade?" asked the Colonel of his boy.

"In the room off the main hall where our luggage is stored, sir."

Ruth looked up from her work and stared at the tool, which she must have misplaced in the anteroom rather than in the sewing parlor. She said nothing. Her heart was racing. She felt suddenly feverish.

Krause kept at it: "After you brought your find to my attention, Asher, and we both went to check our possessions in the anteroom, what did we find?"

"The knots were loose on one of the gift cases," said Asher, employing a bolder voice than the one used before.

"What say you about this, Miss Mount?" asked the Colonel in an interrogatory tone. "I have ascertained that you were the last to leave the luggage room at banquet time . . . am I correct?"

Ruth's mind was racing. She clutched needle and thread tightly and wished she could run from the room. She lifted a quivering hand and wiped a bead of sweat from her brow.

Finally, she summoned the courage to speak. "I may not have been last, Colonel Krause. After I tidied up the anteroom, I left to attend to my next assignment in the warming kitchen. I may have left the door ajar. There is no lock on it. Any number of guests could have entered that room, perhaps in search of a new bouquet or to return one they had tired of."

"Servants in the kitchen say you were tardy getting to your second chore," Krause insisted.

"Tidying up the anteroom took longer than I anticipated.

Besides, I was not feeling well. I was slow to finish."

"You seem to have an excuse at every turn, Miss Mount." The Colonel sighed, then inhaled deeply. "I do admire your skill with your tongue. It is equal to your skill with your fingers. You have allayed my suspicions but little, Miss Mount. However, it appears nothing was disturbed or taken from my possessions. Still and all, I must discuss this matter with your master."

"I can understand your concern on the eve of your departure," the seamstress said softly.

The Colonel waved a hand as if shooing a fly and took a step closer to the table. He deposited an item on his unfinished flag—a fist-sized purse of coins judging by the chink it made against the wood.

Krause employed his deepest voice: "I have a favor to ask of you, Miss Mount. If you respond well to my request, then I shall not mention what we have just discussed to your master."

"Anything, kind sir," Ruth said unhesitantly. She already regretted saying so.

The Colonel offered a predatory grin. Then he frowned.

Ruth read him well. She sensed the man had something execrable in mind. Trouble seemed in the offing. She squirmed in her seat and pretended to review her straight stitch on the third bar of the flag. She wished the guest from St. Croix had nothing left to say. She hoped the Dane and his young slave would leave and allow her to complete the flag. That hope failed to materialize.

"My boy, Asher, here found a kitchen wench to his liking yesterday in the midst of the banquet feast held in my honor. Unfortunately, the twelve-year-old Afric took no fancy to my boy. She resisted his advances; so says Asher, and ran to her mother who is one of the hearth cooks for the Markoes."

"Why are you telling me all this?" interjected Ruth, as if she was talking to an equal. "I care not about the games of children."

"Well, as you can see, my Asher is no longer a child," spouted the Colonel. "He is ready to prove he is a man . . . he longs to be roused by a woman."

Ruth glanced at the young mulatto. His head was down. His lips were shut tight. He seemed more a shy boy than a rutting man. Miss Mount was not liking where Krause's words were headed. She sensed that Asher felt the same.

"He will gain his opportunity in good time," said Ruth. "Men always do."

"Do not be flip with me, woman," Krause snapped. "Remember, I have yet to decide whether or not to tell Captain Markoe about the loosened knots on my case in the anteroom. What I tell the Captain could determine your staying or departing from this employ."

Ruth's heart returned to racing rapidly. Her palms began to sweat. She wanted to say the correct thing, but, for the life of her, she did not know what that thing was. So she said nothing.

The Colonel continued: "Please notice I have placed good Danish coin on your table. Do what I say and I will promise to put in a good word for you when I confer again with Captain Markoe. But first, you must service my son by acceding to his desires. I will sit and watch to ensure that my money and my time has been well spent."

"I will not do this," Ruth declared adamently. "Your boy is young enough to be my son."

"He requires a woman of experience, Miss Mount," said the Colonel smoothly. "Jah, I can tell you are suitable in that regard. Waste no time here . . . you need to get back to your stitching."

Ruth fixed a stern gaze on Asher. She set her needle and thread down on the table. She rubbed her hands on her apron until they were dry. Again, she looked at the shy and pitiful boy. Ruth felt sorry for the fourteen-year-old. He was not yet ready to be a man.

"Lower your breeks, Asher," demanded Krause in military fashion. "Tell Miss Mount what you desire . . . her hand upon your pestle . . . or is it her lips you prefer?"

Asher started worrying a pearly button on his flap front. His head was still bowed. He said nothing.

"Speak up, Asher. Don't be shy," coached Krause. "Miss Mount shall bring your manhood to life. Now is the time to take the chance. You shall remember . . ."

The Colonel was unable to complete his sentence. A knock on the door changed everything. The door opened and Anna McClew walked in. The Markoe baby was in her arms, very much awake and squirming defiantly.

"Please forgive . . . sorry for bargin' in," blurted Anna, after bending a knee. "Did not know you had visitors, Ruth."

The nursery maid turned to go.

The Colonel leaped up out of his chair, rushed to the table, and snatched his bag of coins. Then he grabbed Asher by the arm.

After clearing his throat, Krause exclaimed, "We were just about to leave, Miss . . . here but a moment to check on progress regarding my flag."

The odd pair hastened out of the sewing parlor and headed down the hall. Their footsteps faded quickly.

"You should have come earlier, my dear," Ruth said, soon as she felt it was safe to speak. "But I'm glad you interrupted when you did."

Anna was struggling to hold the uppity child who wanted to escape her grasp and play on the floor. "What, pray tell, did I interrupt?"

Though her hands were shaking, Ruth picked up her needle and thread and went back to sewing. "You don't want to know, my sweet," said Ruth in a motherly tone. "T'was all about men showing their true colors . . . nothing more."

22

A BIT OF REVENGE

(Sunday, August 6, 1775)

For some unknown reason a cart man and his horse came to a halt in the middle of the Upper Road where Adrian Manley's Tavern stood on the Somerset County side. It was far from a peaceful Sunday, late in the afternoon. The wind was blowing fiercely and a light, biting rain was angling down from a brooding sky. Water pooled around the wheels of the man's cart. The horse remained motionless with its head low. The wayfarer, dressed in thoroughly soaked alongshoreman's garb, studied a dry pair of men sitting on a bench on the porch of the tavern.

"Mayhaps that bloak is stuck in the mud," said Puddin' John Barricklow to the other fellow. "I will not tolerate such an affront to my authority."

The yeoman sitting next to the self-appointed ward of the King's Highway offered keen advice, after spitting some tobacco juice beyond the porch. "Give the poor fellow a pull or a push, Puddin' John. 'Tis your responsibility to do so. Treat a stranger kindly . . . he'll return the favor."

"Ain't goin' out in a storm to help a bloak I don't know."

"Look, he sets there like a headstone," said the farmer. "He's makin' no move to help hisself. The man needs your help."

"Nope," Barricklow proclaimed. "But I've a mind to venture out in this storm 'n scold the bastard. I'll order him to move on."

"By the looks of him," offered the yeoman, "I think you'd be makin' a mistake."

Puddin' John arose from the bench, adjusted his wide-brim hat, and stepped off the porch. He sloshed through the mud, avoiding the largest water-filled ruts, and approached the living impediment in his road.

The stranger kept fierce eyes on the one he remembered as being called the ward of the King's Highway. He did not look forward to putting up with the fool's nonsense again.

Puddin' John stopped a safe distance away. He took a moment to stare at the cart's nearest wheel. It was not deep enough in the mud to be stuck.

"By order of the King, you'd best be movin' on," Barricklow advised the cart man curtly.

Pip James kept to his glowering and failed to respond.

"Move on, I say, or face the consequence," added Barricklow.

By now, two more men had emerged from the tavern and stood on the porch watching Puddin' John put on his show.

The Philadelphian on the cart finally blinked an eye. He tilted his head slightly. A few drips of rain water sluiced off his seaman's cap and splattered on the seat board. Pip never took his eyes off the fool. He grinned, revealing a crooked row of yellow teeth and a gap where two teeth should have been.

"You 'n who else of your kind are orderin' me to move on?" growled the man whom Barricklow did not recognize.

"Me alone, stranger," declared the guardian of the road. "You are obviously not familiar with the King's rules. But I'm the one who is. You will learn them quick enough. So move along now. Be quick about it so you will suffer no consequence."

"What if I wish to slake my thirst at your fine tavern 'n dry out?"

"Too late for the likes of you," countered Puddin' John. "Besides that there publick house ain't mine . . . just the road."

"What if I pull off your road and hitch my rig to a post in front of the tavern?"

"Need to pay me a fee for such a luxury," claimed Barricklow soberly.

"I don't think that's the way it went, last time I was here," said Pip, as he slipped down from his perch and stood before the irritating man. He towered over the ward of the road. "Remember when you caused a ruckus back in June," said Pip, as he raised his mended arm slightly. "I ended up breakin' this here limb."

Barricklow stood his ground. "Rememberin' things ain't my strong suit, mister. Enforcin' the King's Law is."

"So you don't recall the two bloaks who came to your rescue after I laid you low in this very same miserable road . . . the ones who stole my pistol and my knife?"

Puddin' John studied the man's face again. A vague recollection gimped across his mind. "You was in General Washington's train, I bet. The one drover which took offense at my order to move on. Yes, I remember now."

Pip James managed a bitter laugh. "You picked on the last waggon in the train, little man. Kind of stupid to do so since I wasn't goin' anywhere that day till the first waggon began to roll. You were barkin' at the wrong end of the train that day. I'd say you're more stupid than mad, then and now."

Barricklow ignored the insult. "This day is different. You're both ends of the train now. I want you out of here."

"Are the pair who rescued your arse back in June on the porch or warm and dry inside the tavern?"

"They haven't been 'round these parts since then," confessed Barricklow matter-of-factly. "Cut and Ike are not from near here."

"Too bad," said Pip. "I need to speak to them about my missing pistol and blade."

"Not my problem," insisted Puddin' John. "But you movin' on is still of my concern. I'm runnin' out of patience."

Pip clenched his right fist and hit Puddin' John square on the jaw. The poor fellow dropped like a stone. He flailed his arms as if about to drown in the mud that despoiled the road. Pip reached down for Barricklow, yanked him up by the collar of his shirt, and stood him up. The aggressor let go of the man's collar, but grabbed him by the arm when Puddin' John started to collapse again. All the men on the porch were standing now, but not one dared to make a move to rescue Barricklow.

"The first blow was meant for helpin' you to remember, my good man," offered Pip in a kind voice. "The second will be to make sure you remember nothin' of this day."

With his free hand, Puddin' John felt for his throbbing jaw. All he accomplished was smearing mud on his face. All he managed to say in a slur was: "King'll be 'bashed . . ."

Pip laughed heartily and glowered at the trio of locals who stood frozen in place on Manley's porch. None of them appeared equal to the pair who put him down back in June. He turned his attention back to Barricklow.

"Make this easy on yourself," urged Pip. "Tell me where I may find this Cut fellow and this Ike as well."

Puddin' John frowned. He appeared deep in thought as well as pain.

Mortaine's man shook the fool violently and raised his right fist again.

Barricklow cringed. He raised an arm in anticipation of the next blow. His words spilled out fast: "Ike Higgins serves Mister Wetherill as ward of the swamp . . . Pigeon Swamp. You'll find that Irishman in there on any fair day."

"And the other bastard?"

"The German's a neighbor to Mister Wetherill . . . over on the Cranberry side . . . north of the creek."

"What's the best way to get to 'em?" continued Pip.

"A path follows Six-Mile-Run to George's Road. Long Bridge Road is another way, but roundabout," sputtered Puddin' John. "But I wouldn't try the path with your cart till it stops rainin' . . . narrow and mired is such a way."

"Are the two I seek close by the Lower Road?"

"Closer to it than to here," said Barricklow.

"You've been very helpful and kind," said Pip with a chuckle. He let go of Barricklow gently. "You've brightened my day."

Puddin' John stared at his feet. He said nothing.

Pip continued: "I tell you what—no reason to strike you again, though I strongly wish to do so. How 'bout we try this instead? You lead my horse and cart to the stable 'round back of Manley's. See that my gelding is watered and fed. I'll meet you inside . . . even buy you a pint. We'll dry out and talk some more. How does that sound?"

Puddin' John frowned again. He had descended into deep thought, weighing the consequences of objecting to anything the stronger man said. He flinched when Pip raised his right arm again.

The alongshoreman made no fist this time. Instead, he spoke calmly as a Quaker: "You can tell me more about your rules for the King's Road, so next time I visit, which will be close to never, I'll be better behaved."

Puddin' John managed a nod. He also spoke softly: "I guess the King would not take offense at your offer, Mister?"

"You may call me Hendrick Lau," said Pip, casting an honest eye.

Barricklow bent an aching knee. "Honored to make your acquaintance, Mister Lau."

"What name do you use?"

"John Barricklow, ward of the road we're standin' in . . . appointed by King George hisself. My title's been bestowed for life."

Pip James offered a rare smile. "Wish'd I had such a title to tell, Mister Barricklow. When we're out of this devilish rain, I want to hear how you came by such an honor . . . and how I might catch the same luck."

Puddin' John accepted the reins from the rough man who had played him. He waited until this character took his first step towards the tavern porch. Barricklow then rallied in his own inimical way: "Such advice might cost you a second pint, Mister Lau."

Pip slapped Puddin' John on the back. The blow made the smaller fellow cringe, but remain on his feet. "Such a wee price for your wisdom, Barricklow. Lead the way."

23

A SECOND HELPING

· · · · · · · · · · · · · · · · · · ·

(Sunday, August 6, 1775)

A large pot hung from a hob above the glowing coals of the kitchen hearth fire. The cabbage soup, prepared by Captain Markoe's oldest slave cook, Aurella, was still simmering nicely. All the Markoes and a few members of the horse troop had been served their soup and slices of beef pudding for supper. It was long after eight in the evening—time for the servants to partake of what remained of the last meal of the day. Nothing fancy for hosts, guests, or servants. Just simple fare garnered from what was left over from the dinner served earlier in the day.

Ruth Mount had made it a point to visit the kitchen earlier than usual . . . not to eat just yet, but to help Aurella and her two young daughters prepare the meal, as she had done the day before. Ruth stood by the soup pot stirring its bubbling contents with a long, wooden paddle. She held an equally long ladle in the other hand. Nearby, Aurella's twelve-year-old daughter, Sally, was setting a row of wooden bowls neatly on a stout bench. The soup and bowls were meant for the servants seated at the nearest table.

Ruth set aside the paddle and started ladling the cabbage soup into the bowls. She was sweating profusely from being so close to the cooking hearth, but glad to gain an opportunity for what had to be done. How she would carry out her plan had not yet been set in her mind. The success of her scheme was chancy at best.

Aurella, a castice slave from St. Croix who claimed descendancy from the Akan-Amina, was almost ready to feed the servants waiting patiently at her long preparation table. Their hopeful voices carried loud and clear to those busy at the hearth. All were hungry and looking forward to the evening repast. Aurella removed the last cloth bag from the largest pot dangling over the coals. She cut the cord from the bag and pulled the steaming cloth away from the gourd-shaped flour and suet casing which held tasty meat scraps and spices inside. This so-called beef pudding was one of Aurella's most delicious creations and a staple for Sunday suppers. Just as the cook was about to cut into her last pudding of the day, her other daughter, Chappy—a few days shy of eleven—came bounding into the kitchen with a large tray in hand. Balanced carefully on the tray was an empty bowl and a bare used plate.

"Colonel'd like 'nother bowl a soup 'n slice a puddin'," Chappy declared, "'fore he gits to his asha 'n red grout."

"Oh Lor'," exclaimed Aurella. "He jus' might, woun't he now?" Aurella was employing her distinctive Twi dialect. She gave a hearty laugh, which jiggled her ponderous breasts and shook her fourteen stone frame. Aurella was not done: "Tell de glutter he gots to wait till all de help's been served."

More laughter rang out in the kitchen with Aurella leading the others.

Her daughter turned to deliver word of her mother's order, but Aurella called out to her child: "Git back here, Chappy, 'fore I paddles your black behind. Ain't no way to treat a gues' to be tellin' him to wait on us kind to be served. Mind your manner, girl. Unnerstan'?"

Chappy nodded and stood at attention.

Aurella turned to Ruth Mount. "Miss Ruthie, fetch dat bowl on de tray. Fill it for de Colonel. I'll jus' slice him de firs' piece of dis here puddin'."

Ruth could not believe her good fortune. She grabbed the bowl off the Colonel's tray. With a shaky hand, she reached into her apron pocket and extracted a phial containing a granular substance. She turned to the pot of soup and pretended to search for the ladle which she had propped against the corner bricks of the hearth. As she bent down to retrieve the utensil, she emptied the contents of the tiny vessel into the bowl. No adult or child in the kitchen saw her trick. Ruth grabbed the ladle and scooped enough cabbage soup out of the pot to fill the bowl halfway.

"Puts more in, Miss Ruthie," said Aurella dictatorally. "We not wants dat slave owner complainin' 'bout his portion."

Mount nodded, turned back to the pot, and ladled out more

soup—not all the way to the brim, however, because she did not want to weaken much more what she had added to the bowl.

She placed the Colonel's soup next to the plate which held a handsome slice of beef pudding. As she did so, her hands were still shaking.

"Dare not fill the bowl to the brim," confessed Ruth to Aurella, "because your dear Chappy might spill it."

"If'n she do, she gets a beatin'," clucked Aurella, who waved to her slender daughter and pointed toward the door which led to the passageway to where the Markoes and their guests were seated.

Chappy took hold of the tray with cautious hands. She shuffled slowly out of the kitchen.

"I hopes de Colonel be pleased," said Aurella, as she commenced slicing her pudding for the servants. "I hopes he ask for no more."

Ruth Mount offered a smile, but she kept her thoughts behind it. She went back to filling the empty bowls on the bench and started figuring out how to pour another portion of her crushed castor beans into Colonel Krause's breakfast fare on the morrow.

24

SAD NEWS

· · · · · · · · · ·

(Saturday, August 6, 1775)

Two men sat in the library room. Peter Markoe had retired to his bedroom in order to attack some fresh thoughts about shaping the lines of a new poem. After a pleasant supper, he had excused himself from joining the two men in the library for a customary smoke and glass of spirits. Asher had been ordered to the guest bedroom by the Colonel, who insisted the boy get his rest after packing for the long trip tomorrow. The boy went willingly. The library no longer held any interest for him.

The horse men who stayed for dinner had departed soon after the custard dessert had been served. It was decided during the meal that Will Pollard and Robert Hare would escort the Colonel as far as the city of New York. Both men were among the few who had stayed for supper. They thanked their Captain for giving them another opportunity to escort the esteemed guest. Abram Markoe told them to report in full uniform at dawn. Then he wished the pair God speed and good luck on the journey.

Thus, the Captain had only a well-fed Colonel Krause to contend with in his library. He was not aware of the woman hiding behind the panel which led to the stairs to his private bedroom.

Krause failed to pick up his pipe, nor did he lift the apple brandy to his lips. He appeared deep in thought, yet a wee bit fidgety. He was weaving his fingers together as if to make an imaginary knot, then freeing them only to start on another knot.

Markoe lit his long-stem pipe and took a few puffs. It relaxed him while he savored a moment of silence. The Colonel was usually quite talkative and overbearing more often than not, especially during and after a meal. This time was different. The Captain did not bother with his brandy. While at supper, he drank more than his usual amount of a fine Danish beer while the Colonel was downing his second portion of beef pudding and cabbage soup. He had to admire a man who possessed such a robust appetite. Markoe wished he could do the same and still mount a horse without assistance.

Eventually, he was moved to start the conversation. "I sent a member of my troop to find Oswald Eve at Frankford Mill."

"Jah, did you now?" asked the Colonel, who reached for his glass of brandy. He took a sip. Krause followed his tasting of Markoe's best with a strong belch.

The Captain continued: "Appears Miss Mount's brother is telling the truth. According to the Private I sent, Mister Willett did visit the miller and inquire about the gunpowder on hand. Willett also asked about how much powder the elder Eve planned to produce during the next few months."

"So you approve of this fellow who will be accompanying me to New York?"

"With reservation, yes," said Markoe. "I also inquired about his renting a room at the Tun Tavern."

"And?"

"Minehost recalls no Azariah Willett paying for a room."

Krause smacked his lips after taking another sip of his brandy. "In Mister Willett's line of business as a procurer of munitions for a fledgling rebel group, I would suspect the chap of changing his name often every place he goes."

Markoe considered the Colonel's explanation as he took another pull on his pipe. "You may be correct, Johan. I might be accused of being overcautious."

"Don't worry for my sake, Abram. I can take care of myself. Before I reach New York, I will know more than I need to know about your sewing maid's brother."

"Be careful, my friend," advised Markoe soberly. "These are troubling times and such a challenge knowing who to trust and who not to trust."

The Colonel waved his large hand in front of his face as if swatting at a pesky fly. "By the way, has the seamstress finished with my flag?"

"Far as I know, Miss Mount is near done with it. She is probably finishing up on it as we speak."

Ruth Mount squirmed a bit behind the panel. She smiled to herself, for she had completed the stitching on the flag shortly before sneaking into her master's bedroom to find the secret stairs. The gift, meant for the Colonel, lay complete on the work table in the sewing parlor.

"She is a strong, principled woman," said Markoe. "I admire her work habits."

The Colonel replied: "Do you trust her to return?"

"Certainly," said Markoe. "My wife trusts Miss Mount and so do I. Besides, our sewing maid has taken a liking to Miss McClew . . . treats her like a younger sister. Miss Mount is very protective of our nursery maid. She has reason to return to us."

"Their bond may be stronger than you think," added Krause with a leer and another belch.

"All the more reason for Miss Mount to return," said Markoe. "I have nothing against a woman's affection for another woman."

"I do," admitted the Colonel. "But it is one of the few slight differences between us, Abram. Here's another—I lust after many women and you lust for a few . . ."

"Only one, since coming to Philadelphia," corrected Markoe. "You may say the same for all your appetites, Johan. I am a gourmand and you are a gorger."

"Suit yourself, Abram," sighed the Colonel. "But I have seen more of the world than you . . . and I am wiser for it. I am telling you to tame all your women, especially your sewing maid. Give her a sound beating with a bangalar stick . . . then take a turn at making her a real woman."

Ruth Mount was trying hard to remain silent. She gritted her teeth and clenched her fists. She wanted to fling open the secret panel and pummel the loutish Colonel with anything she could get her hands on. Better to remain a mouse than turn into a lioness, she thought.

Ruth's master offered a tepid defense. "Miss Mount is a paid servant, not a slave."

"Jah, but a woman is a woman, free or not," observed Krause. "God puts 'em here to serve and service a man. They have to be taught."

"Beating a woman is not for me," Markoe said evenly. "I will handle my servants as I see fit and fair."

"As you wish, my friend. I shall keep my thoughts and desires on the matter to myself. But, at least, you must admit I have a better appetite for motts and meggs."

The Captain held up an opened hand of resignation. "Of course I agree. You have a larger appetite in all things scrutinized by the Lord."

The Colonel laughed, but, at the same time, squirmed a bit. He placed a hand on his prodigious belly and kept it there. "Correct you are, my friend. God knows, I must have devoured too much at sup. My stomach is rebelling." Krause paused to belch again. Then he started up again: "Speaking of rebellion . . ."

Markoe interrupted: "Leave rebellion out of our conversation, Johan. I'm in no mood to talk about liberty's chances . . . too early in the game."

"But that is why I have agreed to stay up late and converse with you, Abram. No need to remain silent 'bout a cause you are committed to."

"My dear Johan, you know where I stand in the struggle 'gainst Parliament and the King of England. Of course, I am all in. There is nothing more to say. The question is where do you stand?"

"I am a Danish subject first. So are you. Do not forget."

"True," said Markoe. "But even Danes in the homeland are divided over the American struggle. Many on St. Croix are sweet on the rebel cause."

"You speak of rumors and impressions, Abram. No true Dane is going against his King, even if ours possesses an addled brain. Long as Christian's advisors hold the reins and the common folk remain loyal."

"So then, what is the bad news you bring me on the eve of your departure?" Markoe asked.

"Not bad news at all," countered Krause. "More along the lines of convincing Danish subjects, like yourself and Christian Febiger, to come to your senses."

"It took us long enough to do just that," snapped Markoe. "I cannot speak for Mister Febiger, but I decided to join the cause when a group of local merchants asked me to form a horse troop to guard this city. I was flattered to be asked and glad to accept the challenge. General Washington has praised my men, my flag, and me. Nothing convinces the spirit more than praise. I am in this fray to the end."

The Colonel did not respond. He commenced rubbing his belly.

"You cannot convince me otherwise, Johan," concluded Markoe.

The Colonel cleared his throat, took a sip of brandy, and then spoke softly: "I have come to warn you, Abram, not to turn you one way or the other. The final choice is yours to make."

"And what is the nature of this warning?"

"King Christian will be forced to sign an edict, a few short months from now, forbidding all Danish subjects from participating in the pending war. England wants Denmark to side with them. Certain neighboring powers object to this. A small minority of subjects desire siding with the colonies. Thus, neutrality looms as the path Denmark will take. All Danish subjects will be ordered to stay out of the conflict. If they do not, then they will face dire consequences."

Captain Markoe scoffed at the idea. "Bah, such an edict will come too late. Besides, how bad can the consequences be?"

"Us islanders who choose to side with the rebels may have plantations confiscated. Family members might be punished for our stance taken."

"You are using 'us' and 'our', Johan. Am I to believe you have come to your senses and have taken God's side?"

Krause chuckled at the jibe. "Let me put it this way. I plan to remain neutral throughout the conflict. But, as a fence sitter, I can play the fiddle and be heard on both sides. There is great profit to be made in wartime. Of course, in the process, I may help one side a bit more than the other."

"There is no slight difference between us on this matter," Markoe answered quickly. "So go ahead and remain neutral. I will continue my whiggish ways and lead my troop of horse. I am in too deep, Johan. I can't back out now."

"I pray you'll come to your senses, my friend . . . before it's too late. Till then, I have left for you a taste of what a neutral can do for your cause. As I stated before, open the gift meant for you—the two cases in the anteroom. Open them after I have departed. I have hidden a message for your eyes only in one of the cases. Heed my directions and thank me after I have returned to St. Croix. Once I find Febiger and give him the same treatment, I plan to return to New York then sail for St. Croix.".

"For a neutral, Johan, you are indeed a man of mystery."

"In life and in death, Abram, if I have any say in the matter."

Ruth Mount heard the laughter and the trail of bad jokes about life after death. She then heard the shuffling of feet. She quickly got up, lifted her skirts, and ascended the secret stairway. The sewing maid had learned what she needed to know. Still, she was upset about one thing. The bits of castor bean had not worked as well as she had hoped. The Colonel sounded none the worse for wear. Ruth was already thinking about sneaking a larger dose into Krause's morning meal . . . enough to disable a fence-jumping stallion or a detestable beast such as Krause.

25

A GUESSING GAME

(Monday, August 5, 1775)

An hour after sunrise, the crossing of the Delaware River at Cooper's Ferry was accomplished without incident. It was broodingly cloudy, but the wind out of the northeast was doing its darnedest to sweep the gray gloom away. The cool morning air whispered that a clear and pleasant day was in the offing. However. the Lower Road was, as expected, sullied and troubled from the previous day's rain. Progress by Captain Markoe's coach and four was slack and slow. Burlington, the old West Jersey capital, was not reached until close to ten in the morning.

Everyone making the journey to New York, save for the spiffily dressed coach driver and Asher, the Colonel's boy, was vexed about the snail's pace. The pair of optimists shared the seat board above the horses. The coachman let the young mulatto hold the reins on a few straightaways. They were the only ones enjoying the jaunt through the Jerseys.

Two of the passengers attempted to forget their misery by using ample time to converse on many subjects. Colonel Johan Gottfried Krause—watery-eyed, red-faced, and sweating—sat alone on his side of the coach's interior. He propped his shiny boots on one of the two wooden cases intended for the Danish rebel officer in Cambridge. No matter how he shifted his weight, the bulky Dane could not get comfortable. Talking to his travel companions served as the only distraction that made him forget his troubles.

Enoch Mortaine, now calling himself Azariah Willett, sat opposite the Colonel. He was serving as a polite, captive listener. Mortaine's less than impressive dull broghams were propped up on the other case which was wedged against its twin on the floor of the coach. The swaying of the vehicle was giving him a headache.

He tried to hide his misery with probing questions and insightful comments. So far, he had learned nothing new from the chatty Colonel. But he was not about to give up. There were many miles still to go.

Ruth Mount sat next to her sham half-brother. She avoided eye contact with the boorish Dane from St. Croix. She was trying her best to ignore the conversation between the two men. Ruth kept smoothing her blue and white striped skirt, making sure it covered her ankles. She did not feel at ease propping her feet up on a case of rifles—especially in the presence of a Lothario like Colonel Krause. But she had no choice. Besides, her laced shoes were too tight and her feet were killing her. If the Dane was absent, she would have removed her shoes and rubbed her toes. She did not even trust Mortaine to do that chore. Ruth also regretted donning a corset for the journey. The stays were pinching where pain could not be avoided. She deemed herself the most miserable passenger in her master's coach.

All the seamstress could think about was the measure of smitches of castor bean she had stirred into Krause's second bowl of gruel at breakfast time. It had been a challenge completing the task in the serving kitchen, because a suspicious Aurella was watching the sewing maid's every move. The cook gave Ruth a sly grin after the deed was done. She pulled Mount aside and whispered that she knew something about the game being played. Aurella's younger daughter had told her about Asher's uninvited advances and that the Colonel had encouraged his boy's rudeness.

"Shoulda spiced up de boy's samp too," Aurella confided in a whisper.

"One at a time, Miss 'Rella," Ruth responded with a wink. Then she gave the cook a short version of the embarrassing confrontation in the sewing parlor and the randy conversation overheard in the library.

"Hope de man gits de rapid runs," Aurella declared while fussing at the hearth. "How 'bout we puts some dat magic in this here vittle bag Masser Markos tol' me to fix for de guest's journey . . . de leas' we may do to thanks 'im."

"I do have a few beans left," admitted Ruth. She put the empty vial in the pocket of her apron and extracted two whole castor beans from there.

Aurella snatched the beans from Ruth's outstretched hand. She placed the beans in a shallow bowl and crushed them with a spoon. Then she selected the largest particles and pressed them into the meat of the pork pie. Aurella refolded the doughy wrap on top of the meat and stuffed the treat into the vittle bag along with the other travel pastries and fruit. It was the cook's turn to wink.

She did and then said: "Hope dat boy of his be cleanin' up de mess lef' in de Colonel's breeks for days."

Ruth smiled. "When I return, my sister, I shall tell you how things went."

The cook and the sewing maid embraced. They pressed together for a warm, lengthy time. Ruth finally freed herself from Aurella's ferocious hug and hastened up the stairs. She wanted to share her last embrace with Anna McClew. That she did. Now she was remembering it fondly as the coach rolled along.

Once in Jersey, Ruth Mount gave an occasional glance in Krause's direction. The Dane had belched but twice since the ferry reached the Jersey side of the river. He was red-faced still and sweating profusely. He had loosened the lace around his neck and his waistcoat lay unbuttoned. The Colonel had a habit of keeping his knees wide apart and scratching his thighs with both hands. He was no gentleman, as far as Ruth Mount was concerned—more like a rutting goat on a midden heap. The Dane's odor was spoiling the air trapped inside the coach. Leather flaps were down and secured at each window. Ruth busied herself with raising the flap nearest her and breathing in the brisk, clean air. She enjoyed the view of the Jersey countryside slowly slipping by, as the coach headed towards Black Horse. It was better than having to look at the ursine man sitting opposite her.

Mortaine and Krause droned on about the latest news home and abroad. The former, dressed in a dark brown waistcoat and matching breeks, voiced his concern over Admiral Richard Howe and his fleet of warships anchored in the Boston port. He also mentioned the rejection by the Continental Congress of Lord North's proposal for reconciliation. As he saw it, the Congress was continuing to blame Parliament first for causing all the trouble, and second blaming King George III for adding fuel to the fire.

Mortaine, posing as patriot Azariah Willett when in the presence of Colonel Krause, was adamant about the looming possibility of war. He noted that thousands of militiamen from various colonies were marching to Cambridge to join General Washington.

"It won't be long now, Colonel, before your Denmark will have to choose sides."

Krause squirmed a bit and fidgeted with the window flap on his side. He rolled it full up and bound its strings in place on a brass peg.

"Warm in here, Mister Willett," said Krause, mopping his brow with a large linen handkerchief. He kept his eyes on the dull-clad man sitting next to Miss Mount. "Your sister has the right idea about letting cool air in."

Mortaine did not move to roll up the flap that covered his window. He was quite comfortable and only wanted to get Krause yapping about his purposes and plans. He kept to the subject he had raised: "What say you about your homeland's situation?"

"You may have heard of our dear Queen's passing," started Krause.

"No, I am sorry to hear this . . . tell me more."

The Colonel proceeded to fill Mortaine in on all that he told Abram Markoe about the Danish Queen's demise, Johann Strunsee's downfall, and the seizing of power by Andreas Peter Bernstorff, current Head of Foreign Affairs.

"The best you colonists can hope for is Denmark failing to give aid to Britain," said Krause. "But this does not mean Bernstorff intends to favor the colonies in their striving for independence. This man pulls the strings on our puppet King . . . Christian dances to Bernstorff's gelded tune. Spain and France applaud such music of neutrality. Russia does the same."

"There is such a thing as a friendly neutral, Colonel Krause."

"Jah," said the Dane, "I guess that might describe me."

Mortaine sensed an opening and took it. "How so, sir?"

"Your feet are firmly planted on my contribution to your cause," admitted Krause, as he looked down at the two cases which sported Christian Febiger's initials.

Mortaine also glanced at his feet. "May I ask what lies therein?"

"You may, Mister Willett, but I'd rather have you guess all the way to New York." Krause leaned back against his hard seat and winced. Pain was blossoming in his gut. "As a munitions procurer, you should be able to figure out the nature of my generous game."

Mortaine pretended not to have a clue as to what was contained in the two cases. "How generous could these two boxes be? Are they filled with Spanish gold or the bones of long-dead saints?"

Krause erupted into thunderous laughter which startled Ruth Mount and made her cast another furtive glance at the man she despised the most. She quickly returned to what her window offered.

"I take it my first guess is incorrect," said Mortaine.

"Jah," said Krause. "Hiding in each box is something worth much more than gold or relics as far as the coming struggle is concerned. Hiding in one of these boxes are the instructions about how to obtain more than two cases . . . hundreds more."

"I'm enjoying your game, Colonel," said Mortaine. "How about a few clues to make my guessing easier?"

"Of course, Mister Willett. I am a fair man. In the end, you may be able to help me connect with independent agents who would be most interested in what I can easily put my hands on in the months to come."

"This small journey might turn out to benefit the both of us," posited Mortaine. "Is there a profit to be gained?"

"Jah, I do hope the same," said Krauss. "I will start by telling you my source. Consider this a dilemma for the Norwegian military . . . involving something the Danes supplied them with . . . something deemed obsolete. Too heavy. Too cumbersome. Many of which are in need of mending. Thousands and thousands. Soon to be replaced by something better . . ."

"Boots," interrupted Mortaine, still feigning sincerity.

The Colonel roared with laughter again. This time Mortaine's window flap trembled.

"You can do better than that, my friend," said Krause after he caught his breath. He belched and brought his left hand to his lips.

"Give me another clue," implored Mortaine.

"Bigger and blacker than a Dutch/Liege," said Krause.

"Many things are crafted in Liege," groused Mortaine. "Give one more clue."

"One-and-a-half meters long. Five kilograms in weight. For infantry, sniper, or drill."

Mortaine gave an actor's look of surprise and held his breath for a second. "So, you are carrying samples of Norwegian firearms to your fellow Danes in the colonies."

"Jah," said Krause, smiling with pride. "You guess true, Mister Willett. Keep this a secret. Only you and your sister are privy to such knowledge. My friend, Abram Markoe, has probably opened his two cases of flintlocks by now. He may be puzzling over my coded message to him as we speak."

"And this Febiger fellow is receiving the same, once you find him?"

"Jah."

"Why are you doing this?" asked Mortaine.

"I am merely a messenger in this scheme . . . a messenger for gain, of course," confessed Krause. "Certain agents and profiteers are involved in this game. If you wish to join in, I will tell you more in due time. This is a delicate matter involving contacts in Oslo, Helleback, Amsterdam, St. Eustatius, and St. Croix, as well as contacts here. When we get to New York, I will tell you who to contact."

"Why not tell me now, Colonel Krause" said Mortaine with the eagerness of a child. "My sister and I can be trusted with your secret."

Krause waved him off and reached for the vittle bag resting at his side. "This guessing game has made me hungry, Mister Willett. I must eat or die."

Mortaine chuckled, but Ruth Mount kept tight-lipped and pensive. She stared out her window and took inventory of dark thoughts.

The Colonel held up a pastry and offered it to Mortaine. The man declined. Krause took a large bite of the pork pie Captain Markoe's cook had prepared just for him. He smacked his lips and devoured the rest of it, crust and all, in quick time. He then opened a canteen of cider and took a few slugs to wash it down.

The conversation between the two men switched to events on St. Croix, the suitability of George Washington as the leader of a fledgling army, and the military superiority of Britain on land and sea. Krause led the way. Mortaine failed to steer the Colonel back to the weapons.

Ruth Mount contributed less than nothing, but she took time to study the Dane. She was looking for telltale signs that proved the castor beans were working. In her heart of hearts she hoped for the worst . . . or was it the best?

26

A SOURING OF LUCK

(Monday, August 7, 1775)

Pip James, now comfortable with the Hendrick Lau monicker, awoke from a restful sleep in a room he had paid for at Manley's Tavern. He dressed quickly. His coarse clothing had dried out and felt good against his oft-scarred skin. He knew he needed a bath, but that would have to wait till he returned to Philadelphia. There were more urgent matters to attend to.

Mortaine's hireling needed to be at his best to successfully navigate the Six-Mile-Run path that would get him to George Rescarrick's Road. Puddin' John Barricklow had promised the alongshoreman from Philadelphia that Rescarrick's Road was the quickest way to old Lawrie's Road, known by most folks as the longest stretch of the Lower Road. Pip was happy with this route because it meant he could kill two birds with one stone. For the hireling, this quaint saying held double meaning. The route allowed him time to track down the two thieves he intended to dispatch, while, at the same time, allow him to meet up with Enoch Mortaine. Judging by the poor condition of the roads, Pip knew he could devote a few hours of this crisp and cloudy Monday to finding Ike Higgins and Cutlope Hancock.

Rescarrick's Road turned out to be plenty wide for his cart. The horse had stumbled a few times on the narrow Six-Mile-Run path, but now was trotting along at a lively pace. Pip pulled up, a little past ten, in front of the Whitlock Inn. He had made it to Cross Roads in good time. Puddin' John had told him the Lower Road lay just a few miles east of this hamlet and that folks around here would know where to find the two bastards who stole his weapons.

Pip slipped down off his seat, tied his horse by a watering trough, and looked around. Whitlock's seemed to be the logical place to start asking. The Inn was a solid, stately structure made of brick and trimmed in green. Its green and gold sign was freshly painted and swaying ever so gently in the breeze from the northeast. On the opposite side of Rescarrick's Road sat a small-framed tavern sorely in need of a coat of paint and a new sign. Pip could not even make out the letters on the sign. There were a few other structures at Cross Roads, but nothing that could compare to the structures in Pip's beloved Philadelphia. He felt he was on the wrong end of a wilderness and definitely not in a place he would want to set down roots. The sooner he accomplished what he came for, the quicker he would leave this dismal place behind.

Pip bounded up the stairs of the Whitlock Inn, quickly opened the door, and stepped briskly into the welcoming room. In a minute's time he emerged and strode across the road, following the instructions given to him by minehost of Whitlock's. Pip was told he could find Ike Higgins at the Wetherill Tavern. Pip recognized the Wetherill name from what Puddin' John had told him. He smiled to himself. Luck was still riding with him.

Mortaine's man entered the humble tavern and found the interior much more to his liking than the exterior of the place. The floor was amply stained with wax drippings, spilled liquor, boot scuffs, and more. A husky woman and a mulatto boy were cleaning off tables used by breakfast patrons. A tall, thin man, sporting a billowing apron, stood inside a modest bar cage cleaning mugs and bowls with a damp cloth. Pip approached the bar and announced, employing his usual gruff voice, "I'm lookin' for a lifter who'd stole somethin' from me. Minehost 'cross the way told me I'd find 'im here."

"Who might you be looking for, my good man?" said Thomas Wetherill in a civil voice that only hinted at a bit of suspicion.

"Actually, two bloaks," said Pip, correcting himself. "One Irish, the other a cabbage head . . . the first is Ike Higgins and the second is Cut Hancock, 'cordin' to my source at Manley's."

The stout woman stood bolt upright. Her mouth was agape. She took a step towards the man asking questions. The boy dropped his rag. He stood, frozen in place. Thomas Wetherill clung to his rag and kept polishing away.

"Which one are you accusing of theft, sir?" said Wetherill cooly.

Pip frowned at minehost and placed his good hand, grimy though it was, on the freshly polished bar. "Don't be playin' with me now," growled Pip. "I'm holdin' both responsible as I see it. Where can I find either of 'em or both?"

"Well, let me see," said Thomas Wetherill, feigning deep thought and sincerity, as the boy retrieved his rag and rushed over to the woman's side. "In all likelihood, you will find Ike Higgins deep in the swamp. He has my two best hounds with him, scouting the possibilities for an upcoming hunt by the local gentlemen in these parts."

Pip kept his frown in place, He did not like what he was hearing. "When will the Irishman return?"

"Before dusk, I imagine," said Thomas. "That's when he usually returns . . . but he could be delayed."

Pip raised his meaty hand and slapped it down hard on the bar. Mugs and bowls jumped. The woman, watching warily as an owl, quickly wrapped her polishing rag around her right fist and took another bold step forward. The boy moved the same way in her shadow.

Thomas Wetherill stopped her by raising his hand, palm out. He used his other hand to reach under his bar for a truncheon he rarely had to use on obstreperous patrons making fools of themselves in his tavern.

"Can't wait long," snarled Pip. "I'll be returnin' though. Tell the mongrel bastard to wait here for me."

"Whom shall I say is looking for Ike?" said Wetherill calmly.

"Name ain't goin' to matter much," said Pip. "But, if you must know, I'm goin' by Hendrick Lau these days, and I'll be back afore the sun dies."

"I will be sure Mister Higgins gets your message, Mister Lau," promised Wetherill calmly. "Anything else I can help you with?"

"Where can I find the German?"

"Hard to say," answered Wetherill while picking at his clean-shaven chin. "Cut does not grace us with his presence much . . . only visits when the hunt club has a meeting here."

"When's the next meetin'?" demanded Pip.

"This night, according to my cousin's request," replied Wetherill. "All members of the Ratters will be bringing their firearms to clean and make ready for the upcoming hunt."

"Christ be damned!" Pip cursed in a loud voice that made the other three in the room cringe.

Thomas Wetherill did not respond to the man's outburst with words. Instead, he gripped his truncheon firmly and took a proper stance behind his bar. But then he decided to continue using words instead of resorting to blows. "Yes, 'tis going to be quite warm in my place after the sun goes down, Mister Lau. I sure hope Ike returns in time for the meeting. He will have word on the best places to roust game."

"Shyte, shyte, shyte!" bellowed Pip. "Don't care bout all those men gatherin' here with their guns. I'm no fool. Just tell me where I can find the cabbage head while the sun still ain't been swallowed up."

"His plantation lies along the Lower Road north of Cranberry Creek. Best to take the path you are on to its end . . . then head south. But, more than likely, Cut's delivering produce up in Brunswick Town. He always goes there on a Monday. That fellow should be rolling his waggon back before dusk in order to make it to the meeting tonight."

Pip had heard enough. He asked for no drink to quench his thirst and he gave no thanks for information gained. He wheeled about and stomped out of the place, slamming the door behind him. He freed his horse from the tether post and climbed into his cart after crossing the deserted road. Pip slapped the reins against the rump of the gelding and coaxed the horse east along Rescarrick's Road. Luck had soured for Mortaine's hireling. Pip saw no chance to find Ike or Cut until the evening. When and if he did find them, he would be outnumbered by a group of armed men. Maybe it would be best to wait for Captain Markoe's coach and four to pass on the Lower Road. Follow close behind to its destination for the night. Return to this godforsaken place another day.

Back inside the Wetherill Tavern, things had not yet cooled down. The boy got back to work, but the woman approached Thomas Wetherill. She was none too happy and none too satisfied with how minehost had handled the stranger.

"Why'd you stop me, Mister Wetherill?" said the woman in her best demanding voice.

"For your own benefit, Mary," said her boss, who was back to polishing cups and bowls. "And for Little Ned's sake."

"I can take care of meself," protested the boy from afar.

"Hush your mouth," scolded Good Mary. She retreated back to the tables, took hold of Little Ned's shoulder, and gave it a pinch.

The boy flinched, but he uttered no sound.

Mary returned to the bar. "I wanted to show that scoundrel a fist or two after he'd been slightin' me mate."

"Judging by the size and mood of the fellow, I'd say we were all outmatched this day," declared Wetherill. "Best to let him go on his way. After I stretched the truth about your Ike and Mister Hancock, I doubt the fellow will return. Sometimes you win with words, not fists."

"Hope you're true, Mister Wetherill," said Good Mary, although her countenance spoke of not being completely convinced.

"We should send Little Ned to warn Ike," advised Thomas.

The woman retreated once again and hugged her boy. "You would have to break all me fingers afore I'd let Little Ned roam about alone in that dreadful swamp. Our best hope will be if Ike returns late . . . very late. He's safe for now where he is."

"You are probably right, Mary," said her boss. "Lets get back to our chores and start preparing the dinner meal."

Good Mary joined her son in wiping the rest of the tables clean. Both of them were wondering what Ike and the German had pilfered from a very angry man. Little Ned thought he knew, but he kept his guess to himself.

27

AT RHODE HALL

(Monday, August 7, 1775)

Pip James made slow progress along the southern stretch of George Rescarrick's Road, which took him all the way to Cranberry. Instead of waiting there and quenching his thirst at Handley's Tavern, he decided to head up Lawrie's Road at the same slow pace he had been using since leaving Cross Roads. He never found Cutlope Hancock's steading. No local he asked in Cranberry knew where to find the German. However, one fellow confirmed what minehost at Wetherill's Tavern had said—Cut was probably selling a waggonload of produce in New Brunswick. So far, Pip had come up empty in his quest to find his pistol and his knife. He was none too happy about it. But he knew an opportunity would arise in the near future. For now, he resigned himself to waiting to meet up with Enoch Mortaine. The man's money was good and so was his word. Pip knew the day would not be a complete loss.

A mile north of the rough road to English Town, Pip heard the galloping hooves of a steed approaching fast behind his cart. He turned his head in time to see a uniformed rider grasping a banner pole as if it was a jousting device used by a knight of old. Pip halted his drab gelding and sat there watching the handsome fellow speed by and disappear beyond the bend in the road. The young man looked familiar. So did his steed and the standard he carried. Then Pip remembered . . . this fellow was one of the pair of Captain Abram Markoe's troop of horse who came to the docks to escort the Colonel from St. Croix on the first of the month. They were the ones who kept staring at him when he lugged baggage and cases to the Captain's coach.

Now this particular horseman was wearing such a grim, determined face. He had made no eye contact. The fellow could not have possibly recognized Pip. He seemed on urgent business and was not going to be distracted by a lowly cartman wending his way slowly on a stage road. Pip wondered what the fellow's urgent business was all about. He looked over his shoulder again but saw no coach pulled by a team of four. Nor did he spot any other uniformed horseman. The rest of the party might be approaching soon, calculated Pip. He decided to wait at the shoulder of Lawrie's Road until a coach came into view. He would let it pass. If it was Markoe's coach, he would follow it at a safe distance. Pip slipped off his seat board, turned his back to the road, and pretended to inspect a bad wheel.

The horseman, making quick time on the Lower Road, was indeed one of Captain Markoe's favorites. This one was Robert Hare, the designated flag bearer, who was now taking orders from a stranger—the male traveling companion of the Colonel. This one called himself Azariah Willett. North of Cranberry Brook, the coachman had brought the four horses to a halt. Hare noticed that the team stopped following him. He turned back, fighting his horse's desire to continue northward. Hare wanted to see what was the matter. The Colonel's boy had scrambled down off the drover's seat. He was conferring with Mister Willett about a matter of seemingly grim importance. The Colonel's companion was raising his voice and waving his arms in a menacing manner. The boy ignored the rant and peered into the coach.

Pvt. Hare came rushing up, halted, but did not dismount. "What is wrong?" he shouted.

Mister Willett speared him with smoldering eyes. "'Tis Colonel Krause," exclaimed the animated passenger. "He doubled over and began speaking in tongues. My sister and I tried to right him but he fought us off. She's still in the coach recovering from a blow to her head."

Hare remained on his charge. His partner, Will Pollard, came trotting up from behind the coach to see what all the fuss was about.

Willett continued talking: "The Colonel passed out. But now he's up and babbling about stopping for the rest of the day. Speed on ahead, fast as you can, Private. Find a suitable place where the Colonel can rest his bones. Hurry, my good man. We'd only be wasting time by turning back to Cranberry."

Robert Hare obeyed the man's orders immediately. A few miles up the road he found a modest ordinary, fashioned from a private house, standing by its lonesome just beyond a lesser road winding back towards Cross Roads. The wooden structure, which had been added on to at one side and in the back, was surrounded by relatively flat expanses of sandy soil where trees were scarce and cleared fields reigned. North and west of the place lay the notorious Pigeon Swamp. Some called this stage waggon stop the Half Way Inn . . . most others called it the Rhode Hall Tavern, or Williamson's, after its owner. It had seen better days when stage waggons ran more frequently between the East Jersey capital of Amboy and the West Jersey capital of Burlington. But when Governor William Franklin decided to settle on living quarters in Perth Amboy, traffic and commerce started coming in second to the traffic along the Upper Road, still referred to by loyalists and neutrals as the King's Highway.

The horseman did not give a fig or a farthing about the status of the main roads through the Jerseys, or what name to call them. Hare dismounted quickly, propped the standard pole against a fence rail, tethered his horse there, and rushed up to the blue door under the Rhode Hall placard. He entered and found the main room deserted. One table close to the bar had not been cleared. Evidence of a nearly completed dinner lay strewn about on the thick boards. Hare clomped his riding boots across the sanded floor and rang a serving bell which was stationed at the pocked and scarred bar.

In an instant, a large, barrel-chested man, wearing an unbleached osnaburg shirt, Russian drill trousers, and a raven's-duck apron, came sauntering out from behind a curtain where a door should have been.

"Do you have a spacious room for a weary traveler?" asked Hare impatiently.

David Williamson offered a wide grin on his flitchy red face. He swept his sandy blonde hair back with a large hand. "Four rooms have I upstairs, officer, all the same size and none too spacious. You may choose the one which suits your fancy."

Hare pulled off his riding gloves and placed them on a dry

corner of the bar. "I am but a Private in Captain Abram Markoe's Philadelphia Troop of Horse . . . assigned to escort Colonel Johan Gottfried Krause of St. Croix to New York. He has taken ill and may need tending to by a doctor. Is there such nearby?"

David Williamson wiped his hands on his apron, stuck out his right paw, and shook Robert Hare's hand eagerly. "Pleased to meet you, Private. I will have my daughters tidy up the bedrooms and clean off the dinner mess left by the travelers on the last stage waggon to leave here. As of now, you and your entourage may have use of all four rooms and any table in my main room."

With that said, Williamson called out the names of his daughters. The three of them marched out single file from behind the curtain.

"Mary, take Eleanor with you and check to see if the bedrooms are neat and nice. We have a distinguished guest coming soon. Lydia, clean off the table last used and make it presentable for the guest and his entourage. Be quick about your business."

Two girls climbed the stairs. The youngest one darted to the table in need of cleaning. Minehost turned his attention back to the handsome man in the uniform—the one who had caught the eye of all three blushing daughters.

"You say your Colonel may need a physician?"

"I have no doubt he will," said Hare. "Those traveling with Colonel Krause say he appears in great distress and has passed in and out of consciousness. I would definitely say the poor man needs to be looked at by a doctor . . . a good doctor."

Williamson scratched the prominent scar on his cheek—a reminder of his younger days spent in a copper mine. "You should have turned your coach around, Private, and headed back to Cranberry. The best doctor in these parts is Hezekiah Stites. You'll find him at his steading near Handley's stage house just south of the creek."

"Too late to turn around, Mister Williamson. My orders were to find a suitable place for an overnight stay . . . a place that brings us closer to Radford's ferry crossing to New York."

"Well, I'm glad you found my house, Private, but you are going to need to retrace your steps and fetch the good Doctor Stites on your own."

Hare snatched up his riding gloves and slipped them back on. "I'll do just that, Mister Williamson. I shall leave my troop's standard at your fence so the coach driver sees where to stop for the night."

The horseman turned to exit the place. Williamson called out: "How many folks accompany your Colonel?"

Hare paused at the door. He noticed Lydia Williamson was staring at him. He touched the brim of his hunter's cap and gave her a wink, then he responded to her father's question. "A brother and a sister ride with the Colonel. He has a slave boy riding with the coachman. And a fellow Private accompanies me . . . seven total."

"We'll figure out who sleeps where and the cost for seven when all show up," declared Williamson.

But Private Hare had already exited Williamson's establishment. Minehost's words had only reached his daughter's ears. He wiped the top of his bar again and smiled at his rutted reflection on its surface. He was estimating how much he would gain before the dawn of the next day. Little did he know how far off was his count.

Doctor Hezekiah Stites—fit and trim, clean-shaven and eagle-eyed—arrived at the Rhode Hall Inn shortly after supper. He had skipped his own evening repast in order to follow Private Robert Hare to the place where the ill Colonel Krause lay in a clean, comfortable bed which took up most of a small room in Williamson's place. The Doctor was dressed in professional array for a patient visit. He wore cotton whites for shirt and cravat, which matched his alabaster wig. His silk vest was black, as was the sateen waistcoat. Black linen knee breeches and white thread stockings encompassed his thin legs. Black silver-buckle shoes, shined to perfection, captured candlelight as he made his way to the stairs. He acknowledged minehost as he rushed past the bar by raising his black leather bag of implements and remedies. The good Doctor paid no mind to the coachman, the other horseman, or the few locals nursing their drinks and/or desserts at tables in the dining area. He had no time for spreading niceties.

Stites followed Private Hare up the stairs and into the room where a middle-aged man, a pale woman, and a mulatto boy stood around a low, wide bed. The air was close and held the reek of a recently used chamber pot.

Private Hare introduced the Doctor to those gathered in the small room, then he retreated down the stairs to get something to eat and drink. He was famished and saddle weary. Hare worried that things were spinning out of control. He had not even bothered to lay eyes on the Colonel. The Private was anticipating the worst. He would not be able to stomach any more bad news. He feared having to report such to his Captain.

Back in the room, Doctor Stites immediately took charge. He brushed by the gentleman who had introduced himself as Azariah Willett, who claimed to be a close associate of the sick man and brother to Miss Ruth Mount whose curtsey went unacknowledged by the Doctor. The boy was never introduced, nor did he open his mouth. Asher stood in a corner by the heap of luggage he had brought up to the room. He was a mere silent shadow to the others . . . except to Colonel Krause who called out Asher's name when the Doctor bent down and felt the Dane's forehead with the back of his well-manicured hand. With the other hand, Stites loosened the Colonel's cravat until it fell away from his neck. He noticed that someone had already removed the patient's waistcoat and shoes. Somebody had already unbuttoned his fall front breeches.

"Fetch me a chair," demanded Stites.

The alleged Mister Willett did not bother to assign the task to the mulatto. He went to the room next door and brought back a sturdy, straight-back chair. The Doctor set the chair by the bed, pulled off his waistcoat, and draped it over the back of the chair. He sat down quickly and rolled up his sleeves. First, he checked the Colonel's pulse. Stites frowned. He said nothing. Next, he lifted the Colonel's right eyelid. When he did so, the Colonel tried to swat the Doctor's hand away, but missed. The swiping arm fell to useless at the Dane's side. His breathing grew labored and drool spilled from the corner of his mouth.

Stites leaned in close to catch a whiff of the Colonel's breath. He did not have to lean too far. The Doctor pulled away suddenly and shook his head.

Stites looked up at the two other adults in the room. "Help me with a bit of history here," requested the Doctor in a sedate tone. "When did the Colonel last eat?"

Ruth Mount answered first: "Colonel Krause devoured the entire contents of the vittles bag, which Captain Markoe's cook prepared for him."

"When was this accomplished?"

Before responding to the Doctor's question, Ruth looked at Mortaine, whose countenance spoke of don't dare ask me about any of this.

So Ruth filled the void: "We had to stop at the Crooked Billet Tavern above Allen's Town. Somewhere between there and Cranberry, the Colonel finished his travel fare and emptied a canteen of cider. From what I have witnessed since his coming to Philadelphia is that Colonel Krause is a man of prodigious appetites."

Stites cast a furtive glance at his patient. "I can see by his girth that he has never refused a meal."

"Or a chance at seconds," added Miss Mount ruefully.

"Do you happen to know what the cook prepared for this poor man?" asked Stites of the seamstress.

"Pies mostly . . . mince pies . . . a pork pie . . . and some fruit."

"Nothing you mention appears sinful enough to cause him harm. Save for the pork, which is always suspect," speculated the Doctor. "He seems a robust specimen. What signs did he show of falling ill . . . and when?"

Ruth was more than glad to elaborate. "The Colonel complained of bad vapors and stomach cramps soon as we reached the Jersey side of the Delaware. He may have been complaining before then, but I was not privy to his conversations with his host and my master, Captain Abram Markoe."

"I see," said Doctor Stites, as he poked the patient's abdomen with gentle fingers. "Go on."

"Nothing really. A belch or two. Breaking wind perhaps. But nothing out of the ordinary, until we had passed through Cranberry . . ."

Mortaine, alias Stillwell, interrupted: "Sister, you forgot our stop at the Crooked Billet."

Ruth gave a nod and took a step back from the edge of the bed. "You tell him, brother."

"I volunteered to escort the Colonel to the necessary out behind the tavern. He was bent over, walking with difficulty, and grousing about pains in his gut. I held his arm all the way. The Colonel spent a good few minutes emptying himself. He emerged doubled over and visibly angry over something. I helped him back to the coach."

"Did he say anything to you?" asked the Doctor.

"Nothing I could decipher," said Mortaine. "The man is Dane and often reverts to his mother tongue. Besides, he was mumbling. He did vomit one time before we rounded the house. I helped him climb back into the carriage."

"You did not give me all those details, brother," Ruth scolded, as she stepped forward again.

"I wanted to spare a woman of your delicate constitution from such unseemly matters," confessed Mortaine, offering a bending of a knee.

Ruth did not bother to blush. She said nothing and kept her eyes on the Colonel.

Stites stood and pulled his leather bag up to the chair. He rummaged through it as he spoke: "This is no time to hold any information from me. The Colonel has obviously ingested something which is causing him great distress. Is there anything else you need to tell me?"

"Yes," said Ruth. "A few miles south of here, the Colonel started thrashing about . . . babbling on about nothing we could understand. He doubled over. Fell on his precious cases. In attempting to right the man, I was struck a blow to my forehead."

Ruth paused to pull her mob cap away from her head. She showed the Doctor the red mark left by one of Krause's large rings, high on her forehead.

Doctor Stites took a quick look at the mark, but said nothing. He appeared unimpressed.

Ruth plowed on: "Then the Colonel fainted . . . only to rouse himself into another tirade. By then, we found this place . . ."

Mortaine interrupted his supposed sister again: "Private Pollard and the coachman shouldered the Colonel up the stairs, laid him down, and removed his shoes. We ordered a drink for the Colonel, but he refused it." Mortaine was also keeping his eyes on Krause. "I do believe he has passed out again."

"No doubt you are correct, sir," said Doctor Stites. He pulled a vial and tiny spoon from his bag. "Now we must wait till he comes to. If he should awake after I am gone, make him drink at least a pint of boiled well water. Be sure the water is warm. Then force him to take three spoons of this emetic oil." Stites raised his hands and showed the others in the room the vial and the utensil. "We need to clean out his innards. I suggest you have the boy empty that sour thunder mug. Fetch another. You are going to need more than one for this man."

Stites removed his bag from the chair. He placed the vial and spoon where the bag had sat. Then he continued giving instructions: "I'm predicting a long night for all of you. I suggest you watch the Colonel in shifts 'round the clock. Take charge, Mister Willett. Get the other men to share the watch. Allow your sister to get a good night's rest. She appears to have earned it. I shall give you a measure of laudenum, woman. Put it in a bowl of tea to ease any pains you carry in your head."

Ruth thanked the Doctor for his concern over her condition. She actually felt no different than before the Colonel delivered a glancing blow. But she dared not refuse the Doctor. She was already scheming how to put her alleged condition to some use.

The good Doctor concluded: "I shall return in the morning to check on our patient. Can't say what hour. I shall bring a stronger potion with me on the morrow. For now, let us retire to the dining area and partake of Mister Williamson's fine supper fare. We can discuss payment for my two visits and the cost of my meal."

Enoch Mortaine matched the Doctor's smile. He led Stites out of the room. Ruth Mount trailed behind the two men after instructing Asher to empty the chamber pot out back then return to the room to attend to his master. The mulatto simply gave a nod and stared sadly at the man he had been charged to watch. He was afraid it was going to be a long night . . . especially for him.

Pip James had a fierce thirst. He was sorely hungry as well. Ever since following the coach and four to the Rhode Hall stage house, he had been hiding across the road behind a stand of lofty cedars. The blind kept his cart and horse completely out of sight. From this vantage point, Pip was able to observe the comings and goings of the party that his boss had attached himself to.

One horseman passed him again. He saw Enoch Mortaine directing the coachman and another horseman, who were helping carry a portly man to the door of the establishment. A woman, rubbing her head with her free hand, followed the procession into the place. A mulatto boy, burdened with satchels and bags culled from the coach, went in shortly thereafter.

All was quiet for a spell. That is when Pip fell to thinking about food and drink for him and his horse. Here he was within walking distance of a place offering what he craved, but he dared not cross the road and make his presence known. The horseman who entered the public house and the one he saw galloping south towards Cranberry might recognize him and start asking too many questions. Enoch Mortaine would not like such a confrontation. So Pip stayed in hiding and bided his time.

The horseman who had left the banner pole by the tavern's fence returned in haste with a well-dressed man pursuing him in a carriage pulled by a handsome sorrel. By this time the coach and four had been removed from the front of the stage house by the owner's slaves and led to the stable yard out back. Now the front of the place was occupied by a few horses and the carriage of the latest arrival. The two men disappeared inside. A long wait commenced and was ended when the well-dressed man emerged, climbed into his carriage, and headed down Lawrie's Road in the direction from whence he came.

By now the sky was dark as a cellar. Stars were twinkling in a cloudless sky. The air was comfortably cool.

Pip's stolen horse had found some wild grass to its liking and seemed content. The practiced thief was not. His belly ached and his throat was parched. He could not wait any longer. He had hoped Mortaine would sneak out of the place and look for him. But that was not happening. The coachman emerged from the house and walked around back to check on his team and the vehicle. The boy emerged twice carrying a chamber pot each time. He also went around back and returned swinging an empty vessel. One local, whom Pip sensed was not part of Mortaine's entourage, came out, mounted his horse, and trotted north at a leisurely pace. The time was as good as any to make a move.

Pip untethered his horse and walked his rig across the road. He went around back and found one of minehost's boys to tend to his horse. He decided to try his luck in the kitchen house rather than enter the main house. Pip introduced himself as the indentured servant of the dignitary who had recently arrived in the coach and four. The slave cook, who was in the midst of preparing supper for the help, was duly impressed with the coarse man's account of himself. He dropped some coins on her table to impress her more.

Thus, the starving man was treated to a fine meal of meat scraps, boiled potatoes, and corn pudding. The devil rum, pulled out of hiding just for him, was not bad either.

28

DEATH OF A ONCE-PROUD MAN

(Tuesday, August 8, 1775)

Robert Hare was snoring canorously. His dream of riding a winged horse was sweet. His bed partner, Will Pollard, did not give a fig about the man's dream. It was the snoring and the smell of Ware's feet that caused him to fall in and out of sleep after returning from his hour's watch in the Colonel's bedroom. The Dane never woke while Will was in the room . . . just shallow breathing and an occasional belch. The mulatto slave, wearing the same clothes he had traveled in, was fast asleep on the wood floor next to the bed. Pollard vacated the only chair in the room when the coachman came in to relieve him. They exchanged a few words while the coachman lit a new candle to replace the sputtering nub on the small table next to the bed. Pollard was glad to exit the room. He considered himself lucky since the Colonel had not stirred once. Krause had not called for the jerry pot. Best of all, the man had not vomited on Pollard's watch.

After the coachman's hour, it was supposed to be Hare's turn. Will Pollard gave the fellow horseman a slap on the nearest foot. The heavy sleeper lost hold of his dream, abandoned his snoring, and sat up.

"Time for a turn," hissed Pollard urgently. "May you gain the same luck I had."

Hare stretched and yawned. Said nothing. He donned his jacket over his night shirt and slipped his bare feet into his boots. He left his other clothes on hooks against the wall. It was well past midnight. The air in the room flirted with cool. The Private, overdue for his turn at the watch, glided softly down the hallway, his boots clicking like busy crickets, all the way to the Colonel's room. The door was ajar and the snoring emanating from the room seemed to be trumpeted by a robust bear. Robert Hare thought this odd. Maybe the Dane was rallying.

Hare pushed the door gently and stepped into the candleglow. He found the coachman slumped in the chair snoring loudly. No sound was coming from the bed or the floor. There was no slave boy in the room. Without bothering to rouse the coachman, Robert Hare strode to the bed. He thought it odd that the sick man held both arms rigid over his chest. The horseman leaned in close and studied the Colonel's face. The eyelids were down, but the mouth was agape. There were tears on his pallid cheeks and a trace of drool on both chins. Hare put his ear close to the Dane's mouth . . . nary a whisper of breath in or out. The Private stood bolt upright as if at attention in front of a superior officer, who had obviously been posed after death. He saluted the corpse. It was the only thing he could think to do.

Hare stepped around to the chair and shook the coachman awake.

"Go fetch Mister Willett," whispered Hare. "Hurry, man, the Colonel is dead!"

The coachman struggled to rise from the chair. He stood gape-mouthed, not daring to stare at the corpse in the bed. He busied himself with pulling his drover's coat from the back of the chair and draping it over his shoulders. Then he snatched his hat off a wall peg and held it with a shaking hand. He crossed himself with the other. He scuttled out of the room and made his way down the hall.

In no time at all, the Colonel's room was filled to near capacity. The one claiming to be Azariah Willett, wearing a flimsy nightshirt and nothing on his bare feet, had taken charge. He was barking out orders to others in the crowded room. His face became a rigid scowl. He reddened more and more with each command.

"Rouse minehost, Private Hare!"

"Yes, sir," saluted the horseman.

"Tell Mister Williamson to summon a constable."

Hare sped out of the room and down the hall in search of the stairs.

"Inspect the coach and the horses, drover," snapped Willett. "See if anything has been stolen or tampered with."

After a nod, off gimped the coachman as fast as his bow legs would carry him. He dared not challenge the man's queer command. He was glad to exit the room and avoid questions he did not look forward to answering.

"Where is the young maroon?" groused Willett.

A sleepy-eyed Will Pollard offered: "The boy was asleep on the floor near the bed during my watch, sir."

The man in charge barked: "One of you two troopers fetch the Doctor again. Better not return without Stites."

Pollard backed out of the room after touching his hunter's cap with an ungloved hand. He ran down the hallway in search of Robert Hare, whom he knew would be in no mood for a gallop to Cranberry.

Enoch Mortaine was now left alone with Ruth Mount, and, of course, a very cold and still Colonel Johan Gottfried Krause. The woman had been standing stoic as a statue in a cotton night shift and flowery robe. Calfskin slippers protected her feet. Ruth's hair was loose, cascading off her shoulders. There was no color in her cheeks, but her eyes sparkled with interest which was bordering on satisfaction.

"This is all your fault, Miss Mount," sputtered Mortaine in an angry whisper. "You gave this poor soul enough of whatever it was to slay a horse."

Ruth Mount's smile complemented her eyes. "This bastard was not poor, nor did he ever possess a soul. No woman need fear him now. Krause deserved his fate. I am glad to be rid of him."

"He was going to tell us more about his munitions game," moaned Willett. "I had softened him up . . . almost got him on the verge of revealing his sources and his contacts."

"This dead Dane was playing with you, Mister Mortaine." The seamstress was speaking in a measured monotone, "He was not going to tell you more than he wanted. His list of contacts lies in one of the cases intended for that Febiger fellow . . . I'm sure of it. Everything you require must be on that document. You no longer need the Colonel. You need a code breaker."

"For your sake, I hope you are right," whispered Mortaine.

Mount took a step towards her boss. Her glare was just shy of threatening. "What is that supposed to mean, Mister Mortaine?"

"Stop calling me that," the agent hissed. "I am presently Azariah Willett to you. Someone might hear you using a name I am saving for my return to New York."

"You're evading an explanation for why you just threatened my person," said the seamstress calmly.

"Not at all. In this clandestine business, those who make mistakes pay for their mistakes."

Ruth Mount had heard enough. In her mind, no mistake had been made. She had followed her superior's orders to the letter. Who could account for the gluttony of their target? Colonel Krause had done himself in. Ruth wheeled about, swirling her voluminous robe and gown. She stomped out of the room and proceeded noisily down the hallway. She re-entered her bedroom and slammed the door. There was no need to waste the rest of such productive dark hours. She had accomplished much during them. Now, her second sleep seemed much more important than fretting over the loss of a source of information.

Enoch Mortaine stood alone in the corpse's room. He stared at the remains of the once-proud dignitary—a man who held invaluable secrets that British authorities would have paid dearly to possess. Instead, it had come down to finding the coded parchment assumed to be lurking in one of the cases left on the floor of the coach. Mortaine hoped Miss Mount was correct and that the coachman had found nothing missing . . . nor the mysterious pair of cases tampered with.

Mortaine cursed the Colonel's name, then quickly exited the room. He rushed down the stairs in search of the quickest way to get to the stable. He hoped he was not too late.

David Williamson, fully dressed and wide awake, intercepted the Colonel's associate at the bottom of the stairs. "Mister Willett, what has happened?"

"The Colonel, sir," said Mortaine somberly. "I think he has been poisoned. His boy servant has vanished. He has to be the one who did in his master."

"I will fetch Mister Vanderhoof," offered minehost. "He is the Justice of the Peace in these parts. Let him handle this matter."

Mortaine agreed with a nod and a sigh.

Williamson went on: "But first, if you don't mind, please lead me to the Colonel's bedroom. I need to confirm, in your presence, that the Dane is deceased."

"Krause is most definitely dead," said Mortaine. "I'm not the only who will swear to that. A hand of folks will swear they've seen him dead."

"Still and all, I need to inspect the room with somebody else present in order to testify that I disturbed nothing. It is my room, but I lay no claim to the corpse."

Mortaine said nothing. He wanted so badly to get to the coach and find the precious coded document.

Minehost pressed on: "I shall need to summon Doctor Stites to confirm the manner of death."

"Already sent one of the horsemen to fetch the good Doctor," said Mortaine. "I'd love to follow you up the stairs, sir, but I must first check the coach we arrived in. I want to make sure nothing of value has been stolen by the boy slave. What is the fastest way to your stable?"

"Through the serving kitchen behind these stairs," said Williamson. "When you are done with your checking, please return to help me upstairs."

"Fine," said Mortaine who was already on his way to the serving kitchen.

The agent to the King found a rear door and rushed across the yard. Up ahead, he saw the coachman standing with a lantern in hand inspecting the wheels of the vehicle. A tall man, who was leaning against a stable post stood watching. No one else was up and about in the yard. Mortaine gave the lone spectator a hand signal of recognition, then confronted the coachman. "Have you checked the passenger's compartment yet, my good man?"

"Horses come first 'n this here rig second," said the coachman. "I don't really much care to be blamed for messin' with whatever's inside Captain Markoe's vehicle."

Mortaine flung open the door to the coach and peered into the darkness. "You should have looked in here first, drover. Do one thing right . . . come closer and hold your lantern high."

The agent gasped. The lids of both cases on the floor rested on the seats, as did the ends of the thick binding ropes. Mortaine poked and prodded in between the rifles which still remained neatly arranged in each container. He pulled a few of the weapons from one case and laid them on the seat in order to see if a piece of parchment was hidden there. But what he was looking for was not to be found. The sheet containing a coded message was missing. Maybe it had never been placed in there in the first place.

Mortaine slithered out of the coach. He slammed his fist against the open door of the coach and it screamed on its hinges. As he backed away, Mortaine bumped into the coachman who was still holding the lantern high.

"Get out of my way, you bumbler!" snapped Mortaine angrily.

The coachman staggered back a step or two, but held his tongue. He did not like the sewing maid's brother right from the get go, but he knew his station and he wanted to keep his job. He did not much care for the sewing maid either. Or the deceased Colonel, for that matter. In fact, the only soul on this journey that he took a liking to was the Colonel's boy. The coachman thought it best to keep his likes and dislikes to himself.

Mortaine headed to where Pip James stood. The coachman went back to inspecting the wheels.

"Thirteen stripes," declared the alongshoreman when his boss drew close.

"Cut the humor," snapped Mortaine. "Where have you been?"

"Followin' right behind ever since you passed through Cranberry," said Pip.

"The Colonel died in his sleep," announced Mortaine. "Did you not hear?"

"I was roused from my sleep in the hay down the far end of the stable . . . some commotion in the yard. I saw the lantern by the coach, so I decided to take a look see."

Mortaine accepted his underling's account without comment. He changed the subject: "Before minehost joins us, this is what I want you to do . . ."

"What is your wish?" interrupted Pip with feigned interest.

Mortaine was surprised by Pip's lack of surliness. He changed the subject again. "By the by, what are you calling yourself this day?"

"Still goin' by Hendrick Lau."

"Good. Keep to that. Such a fine German name fits in well 'round these parts. I will introduce you as such to the Justice of the Peace when he arrives."

Now Pip resorted to his usual frown, but he said nothing untoward. He kept his feelings about enforcers of the King's Law to himself. Finally, he said: "So what's it I should be doin'?"

"Find the Afric boy who must have stolen a piece of parchment out of the coach. I'm also blaming that black bastard for poisoning his master. So, once you find him, I do not care if you drag him back alive or dead."

"That same half-breed I saw with the Colonel at the docks?"

"Yes, one and the same," agreed Mortaine. "Are you armed, Mister Lau?"

"A borrowed knife . . . till I find a certain proper blade and pistol."

"I don't give a shyte about what's missing, save for the Afric's hide," said Mortaine balefully. "Without the piece of parchment he's filched, I have nothing to prove with regards to the selling of weapons by the Dane to the rebels . . . nothing but two cases of whatnot passing as gifts to fellow Crocians. That is not enough to convince my superiors of Krause's scheme."

Mortaine stopped talking when he saw David Williamson rushing across the yard. Mortaine took a step closer to the lantern light and waved to the owner of the Rhode Hall house. Minehost skirted past the coachman who was still fussing over bindings and straps on the vehicle.

"Mister Williamson, let me introduce you to a fellow traveler, whom I met by chance back in Allen's Town," said Mortaine. "He happened to follow my coach here."

Williamson eyed the tall, coarse man suspiciously, but he kept his darkest thoughts to himself. "We'll need as many able-bodied men as we can get," said the host.

"This is Hendrick Lau," offered Mortaine. "Strong as they come and eager to please. I am sure he will prove useful."

Williamson did not offer a hand of welcome, but he did say: "Pleasure to meet you, Mister Lau. I like your name."

Pip kept his eyes on the inn owner's empty hand. He spoke in his usual gruff way. "For a meal and a pint, I'll be glad to help in any way."

"Good," said Williamson. He turned to Mortaine. "Anything missing from this coach?"

"A few items," confessed Mortaine. "Nothing of great value . . . must've been filched by the slave boy before he took off."

"So we are looking for a runaway black who may have murdered his master and stole a few items of meager worth," summarized Williamson.

"Appears so," said Mortaine. "The boy must be found . . . preferrably alive."

"Not to worry, Mister Willett," said Williamson with confidence. "Runaways 'round here tend to hide in the swamp. They don't last long in there. I'll be summoning a number of fellows to start the searching. Besides the swamp, they'll be checking nearby farmsteads and outbuildings. I'd say the Afric has less than an hour on us. 'Tis close to sun up, so we've got a fair chance to bag him quick."

"I'd like to have him hanged, if you bring him in alive."

"Hope so, too, Mister Willett," said Williamson. "But I can't promise such. The fellows I recruit will be armed and they'll be primed for a hunt. Folks 'round here do not take kindly to an upstart Afric doing harm to his master. I'll do my best to warn them to capture the boy, not kill him."

"Fair enough," allowed Mortaine.

Williamson continued: "I'll send someone up to Cross Roads to get Tom Wetherill to lend us his best hounds. I understand the Ratters Hunt Club has planned a day in the swamp, so I will recruit them as well. If the boy's hiding in Pigeon Swamp, then we'll find him for sure."

"Good then," said Mortaine. "Now, I need to inform Miss Mount of what has transpired."

"And I need to wait for Doctor Stites to arrive," said Williamson. "I say we go inside. I'll have one of my girls prepare eggs and sausage and a cup of courage for Mister Lau. You and I can discuss the legalities germane to the corpse at rest in one of my rooms. You need to tell me what you can of Colonel Krause. That way we can support one another's account when the Justice of the Peace arrives."

"No problem," sighed Mortaine to give sign that he was growing a bit weary of it all. "Miss Mount knows more about the Dane than I do. I will ask my sister to join us in your dining room."

Minehost's face brightened. He was encouraged by Mortaine's words. He led the two he knew as Azariah Willett and Hendrick Lau back into his house.

The coachman was left behind. He opened the door to the coach and took a peek at the handsome muskets laid out on one of the seats. He grabbed one and hefted it to his shoulder.

"It'd take a strong man to fire one of these here darlin's," said the coachman to himself. "A true rebel sort 'fraid of nothin.'" He placed the long, black Kronberg back on the seat and closed the door of the coach.

The man stood for a moment, alone in the stable yard, contemplating his next move. He wondered about the fate of his new, young friend—a mulatto scared out of his wits and on the run. A mere boy accused of murder and theft. The coachman knew better.

29

SEARCH IN THE SWAMP

(Tuesday, August 8, 1775)

A gang of Ratters crossed into the heavily forested southwestern ridge of Pigeon Swamp close to an hour after dawn. The strong sunlight revealed an army of red maples, pin oaks, birches, and stout sassafras trees. The chosen deer path into the swamp was dry here and the waygoing was easy. Things were looking promising.

John Wetherill, Jr., and his brother, Vincent, both dressed in hunter shirts and buckskin trousers, led the hunt club members who had volunteered for a special mission beyond the solid ground which held the welcoming trees. They had originally intended to follow up on Ike Higgins's recommendation to trace a deer trail north of Cross Roads. This would have led to a grazing area in a dry marsh. But that plan had been abandoned before the sun came up.

At that time, John Probasco, who was David Williamson's newest neighbor, came galloping into the yard of the Wetherill Tavern with news of a runaway slave suspected of hiding in the swamp. This carpenter turned yeoman, possessing a lanky build and straight bearing, spoke in a frantic, high-pitched voice. He waved his hands animatedly with every syllable that spilled from his red-lipped mouth. The man of the soil was all sinew and cord, middle-aged, large-eyed, and ruddy colored. Country life appeared to suit this husbandman well. Though new to the area, he had been welcomed and well-received by all his neighbors. He was recognized immediately by those hunters who had already gathered in the tavern yard. Vincent Wetherill stepped forward to grab the reins of Probasco's horse and calm the beast while its master dismounted.

John Probasco addressed the hunters after hallooing all of them and removing his straw hat. He claimed to have been sent by the

Justice of the Peace, Peter Vanderhoof, to ask, first, for the use of Thomas Wetherill's best hounds—Rapax and Lion. The plan was to take the pair down to Rhode Hall to pick up the scent of a runaway slave suspected of murdering his master.

This news caused a stir among the Ratters . . . and a slew of questions Probasco could not answer. John the younger sent one of the Ratters inside the tavern to fetch his cousin who was busy preparing for early breakfast patrons. Thomas Wetherill, with his serving apron billowing in the morning breeze, came running into his yard. Probasco repeated his request and minehost wasted no time agreeing to loan out his best pair of hounds. He sent Ike Higgins and Little Ned to fetch them from their pens on the shade side of the slant-roofed stable. John, Jr., convinced Cutlope Hancock to help load the hounds into the German's waggon which sat by its lonesome in the yard. He ordered Cut to haul the pair, along with Ike and Little Ned, and follow Probasco down the ridge path to Rhode Hall.

At first, Cut refused. He did not want to miss the hunt. Besides, he wanted no association with the unlucky Irishman, who always got him in trouble. The Wetherill brothers took turns trying to convince the stubborn German to accede to their plan. Finally, they convinced Cut to cooperate and swallow his pride. Hancock spat on the ground then stomped off to turn his horse and waggon around in order to follow Probasco out of the yard.

Ike and Little Ned appeared with the two hounds straining on chain leashes. Ike had taken charge of the much larger hound, Lion. Little Ned followed with the lesser Rapax. Both humans and dogs seemed eager to please on such a fair hunting day.

Cut helped lift the hounds into his waggon. He also helped Little Ned scramble over the side board. Ike was ignored by the German. When all four passengers were ensconced in his waggon, Cut propped his hunting rifle and gear on the seat board where either Ike or Little Ned should have been invited to sit. But Cut wanted nothing to do with companionship or conversation on the way to Rhode Hall. As far as he was concerned, he was carrying four curs to a destination that interested him not in the least.

Thus, the two handlers crouched in the well of the waggon with the hounds. Ike was glad to have been assigned such an important responsibility. He carried only a knife at his belt, since he had assumed the Wetherill brothers wanted him on the hunt simply for rousting game in the swamp. Little Ned was supposed to have been used in like manner. But now they were about to tackle a new and exciting assignment. Both felt up to the task.

Ike was dressed in a tow homespun shirt, which Good Mary had sewn for him recently . . . and a newly patched pair of corduroy trousers. Little Ned sported patches on patches on a frayed linen shirt and dirty trousers. This was the same outfit he had worn the last time he had been allowed to accompany Ike into the swamp. He clutched the same satchel he had lugged there as well. Little Ned smelled as ripe as the hounds. Ike was no rose either. This was another reason why Mister Hancock was in no mood to share his seat board.

John Probasco finished negotiating with the Wetherill brothers. All Ratters had agreed to help with the search for the runaway slave. The scheduled hunt was abandoned. Probasco mounted his dray horse and sped off, followed by Cut Hancock and his waggon, containing odorous humans and hounds.

The Wetherill brothers, Benjamin Hull, John Caywood, Robert Marshon, and Abraham Dean were left standing in the tavern yard. Within a minute's time, the hunting party was on the move and headed for the southwest ridge of the swamp. When they reached spongy ground, they split up. Vincent took Ben and Rob with him and headed west. John, Jr., took Caywood and Dean and headed east. The hunt was on, but not for deer or any other usual prey. They were tracking a human now—not a mere runaway slave, but a murderer. At least it was good tracking weather—fair and clear and comfortably cool. But luck hid out of sight in the shadows for both parties. They spotted nothing but frogs and toads and a few brown snakes. It was going to be a long day.

Preparations by the search party in the stable yard behind the Rhode Hall house were chaotic at best. No one, save Pip James, was eager to venture into the swamp before the hounds arrived. Actually, Pip wanted no part of the hunt for the runaway slave. He would have preferred running his cart up to Cross Roads to confront the scoundrels who stole his weapons. But that was not his choice to make. Instead, Enoch Mortaine ordered him to transfer the musket cases to the cart Pip had stolen in Trent Town. Then he was to get a head start over the others recruited by David Williamson and Peter Vanderhoof.

"Slip away, unseen, Pip," instructed Enoch Mortaine. "Be the first to find that maroon. Do him in, clean and quick. Leave his half-piece arse to rot in the swamp. But most important, bring the parchment back to me."

"What's in it for me?" posed the taciturn alongshoreman.

"More gold coins than you can imagine . . . if and when we make it to New York."

"How much is the parchment worth?"

"Priceless, my man . . . priceless."

Pip said nothing more. He turned about and disappeared behind the stable. Only his boss saw him depart. He was missed by nobody.

Close to an hour later, John Probasco returned with Cutlope Hancock's horse and waggon close behind. They were greeted by cheers from the recruited searchers. The hounds were brought up to the room where Doctor Stites and the Justice of the Peace were conferring over particulars germane to the corpse in the bed. They were debating how long they could wait before Colonel Krause had to be buried. A few scented candles were already lit in the room and the one window was open wide. The question turned from when to where before the dogs finished sniffing the floor where Asher had slept. Ike and Little Ned were pulled by Lion and Rapax down the stairs, through the dining area, and out the front door. The canines strained against their leashes and pulled their trackers south along the west shoulder of Lawrie's Road.

By now, all the recruited men followed the hounds. Weapons in hand. Eager to get this chore done with. Most were dressed in yeoman's garb or hunting leathers. Included in the Rhode Hall entourage were John Probasco; Gilbert Van Pelt; John Van Dyke;

David Vanderhoff, son of the Justice of the Peace; and, bringing up the rear, a gimping Moses Gulick who had turned his ankle back in the stable yard.

Remaining behind at Williamson's house were Cutlope Hancock, the coachman, and the man who called himself Azariah Willett. All three kept to themselves, exchanged no pleasantries, nor made eye contact. Hancock remained on the seat board of his empty waggon. The coachman went to check on his team of horses that had been led out to a nearby grazing field. Willett stood by the rear entrance of the house waiting for Markoe's horsemen to return from their patrolling of the stage road. He had ordered one to head north four miles out and the other to head south all the way back to Cranberry. He wondered what was taking them so long. Perhaps either one had found the boy.

Minehost Williamson had retreated into his establishment to light more scented candles in the Colonel's bedroom. This gave him an opportunity to consult with the Doctor and the Justice of the Peace, and to check on his daughters who were taking care of a few morning patrons. One of them was Ruth Mount who had refused to come outdoors when requested to do so. She dined alone in the quaint side room set aside for female guests. She was savoring a bracing black tea, and the solitude in a bright room. Ruth continued to pretend to be ill, especially with the return of Doctor Stites. Feigning illness fit well with her scheme. Plus, she was glad to have avoided the commotion that had erupted outside and woken her so rudely. Men's foolish fox and hound games be damned. Ruth's game was better.

A mile down Lawrie's Road, the hounds veered west and crossed Probasco's fallow field. Everyone in the search party knew where they were going—knew which way the slave boy had chosen. The field abutted the eastern extremity of what the locals called Mary Pigeon's swamp. Where the waygoing became crowded with golden bells and Queen Anne's lace, the two hounds slowed, sniffed frantically about, then zigzagged through the underbrush. The Crocian runaway was not following one of Ike's trails, nor even a deer trail. In the dark before dawn, Asher must have made his own trail through difficult brush and brambles. That meant slow going on his part. It also meant a distinct advantage for his pursuers.

David Vanderhoof—tallest and lankiest, with sandy blond hair and piercing blue eyes—had been put in charge of the search team by his equally handsome father. What set the son apart from his followers was a beaver hat worn at a jaunty angle over his golden mane. The young leader declared that the Afric had to be in bad shape by now—cut, bruised, exhausted, and slowed to a stumbling crawl. He pronounced confidently that the hunt for the boy would not take long. His men shouted their 'huzzahs' in unison and followed the hounds confidently as well.

Ike was the man in the fore. He was beginning to have his doubts. Lion came to an abrupt halt at the edge of the largest marsh pond in the swamp. Ike knelt by the hound to check the ground for clues. A red tail hawk circled overhead, revealing no secrets. Rapax and Little Ned caught up with Ike. Both hounds worried the sandy soil with eager noses and slobbering tongues, but they always returned to one spot at the edge of the murky green water. Ike offered words of encouragement to his Lion. Little Ned, arm weary and footsore already, did the same with Rapax. While doing so, he shifted the strap of his satchel to the other shoulder to lessen the pain which had been bothering him most of the way.

Gilbert Van Pelt—a stout. good-humored fellow—noticed the boy's discomfort and offered to relieve Little Ned of his tracking duties. Good Mary's son refused at first with a vehement shake of his rufous head, but Ike ordered him to hand the leash over to Mister Van Pelt. The boy did so with mixed emotions. He uttered a sigh of relief after a grunt of embarrassment. Little Ned had still wanted to prove he was a man. And here he was, losing another chance.

Ike turned his leash over to John Van Dyke—a taciturn fellow who never complained about being asked to help. Van Dyke was a large, muscular farmer who was capable of handling Lion. Ike was glad to be free of the task. He decided the hounds would be useless if they had lost the scent of the slave. It was obvious to the Irishman that the runaway had either tumbled into the water and drowned, or cautiously strode in and decided to wade across the pond to avoid capture.

Higgins smiled to himself. He had to admit that the fleeing bloak was sharper than the young Vanderhoof was giving him credit for. First, the ploy of sticking to the road for a mile or so. Second, a daring wade across a pond in the dark. Ike did not know how deep the water was out in the gloom, but he guessed it shallow all the way. The boy had left no sign to convince Ike that he was correct. A drowning was still a remote possibility. Whatever the fate of the runaway, Ike thought it best to skirt the pond and hope the hounds could pick up the scent on the other side. The ward of the swamp suggested the search party split up and encompass the pond—one dog with each group. Vanderhoof approved of the idea. He had nothing better to suggest. Gil Van Pelt led to the right with Rapax's chain in hand. John Van Dyke pulled Lion to the left. Ike, Little Ned, and Moses Gulick followed Van Dyke. The rest followed Van Pelt.

The roundabout way for both parties proved difficult and daunting. Muck and mud clung to boots. Thorn bushes tore at clothing. Any hope of picking up the trail at the other end of the pond was dashed by a vast bog, sporting cattails and lily pads, as far as the eye could see. The two parties ended up being separated by a hundred yards of impenetrable swamp. They found not one footprint. No bent twig. No piece of torn clothing dangling from a thorn bush. The hounds sniffed and snorted feverishly but came up with nothing. Neither party held to any optimism.

"The black bastard drowned," surmized Moses Gulick in disgust, as he leaned against the trunk of a stunted sassafras tree in order to ease the pain in his swollen ankle.

"What's to be done now?" asked Johnny Van Dyke with equal disgust. He had removed his battered tricorn and was scratching his close-cropped pate, while, at the same time, restraining Lion. "Must we wait till the boy's body rises to the surface of the pond?"

"Ain't deep 'nough fer drownin', 'cept if'n the boy was fierce drunk," concluded Ike. He was peering off into the dark, gloomy distance. "Once'd the boy tried the water, he must've kept to it. Most likes, he's up to slow goin' all the way cross this boggy stretch ahead. Me thinks he's tryin' for Fresh Ponds without even knowin' what waits there."

"Then we're wastin' our time here," argued Moses Gulick. "Best we head back and come 'round to Fresh Ponds."

"Gonna take some time in the doin'," observed Van Dyke, "but I guess there's not much else we can do."

Ike agreed, but added that he and Little Ned were going to take a chance at finding a straighter way through the swamp and meet up with the others at Fresh Ponds.

Van Dyke and Gulick had no problem leaving Ike to his own devices. After all, old John Wetherill had appointed the loner as ward of Pigeon Swamp, so this Irishman was supposed to know this dismal place better than anyone.

Gulick employed his booming voice to holler out to the other group standing across the way. He told them to turn back. David Vanderhoof shouted a positive response. Soon, his team disappeared from sight. So did Gulick, Van Dyke, and Lion.

That left Ike and Little Ned alone to ponder the next move forward. The Irishman was still discerning which way was best. Little Ned was wondering what would go wrong next.

"The feller we're chasin' sure is crafty, Neddy," said Ike finally.

"Not as keen as you, Mister Ike."

The Irishman reached out with a calloused hand and gave Good Mary's boy a playful Dutch rub.

Little Ned did not even flinch. He was used to such treatment. He trusted his mother's mate not to take such games too far.

"Yer speakin' truth 'bout the likes o' me alway,—Neddy, me lad," grinned Ike. "I know secret trails which'd I expect no other chap to ever learn in here . . . 'cept fer you to know 'n use when I'm gone."

"Where're you disappearin' to, Mister Ike?" said Little Ned with curiosity knitting his brow and innocence motivating his concern.

"I ain't a worm's meal yet," said Ike with a chuckle. "Follow me, Neddy. Us alone are gonna find that there runagate, no matter how cunnin' he thinks he be."

Enoch Mortaine found his accomplice sipping her morning tea in the side room reserved for women. Ruth Mount sat alone, as she preferred. She was dressed in her traveling outfit, sans corset. Her comfortable slippers still encased her feet. Ruth looked up when her boss entered the room, but she offered no smile. After all, it was a grim day with the tragic passing of the one Mortaine wanted to keep alive and the all out search for a runaway slave whom Mortaine wanted dead. Her boss wore no smile either. He sat down opposite his partner in crime. Said nothing. Simply stared at his hands with unreadable eyes.

"How goes the search, Mister Mortaine?" asked Mount with feigned curiosity and concern.

Mortaine looked right and left, but there was no person in the room except himself and the woman asking the question. The King's agent replied in a whisper: "How many times must I tell you not to call me by that name. I am Willett to you here. I am saving my former name for New York and for Mister Bancroft, who pays me to pay you. The least you can do is simply call me 'brother.'"

Ruth Mount had never heard Mortaine mention his boss by name before. She thought it curious that the name of a high-level tory operative be mentioned now.

"I am still your brother around here, so keep to the name you gave me."

Mortaine looked Ruth in the eye. She stared back with equal intensity.

The man continued: "We shall be leaving shortly. Soon as Mister James returns with the Colonel's parchment which the slave boy stole from one of the cases before fleeing into the swamp."

"You think so?" prodded Ruth, after taking a dainty sip of her tea. "One of minehost's daughters told me the Colonel's boy escaped out the front entrance and fled down the road."

"Before he disappeared, the boy must have gone 'round back to fetch what his master had told him to find. This should show you how valuable that paper was to the Colonel and how valuable it is to us. We get that coded document and bring it to the higher-ups, then we can expect a handsome reward for our efforts."

Ruth Mount shifted in her seat. Even without the restrictive corset, she was in some degree of discomfort. She took a deep breath and let it out slowly.

"I've had a change of heart, Mister Willett."

"What do you mean, sister?"

"The Colonel is dead . . . my work is done. I want out of this game."

Mortaine felt insulted. He said as much: "You cannot abandon me so easily, Miss Mount. I have seen to it that the muskets be returned to their cases and properly bound with rope. When my man returns with the parchment, he shall cart the musket cases to Radford's Landing on the Raritan. We shall cross the river and take the next stage waggon which has seating available. We will catch up with Mister James and ferry across to Staten Island. Once in New York, we will present our findings to Mister Bancroft."

"You don't need me for any of that," said Mount.

Mortaine's face reddened with anger. He slapped the table and rattled Mount's teacup. She reached for it and held it firmly.

"I wish to return to Philadelphia in my master's coach," hissed Mount.

"You miss your sweet Anna McClew, do you not?" asked Mortaine with a sneer and a look of disgust.

"Yes," is all Mount needed to say.

"And you are willing to forfeit the rest of your pay?"

"Yes," said the seamstress without hesitation.

Mortaine pushed away from the table, stood quickly, and turned his back on the woman. Seething in silence, he walked out of the room.

This brother and sister would never speak to each other again.

30

DRY ISLAND

· · · · · · · · · · ·

(Tuesday, August, 1775)

Way past noon, Ike Higgins and Little Ned found what they were hoping for. They had successfully traversed the heart of the marsh by following a soggy trail the Irishman had marked last winter when the ice was thick and the way was easy. His runic carvings on the trunks of stunted trees pointed the way to a dry island. This patch was a few thousand yards square and not far from the high ground forest which ran to the waypath used by the farmers at Fresh Ponds.

The leg weary pair were glad to climb over a husbandman's cut of logs which lined the rim of the island. They selected one to sit on and spare a few moments to rest. Ike surveyed the harvest of trees. He was not pleased. Only a score of gnarled, wind-twisted trees remained standing guard over their straighter fallen peers. Trunks and limbs had been cut to various lengths and stacked like tinder here and there. Ike guessed that the Van Dykes of Fresh Ponds were responsible for such a drastic slaughter. Unfortunately, he was not in charge of this stretch of the swamp. He had no authority in these parts. But with all the trees gone, the marsh water was sure to claim the island. Ike was keenly aware of the destruction coming. He would have to tell Mister Wetherill about it. The Van Dykes were inching close to his master's property. They would have to be warned. For now, Ike Higgins had to make sure nobody poached on Wetherill holdings. He would be ready if any Van Dyke lad tried.

Little Ned was getting restless. He wanted to explore the island. Ike told him to be still and remain seated under the shade of a spared maple. They were both soaked and mud-smeared from the knees down. Faces and hands cut by nettles and thorns. Clothing ripped by the same. But, worst of all, they had found no sign of the runaway slave.

The boy removed the satchel strap from his shoulder. He reached in and pulled out a pair of corncakes his mother had packed for them. He handed the bigger prize to Ike and kept the lesser one for himself. They ate in silence.

Finally, the Irishman spoke: "Mary'd put a canteen or flask in yer bag, Neddy?"

The boy peered into the bag. "None," he said, "but a few of Master John's ripe 'n red pippens."

"Better 'n nothin'," mumbled Ike sadly. "Hand me one o' them beauties."

Little Ned tossed the Irishman the biggest apple. Ike followed the arc of the fruit but failed to catch it. Something glinted next to the trunk of the largest standing tree on the island. Ike scrambled to his feet, pulled his knife from his belt, and stepped slowly and cautiously towards the largest tree. Little Ned concerned himself with attempting to retrieve the apple.

"Come out from behind there!" commanded Ike as loud as he could. His words were followed by a phlegmy cough. The swamp air had never been kind to his lungs. "I see you, boy . . . yer runnin' game is nigh up."

The glint had come from a stout knife blade, held low by a large man, who suddenly came out from behind the tree. He sported a crimson seaman's cap and a wide smile. This fellow looked vaguely familiar to the Irishman.

"Where's my pistol, you piece of shyte?" growled Pip James. "And where's my knife?"

Ike decided to stand his ground. He stood erect as he could manage and anticipated the worst. His knife was clutched firmly in his hand.

The Irishman called out to Mary's boy: "Run 'n hide, Neddy!"

Little Ned started to dash away, but stopped and returned to the maple in order to retrieve his satchel. Then he took off like a chipmunk fleeing a hound. Twenty yards away he found a stack of logs to hide behind. To his astonishment he discovered that he had to share his hiding place with another mulatto boy—one looking a few years older, dirtier, wetter, and more scratched and tattered.

He was looking none too happy to be sharing a tight hiding spot. No words were exchanged. This was no time for introductions. Both of them peeked out from their hiding place in order to see what the two grown adversaries were fixing to do to one another.

Ike was keeping his eyes on the man's weapon. He now remembered when and where he saw this fellow last. "Looks like ye already found yer blade, drover."

Pip James was still moving forward, but at a more cautious pace. "This here pigsticker is borrowed . . . meant to cut your heart out if'n you don't hand over my pistol 'n blade. The knife you're holdin' is not the one I'm lookin' for."

"This one I'm holdin' is meant for defendin' meself 'n the boy, drover," said Ike with a confident voice. "By the by, I ain't carryin' yer pistol 'n I ain't seen yer knife ever since ye dropped it into yer own waggon. As I recall, old Cut helped ye drop it in there after he broke yer arm."

Pip growled and started circling to his left.

Ike kept wary eyes on the man's weapon. "I guess a chance were lost to search yer rig after the German was through with the likes o' ye."

Pip growled again. "Look, you bastard, if you remember the fate of my knife, then you must remember the pistol. The dueling piece is more important to me."

Ike offered a sly grin. "Me memory ain't as good as 'twas. Guess I survived too many a knife fight . . . too bad them which'd faced the likes o' me didn't."

Pip took another step forward and extended his arm that held his weapon. "This'll be your last one, Irish."

With that challenge said, the knife fight in the swamp began in earnest. Pip lunged at Ike's head with his blade but caught only air. Ike dipped his head low and quickly moved to his right. He remembered that Cutlope Hancock had broken the man's left arm. Ike swiped at the limb with his weapon and tore the sleeve of the man's Russia shirt. Blood painted the cloth around the tear. Pip gave the flesh wound a cursory glance then bull rushed his opponent. He slammed into the Irishman with all his might. He was bigger and stronger . . . and amazingly quick on his feet. Cutlope Hancock could match the man, but Ike did not stand a chance. The Irishman went down . . . flat on his back, but still holding tight to his knife. He waved it at his opponent to keep the man at bay.

Pip took a step back. He circled to his right now. Then he jumped in close and kicked the knife out of Ike's hand. He plunged his own blade into Ike's shoulder above the heart. The Irishman rolled to his side and took Pip's knife with him. Pip roared his anger at being empty-handed. Then he started kicking Ike's ribs with his heavy boots. Mary's man gasped and groaned. He failed to fight back.

Pip stopped kicking all of a sudden. He stumbled back away from the man he accused of being a thief. Something fierce and screaming had climbed on his back and was clawing his face with one hand and choking him with the other. Pip fell to one knee, reached behind with the hand that had held the knife, and threw the attacking critter to the ground.

"Well, well," gasped the alongshoreman, as he struggled to catch his breath. "Look what the swamp has brought me . . . a stray bear cub!"

With that, Pip stood and planted a wide, hob-nailed boot on Asher's chest. "Where's the prize parchment, boy?"

The Colonel's boy cried out in pain. He spit like a cornered beast and writhed under the large man's foot. He flailed his arms, but to no avail.

Ike could not help him. The Irishman was out cold and bleeding.

Pip repeated his question. He pressed down hard with his heavy boot.

Asher screamed again then managed only a few words in a gasping breath: "I carry nothing but the clothes on my back."

Pip leaned in and laughed in the boy's face. "Then I slay you here. I'll rip off your clothes to find what you stole from one of the cases in the coach. Then I'll leave your sorry arse here to rot."

"I took nothing from my father!" cried Asher.

Pip stood bolt upright. His mouth was agape in disbelief. He lowered the fist that was supposed to have delivered a death blow. Out of the corner of his eye he spotted another mulatto—shorter and younger than the one underfoot, but standing boldly just twenty yards away. A fine pistol, primed and cocked, was held in his two trembling hands. The boy and the pistol looked familiar.

Mortaine's man wanted to cry out and thank the fates for his good fortune. But he was too late. A lead ball cored his left eye and found his brain. Another piece of lead entered his left leg and kissed bone. Pip James, alias Hendrick Lau, fell like an axed tree—face up with his remaining eye preoccupied with measuring the depth of clouds. He was done for the day. Pip was of no use to anyone, now or ever.

Cutlope Hancock emerged from his blind, which was a mere fifty yards from the man he had shot dead. Shouldering his trusty hunting rifle, he strode slowly towards the three survivors. Cut reached Little Ned first. The boy was inspecting the corpse and puzzling over the two holes therein.

"You done well, boy," said Cut avuncularly. "Made your mama proud this day . . . shot this bastard right in the eye."

Little Ned looked up at the German. He cast inquisitive eyes. "You sure, Mister Cut?"

The German patted the ten-year-old on the head and lied again. "Ya, my shot got him in the leg . . . your shot did him in."

"Does that make me a man?" asked Little Ned.

"Makes you a better shot than me, boy," said Cut. "Just don't brag or boast 'bout it . . . promise?"

"Why can't I?"

"'Cause folks 'round here don't tolerate no black man slayin' a white man. You let me take care of this mess. Neither one of us is gonna dare confess whose lead went where. Don't even tell your mama or that deuce of an Irishman sleepin' under yonder tree. You swear?"

"Guess I got no choice, Mister Cut." Little Ned placed the pistol back in the satchel. He turned and hurried over to check on Ike.

The German went to the other boy and lifted him to his feet. Asher shook his head in an attempt to come out of his stupor caused by being thrown on his head by Pip. The Colonel's boy was a sorry sight—wet leaves and burrs sticking to his once fine outfit. Both sleeves were torn. The shirtfront soiled and stained. Breeches streaked with mud. No shoes on his feet. Sopping hose sagging down around his ankles. The swamp had been unkind to the boy.

But Asher had recovered his voice: "Thank you, kind sir, for appearing when you did."

"Think nothin' of it, my boy. Been followin' that dead bloak since I'd picked up his trail behind the stable at Rhode Hall. Such an easy one to track. He never once caught wind of me. You can thank him for leadin' me to you three."

"If my father was alive, he'd be sure to pay you well," determined Asher.

"So you're claimin' to be the Colonel's son?"

"Jah," answered Asher with a Danish lilt. "My mother is one of his favorite servants back in St. Croix. He picked me to accompany him on his journey to the British colonies."

"I'm almost near to believin' you, boy," said Cut. "The search party will want to know your tale . . . especially the Justice of the Peace and the Wetherill brothers. But that comes later. For now, come help me lift old Ike."

The odd pair joined little Ned at Ike's side. Cut barked out instructions: "You two boys are goin' to have to shoulder him over to Fresh Ponds. There's a log bridge to the north that'll get you beyond the swamp and on to higher ground. They'll be folks there to help all three of you back to Rhode Hall by way of the mill road."

"Aren't you leading us, mister?' asked Asher hopefully.

"I'll catch up to you before you reach Fresh Ponds," said Cut. "For now, I've some cleanin' up to do. I won't take long."

Before the boys and Ike took off, Hancock pulled the knife from the Irishman's wound. It was bleeding some, but not enough to put the man's life in jeopardy. Cut yanked the shirt off Pip's corpse and ripped both sleeves off it. He used the cloth to bind Ike's wound tightly in order to stall the bleeding. When the German was done, he ordered the boys to guide Ike to the log bridge. The wounded man was wobbly on his feet. He was glad Little Ned and Asher were there to help him on his way. Cut watched the trio until they were out of sight, then he got to work.

The German made his way to the water's edge at the south end of the island and lifted several logs out of the muck. He fetched Pip's body and pulled it to the water that had seeped in where the logs had been. He laid out the corpse in the miry crease. Cursed the man's name. Then Cut heaved the logs back in place over Pip's bones. He took his time in between logs in order to catch his breath.

After he was satisfied with the results, Cut scoured the area where the knife fight had taken place. He wanted no trace of the incident to be discovered. He spread dead leaves over the bloody ground where Ike had fallen. He also tossed the food scraps Little Ned had left behind into the water. Cut retrieved the two knives and slipped them behind his belt. Satisfied with his efforts, the German headed quickly for the log bridge. He wanted to keep his promise to the Colonel's son. That boy was worth saving.

❖

An hour later, the Ratters team, which had taken the long way west over Lawrence Brook, finally reached the log bridge. They had been drawn to the area by the sound of gunfire. Vincent Wetherill, followed by Benjamin Hull and Robert Marshon, sped as fast as they could across the bridge and on to the dry island. They milled about for several minutes but found nothing worth bothering about. Marshon did find a ripe apple on the ground near a maple tree and wondered how it got there. In the next minute, he tossed it into the water and caught up with the other two searchers who had started back to the bridge.

The discouraged party found dry ground beyond the bridge and headed towards Fresh Ponds. All three weary men were glad to give up the hunt. They were convinced the swamp waters had claimed the runaway.

31

CHAOS IN THE STABLE YARD

(Tuesday, August 8, 1775)

Ominous reds and brooding violets painted the western sky. One golden eye peeked through blushing clouds and counted all the men gathered in David Williamson's noisy stable yard. Minehost was overjoyed to welcome so many potential paying customers to his humble establishment. Tethered horses, coaches, waggons, and carts were scattered at the fringes. Women and girls peeked out the windows of the Rhode Hall house, curious about the commotion in the yard. A smattering of the eligible fairer sex were hoping certain eligible men would cast a glance their way. Why they had gathered seemed not to matter that much. A few idle house servants stood outside the serving kitchen door. A goodly number of field slaves stood in the shadows under the eave of the stable barn. All were anticipating a major event—something to liven up the mundane daily existence of locals of every stripe in the South Ward. Perhaps something even better than a tar and feathering.

In the yard, small groups had formed based on status, opinion, or conviction. Outsiders—such as Enoch Mortaine, still pretending to be Azariah Willett, the pair of Philadelphia horsemen, the taciturn coachman, and a pair of curious travelers on the latest stage waggon up from Burlington—formed a separate group in the shadow of Captain Markoe's coach. Few words were being exchanged here.

Robert Hare, having rescued the troop banner from where he had stored it in the vehicle, unfurled it and held its staff firmly planted on the ground between his shiny boots. The coachman climbed up on his seat board to get a better view of the proceedings. Mortaine took a seat inside the coach in order to brood. He was mulling over whether or not to instruct Pip James to dispatch the sewing maid. That woman was useless to him now. Ruth Mount had retreated to her room. She obviously wanted no part of watching the hanging of an innocent slave. Mortaine was worried she might talk and put the English spy network in the colonies and his clandestine project in jeopardy. After all, she now knew the name of his boss, thanks to a slip of the tongue. Better to have her wagging tongue silenced than set free to stir up woe.

Mortaine was also irritated that Pip was taking so long to return from the swamp. The usually dependable lackey was way late. After the alongshoreman did return with the coded parchment and Ruth Mount had been silenced, then Mortaine felt he could leave for New York. Pip was to take the cart burdened with the firearms cases and Mortaine would take the stage waggon which had just arrived from Burlington. But this all depended on Pip's success in the swamp. But he was missing. His boss was deeply concerned. Things were not going quite as planned. Enoch cursed under his breath and stared out at the crowd. His mouth was down-turned. A scowl formed on his face.

Many others, such as half the Ratters and most of the Rhode Hall search party, had already reported in. They had returned empty-handed and were in a foul mood. They clustered in the center of the yard and exchanged accounts of their failures in the swamp. A group of local dignitaries stood apart from the searchers. They were patiently waiting for the contingent from Fresh Ponds to arrive ever since a horseman had galloped into the yard with news of the boy's capture. The conversation of those of high status was being consumed by the fate of the corpse. They spoke in low tones and frowned often.

The Van Dyke lad, with golden hair unclubbed and wildly flowing down to his shoulders, had announced that two waggons were on their way. Most of those on the boards were the other searchers. He also announced to one and all an untrue tale of how the Colonel's boy had been captured, and that only one searcher had been injured in the process. Upon his telling, the yard exploded with lusty cheers and crude songs. Two stout men with grim faces immediately proceeded to work a thick rope over one of the rafters in the stable in anticipation of a quick hanging. This action was taken without the approval of the authorities supposedly in charge.

Peter Vanderhoof, dressed in officious black and grays which befitted his station as the local Justice of the Peace, was not made aware of the hanging plans. Neither was David Williamson, who had donned a clean white apron for the occasion. He stood next to Vanderhoof in the shadow of his house. Both ignored the calls for a lynching. They focused, instead, on the words of Doctor Hezekiah Stites who was still explaining the intricacies of his post-mortem examination of Colonel Krause's body. Vanderhoof and Williamson posed key questions and concerns, and Doctor Stites, serving as the coroner, offered expert information and cogent opinions. Midway through the deliberations, John Wetherill, Jr., sauntered over and joined the men of high status. He was accepted readily because he was the elder son of their Assemblyman, and respected in his own right.

The younger John listened politely as Stites concluded his summation. Wetherill had only one question for the three gentlemen: "When will the Colonel's burial take place?"

Peter Vanderhoof responded quickly, putting his commanding bass voice to good use. "We have to determine where first. Pennsylvania does not permit a corpse from the Jerseys . . . likewise New York. No ship will be willing to transport the Colonel back to St. Croix, whether the jack tarrs be superstitious or not. So we're stuck with the Dane."

"And he's begun to stink," added Williamson. "The loss of a room is costing me dearly."

"I am sure my father will cover all expenses," proclaimed John Wetherill's older son. "He has aspirations of being a colonel himself when the fighting starts, so his honoring of such a dignitary is something I know he would gladly do."

Doctor Stites and minehost Williamson raised wary brows. They knew the penny-pinching Assemblyman better than his own son. They thanked Wetherill for his father's generosity. After all, Stites and Williamson would be the main beneficiaries of such largesse.

Vanderhoof seemed the most concerned with the question John, Jr., had raised. "The morrow at dawn is the earliest we can put the Dane in the ground . . . but the place for his burial has to be decided first."

"I have an idea," posited Williamson.

"You want Colonel Krause on your property?" queried Vanderhoof.

"No, definitely not," exclaimed Williamson. "A man who dies in an ordinary, no matter the circumstances, should be buried far away. Having the Dane's ghost haunting my property would be bad for business."

"Who around here has a suitable patch of untamed land?" asked John, Jr.

"John Probasco is my newest neighbor," said Williamson a bit too eagerly. "He has started clearing trees near the ridge, but he has a long way to go. I suggest we call him over for a talk."

Wetherill returned to his original group of searchers who stood in the center of the yard. They were most responsible for the shouting and cheering in favor of a hanging. Faces of outrage and anger confronted him there. His two Ratters stood with a pair of Williamson's recruits—Gilbert Van Pelt, in a snuff-colored drugget coat, and John Probasco who had failed to return to his farm chores.

Wetherill signaled Probasco and led him over to the three men in charge. Pleasantries were not exchanged. Vanderhoof got right to the point. He explained the burial predicament to the husbandman. Without hesitation, Probasco accepted the responsibility for finding a suitable burial site on his property.

"I'd be honored to put the Colonel to rest on my land," said Probasco, holding a Quaker hat in his hand. "But don't ask me to do the same for his slave's bones."

Vanderhoof thanked the man for his generosity, but scolded him for his presumption regarding the slave. "When the mulatto is brought in, he will need to be questioned. He must account for his actions. Some of your fellow hunters have found the boy, so I have been told. Therefore, your searching task is done. Now the accused's fate lies in my hands. Your implication of his guilt is unacceptable in the eyes of the King's Law. You need not worry about the fate of the boy's bones. I will not ask you to bury the slave on your property, Mister Probasco. It may turn out that the Colonel's boy may not need be buried anywhere by anyone."

John Probasco nodded that he understood, though in his heart he felt the same as before Vanderhoof's scolding. He promised to start digging a suitable grave at sunrise on Wednesday. His son, John the younger, would help him. He suggested that the burial be set for mid-morning. Vanderhoof agreed to such a time.

Probasco returned to the huddle of searchers in the middle of the stable yard.

Doctor Stites was about to say more on the results of his examination of Krause's body, but he went silent again when the two waggons from Fresh Ponds rolled into the Rhode Hall yard. Curses and shouts of anger greeted the folks in the vehicles.

John Van Dyke was at the reins of the first waggon. He brought his team of horses to a halt in the middle of the yard. Vincent Wetherill, Ben Hull, Robert Marshon, and Moses Gulick scrambled out and were greeted warmly by the rest of the Ratters. The second waggon, driven by David Vanderhoof, pulled up right behind the first waggon. Nobody got out of this one. Ike Higgins was laid out prone on the boards and out of view of those who started to surround the second waggon. Little Ned and Cutlope Hancock stood but did not make a move to exit the waggon. The runaway squatted next to the Irishman. He was bound and tethered.

Cheers and shouts in favor of a lynching started up. The angriest men, brandishing fists and weapons, pressed close around the second waggon. Those who had spilled out of the first waggon, save for Vincent, joined the others in crying for swift justice and a quick hanging.

A minority of men refused to support the consensus in the yard. The Justice of the Peace, Doctor Stites, and minehost Williamson made their way through the filthy men who reeked of the swamp. Vanderhoof and Stites climbed into the surrounded waggon. Williamson stood his ground by one of the waggon wheels—his bad leg prevented him from following the other two.

The senior Vanderhoof ordered his son off the seat board and proceeded to stand in his place. He raised an open hand to quiet the rousty crowd. Meanwhile, Doctor Stites concentrated on examining Ike's wounds.

When silence was achieved, the Justice of the Peace addressed the surly throng by using his best arrogative words: "We must do right by the King's Law. Any whisper or shout smelling of 'lex talionis' shall not be tolerated. Justice will prevail always in the

South Ward . . . long as I am standing."

There were an uncomfortable number of boos and hisses, but they were mostly directed toward the hated monarch. Vanderhoof raised both arms and waved open hands. He cast an indignant stare. Silence was achieved once more, but it took a bit longer.

"My two admonishers and I shall interrogate this found slave inside the Rhode Hall house. After doing so, I will decide what shall be done with the boy. This is my call, lads, not yours."

A voice in the crowd called out: "We're wastin' time! Got to get home! 'Tis harvestin' to be done on the morrow!"

These sharp words were followed by supportive cheers and loud objections to Vanderhoof's plan

"Question that scorched boy here and now!" cried another angry voice. "Time to get on with what to do with this here good-for-nothing limb of the devil!"

Vanderhoof appeared flustered. He wanted so dearly to avoid mob justice and give even a lowly slave a chance to clear himself. However, his wish did not seem to be gaining any traction.

Cutlope Hancock moved up close to the Justice of the Peace. He was fussing with his jaeger hunting rifle, which he had raised for all to see. All eyes shifted to the weapon.

Someone in the crowd cried out: "You gonna shoot the manqueroon, Cut?"

"Nein," snapped the German. He singled out the shouter and cast an angry stare. "Goin' to shoot any fool who tries to stop the judge from questionin' the boy. Four folks know the truth 'n they're all waitin' in this wain. Soon, you'll know the truth. This boy, Little Ned found, ain't bein' seized by any of you."

Another raw voice in the crowd shouted: "A slave's word ain't worth a turd, Hancock. You know it. 'N the word of Good Mary's boy is worth the same."

This was followed by another accusation: "Ike Higgins is a liar. His word's not to be trusted!"

Cut grinned at the last man daring to speak up. He raised his rifle to his shoulder and aimed it at the man's broad-brimmed hat. "Guess that leaves me for the tellin' of what I seen 'n heard in the swamp. Should be enough to clear things up."

Many in the crowd were not satisfied with Cut's stance. They were not cowered by his rifle, as long as it was not pointed at them.

One voice ascended above the others: "The buck has to be guilty of somethin' worth hangin' for!"

Another hollered: "You can't stop us all, Hancock!"

"Yup," said Cut calmly. "'Cept for the fool tryin' me first."

"The boy's a runaway . . . least he's guilty of somethin'," cried a voice way in the back of the crowd.

"Which side you on, cabbage head?" yelled another closer by.

Vanderhoof remained stoic and silent during the harangue against the German. He was glad to share the responsibility for taming the crowd with Cut. The Justice of the Peace gave Cut a supportive nod and urged him to finish speaking his mind.

Cut continued to glare at the challengers. He was making no friends, but he still held their attention. Nary a one dared to climb into the waggon.

Cut aimed his rifle at the man holding the noose under the stable eave. As he did so, he said something which caught his audience by surprise: "The boy tells me he's the Colonel's son."

Half the crowd was stunned into silence. The other half resorted to obscenities and epithets.

One voice screamed: "Blasphemy on a good man's corpse!"

The German ignored the last accusation. He kept his rifle trained on the man holding the hanging rope.

Vanderhoof quieted the crowd with another wave of his hand. Strangely, the locals gave him what he wanted. "Unsubstantiated claims at this juncture change nothing, my good men. I will interrogate each soul in this waggon and glean the truth from them. There is nothing more to be said on the matter. Make way now. Allow us to move peacefully indoors."

Those closest to the waggon pulled back grudgingly. Cut lowered his rifle and stepped back to confer with the two boys.

Vanderhoof, aided by his diligent son, scrambled down from the seat board after giving orders to those in the waggon to follow close behind him.

Cut untethered the runaway, pulled him up to his feet, and lowered Asher down to minehost Williamson's waiting arms. Cut shouldered his rifle and jumped out of the waggon to assist with protecting the Crocian boy from the crowd.

Doctor Stites and Little Ned helped Ike Higgins up from the floor boards of the waggon. They lowered him to the ground, but he slumped to his knees before two members in the crowd raised him to a standing position. Stites and Little Ned clambered out of the waggon and rushed to Ike's aid. Each took hold of an elbow and led the Irishman to the house. Minehost Williamson led the procession into his establishment.

Eventually the disgruntled crowd began to disperse. Some convinced themselves that no hanging would take place until the next day—at dawn most likely. They headed for their horses and vehicles. The Ratters from Cross Roads, save for John, Jr., were able to convince John Van Dyke to take his waggon the long way around. This allowed them and their hounds to avoid walking back to the Wetherill Tavern.

John Wetherill's older son decided to remain behind at Rhode Hall. He entered the Williamson house along with the two Philadelphia horsemen, the travelers from Burlington, and the coachman. They were all looking forward to a warm supper and a stiff drink in the dining room. They also hoped to be the first to hear the decision by the Justice of the Peace.

Nobody seemed to notice the gentleman who had remained all this time ensconced in Captain Markoe's coach. He sat alone, contemplating his next move. He kept his eyes on the noose which still hung from the stable rafter. But thoughts of a convenient hanging were fading from his mind. He had to save his own skin and he had to act fast.

Enoch Mortaine remembered the trackers talking about the route Krause's slave boy had taken based on the scent followed by the hounds. That meant the boy, claiming to be the Colonel's son, had never been near the stable or Markoe's coach at the start of his escape. Asher could not have stolen the parchment, which contained the coded message meant for that Dane, Febiger, in Massachusetts. So who was left to blame for filching it from one of the cases of muskets? The only man in the yard last night, who might have known of the secret document, was Pip James. And he was gone. Vanished. The only searcher who failed to return after the runaway had been captured. One had to assume the obvious. The person Mortaine had come to trust the most must have absconded with the Colonel's coded missive!

The one who claimed to be the King's agent slipped quietly out of Captain Markoe's coach. Only one person was watching him—a woman staring out a second-floor bedroom window.

Mortaine, burdened by luggage culled from the coach, shuffled down to the far end of the stable barn. He tossed his bulging satchel into Pip's stolen cart, which was already weighted down with a pair of long, wooden cases. He hitched the stolen horse to the cart, assumed an uncomfortable position on the seat board, gave the reins a snap, and disappeared around the north side of the house.

"Good riddance, brother," said Ruth Mount to herself. She turned away from the window. A smile lingered on her lips. "Give my love to our dear mother."

32

QUESTIONING SLY FOXES

(Tuesday, August 8, 1775)

David Williamson ordered two patrons at cards out of his game room. He ushered those who had followed him in from the yard to take seats on spindle-back chairs at the small tables. One of his daughters rushed in to take requests for beverages. Minehost promised all in attendance that supper would be served to them in the main dining area once the interrogation proceedings, to be conducted by the Justice of the Peace, had concluded. Another daughter brought Doctor Stites his bag from the upstairs bedroom where the corpse lay in repose, so that he could finish patching up the Irishman and check the cuts and bruises on the Crocian boy. Before Williamson left the room, Stites requested a pot of boiled rags and a pair of tongs. All was set for the interrogation to begin.

Peter Vanderhoof opened the proceedings: "Before I question the boy about the death of the Colonel, I need to ascertain whether or not he be accused of having anything to do with the accosting of Mister Higgins in the swamp."

His opening remark was greeted with an awkward silence and pairs of eyes darting from one participant to another.

The Justice of the Peace turned to Ike Higgins as soon as Doctor Stites had removed the man's torn hunting shirt. All eyes fell on the wounded man who was now fully awake but woozy. Ike's account could ruin the tale Cut and Little Ned had cooked up.

"What say you, Ike Higgins, about the assault on your person?" said Vanderhoof in an officious voice.

Ike looked up from where he was seated. He winced when the Doctor poked around his bloodied shoulder.

"Don't recall nothin'," mumbled Ike.

"Who might you accuse of attacking you?" queried Vanderhoof.

"None here." said Ike. "I was out cold fer most all o' it. The critter which'd attacked me bones was a fierce shadow."

Vanderhoof gave a raking glance at the others who had followed him into the room. "Mister Hancock, what did you see?"

"Came late," offered Cut. "By the time I got to Higgins he was out 'n bleedin'. So I got to see the end of it."

The Justice of the Peace was reluctant to ask a ten-year-old half-breed what he witnessed, but he did anyway.

"What did you witness, Little Ned?"

Mary's boy offered up wide eyes and a runny nose. He directed his gaze to the German, then to Vanderhoof. Little Ned squirmed in his seat. He was a sight after his adventure in the swamp—soaked and filthy—but ready to provide a fantastic explanation for everything. Ike Higgins had mentored the boy well in the field of malarky. And Cut Hancock had provided a few contrived details.

Little Ned showed no sign of struggling to find the words. "This big, black mama bear—biggest thing I'd ever seen 'n way darker than me, came chargin' out of nowhere. Me and Ike must of come too close to her cub which was sniffin' 'round a blueberry bush close to where we was headin' to dry ground. Next thing I know'd, the mama bear was strikin' Mister Ike a fierce blow with her dagger claw, followed by other swipes with that same sharp paw. Afore Ike went down hard, he was screamin' at me to hide . . . which'd I done." Little Ned pointed to the older peer in the room. "That's when I found this runaway over there, hidin' where I came to."

Mary's boy gave Asher a wink of support. He offered the same to Cut.

The Colonel's boy held his swamp-soiled head erect and offered no sign in return. But he did listen intently to the younger mulatto's every word.

Hancock did the same.

Little Ned continued with his tale: "The Colonel's boy did not run from me. He showed no fear in his eye. Instead, he grabbed a cut limb with leaves still on it 'n charged at the mama bear. I stayed hid behind a log . . . scared to move. But I peeked out 'n saw everythin'."

"Was the boy successful in distracting the beast?" asked Vanderhoof in a fatherly tone.

"Sure," responded Little Ned crisply. "The mama bear reared up then turned away from Ike to face this boy with the limb. That's when we heard a rifle shot. The mama bear 'n her cub took off quick as lightnin', splashin' through the shallows, never to be seen by us again. Mister Ike was left all bloody 'n spent . . . yet still alive thanks to this here Crocian."

"Who fired the weapon?" asked Vanderhoof with a momentary frown of skepticism possessing his clean-shaven face.

"There was one warnin' shot 'n it came from my piece," interjected Cut. "I heard a man cryin' out . . . someone in pain. Couldn't see 'em yet, but I figured I'd distract what I saw . . . 'n that was the bear. The Colonel's boy had beat me to it in menacin' the beast, but I finished the job. Got off a round . . . then came runnin'. Guess it worked."

"Are you sure you saw a full-grown bear and her cub?" asked Vanderhoof.

"The bear, yes," answered Cut. "Little Ned told me 'bout the cub. I had to believe him 'n I still do. Believe the other boy's account too . . . all of it. These two burr heads, I've come to trust."

Doctor Stites threw in a concern: "What I do not understand is how a black bear, full-grown or not, managed to stomp on poor Ike's ribs and kick him in the head . . . looks more like he was hambling a horse."

"What say you, Little Ned?" asked Vanderhoof after a measure of bemused hesitation. He was already leary of the boy's response. "Make a mama bear angry 'n you gets what you deserve," offered Little Ned, with wisdom and evasiveness beyond his years. "Mister Ike know'd it well, since he's had to deal with my mama for years."

Little Ned's words were greeted with grins and guffaws by the adults in the room. The Irishman was nodding.

The Justice of the Peace decided not to pursue the subject any further. He chuckled and asked a pointless question anyway: 'Ike, do you wish to draw charges against this runaway for eluding you so skillfully in the swamp?"

"No," said Ike adamantly. "That one save me life 'n helped me make it out in one piece all the way to Van Dyke's plantation. He's been on me right side . . . same as Neddy. Neither o' them had nothin' to do with me not defendin' meself proper like."

Vanderhoof sighed. "Good then. Lets move on to the delicate matter of the Colonel's demise. Mister Hancock, you may leave now. Enjoy your repast."

"Yup," said Cut. He got up and exited quickly. The rifle he had used to slay Pip James was still in his hands.

"Little Ned, you stay to help Doctor Stites," ordered Vanderhoof.

"I ain't hungry yet," boasted Mary's boy. He still clutched the satchel containing scraps of food and the prize pistol.

"Good," said Vanderhoof. "And thank you for sharing your tale. I trust you learned something from your small adventure today?"

"Many things," observed Little Ned, flashing the serious look of a scholar. "Mostly on bein' careful with your tongue 'n watchin' what you say. But more important, how to be a man . . . which'd I done, but was still told I have to wait some. This here Crocian beat me to it this day."

Vanderhoof and Stites chuckled over Little Ned's weighty words. Neither forced a comment, for then, a coal-hued servant rushed in with a large steaming pot held in gloved hands. A pair of tongs was dangling from his belt. Doctor Stites pointed to where he wanted the vessel of boiled rags placed.

Right behind the servant came Williamson's daughter with a pair of pewter mugs filled to the brim with house ale. Vanderhoof sipped from his. Stites ignored his. He picked up the tongs off the table where the servant had placed them. He used them to extract a steaming rag from the pot. He was now ready to finish with Ike's wounds and the ugly cuts on Asher's bare feet.

Vanderhoof put down his mug and started his questioning of the mulatto from St. Croix. "Why did you run, Asher?"

"My father ordered me to flee," stated the fourteen-year-old without hesitation.

"Doesn't your father live far from here, boy?" queried Vanderhoof with a puzzled look on his face.

"My father is dead."

"So your father's command came to you in a dream?"

"No, of course not," insisted Asher. "Before he met his fate, he told me to run and hide in order to save my soul. I have obeyed him in all ways. Now my father is dead. I am alone."

"I do not understand you, boy," said Vanderhoof. "You are

making no sense . . . nor are you helping your cause."

Asher presented his most serious face and spoke with a twinge of irritation. "My father's body lies upstairs. He awoke when Matt, I mean Mister Timmons the coachman, was on the watch. I was awakened by the sound of my father's voice. We both heard his last words. Then papa stopped breathing and we knew he was gone. Mister Timmons said he would take care of things. The coachman told me to flee, which I did because I obey those I trust."

Vanderhoof was speechless. Things were coming clear to him, but not yet completely so.

"You're telling me Colonel Krause is your father?"

"Yes," said Asher. "I am a Crocian Dane and a Bukra by half. The Colonel allowed me to accompany him to the colonies so long as I played his servant."

"Who can confirm this?"

"Ask Matt Timmons."

"Pray tell, where is Mister Timmons at this moment?"

"The coachman came in from the yard . . . I saw him come in," said Asher. "He's the only one who can vouch for all I have said."

Vanderhoof excused himself and headed for the door. He swung it open and hollered out into the dining area: "Anybody know the whereabouts of Matt Timmons, the coachman from Philadelphia?"

There were rumblings of the men slouched over their evening repast.

Vanderhoof addressed all of them: "Find the man and bring him to me immediately."

The Justice of the Peace had to wait but a moment before a bow-legged, leathery-faced man shuffled towards him. The fellow held a black castor hat in his hand. He wore a spot of gravy on his whiskered chin.

"And you are?" asked Vanderhoof in his best authoritarian voice.

"Works for Captain Markoe, sir," said the coachman. "Matthias Timmons is the name."

"Step into the game room, Mister Timmons." Vanderhoof pointed to the door leading to the game room. "I am the law around here. My name is Peter Vanderhoof. I have a few questions to ask of you."

"Pleased am I to meet you, sir," said the coachman with a bow.

Timmons entered the room with a noticeable limp, nodded at the fourteen-year-old, and sat down next to him. He placed a large, calloused hand on the boy's knee.

Vanderhoof went back to his chair, sat down, rested his elbows on the table that hid his knobby knees, and steepled his fingers.

"How is it you never came forward before now, Mister Timmons?"

"No one ever asked till now, kind sir," said the coachman. "Not one bloak 'round here ever dared ask my name. Just afore now, I've been sittin' by my lonesome in the large room next door."

"Asher says he knows you well and trusts you," said Vanderhoof.

The coachman smiled, eyed the boy, and gave him a gentle pat on the knee. "Asher rides with me up on the boards any chance he gets. He's a good boy . . . listens well. Almost grown. Free as I am and one to be trusted, accordin' to his poor, deceased father."

"How did you come to be privy to this boy's lineage?" asked Vanderhoof.

"When his father introduced him to me on the docks in Philadelphia," replied the coachman. "Since then, the Colonel told me at least three more times that I'd better take good care of this boy since Asher, here, is his son . . . born of a favorite servant in the Colonel's house. The boy's been pretendin' to be the Dane's slave all along, 'cause he was obeyin' his father. Even Captain Markoe don't know."

All in the room were listening to the coachman's words. Not one wished to interrupt him . . . not even the Justice of the Peace.

"Last time the Colonel spoke to his Asher was when he awoke while I was on watch in his bedroom."

"What did Colonel Krause say exactly?" asked Vanderhoof.

"Said some things I did not understand . . . words in Danish I assume. But then he spoke some English, which I did understand. He told us both 'bout fixin' to die . . . said he ate too much of some reechy food. He was in great pain at the time. Then he tells me to take care of his kin after he's gone. Then he changes his tune . . . all fear-eyed and such."

"What do you mean?"

"The Colonel spits up some blood. While I'm reachin' for a rag on the bedpost, he orders the boy to flee fast as he can."

"Did he give a reason?"

"All 'bout not trustin' folks here and there. The Colonel felt Asher'd be blamed for causin' his death. He wanted his boy kept free after he passed."

"What happened next?"

"Asher was ready to obey his father, Mister Vanderhoof. He was already dressed and scared as a rabbit. But the boy stayed put till his father stopped breathin'. Then he bolted out the door. I didn't have it in my heart to stop him. May have told him to run, myself, though perhaps I shouldn't have. Instead, I wiped the Colonel's blood from his face, thumbed his eyelids closed, and folded his arms over his chest . . . nice and neat. Then I sat in my chair, like I was before, and shammed a sleep."

Vanderhoof was not quite finished with his questioning of the coachman. He paused to consider his next question, then he said: "How is it you said nothing of this to the man who came in to relieve you?"

Timmons was quick to respond: "Wanted to give Asher more time to get away."

"Well, it worked," said Vanderhoof with a slight smile. "But Krause's boy almost got himself killed this day."

"We was only followin' the Colonel's orders, mister. Both of us was sore afeared of certain consequences at the time."

"I understand," concluded Vanderhoof. He turned to Doctor Stites who had finished treating Ike and was now tending to Asher's wounds. "Does all this fit your assessment, Doctor Stites?"

"I have my reservations about the bear attack, but, other than that, everything else appears quite plausible," observed Stites. "Krause ingested something which caused his death. Tainted meat, perhaps. The quantity he consumed may have contributed to his swift demise . . . usually, gluttony does not go unpunished. Before I depart, I shall write up this cause of death for you, Peter. And I shall list my fees for services rendered as physician and coroner."

"Thank you, Hezekiah, for all you have done last night and this day. I think I saw the younger John Wetherill at sup in the dining area. You may give your list to him before you go."

"Almost finished with this brave lad here," said Stites, patting Asher on his head.

"I am brave too," blurted Little Ned as he squirmed off his chair and stood proudly, holding the bag which hid the weapon he had purposely failed to mention in his tale.

"Indeed you are, boy," declared Vanderhoof, who rose from his chair. He towered over Good Mary's child and used a large, well-manicured hand to tap Little Ned on the shoulder. "And well on your way to being a brave man."

Everybody else in the game room eased out of their chairs. Ike fell back down, but Little Ned caught him by the arm. This allowed the Irishman to right himself and rise again.

"Could use a stiff pint," said Ike with a shaky voice. "Mayhaps, more 'n one."

The Justice of the Peace allowed a warm chuckle. "Has been a long day for all of us. I say we all head for the dining area and order whatever we want since our dear John Wetherill, even though he doesn't know it yet, is paying."

Vanderhoof's words were met with a laugh or two.

He continued: "Let us celebrate Ike's survival and Asher's escape from the noose. The time has come to spread the word that there will be no hanging today or tomorrow."

All voices in the room were in agreement. Little Ned and Ike led the procession to the long tables in the dining room. Asher followed the coachman to his table. They were joined by Little Ned and Ike. Vanderhoof and Stites joined the two horsemen from Philadelphia at the nearest table to the survivors of the ordeal in the swamp. John Wetherill, Jr., and Cutlope Hancock sat closest to the door, discussing the likelihood of war with the pair of travelers from Burlington. Their exchange of hot words cooled down when the Justice of the Peace stood to announce his decision on the fate of the Colonel's son. His decision received a tepid response. However, no voice was raised in opposition.

Peter Vanderhoof sat back down and called the younger John Wetherill over to his table to discuss who would pay for what. Wetherill excused himself from the resumed discussion of the possibility of war and huddled with the Justice of the Peace and the good Doctor Stites. There was nothing heated in this discussion. Mister Wetherill voiced no objection to the distinguished gentlemen's demands.

All the while, the Williamson girls were bringing food and drink to the patrons of the Rhode Hall establishment. When trenchers and mugs were brought to the coachman's now crowded table, Ike scolded little Ned for putting the satchel on the boards. He told Mary's boy to hide it under the bench. Little Ned did as he was told.

Will Pollard sat with his back to the mulatto boys, who were next to each other. This was the closest the horseman would ever come to recovering his lost pistol.

33

ONE LAST THING

· · · · · · · · · · · · · · · ·

(Wednesday, August 9, 1775)

The coachman, Matthias Timmons, did not have the stomach to help prepare the corpse for burial. He stood outside the open bedroom door waiting to assist in carrying the closed coffin box which had been hastily constructed and donated by the same John Probasco who had volunteered to dig the grave on his property. Besides his farming endeavors, Probasco was still a carpenter by trade. He had quickly developed a favorable reputation in the area. He also possessed a queasy gut when it came to working on a corpse. Therefore, he joined the coachman in the hallway. They discussed pending showers and the upcoming harvest. Not one word about the Colonel's corpse. Mister Timmons mostly stared at the floor, feigned interest in things agricultural, and listened politely. No matter how hard he tried, the coachman could not ignore the sickly odor emanating from the room which held the corpse competing with Williamson's scented candles.

Inside the bedroom, Asher Krause and the two Philadelphia horsemen prepared the Colonel's body for placement in the pine box which sat on the floor at the foot of the bed. Ruth Mount should have helped, but she was still feigning an illness of unknown origin and keeping to her room down the other end of the hall. She wanted no part in the preparations or the actual burial of a man she had come to despise. Her work was done. She was simply waiting for the coach ride back to Philadelphia. She was done with spying, plotting, and poisoning. Her reward had come with the passing of a less than honorable man, who was now going to be honored by other imperfect men. Ruth Mount wished to play no part in this end game. She longed for one thing—to return to the arms of Anna McClew.

Asher rummaged through his father's belongings, which he had lugged from coach to bedroom on the night of their arrival at the Rhode Hall house. He found clean knee breeches and cotton hose, a linen shirt with full sleeves, a deep green waistcoat, and a brown high-skirted coat with broad collar. Robert Hare and Will Pollard lifted the Colonel's body into position so that Asher could slip the chosen apparel over the banyan Krause had died in. The pair of horsemen then propped up the corpse. Asher pulled his father's hair back and tied it with a black ribband. Then he fitted a full white wig over the natural hair.

Hare and Pollard returned the corpse to a prone position. Asher finished his thankless chore by slipping low-heeled buckled shoes on Krause's feet. He stood back a moment admiring his work.

Will Pollard broke the silence: "Anything else?"

Asher went back to the luggage pile and pulled the striped flag Ruth Mount had sewn from a depleted satchel.

"One last thing," announced Asher. The boy rolled out the flag sporting thirteen stripes of blue and gold. He draped it over Krause's body. He tucked the corners under the limbs of the corpse and pointed to the plain pinewood box.

Hare and Pollard lifted the weighty corpse as gently as they could and placed it in the box. Asher fussed with the lace at his father's neck and the corners of the flag. Finally, the lid was positioned on the box and binding ropes were tied tightly to keep the lid secure. All was ready for vacating the room.

Matthias Timmons was called into the room to help lug the coffin down the stairs. John Probasco went to fetch his fresh-faced son and his black-haired brother, Ruloff, who had been waiting with their waggon out front. Also waiting with the Probascos were David Williamson's two strongest stable slaves.

When John Probasco returned with the four, the coffin was lifted out of the room and down the stairs without incident. The horsemen went out back to prepare their steeds for leading the procession to the gravesite.

Asher remained in the room for a few minutes to gather up the belongings. He left the window and the door open to allow the room to air out. He also left the scented candles lit. Asher was able to get all the baggage down the stairs and out to the coach in one trip. The only one remaining on the second floor was Ruth Mount. She was staring out her window, which overlooked the stable yard. She watched the fourteen-year-old positioning his luggage in the coach. The boy looked quite handsome in his father's voluminous black waistcoat, white lace shirt, and red knee breeches. He wore no wig and he sported no buckles on his shoes. Such a hasty outfit for a funeral, but in Ruth's mind the boy had done the best he could do now that he was on his own. She dreaded having to sit with Asher all the way back to Philadelphia. The thought made her feel ill.

❖

By all accounts the burial procession and gravesite ceremony for Colonel Johan Gottfried Krause of St. Croix was a modest affair. John Probasco's son, Little Johnny, led the way down Lawrie's Road to the Rhode Hall path which allowed the small procession to reach the upland ridge where the grave had been dug. Probasco's son rode a young bay gelding sans saddle. He wore homespun field clothes, but, at least, sported a black ribband on his straw hat.

The pair, representing the Philadelphia Troop of Horse, followed close behind the gelding. Hare and Pollard were in full uniform for the event. The latter held the troop's unique banner proudly. Hare had thought it best to give his companion a turn with the standard designed by their Captain.

Tucked into Will Pollard's waistbelt was the one remaining pistol from the dueling pair he once owned. He had had no luck finding the missing one on this trip, even though he had come so close to the firearm without even knowing it. The bag Little Ned had carried into Williamson's dining area had been placed but a few feet away from where Will Pollard had sat during last night's supper. Yes, the horseman had seen the boy with the bag, but thought nothing of it. He had seen Ike Higgins also, but did not recognize the bandaged man—the only man in the room who knew the true story behind the disappearance of the pistol. A singular opportunity had been missed. Sometimes that is how luck and fate operate. Had Cut Hancock allowed Little Ned to boast in Williamson's establishment, things might have turned out differently. But a mere boy proved he could keep a secret. In so doing, Little Ned was able to keep the pistol.

Behind the pair of horsemen came the waggon carrying the coffin. John Probasco and his brother, Ruloff, sat atop the seat board and guided the two-horse team from road to path. Since it was threatening to shower on a day of gloomy gray skies, the decision was made to cart Krause's heavy body over muddy ground and have the six pallbearers, who were walking alongside the waggon, carry the coffin from the path's terminus to the gravesite. Behind the waggon marched a paltry few dignitaries, all dressed in black, and an equal number of lesser-knowns. Peter Vanderhoof led them. Doctor Hezekiah Stites accompanied the Reverend Thomas Small, whom he had recruited from the Cranberry Presbyterian Church. John, Jr., represented his brother and father. None of the other Ratters were in attendance, save for one.

Word of the Crocian's innocence had spread rapidly. Many were not pleased. Most were still upset that Asher Krause had not been hung.

Cut Hancock was in attendance. He carried his hunting rifle on his shoulder, for he had volunteered to fire a salute to the Colonel at the end of the ceremony.

Ike Higgins was absent. He was on the mend and being taken care of by Good Mary. Little Ned was also absent. Ike was teaching the boy how to clean a dueling pistol.

David Williamson failed to join the procession. Minehost was busy tidying up the bedroom where the Colonel had expired. His wife and daughters remained at their chores. Things were quickly getting back to normal at Rhode Hall. Patrons seemed to have lost interest in the tragedy of yesterday. However, most of them still took umbrage at Asher escaping the noose. They were looking forward to being entertained by a hanging. Now that hope had been dashed by Vanderhoof's decision. It was time for the locals—those who had participated in the search in Pigeon Swamp and those who had not—to pay the matter no never mind. Mob justice had not prevailed. The King's Law had.

The pallbearers were the same six who took Krause's body out of the bedroom. Matthias Timmons was the only stumbler who faltered before reaching the gravesite. He recovered quickly and represented himself well the rest of the way. Reverend Small spoke few words of his own and kept to chapter and verse from a St. James Bible he carried. Peter Vanderhoof followed with paltry praise, and the sanctity of life thrown in as a final thought. Asher wanted to say something, but he was not allowed. Cutlope Hancock fired off a single, solitary round. The thunder clap from his trusty rifle signaled that the service was done.

The dignitaries and whoever else could cram into the damp waggon were driven back by Ruloff Probasco to the Rhode Hall house.

John Probasco, his son, and Williamson's stable slaves remained behind to lower the coffin and fill in the hole. Once this chore had been done, the elder Probasco produced a cross he had fashioned from wood left over from constructing the coffin. He planted it in the soft earth piled on top of the grave, then pounded its crown a few times with his shovel.

Probasco stepped back and admired what he had carved in the wood of the temporary cross. It wasn't much:

'Col. Krause, R.I.P.'

His son voiced a sober opinion: "A good man deserves a handsome stone."

John the elder put a large, calloused hand on his name-sake's shoulder and said: "Maybe one day, when you lay my bones to rest up here, Little Johnnie, you'll place a handsome stone o'er me and a handsome stone atop the Colonel's bones."

Probasco's eldest son looked up, studied his father's soft brown eyes, and gave a curt bob of his head. It was almost a nod . . . nothing more.

34

LETTERS AND NUMBERS

* *

(Wednesday, August 9, 1775)

No time was wasted by those who were eager to return to Philadelphia. It was still showering when Matthias Timmons, with Asher's help, brought the coach and four out to the road. The coachman and the boy had donned full-skirted seal-skin coats for the journey, because there was a distinctive chill in the August air. They sat together on the seat board waiting for their sole passenger to emerge from the Rhode Hall house.

Will Pollard and Robert Hare had gone in to fetch Miss Mount. One helped her down the stairs. The other followed with her luggage. Ruth Mount wore a dun cape over a Brunswick dress with rose-colored hood. She favored no corset and just a single petticoat for the return trip. All she carried was her sewing bag in one hand and a fichu in the other.

As soon as Miss Mount was safely helped inside the coach, Private Hare went back to settle accounts with minehost. Earlier, Asher had turned over the Colonel's purse to the Private. Now Hare counted out Danish coins and paid David Williamson what was owed. With a final farewell and a word of gratitude, Private Hare strolled to his horse, mounted skillfully, and called out to Will Pollard to get things going. It was past noon and the party heading south would be lucky in the rain to get to Burlington before dark.

Ruth Mount sat alone in her master's luxurious coach. All the leather window flaps were down and secured. She smiled at her situation and paid no mind to the weather. She was looking forward to a safe return to her master's manse and her lover's arms. Fate had treated her better than she could ever have imagined. But fate is tireless as rust and also oftentimes pitted. It was also devilishly unpredictable.

Mount had a few more lies to tell. A major one was convincing the Markoes that she, too, fell ill and dared not continue on to see her dying mother. She planned to say that her brother understood her predicament and agreed to take care of things himself. Ruth knew the Markoes would accept her account. After all, they did want her back as soon as possible. They would be relieved that she was returning after a remarkable recovery in light of what she had to report about the demise of Colonel Krause. Feigning remorse over that one's passing would be an easy challenge Ruth was prepared to tackle. The sewing maid smiled again. She felt she was getting very good at this game.

Before the coach reached Hide's Town, Ruth Mount decided to pull a creased sheet of parchment from her sewing bag. She unfolded it carefully and smoothed it on her lap. She had already studied the letters and numbers a few times in her room at Rhode Hall, after having pulled such a treasure from the first case she opened in the coach an hour before Colonel Krause was discovered dead. Dressing in man's clothing, which she had brought along for use when needed, had worked. No one noticed her in Williamson's yard that night. Finding the coded missive and slinking back to the room had gone so smoothly for Ruth. She could laugh about it now, alone in the coach . . . and she did—soft as a whisper, stealthy as venom.

The paper in her hand meant she had won the game. Not Enoch Mortaine. Not Pip James. Not some mysterious other. Now Ruth had to decide what to do with the prize. It might help if she could figure out the Colonel's coded message. Then she could determine its import. Determine its value. Ruth wondered how much the thing could be worth. Was the message in Danish or English? She knew not a word of the former, and, so far, she had gotten nowhere relying on her mastery of the latter. Without a cipher she was lost. But she decided to give it one more try.

Mount carefully studied the lines on the paper. They were written in a good hand. She started reading aloud in a low voice what had been written most likely by Colonel Krause:

"CF • T5N TH1521 KR15NB5RG BL1CK 9NF1NTRY M21SK5TTS

21s5D L555 F9V5 H21NDR5D N55D R5Pl9R •

5NR1521T5 Nl5RW1Y • HlMM21RM15LL5N

FICTl5RY • H5LL81CK • Fl5R R5F9TT9NG •

9NT5RC5PT 85Fl5R5 15 55P 75 •

D9V5RT 1RMS PR15C21R5R5

H15LL1ND J V1N 5Z5LL

521STlT9215 • J CR15Hl5N

CR159X N T219T5

81LT9Ml5R5 • J SP51R

9N9T91T5 SlL5 • Cl5NT1CT • S9L1S D51N5"

The sewing maid stared at the letters and numbers until they became a blur. The jostling movement of the coach did not help. One mile later, Ruth refolded the parchment and slipped it back into her sewing bag.

She had thought of ripping the find into pieces and tossing them out the window. But with Private Hare taking his turn at trailing the vehicle, defenestration was not a good idea. Keeping the thing or turning it over to Captain Markoe were still viable options. Selling it to an interested third party was a possibility. After all, her boss had said the document was worth a great deal to certain parties.

Ruth Mount debated what to do until her head hurt. Finally, she leaned back, took the last drop of the laudanum Doctor Stites had given her, and dreamed of walking arm in arm with Anna McClew around the pond in Southwest Square. Maybe twice . . .

EPILOGUE

· · · · · · · · · ·

Rivington's NEW YORK GAZETTEER, No. 122, included a modest notice on the passing of Colonel Krause. It read as follows:

> 'New York, August 17. On Tuesday the 8th instant, departed from this life, on his journey from Philadelphia to this city, at a place called Rhode Halls (sic), at the house of Mr. David Williamson, on the Burlington Road, fifteen miles from South Amboy, Col. Johannes Godfried Krause, of the island of St. Croix. He was a gentleman eminent in his profession, amiable in his private, as well as public character, and it may with truth be said that, as he lived universally respected, so he died universally beloved.'

Krause was probably 46, or 47, when he died. Nothing was mentioned about the cause of death or Krause's reasons for visiting Philadelphia and then heading for New York by using the Lower Road through New Jersey in 1775.

What is known about the man is meager. Krause was born in Silesia in 1728, the son of Johann Gottlieb Kraus(e). He ventured first to the island of St. Eustatius in the West Indies prior to 1760. In that year, he married Anna Caroline Heyliger (c. 1740-1820). The couple went to St. Croix by December of 1760. He established sugar plantations on this island. The main one he called Annaberg (Anna's Hill), named after his wife. He served in the Danish military as a Captain at Fort Christiansvaern, Christiansted, on the north coast. He was a Major by 1765, and a Lt. Colonel during the 1770's. He was instrumental in organizing the Planters Civilian Militia (aka: Civil Guard). In 1766, Krause was given title to the saltwater pan south of the Anguilla settlement by King Christian of Denmark. This was renamed 'Krausses Lagune'.

His documented children were Peter Heyliger (1760-1790); Johan Gottfried (1761-1826); Christian Sigismund (1763-?); Maria Aletta (1764-1830); Martin Ludwig (1767-1831); Johanna Rosina

(1768-1818); William Henry (1769-1841); and Anna Christina(?-?). There is no record of Krause's children born of his slaves.

Colonel Krause had business dealings in several ports around the world. He had dealings with the Danish West Indian Company and the Dutch East India Company. He traveled extensively, mostly to ports in Europe. One of his trips took him to Philadelphia—unfortunately, his last one.

It appears that Colonel Krause was the first to be buried in what became known as the Probasco family burial ground (aka: Conover Cemetery). An unknown number of years (but most likely many) passed before a proper headstone was placed on Krause's grave. The inscription on the stone reads:

'Krause, Godfrey, Colonel, d. Aug, 8, 1776 (incorrect year), aged 49 years of the Island of St. Croix' (date of birth not legible)

It is not known who paid for the stone, who prepared the stone, and/or who placed it on his grave.
Unfortunately, all the other grave markings at the site have vanished, or possibly buried under soil and debris. When the Probasco family was tending to the site, the following stones were in place:

'Probasco, (Es)ther, wife of J(ohn) Pro(basco) in fragments; Probasco, (G)arret, d. Sept, 14, 1806, in 43rd year; Probasco, John, d. 1803, aged 74 (fieldstone); M. P. (footstone); OT d. May 20, 1826 (fieldstone); IWV (fieldstone); and d. Mar(ch) in the ________46th year of her age (fragments).'

All these stones and fragments, except for the Colonel's headstone, may have been moved to an unknown location, or are buried under tree roots, soil, and debris, or were taken by vandals. It is possible that no corpse lies in the ground assumed to be the burial site. The actual burial site has yet to be definitely determined.

The sparse chronology of the interest in the Probasco burial ground, since the year a local citizen felt moved to put a proper headstone on Colonel Krause's grave, is telling. Inscriptions on the existing Probasco cemetery stones were first copied in 1940. These records, gathered by the Genealogical Society of New Jersey, were turned over to the Special Collections Department of the Alexander Library at Rutgers University. It was reported at this time that the gravestones had been subjected to much damage.

In 1952, Edward J. Raser completed his study of the graveyard and gravestone inscriptions locators in Middlesex County. This was the first study of its kind in the State of New Jersey and long overdue. The Probasco burial ground is mentioned in this effort as dating back to 1776, and unused after 1826. Raser was in error by at least a year with his inception date, because Colonel Krause had to have been buried in 1775. The 1826 date may provide a clue as to the decade in which a proper headstone was placed on Krause's grave.

Raser happened to quote a former local historian on the Krause matter: "The origin of this nearby graveyard is unknown, and the destruction of so many gravestones makes it uncertain if it actually was a community burial ground from the start. Its earliest known and most prominent occupant is Col. Johannes Godfried Krause . . . Krause's stone has led some to mistakenly call this place the Revolutionary War Cemetery. It has also been called the Conover Cemetery and the J. S. Bennett Burial Ground."

When Raser visited the site in 1952, he reported: "The cemetery occupies a hillside on which cows have been let to graze . . . covered with tree stumps (from) recently pulled (trees) having been dead (a) long time as if the land is to be cultivated. Only three reasonably whole cut stones could be found. A good two dozen fieldstones, probably most all without markings, are still rooted in the ground. Others lie loose about. Several dozen pieces of old gravestones (red sandstone, similar to two Probasco stones) lie about, none bigger than a fist, evidently the work of a person deliberately trying to destroy the plot. (The) D. T. Dye stone was loose. Many animal holes about, and I have no doubt that parts of stones have been dumped into them."

In September of 1977, Janet T. Riemer, printed her study of the three phases of cemetery development in South Brunswick Township. The Probasco family burying ground was listed among the fourteen cemeteries in the first phase. At the time of her study, Riemer noted: "A few, broken headstones are still visible in the southern part of a small woods." The Krause stone was among them.

In the latter months of 1988, New Jersey Turnpike road-widening activity, cutting through South Brunswick Township, was halted for a week after road workers stumbled upon the Krause gravestone and a few others.

Home News staff writer, Alice Gallagher wrote the following account on September 28, 1988: "After 212 years (actually 213 years) of relative obscurity, Col. Godfrey Krause has gained the attention of state and local officials. Krause's gravestone was one of several found yesterday off Deans Rhode Hall Road by contractors widening the New Jersey Turnpike between interchanges 8A and 9."

Allen Lewis, Senior Engineer on the project, was of the opinion that at least one grave was there. He assumed, correctly, that the site had to be a family cemetery. A number of gravestones, mostly fragments, were found by Charles Kerzan of Sayreville, who was employed by D'Annunzio & Son, Inc., of Fanwood. These stones were not located on land designated for the widening project. Kerzan had been warned by a local resident to be careful about old graves, possibly ten to fifteen, buried in the area. The workers could not tell if the stones found were on the original burial site or had been moved to where they lay. The workers did not dig deep enough to find any graves.

At the time, Township Health Officer, Stephen Papenberg, stated that there was no record of a cemetery at the site where the workers found the stones. This contradicts the findings and documentation going all the way back to 1940, including Raser's and Riemer's studies. The implication was, and still is, that the Probasco burial ground has been ignored and neglected for decades. In 1988, the land on which the cemetery sits was owned by Construction local 825 which operated a heavy-equipment training site. This outfit was not interested in attending to the upkeep of the burial ground.

The Turnpike Authority executives called in an archeologist to determine if there might have been any graves buried under land involved in the widening of the highway. The Senior Engineer, Allen Lewis, was convinced that remains were under the grave markers. However, the executives had no plans to dig for coffins and corpses. Lewis suggested that the Township put up some sort of historic marker.

Another Home News reporter, Lenny Melisurgo, wrote that more archeologists visited the site in the following month. Some had been hired by the Turnpike Authority, while others represented the Preservation Coalition of New Jersey. The latter group planned to dig at the edge of Deans Rhode Hall Road to search for signs of graves. The suspicion of these archeologists was that as many as fifty graves might lie near the road.

According to two members of the Preservation Coalition, soil and grass indicators led them to consider that some gravestones had been moved from the Turnpike work area and placed more than fifty feet from the road. Turnpike Authority archeological consultants disagreed. They maintained that the topsoil in the work area was uniform and the ground in question undisturbed. The stones the workers found were at least a hundred yards from the Turnpike construction. This variance of opinions over the gravesite situation led to much rancor between the Turnpike Authority, authors of a highly criticized 1987 environmental impact study, and members of the Preservation Coalition. This left a measure of doubt as to whether the Krause stone rests in its original location or had been moved one or more times.

The New York Times added its two cents with an article in its Sunday, October 9th edition by Kate Sheehy. She wrote: "A 271-year-old sugar trade magnate from St. Croix brought part of the New Jersey Turnpike's project . . . to a halt last week." Sheehy went on to write that Turnpike Authority archeologists proclaimed, "Krause's nearby presence should not delay the project."

However, Turnpike officials did call workers off the site for ten days after Krause's headstone had been 'discovered' in an "isolated clump of trees about 200 feet from the road." Also found were the partial stones representing five others. Authorities claimed the Turnpike widening was at least a few hundred feet from where the gravestones had been found. The Senior Engineer, Allen Lewis, downplayed the possibility of encroachment on the historic site, by saying: "South Brunswick didn't even know the cemetery existed."

Locals, Township officials, and preservationists in the state were not buying the Turnpike Authority's rush to judgement. Thomas

Sadlowski, Chairman of the Preservation Coalition of New Jersey, believed the headstones had been moved from the graves. He stated: "As typical in the Revolutionary period, burials occurred on high mounds and as close to the road as possible." He did admit that local records at this time and Rutgers University archival records did not specify a graveyard at the site in question. Therefore, it remains a guess as to whether or not the site for the Probasco family burial ground is in the right place, much less Krause's headstone.

Work resumed after authorities determined that interments had not occurred in the path of the actual roadway, but a distance from it.

In the summer of 2004, a large distribution center was constructed adjacent to the alleged Probasco cemetery. The south end of the hill on which the remains of the burial ground stood was cut down to the new building's floor level. A high retaining wall was erected on the other side facing Deans-Rhode Hall Road. Concerns were voiced over the land-owner's (at this time, Keystone of New Jersey c/o Deloite and Touche) plans for the land on which the cemetery sits. Certain parties feared destruction was in the offing. The company allayed such fears by announcing plans to fence in the cemetery site and a promise to protect it from ruin.

In 2008, the Probasco burial ground was surrounded by a black simulated iron-bar fence. The space between this site and the distribution center was filled in and landscaped by the property owners. Since then, the only stone visible appears to be the broken Krause stone, face up, within the fencing and close to the southwest corner. Whether the stone actually lies atop Krause's grave is open to conjecture. In earlier photos, the stone was propped up against a tree. At this juncture, there is no telling where Colonel Krause's bones lie.

In 2007, an updated report on the cemeteries of South Brunswick Township was put out by the South Brunswick Historic Preservation Commission. Included in this report is a photo of the Probasco family burial ground taken from the Deans-Rhode Hall Road side. The update was not promising: "In 2001 a few stones were spotted within the cemetery . . . as of 2006 none have been found. An iron gate has been placed to protect the remains. Approximately three stones were known to be in this plot." There was no mention of the Krause stone in this report.

To date, the Probasco burial ground takes up a small corner of a 49-acre property at 354-380 Deans-Rhode Hall Road. The land is owned currently by Prologis c/o Thomson/K. Fahey, Denver, Colorado. The black metal fence still surrounds the burial ground. Only one stone is visible—that being the Krause stone—positioned face up in three pieces, and badly weathered. This neglected site is virtually unknown to residents in the Township. Just as Colonel Johann Gottfried Krause sleeps forgotten—neither a Revolutionary War hero nor a Hessian officer, but a notable just the same—so has his final resting place . . . that is, his assumed resting place.

Public access to this cemetery may be gained by obtaining permission from the property owners or by contacting the South Brunswick Township Public Works Department. There is no public parking available.

Probasco Burial Ground, Rhode Hall area

In 1952 Col. Godfry Krause's stone lay on a relatively open hilltop with various gravestone fragments nearby. Many mysteries surround his presence here—what was he doing in America at this time; what were the circumstances of his death; and who belatedly provided his gravestone?